A GOBLIN OF THE GLADE

A NUMINA PARABLE

MCKENZIE CATRON

A Numina Parable

A
GOBLIN
OF THE
GLADE

McKENZIE CATRON

Whimsical Publishing

To my nieces and nephews – may you always embark on sibling adventures, even when you want to throttle each other.

The Glade

*I*t's not that I don't love my sisters, I do, they've just been on my nerves since the three of us shared a womb. And right now, they're squabbling again. Poppy complaining that Posy gets too engrossed in her studies and slacks off around the glade, while Posy huffs and rolls her eyes--she's not one for words but the sass still oozes from her. It's a one-sided, semi-silent argument but it's bickering all the same. I try to ignore them but when Poppy trips on the hem of her too-long cloak, bumps into me, and makes the pile of wood in my arms fall to the ground, I lose it.

"One more word, Poppy, and I swear to Fate..." I groan, irritation clinging to my back like a heavy knapsack.

Poppy and Posy look at me with their identical faces, my face. Their emerald-green goblin skin is all aglow in the morning light as their long, rippled ears blush and full dark brows rise. Their swooping lips pull up in innocent mask-like smiles, and Poppy begins to protest, "But Rose—"

I don't let her finish. "You dodge your chores by playing with the changeling babes almost every day, you chatterbox." I swirl an accusatory finger around her face. She bats it away as I turn to Posy whose firefly eyes twinkle with mirth. "And I'm sure you cleared the rest of the autumn harvest just like Rush asked before you transcribed that book for Hazel. Didn't you, Posy?"

The glee over Poppy's reprimand fades as Posy's gaze darts around.

My annoyance fades––of course she got caught up in her task for Hazel. Posy's special interest has always been gathering information, and the Elder Mother has been something of a mentor to my quiet sister. Posy enjoys the work; even craves the knowledge she absorbs and stores away inside her flawless memory. Though she has never expressed it, I think her fact-finding provides her comfort and a sense of purpose, especially after everything we've been through the last ten years.

"Go get it done. I'll cover for you if dear old brother asks," I sigh, knowing if she gets in trouble, she'll find a way to drag me and Poppy into the fray.

Posy gives me a dazzling smile in thanks before spinning on her heel to leave. I grab on to the tails of her coat, stopping her when I see the bulge of a pocket-sized book and her spectacles stuffed inside her vest pocket. Sticking out my hand and flexing my fingers, I motion toward the book.

"Not so fast, hand it over." I narrow my eyes. "I know better than to let you walk away with unfinished work for the Elder Mother."

With a pout, and extra care, Posy places the old book in my waiting hand. Then, being careful not to smudge the blue tinted lenses, she puts her wire spectacles on top of the old brown leather as well. Poppy gives her a mocking wave as our triplet follows the stone path to the garden where Fern and the rest of the gnomes are waiting for her help.

Tomorrow is the first day of the last month of the year and the glade is getting colder. Pumpkins and gourds are going out of season along with the sunflowers, while the winterberry holly bushes are newly teeming with red. There's a lot of work to be done before the first snowfall rolls in these next coming weeks, and everyone needs to pitch in before Christmastide arrives, even Posy. My thoughts flit to Sparrow--no doubt she's already decorating; she loves Christmastide.

Before they got married, Rush, with the help of the glade, built them a cottage at the end of the stream by the watermill. It was my half-brother's wedding gift to his changeling bride, a home of her own with room to expand, accessible for her and her magic elder tree wheelchair, and close enough to Sparrow's old house but far enough away for privacy.

They had their wedding in the fall when Sparrow turned twenty. Posy, Poppy, and I were nine and ecstatic to have The Changeling Queen, Slayer of Witches, our liberator, as a sister.

It didn't take long for their family to grow because Sparrow made use of all the changeling hearts that had been stashed away by her and Aspen many moons ago. I don't think either of them knew the twigs would ever be useful. Mainly because the pair confiscated the hearts from the trolls to discourage the burly old faeries from creating changelings to swap for human babes. But I suppose the efforts to stop the trolls' kleptomaniac tendencies ended up being a blessing.

The three of us girls were there when Sparrow and Rush took the hidden hearts from the chest beneath Aspen's bed and brought them to the eldest troll, Bramwell. They asked him to charm the woven elder twig hearts, and together, the trolls took up their magic once more. After a few years, the mossy faeries created a whole gaggle of nieces and nephews, an adorable group of changeling babes.

Some of them run past Poppy and I with red, frost-tipped noses and bright laughs while their slow grandparents lumber after them on thick, lazy limbs. The trolls wave at us in synchronized motion as they follow the children. My sister looks at the giggling brood with her watchful, raspberry eyes. She loves our makeshift family more than words can say and prefers, above all else, to be their caretaker. While Posy is the scholar, Poppy is the maternal one, content to wipe snotty noses and bandage scraped knees while she dreams of having kids of her own. And right now, while she watches the children fly by, her face betrays it all.

I look down at my boots––then there's me––I'm not really the dutiful sister I appear to be. Honestly, I prefer adventure in far-off places, and journeys that don't involve mundane chores. But it seems that it's my turn to be the responsible one today. My eyes lift. "You go, Poppy, Bramwell is too old to chase after them. Especially Lark; she's going to give that old-timer a heart attack if she tries climbing the maple trees again. He almost threw out a hip wrangling Starling out of an imp's nest in the barn yesterday."

Poppy kicks the wood still scattered over the crunchy, yellowed grass as she sprints after them, flickering in and out of sight, using her goblin ancestry to sneak up on the kids. "You're the best, Rose!" She shouts this over her shoulder before she disappears entirely.

"You owe me your dessert tonight," I yell back, a playful threat coating my words. My sisters know better than to mess with me when there's sugary sweets involved. I've been paid with delicacies for chores and secrets many a time.

Thinking of layered cake slices makes my stomach moan as I pocket Posy's things and bend to collect the fallen firewood. My breath billows in the crisp air when I finally head down the smooth, snaking path ahead. It's not too cold outside in the daylight, at least not for me, but for others it's intolerable. Aspen requires more heat as of late, and that means more wood for bigger, longer burning fires in her hearth.

Her health has been poor these past few years, but it wasn't until this past summer that she started to truly decline. Now she's become frail and tired, mostly bound to her bed as the moon changes cycles. Sometimes it's even too much for her to talk or pick up her sewing projects, and she hasn't been outside since Hallowtide. She's dying. I know it. Sparrow knows it. We all know it, but none of us know why, or how long she has left.

Hazel and Posy have been researching, scouring every book, tome, and crumbling scroll for an answer or clue. Sparrow even begged her mother to let the trolls make her a new body, to infuse her soul into a changeling heart, just as Sparrow herself came to be, but Aspen refuses. She told me that she'd played with Fate by recreating her human daughter, and knows better now. *"When it's my time, darling, it's my time,"* she'd said.

Aspen is headstrong, but I look up to her. And over the past decade she's been a surrogate mother to us triplets, gathering us beneath her wings, loving us and trying to help us heal after the horror of Black Annis. None of us like to talk about our time in that cold iron cage though...it broke our Pop's mind, and the trauma lingers over me and my sisters too. Most of the time I repress the memories; it's just easier if I shove them deep inside--so deep that they, like the night-crawling bogeys, cannot see the light of day. I know they're not gone, no matter how deep I push, because similar to the creatures that haunt my daytime periphery like hazy impish ghouls, they linger.

I ignore them all though, shaking them off along with the shades of dark, blue belladonna-soaked memories while I wipe the soles of my travel worn boots on the doormat outside Sparrow's childhood home. Balancing the wood in one arm is a juggling act that includes using my chin as I reach for the doorknob blindly. When the front door opens, a wall of heat slaps me in the face, but I'm quick to close it all in with a kick, making sure the precious warmth doesn't escape. The chopped wood gets dumped in the log rack against the wall, and then I survey the room.

It's one of Aspen's better days because I see she's sitting up. It's a welcome sight. She's bundled in the chair next to the blazing hearth, and Sparrow is pouring her something hot in a chipped cup.

"Ah, my two favorite people. How are you ladies doing this fine morning?" I ask, pulling off my scarf and hanging it on a hook protruding from the wall.

"Hello, Primrose," Aspen chuckles, keeping her attention on the needlework she holds in her shaky hands.

I hear a thump from behind the open cupboards in the kitchen. "I thought *I* was your favorite person," Rush's voice calls. He must be making a post-breakfast snack because the smell of yeast and sugar floats through the room like sweet, powder-dusted sprites. Sparrow has taught him a thing or two about baking since their wedding day, and thank goodness for that since the things he tried to feed Posy, Poppy, and I as kids were vile.

"Your wife won that spot ages ago, brother," I call back, a lightness from familiar banter filling my chest.

Sparrow laughs, wheelchair gliding over the scratched floors to put the kettle back in the kitchen. "Darn right I did," she says over her shoulder. "I plied you girls with enough sweets to earn your favor for a lifetime."

This invokes a playful argument between Rush and Sparrow in the kitchen, but I head for Aspen, crouching by her chair, hands clutching the armrest. "How are you feeling today?"

She lays her work in her lap, the bright, colored threads splaying across the quilt that covers her legs. She smiles at me with fond wrinkled eyes before tucking an errant curl behind my pointed ear. Her fingers quiver. "Better than yesterday, darling."

While that may be true, I fear that tomorrow will be worse. She looks tired, so tired that I can feel the sag of it in my bones. Her posture reminds me of a storybook in Sparrow's collection about a man condemned to hold up the heavens on his back. There's a curve in between her shoulders where they meet her neck, like the strain of keeping herself upright weighs on her body.

Settling my chin on my hands, I look up at her the same way I did as a child. My sisters and I don't remember our mother, so Aspen has been the closest thing we've ever had. I love her. "Is there anything I can get you?" I ask, eager to make her feel better.

"See if there's any biscuits you can sneak me to dunk in my tea, will you? Sparrow seems to think too much sugar will bring me to Death's door faster. I keep telling her, I'll go in my own time."

I shake my head, always so surprised by how poised she remains through suffering. She speaks about dying so frankly, so at peace––it's something I will never understand.

"Three or four?" I whisper as I stand, knowing her soft spot for baked goods almost matches mine.

A grin lights up her wane face, freckles almost hidden by her pallor. "As many as your pockets will fit."

With a snort, I make my way to the suspiciously silent kitchen. I saunter in as loud as I can, but I still catch the love-birds with their lips locked. My half-brother is leaning over Sparrow, letting the handles of her wheelchair behind her shoulders hold his weight. She runs her palms over his short hair and cups his scruffy face with tender hands. The silver band on her left ring finger winks before I cover my eyes with dramatic flair. "Come on, not by the food, you two. You have your own house, leave this one unsullied for all our sakes, please." I search blindly for the table that holds the biscuit jar.

I hear Rush pull away from Sparrow with an exaggerated smack of his lips, and when I uncover my eyes, I see his dark umber skin is flushed with happiness. "You know, Rose, one day you'll find someone who––"

Pressing my hands to my ears, I crinkle my nose with a shiver. "Nope. Hard pass, I'd rather be a spinster. I'd sooner run thousands of miles back to the beach towns before I subject myself to *that*."

"Aw, you just got back a few weeks ago, don't leave me alone with your siblings again until after Christmastide," Sparrow pleads with a quirk to her reddened lips. She may be pushing close to twenty-nine but when it comes to Rush, she looks like a lovestruck teenager again.

Speaking of the devil, it was my brother who passed on his spirit for adventure to me; he had no more use for it after courting Sparrow. And as soon as I was old enough and weighed down with all the salt Aspen could make me carry, I set out to see the world. I went west to discover the seas made of sand before wandering east to the moon-churned oceans. Once I tried to go south but I couldn't make it past the birch trees that grow before the pine forests, their white bark reminding me too much of the banshee trees surrounding that old, harrowing cave––the one that will forever haunt me. I had to turn back. After that I sought solace in the black sanded beaches I'd left in the east; it helped, a little.

The holidays called me back home to the glade before I could meander north. This faerie laden land is where I belong, but I will always love to roam. New journeys call to me, my keen sense of goblin smell leading the way. I want to see the whole world someday. But family comes first. I don't see myself leaving anytime soon, not with the state Aspen is in. If anything happens to her, I'll need to be here for the aftermath, to be a part of the glue that's going to hold everyone together in their grief.

In the meantime, I'll putter around the glade and pick up my triplets' slack when needed, all the while dreaming of greener hills and warmer weather. I'll pester Rush when Posy and Poppy pester me, and I'll brood with the brownies in the barn when I want some peace and quiet. Maybe I'll even play with the cute little booger-faced changelings and sneak off to Hazel's cottage to raid her elderberry wine stash once I've reached peak boredom.

I stick my hand out to my sister-in-law. "Don't kiss my brother like that in front of me again and I'll think about sticking around."

Sparrow's pale hand slips into my green grasp. "Deal," she says with a firm shake. Her pristine, black lacquered chair, enchanted by the Elder Mother herself, spins from her husband and leads her back toward the sitting area.

"Honey—" Rush sulks at the prospect of kisses being withheld.

"Don't forgot to take the bread out of the oven, my love," Sparrow laughs. "You wouldn't want to burn your masterpiece."

He grumbles as he turns his attention to the clay oven, the source of the yeast and sugar scent. I think I spy a lopsided braid-like loaf bathed in spotty patches of egg-wash inside.

Under the guise of sympathy, I give him a heavy pat on his shoulder while my other hand reaches for the biscuit jar. Once I have my prizes tucked into my other pocket, free of Posy's belongings, I dash from the kitchen, hoping Rush doesn't see the crumbs falling in my wake.

The front door flies open when I return to Aspen's side, bouncing off the wall as tiny feet run inside. A trail of wet prints are strewn across the wood floor as a changeling child cries, "Mommy, Mommy!" Robin flings her arms around Sparrow's thin legs.

The youngest of Rush and Sparrow's children would be the spitting image of her mother if it weren't for her silver eyes. She has Sparrow's ivory skin, dark wavy hair, and button nose. Robin even has the same heart made of elder twigs cloaked in a troll charm sitting inside her chest, but she has her father's gaze.

Rush comes stumbling in, silver eyes wide with panic. "What is it? Where's the fire?"

"Starling pushed me in the stream again." Robin gives a pitiful shiver, bottom lip quivering.

"Did you push him back?" I ask.

"Rose," Rush hisses. "Not helpful."

Shrugging, I slip Aspen one of the chocolate-iced biscuits and grab one for myself. We nibble as we watch the parents at work.

"I'm sorry, sweet girl, that wasn't very nice of your brother. Where is he now?" Sparrow pulls the cold, soggy child into her lap, wiping away her tears.

Robin sniffles. "Auntie Poppy put him in a timeout after making him say sorry."

With a long-suffering sigh, Rush kneels to rub warmth into his daughter's back. Robin plays with Sparrow's almost waist length hair as she leans against her chest, brows sad and furrowed.

"Remember what Daddy said about playing by the stream?" Rush asks.

"Someone could get hurt or taken by Nelly Longarms," Robin mumbles.

I hold back a laugh, thinking of the witch who's trying to steal Jenny Greenteeth's notoriety for stalking lakes and rivers for victims. Hearing about the story of how Rush and Sparrow had slain Jenny, I grew up without caution for most water. The glade's streams and the world's oceans were safe. Rivers and lakes on the other hand are always a gamble, even after news of Jenny's death spread like wildfire and the story of the elusive Changeling Queen grew. Witches became afraid of the figure that felled her *and* Black Annis. Though Nelly Longarms is said to be testing her luck by being on the prowl, and her existence is now used as a tactic to get kids to behave around water.

Sparrow rolls her eyes at Rush before turning her gaze back to her little girl. "Daddy will take you home to get changed and cozy, okay? I'll be there by lunchtime."

Rush points at Aspen. "I'll be back for our sewing time. I have a new project for us, lots of buttons to reattach to the kids' jackets." My half-brother scoops up his daughter and turns for the door. Quickly, I slip a biscuit from my pocket with a finger to my lips, planting it in Robin's chilly fist as Rush carries her away. She gives me a toothy grin, then munches, spilling crumbs over her father's shoulder all the way out the door. The pair pass both Posy and Poppy making their way inside the home.

"Special delivery," Poppy chirps, twirling her way inside to plant a kiss on Aspen's cheek. She's moving towards Sparrow when she sees the dark splotch covering the woman's cream-colored trousers and earthen sweater. "You're wet," she states, confused.

"Well spotted, genius," I say around a mouthful of choco-latey-biscuity-goodness.

Posy crosses the floor with more grace, kissing both Aspen and Sparrow on the cheek in greeting before setting a basket full of autumn harvest on the scuffed kitchen table. Poppy and I are making unpleasant faces at each other when Posy shoves her hand in my pocket to retrieve her book and spectacles. I don't even get in a word before the blue eyeglasses are perched on her nose and her book is open. She plops down to sit on the table-top, foregoing an actual chair. I try to distract Posy from read-ing, retaliating for my rudely picked pockets while Poppy roots through her basket. She organizes some pickings, setting them aside for canning and pickling while Sparrow mops at her damp lap with the sleeve of her sweater. Aspen beckons her closer to the fire, telling her to get dry before going out into the cold to make the short trip home. We settle into a quiet sort of concur-rence until a sudden sharp scratching at the window makes us all jump in surprise. I look, expecting one of my nieces or nephews with a stick in hand, but instead there's a black cat. It sits on the windowsill perched in smoky shadow, not unlike the ones always flickering at the perimeter of my gaze. Except, there is no real shadow darkening this animal, it's only the inky fur on its body floating in the non-existent wind.

My memories spark. There was a night, many years ago,

when my sisters and I were little enough to share a bed, when Sparrow and Rush sat in our room telling us a story. They told us of a giant wolf-like dog that turned into a spectral horse with sulfurous eyes, a creature draped in chains and whispers. The feline eyes that stare at us through the window are glowing yellow, unnatural in their luminescence.

It's a Pooka, and it looks like it wants to come inside.

The Pooka in the Window

"Is that what I think it is?" Poppy asks aloud. Who she's asking I'm not sure, but we all nod as we stare at the creature on the other side of the glass.

"I haven't seen a Pooka in ten years, but their presence is never good. They don't come around unless they have a message." Sparrow sounds lost in her harrowed memories. I can see her rubbing the long-healed scars on her chest through her damp sweater. Like the rest of us, Sparrow also has lingering damage.

The chair Aspen sits in creaks as she leans forward, trying to get a better look at the black cat with her aged eyes. "If my memory serves me, Pookas carry prophecies." Her statement sounds more like a question, and it's aimed at Sparrow. But when I peer at her, she's not present; she seems far away. "Little bird?" Aspen prompts.

The nickname shakes the changeling woman out of her stupor, her absent hand dropping into her lap as she blinks the past away. "What? Oh yes, sorry, Mother. You're correct, but remember, prophecies are elusive things, hard to interpret. I originally thought the last one was about your death."

"When in reality it was about yours," I remind my sister-in-law.

Sparrow hums in agreement and we all turn back to look at the cat. It appears distinctly unimpressed, gazing skyward as if rolling its eyes with a huff. The next thing we know, the faerie materializes through the glass in a smoky puff and drops to the ground on four stealthy paws.

There's safety in numbers, so Poppy skitters over to where Posy is still perched on the table. Posy's precious book is clutched to her chest as she stares with equal parts fear and intrigue at the Pooka sauntering toward the hearth. I can almost imagine the gears in her head spinning, searching through all the information she knows about this creature, whether that be from books or the mouth of the Elder Mother.

I'm torn between going to my sisters and staying by Aspen's side, but when my body inches to stand between the ailing woman and the Pooka, my decision is made. With my silver eyes narrowed and hand on the hilt of the elder wood knife sheathed at my hip, I watch the faerie disguised as a harmless cat. There's no doubt that if Rush were here, our matching gazes would both be like steel.

There's a sense of foreboding hanging over the creature. I don't trust it one bit.

Sparrow pushes her wheelchair toward the Pooka who now sits backlit by the blazing fire—a dramatic front if you ask me. Sparrow doesn't seem afraid though, more wary, like going into a battle she's fought before. Her voice doesn't even tremble. "I'm surprised you were able to get past the salt barrier around this glade."

"I may be made of darkness, Daughter of the Trolls, but evil was not what formed this body. Your salt is nothing but mere decoration to me." The Pooka's voice sounds layered, an accumulation of male gravel-like whispers that drift throughout the

14

room in echoes. It makes the skin on my arms ripple with bumps despite the warmth of the house.

The white scar that runs through Sparrow's brow, thanks to Jenny Greenteeth, pulls when she frowns. "Have we met before?"

"We have not, nor am I here for you." The cat turns its spectral eyes on Aspen. "Or you."

"Then why are you here?" the older woman presses from her bundled quilt.

"Fate has a message for the goblins of the glade." The Pooka looks at me, and a whisper of cold, bottomless intelligence hits me when our eyes lock. I shiver as the creature turns away to look at my sisters. Instinctively, I step forward, a hot possessive feeling burbling in my stomach as I draw the creature's attention back to me, and to my blade. The Pooka's flowing hackles go stiff at my sudden defensive move.

"Yeah, right, if *Fate* speaks to you then I'm a long-lost princess," I snap. The light of the fire dances along the rose filigree magically carved into my knife.

Fate is just a personified term for so-called *destiny*, for the things we want to seem "meant to be." Just like Death is a friendly face to greet us in the end, Time a cruel master who never gives us enough, and the Sun and Moon ever present and watching lights. These omniscient things aren't real people. They're all just figures of speech, or god-like myths made to make us feel less alone in the world. Using them as names is almost a language that's been passed down to us, like old stories the world heard whispers of centuries ago.

"What do you really want, bogey?" I ask, eyes narrowing further as my hand clutches my weapon.

If cats could raise a brow, that's what this creature seems to be doing. "Watch your words and your blade, Primrose," it purrs.

Hearing my name and the quiet threat on the ghost-filled

wind of its coarse voice feels like winter ice down my back. Stepping out the door into the budding cold would feel warmer than I do right now. When Aspen takes a shaky hand from her blanket and touches my elbow, I pull in a long breath of toasty air, attempting to thaw my soul. Her gentle touch tells me everything her silence doesn't. *Stand down.* My body can do nothing but listen to her. We don't know why this creature is here and my aggression could get my family hurt. You never know what might happen if you pull a weapon on the wrong Pooka.

"It would seem you've all forgotten your manners, along with your knowledge, over the years. What a shame." The Pooka's words curl around my neck as it rolls its yellow eyes skyward, bored.

As I sheathe my knife, I hear movement behind me and when I turn, I'm surprised to see Posy at my shoulder. She has a deep furrow between her brows, and the spectacles on the end of her nose are slipping. "What are we forgetting?" she asks, petal soft.

If there's one thing Posy is known for, it's her memory. The way she catalogues facts, stories and creatures, words and their origins, every bit of information she can find. Her memory will never cease to amaze me. That's why I know this statement from the Pooka bothers her, *a lot*. If there's something she doesn't yet know, she'll do everything she can to learn about it. But forgetting…that has never happened. Ever.

"Well, it's not entirely your fault, much of history died with Lady Luck centuries ago, but there is someone left who possesses all of those secrets, albeit unaware." The cat looks at every one of us as if trying to get a very important point across. "Someone whose many faces you know well."

Sparrow and her mother share a knowing look while Poppy tries to pull Posy back into my shadow. This creature said it was here for us; whether the message is bogus or not, I won't lie, I'm interested now. The last prophecy that was given to my family a decade ago was a warning; according to my half-brother's account of their run-in with a Pooka, it's *not* something to be ignored.

"Out with it then." I cross my arms, trying to look disinterested, but on the inside, my heart is speeding up, a seed of worry growing. Could it be another warning of death? Maybe Aspen's impending departure from this earth?

The Pooka stands in a lazy stretch, muscles taut and tail high before it sways closer on dark, silent paws, whispers of smoke trailing behind it. *"Beware, triplets, for the memories of the past are buried. Follow Time's words to return him to his lost love, and recover The Numina or unravel the thread to the forgotten forever."*

I laugh. That didn't sound like a warning about death at all. I knew this faerie was full of nothing but bosh and bilge. "The Numi-who? This sounds like a dumb cheapjack scavenger hunt for a love letter and a piece of string."

An exasperated symphony of my name plays out as not only Aspen, but Sparrow and Poppy scold me. But I see a glimmer in the Pooka's face, and the slits of its feline eyes show a fragment of amusement.

"Find the book hidden behind a door no one would look, beneath a place that has not seen light in six hundred years. And please, do tell the Elder Mother her old friends say hello." The cat says all this before dissolving into a black cloud that disappears underneath the seam in the front door.

I'd applaud the theatrical exit, but I have a feeling, by the tension in the air, that now is not the time for sarcasm again. Sparrow looks grim and Aspen, poor Aspen, looks drained down to the dregs. She needs to go lie down.

I'm about to suggest Aspen's had enough excitement for the day and needs rest when Poppy speaks up. "It sounds like we're going on an adventure." Her green skin had gone a little wan in the presence of the misty creature but now she seems jittery, excited.

"Perhaps..." Sparrow shakes her head, rubbing absentmindedly at her littlest finger. "Hazel said that the Pooka who cornered your brother mentioned something about Fortune and these paths. And I've seen the red threads of Fate with my own eyes. I'd even swear I've met her and Death when I floated in the space between life and whatever comes after-- when my chest was cleaved wide open." She stares at me and my sisters in turn. "At the very least, this visit should not be taken lightly."

Aspen nods in agreement with her daughter, giving us a stern mother-ish look.

Poppy and I sober. She stops bouncing on her toes, instead humming a nervous tune while my glib attitude hardens to stone. Posy looks like she's rummaging through her memory bank though she's still attentive to the changeling sitting in front of us.

"Consider the message carefully, comb through every word until it's burned into your brain." Sparrow sighs, letting her muscles relax into her wheelchair as the sternness slips from her tone. "Pookas are cryptic, but I think we all know where you need to start."

She's right. Hazel's cottage.

—

FOR A TIME, we all went our separate ways, Sparrow returning to her home to change her wet clothes and wrangle her family for lunch while I ushered Aspen back to her room for a nap. Poppy went to go check on Pop, hoping he'd moved from his beloved rocking chair and stopped staring into space, while Posy packed our knapsacks for the short journey to Hazel's.

Years ago, after Sparrow's twig heart had mended, the Elder Mother, Hazel, returned to her responsibilities as the caretaker of the elder trees. However, the long day of twisty travel through the forest that separated Hazel from her new family eventually became too much for everyone. So, with the help of the glade's occupants, the Elder Mother discovered a more direct route and together they built a stone path, one smooth enough for enchanted wheels and little feet. And it's no ordinary path. Some of the surviving goblins from the attack had the brilliant idea of adding salt into the wet mixture that would solidify and pave the way between the glade and the hidden cottage. They engineered a way for safe travel where no bogeyman, creatures of evil and witchcraft, could harm the traveler. It's made our weekly visits there much easier.

We three girls loved visiting her while growing up, because in the mornings Hazel was almost the same age as us and could act as a playmate. As she aged throughout the day, she'd become more like an older sister, then by afternoon an aunt-like figure, all the way to a grandmother and mentor by nighttime.

Back then, we thought Hazel knew everything, but as we grew we learned the sad truth: Hazel has no memory of her own past, at all. She doesn't even know how long she's been the mystical Elder Mother. She's only been able to keep track of a handful of centuries, but anything before that is a blur.

Still, the Elder Mother is a well of information. And when all the glade's survivors returned home from that cave ten years ago, Hazel gave not only Posy, but all three of us, some stability in the form of knowledge. When the sun set, and we finished our dinner with numb minds, she would gather my sisters and I and breathe life back into us with Floriography. The secret language of flowers. It distracted us, in short spurts, from the memories of dark horrors and replaced our haunted thoughts

19

with something soft and sweet. We loved it. Especially considering we were all named after flora. It felt special, like the information was our birthright.

Poppy means eternal sleep and when paired with snowdrops it shows love for a person you've lost. Posy is a gift meant to show sentiment and communication. Primrose represents youth, and when given to someone, it means you can't live without them.

We learned how to create bouquets that mean friendship with apple blossom, pansy, and eucalyptus, bitterness with petunias, pansy, and thistle. We used flowers to convey our feelings when words were too hard, or the days too much. Hazel kept us busy until the wounds no one could see had time to scab over.

When we got older, we used our special language less. It wasn't until I came home to the glade and found out Aspen was sick that I gave her a bundle of gladiolus for strength. That was the first time I'd dipped back into Floriography in years.

I reminisce about all of this now as my sisters and I make our way down the salt-infused path to the Elder Mother's cottage, passing little sprigs of snowdrops with their sad, droopy white heads sprouting through the cold winter earth. We should make it there well before dinnertime since we don't have to weave through looping trees or skitter down frost-hardened slopes anymore.

Poppy is ahead, bopping along her merry way, whistling a tune. She can never stay quiet. Of course, Posy tries to read while she walks. I stay at her elbow, steering her so she doesn't stumble off the path and twist an ankle on the slippery moss flooding the forest floor. At times I feel tempted to let her fall, just to see the surprise on her face, but I resist the sibling-urge knowing the power of the silent wrath I'd face if something were to happen to the book she's transcribing. It wouldn't be pretty. I stay at my post, watching over her from just a step behind. It's best I'm at my sisters' backs keeping a watchful eye;

I can't keep up with Poppy's light feet and I don't want to listen to her tune up close or the song will get stuck in my head. The snatches I can hear are more than enough. I'm content to keep my hands in my pockets as I stroll, adjusting Posy's direction when needed, while I daydream of sandy shores and trees with fronds twice the size of my body.

My pleasant thoughts are interrupted when Poppy sings louder. "For lo!" She turns to face Posy and I as she continues walking backward, throwing her arms out. "The days are hastening on, by prophet seen of old—"

"Poppy," I say, a low warning in my voice. She's doing this on purpose to be a nuisance, and I know she'll only grow more boisterous the longer I let her sing.

She gives me a cheery grin. "When with the ever-circling years shall come the Time foretold—"

"Knock it off," I groan. "Your voice is loud enough to make my ears ring."

Posy lets out a huff in agreement, putting her thumb in between the pages she's reading and closing the book around it to keep her place.

Poppy trips a little but keeps on her incessant off-key singing. "When peace shall over all the earth the ancient Numi —" Her singing cuts off in a giggling scream when I break out into a sudden run, pushing past Posy and rushing toward her. Poppy turns back around and runs down the path with me chasing after her. I hear Posy follow with a groan. She's hot on my heels as her long boot-covered legs keep her from being left behind.

—

WE ARRIVE at the Elder Mother's property sooner than hoped, laughing and out of breath with wind burnt cheeks. The path cuts through her own personal woods of elder trees and shrubs, and there's so many of them that it's a maze to those unfamiliar with the area. But we pass right through, the naked branches of the silver trees hanging above us, forming lattice-like shadows over the ground. I see another shadow too, a smokier cat-shaped one running along the tree limbs. The Pooka has been following us. The faerie blends in amongst the other dark shapes that have plagued my periphery since childhood, but I don't pay them or the trailing spy much mind. My sisters have never been able to see my ever-present shadows, no matter how many times I've tried to catch or describe them throughout my life. And right now, they're both too distracted shoving each other with their shoulders to notice our stalker either, so I stay quiet. Besides, I won't give the shady creature the satisfaction. The Pooka wouldn't be skulking behind in the shadows unless it thought we were incapable of following directions.

So I immerse myself in my heightened goblin senses until I can smell smoke wafting from Hazel's chimney; it smells like she's steeping mulled spices over the fire in her cauldron. The gentle burn of cardamom, star anise, cinnamon, and clove fill my nose, and it feels like Christmastide morning. I'm tired from all our sprinting after Poppy, but the nostalgic scents give me one last burst of energy. I quicken my steps.

By the time we break through the trees and see the Elder Mother's ivy-covered stone cottage, the carved door is already open and Hazel stands in the doorway wrapped in a thick shawl and a long, black wool dress. Her braid, threaded with gray, lies over her crossed arms. At this time of day she appears almost fifty, and she looks quite concerned, judging by the combination of surprise and confusion scrunching her progressively aging features. We drag ourselves closer and I can see her one brown and one blue eye assessing the three of us.

Her search will come up empty seeing as we're not running toward her home in a strange panic or carrying anything unusual that could give her a clue as to why we're here. All she can do is speak with conjecture the moment we darken her doorstep. "What have you done?"

The Beast Under the Floor

I huff at Hazel. "What do you mean what have *we* done?"

"With you triplets, there is always something," she says while shifting sideways and gesturing us inside with a hand. We skulk past her into the cottage, hanging our coats and scarves, making ourselves right at home. Poppy goes straight to the kitchen of the large, one roomed house, looking for elderberry snacks while Posy perches herself on top of the table. I take up the taller of the mismatched floral chairs sitting by the hearth. The bubbling cauldron hanging over the fire imbues my senses with cozy spices as I slouch downward and sprawl my legs out.

Hazel clicks her tongue as she closes the door behind us. "Poppy, wash your grubby little hands before you touch my food. I know you've been with Sparrow's little flock; I will not have you passing on their germs."

Next, she looks at Posy with a lifted brow.

Blood floods my sister's green cheeks as she slides from the tabletop into one of the many chairs sitting around it. She tries to look as casual as possible, like she didn't just get a silent reprimand from her prized teacher. She fails.

"And you," Hazel sighs, kicking my ankle as she passes,

intent on occupying the overstuffed chair beside me. "Would it kill you to sit like a lady, Primrose?"

"It will if you keep calling me Primrose; makes me sound like an old lady." I wiggle my way upright, like a proper person.

"She only lets Aspen call her that." Poppy shouts this through a mouth full of what looks like a scone. Wrinkling my nose as half-chewed pieces fly from between her teeth, I stick my tongue out at her while the Elder Mother's back is turned.

Posy rolls her eyes at us.

When the older woman turns back around, my face is a veil of innocence, but Hazel knows, she *always* knows. "Rose," she drawls as she settles deep into her chair, crossing one leg over the other. "Care to share what brings you three to my door so early this week?"

I give her an extra toothy grin, but I can see by her serious expression that she's not buying it, so I slump back into the chair. "Can't we just be here for a visit?"

"Your sister over there"—Hazel sends a pointed look in Posy's direction— "didn't go for my books as soon as she walked in. Plus, all of you were here a few days ago and I'm supposed to be in the glade tomorrow. This isn't a casual visit."

"We need your help," I admit, the blasé air I usually carry leaving my words.

Hazel leans forward.

Poppy is the one who beats me to the punch. "We were visited by a Pooka," she states, scone crumbs covering her lips.

Eyes wide, the Elder Mother falls back in her chair, hands clutching onto the armrests. Whatever she expected us to say, it wasn't this. I can imagine what she's remembering as she holds herself steady, the prophecy she, Sparrow, and Rush received thinking it was about Aspen. Then, discovering it was about Sparrow as she lay dying, bleeding out on the cave floor as Hazel tried to heal the broken changeling heart lying in pieces all around them. I can picture it because I was there too, standing off to the side, helpless with my sisters, Pop, and the rest of the faeries who'd been caged.

After a moment Hazel clears her throat. "What did it say?"

"Nothing very helpful in my opinion." I shrug. "Just some stuff about memories and lost love. But it did tell us to find a book."

"Don't forget it said to tell the Elder Mother her old friends say hello," Poppy adds, her mouth blessedly empty now.

Hazel's thin brows furrow, her olive skin crinkling not only as she ages before our eyes, but in confusion. "Old friends? I don't have any friends, well, except your brother and Sparrow of course, but they don't count."

I force myself to hold back a laugh.

"What about from before?" Posy all but whispers.

That's when Hazel's face drops. She doesn't remember her life before she became the Elder Mother, but she must have had one. There's no way she just *poofed* into existence and started growing and protecting all those trees outside. But why wouldn't she be able to recall a time before? She has lived at least six centuries and remembers everything else she's seen and learned--

"I don't...I don't know." The Elder Mother's eyes are glazed, lost.

Sitting up, I lean over to put my hand on her knee, stopping her from trying to force the memories that've never surfaced for her before. The look on her face is heartbreaking. I share a troubled glance with my sisters as they come closer. Posy sits at Hazel's feet, the fire warming her side as she wraps her arms around her knees to rock herself, a self-stimulating habit she's had since we were little. Poppy balances on the arm of my chair like a storybook princess sitting sidesaddle.

"Forget about that, Hazel, that's not what's important right now." I drum my fingers on her knee, trying to break her free

26

from whatever mental limbo she dropped into. "We need help deciphering the Pooka's message."

"Right." She blinks. "Of course."

Poppy twirls one of the small braids she has nestled in her mass of curly, ink-colored hair. She looks concerned, nervous even, as she speaks to Hazel. "The message didn't directly mention you, but the messenger did make it clear that you'd be the one to hold some of the answers to our questions."

With a deep, grounding breath, the Elder Mother nods. "All right, let me hear it."

Glancing at Posy, I expect her and her perfect memory to be the one to recite the so-called prophecy, but she just stares back at me. Her yellow-lime eyes begging me to be the one to say it as her body sways. I can see the guilt about bringing up Hazel's past in the way she picks at the skin around her fingernails.

I shrug, then eye the rafters where dried herbs and flowers hang, trying to recall all the Pooka's wispy words. *"Beware, triplets, for the memories of the past are buried. Follow Time's words to return him to his lost love and recover The Numina or unravel the thread to the forgotten forever."*

Hazel tugs at the end of her braid, fingers smoothing over the leather strip that ties it all in place. The fine wrinkles around her mouth deepen as she mulls over the shapeshifter's dark words. "It would seem I've been caught up in Fate's strings once again," she mumbles.

This again? I've been told enough tales about Death, Fate, and Time by Sparrow to last an eternity. And I know believing in these all-powerful beings is a generational thing—Hazel comes from every one of them, so it doesn't surprise me that she believes. But today's humans and faeries have all but forgotten those old ways.

"What do you mean 'again'?" Poppy asks the Elder Mother.

"Do you remember the stories Rush, Sparrow, and I used to tell you about our journey to bring you back home? How the

Pooka we met said only an elder could restore a daughter of the trolls?"

My sisters and I nod.

Hazel continues, "Well, I was always the one meant to repair Sparrow's heart. It was my destiny. Fate sent her messenger to tell us this, to give us a warning about what she saw in her red threads."

I've heard of this red thread before; it's a childhood memory cloaked in the fog of sleepy bedtime stories. Poppy in her starry-eyed nature had asked Sparrow and Rush, as they tucked us in, how they knew what they felt was true love. Sparrow had shared this fond look with her then-fiancé and told us about a place with bright white light and two women weaving. How Time had given Sparrow a frozen moment with Death and Fate, a moment to make an important choice. She said she chose to hold on to the thread tied around her littlest finger and let it lead her home to our half-brother.

Since then, Poppy has never had a problem dreaming about true love. Posy has remained indifferent to the concept––and me, well, the thought of romantic affection makes me uncomfortable. Having someone to call your forever person is nice, but swapping spit is not. I think the red-threaded stories were just embellished fairytales meant to convince us all to believe in love.

Right?

"Somehow," I begin, voice dripping with skepticism, "if this were even half true and Fate is some magical lady with fancy yarn, what thread and what book are we supposed to find for her?"

"And who or what is The *Numina*?" Poppy pitches in.

From the floor, Posy nods in agreement to our questions and turns her gaze up to Hazel. Who in return rubs at her temples and squeezes her eyes closed as frustration overcomes her.

"Death and Time, the Sun and the Moon, Fate..." She trails off. "There's something more important about them. I've heard little snippets of myth throughout my years, in torn scraps of cloth, in the veins of feathers, old poems and songs. They were called The Numina but that was when Fortune supposedly existed. It seems that the earth has, well..." She pauses. "Forgotten."

"Don't give yourself a headache over myths, Hazel. Let's start with something more practical, like finding this mysterious book." I can't resist a sarcastic flourish of my hands.

Poppy almost falls into my lap as she tries to stand from the armrest of my chair. "Well, there's plenty of books in this house! I'm sure it's got to be around here somewhere." She heads for the shelves, scanning the mass of tomes and timeworn spines, cocking her head to the side, trying to read the vertical titles. From my vantage point, she looks like an awkward chicken with a wonky, green neck.

There's a hum coming from the back of Posy's throat, and it sounds a lot like disagreement.

I nudge her folded legs with a booted toe. "What's up?"

"*Find the book hidden behind a door no one would look.* It's not going to be on the shelves," Posy murmurs. She's given up on stripping the flesh from around her fingernails and taken to playing with the loose button on her vest.

"Ah, good point." Getting up, I tap along the walls, listening for any hollow thumps instead of shallow thuds.

"Rose, what in the world are you doing beating up my walls?" Hazel chides.

I stop, fist poised to knock on the wood with my ear up against the surface. "I'm looking for secret doors."

The Elder Mother snorts. "I can tell you right now the only doors in this house are the front door and the closet."

Posy hops up and goes to the closet in the far corner of the small cottage, right across from the single bed tucked up on the opposite side. Little dust motes flutter through the air when she opens the door and peers into its shadowy insides.

When I come up behind her and leer over her shoulder, I see what I expected. Folded linens on a shelf, a cloak and a handful of black dresses hanging on a wooden rod. Not a single book in sight. My mind flits to the prophecy again—*beneath a place that has not seen light in six hundred years.*

Even with Posy, me, and now Poppy blocking the direct light coming from the fire and dove-gray gloom outside, I can see light is touching every corner of the closet. The darkest shadow in the upper left corner of the ceiling is maybe the size of my hand and there's no secret book hiding there. Though, when Poppy shifts her feet, I hear a creak of the old floorboards.

"Say, Hazel—" I step back, peering down— "Have you done any remodeling in the last half dozen centuries?"

"I haven't done a thing besides the occasional dusting and hanging plants in the rafters to dry," she calls from her chair.

I give my sisters a conspiratorial look, my lips tilting in a smirk. "How much do you want to bet the book is in the floor?" I punctuate my words by bouncing on my toes, listening to the hollow wood groan in complaint.

"I've already lost my dessert to you today. I'm not wagering anything else." Poppy throws her hands up and backs away, unwilling to gamble with me. Coward.

"How about you?" I question Posy, but she's already crouching and running her hands along the floor looking for seams. I guess we're in agreement then.

She glances up at me when her fingernails catch on something. A grin climbs over her swooping lips. Her emerald skin is glittering as she pats at her pockets, no doubt looking for something sharp. I haven't seen her this intent on solving a puzzle since Hazel gave her an old Latin book to translate for Christmastide last year. It's nice to see her excitement, even with the semi-spooky mystery looming, and of course it's about another book, so to her, it's pure happiness all the same.

"Anyone have something sharp?" I all but shout.

When someone pulls the dagger from my hip and offers it to me at my elbow I almost jump out of my skin. With a hand pressed to my chest, I notice Hazel. "Goodness, woman, you and your silent feet. Announce yourself, will you?"

The Elder Mother laughs. "Your goblin ears should have heard me." She moves to tug on the long ears sprouting from my head, but I dodge her, snatching my blade and crouching next to Posy for safety. Hazel just leans up against the doorjamb and watches with the hint of a smile. "Just so you know, you break it, you fix it."

I survey the dagger in my hands. I'm reluctant to use my precious elder knife; I don't want it to chip on the thick, old floorboard. While Hazel was the one to convene with the trees to craft me the intricately decorated weapon, Aspen was the one to suggest it. It was a gift they worked on together, and not only was it meant to protect me in my travels, it was also meant as a piece of home…and now I might ruin it on the Elder Mother's closet floor.

With a deep sigh, I shove my knife into Posy's waiting hand. She rolls her eyes in response before jamming the tip into the faint crack in the floorboard between two planks. By wiggling the blade back and forth, she manages to wedge it in deep enough for the dagger to meet resistance. That's when she pushes down. I grit my teeth, willing my knife to stay strong. Little by little the board pries free, and then with one final crack, the plank separates from the rest of the floor. Both the wood and my knife land a few inches away with a clatter.

The four of us all lean forward, squinting into the dark, uncovered abyss. At first glance, I see no book, but then again, I can't see anything else either. The space beneath the floor looks bottomless and smells musty to my sensitive nose. "I am not putting my arm down there."

"Well, someone has to," Poppy retorts.

I peer up at her where she stands. "Are you volunteering?"

She shakes her head and crosses her arms over her chest. When I look at Hazel, she just shrugs her free shoulder.

"Looks like it's up to you, sister dear." I pat Posy on the shoulder.

With a huff, she rolls up her blouse sleeve and lowers her hand into the hole. Her arm moves as she waves it around, trying to feel for this elusive book. She's reaching even lower when her body is pulled flat to the floor and the side of her face is smooshed into the ground. Her expression is wild, panicked, like a beast from the dark is trying to yank her into the unknown.

Heart and stomach plummeting, I hook my arms beneath her armpits and heave. To my surprise, we fly backward without a fight, as if whatever had hold of Posy gave up and let go, fast. I hold her trembling frame in a protective hug, waiting for something to rise from the depths while using my goblin ancestry to disappear. Squeezing her, I urge Posy to do the same, to hide from the unknown threat, but she only shudders. It takes a moment but when I realize that the shaking I feel in my sister's body is from laughter and not fear, I shove her off, reappearing as I say, "You son of a banshee! I thought a bogey was trying to pull you down to Purgatory."

Posy is lying on the closet floor still relishing her joke with a wrapped, bookish shaped object gripped in her hands. I huff, standing to dust myself off while Hazel and Poppy chuckle. Embarrassment curdles in my gut as I scoop the book from Posy's loose hold and snatch up my knife with the other. Then, with an undignified sniff, I tuck the blade into its sheath and stomp back to the chair I occupied before.

The dusty fabric that covers the book feels like it's going to turn to ash as I unwrap it. It's thin, and very, *very* old. When I uncover it, I'm surprised to find a journal with a soft brown cover worn in spots by loving hands. According to the Pooka, this book hasn't seen the light of day in six hundred years. Nor the hands that obviously loved it so many centuries ago.

I'm flipping through the pages when Hazel and my sisters come to crowd around my seat. We soak in the words of this precious-to-the-so-called-Numina journal--so precious that the fabled "Fate" even sent a Pooka to make us unearth it. The beginning has different writers, told apart by red and purple ink. The harsh edged cursive letters written in red ink are masculine compared to the feminine swooping letters in purple. It appears as though a couple had been writing back and forth, like passing notes within the same book. There are little domestic reminders to the man like: *"please refill the birdfeeders"*, or an *"I love you, have a great day"* to the woman. There's also shared jokes and sugary sweet declarations of love written among sketches of feathery wings and stylized hearts.

When I turn the pages further, I see notes, tons and tons of notes in purple ink about plants and herbs, instructions on how to make medicines like clotting powders and special sleep teas. There are even a couple different treatment plans for what seems like a young patient named Ellery tucked between two full pages just dedicated to cornflowers and a pome fruit. In the margins of these pages, there are sketches of other flowers I recognize like yarrow and wormwood, lavender and chamomile, all done in the man's red ink.

I stop on a page that has a detailed drawing of a large belt entitled, *"Her Herbalist Belt."* It has a satchel, vials, and room for a small blade. "This book must have belonged to a physician before you built your house on top of it," I say to Hazel as I study the fine pen strokes.

"None of this is anything I've seen or heard of a physician studying. They couldn't care less about using what the earth has given us, they're too intent on lining their pockets with expensive and unnecessary procedures or placebo experiments." Hazel frowns. I study her for a moment longer and see that her mind is somewhere else now––something is bothering her, and I don't think its dodgy medical practice.

"Maybe they were a gardener?" Poppy suggests.

I flip back to the pages of notes and the words *"foxglove"* and *"belladonna"* catch my eye. My stomach clenches as I recall the sickly-sweet scent of poisonous berries. Shades of bruise blue dance before my eyes. Shaking off the memory, I flip to another page. "But why would Fate concern herself with a gardener's book?" I almost sound like I'm starting to believe in mythical beings, so I clear my throat and add, "If she's real, that is."

Posy reaches out and taps the words on the page. "I know this handwriting." She nods in self confirmation as she squints and points at the perfect purple loops and curls.

"What?" Poppy and I say in tandem.

"How?" I add.

Hazel shares a look with my quiet sister who's already staring at the older woman in wondrous confusion. It's the Elder Mother who responds. "Because she sees it almost every day." Hazel looks down at the book. "That journal is full of my handwriting."

A Letter from Time

"I'm sorry, come again?" I sputter. "Why didn't you just tell us it was down there to begin with?" I twist in my seat to look at the Elder Mother, and the old book slides from my lap to the floor, landing page side down, the paper edges holding it up like a tent.

Hazel takes a step back. "I didn't know it was. I don't remember writing it, or putting it in the floor."

"How is that even possible?" I ask.

Poppy rounds my chair and stoops to pick up the journal. "It must be from before you became the Elder Mother, the times you can't remember." When her spine straightens, something slips from between the upended pages and flutters to the floor. It looks to be a folded-up piece of parchment.

Posy is the one to snatch it up and unfold the yellowed paper. She pulls her spectacles out of her vest pocket and slips them onto her nose. Her eyes widen as she scans the red inked words peeking through the other side. It looks handwritten, like a letter. Lips parting, a small breath leaves her lungs. "Oh."

"Oh? What *oh*?" I bat at her hands to give me the paper. "What does it say?"

Even Poppy steps forward trying to take it from her, but

Posy pulls it out of her reach too. She looks dead at Hazel, more serious than I have ever seen her, and offers it up to her to read. The older woman only hesitates for a mere second before taking it.

She clears her throat before reading aloud:

Dear Primrose, Poppy, and Posy,

I am writing this letter twenty generations before your birth. By the time you read this, six hundred years will have passed since our imprisonment, and the world will have mostly forgotten us.

We are The Numina. The Sun, Moon, Death, Fate, Fortune, and me, Time. We have existed since the beginning, guiding the world and watching the threads in the tapestry of life unfold. But on the day you finally read this, only one thread will remain, a thread that wraps around the three of you.

Forgive me for being hasty, I should start from the beginning...

Being one of The Numina is an inherited gift. There have been many Deaths, Fates, Fortunes, and Times throughout the ages, but the birth of the first witch (her name was Quince, which is another tale for another day), resulted in the devastating murder of Fortune. When she died, there was no one ready to fill her position and this imbalance resulted in our imprisonment. Without the existence of a sixth Numina, the scales were tipped too far, and this pulled our physical bodies to a plane that we cannot escape alone, not without our missing piece. We are trapped in The Between, which exists in neither your world nor The After. My wife visited here long before becoming the Elder Mother, and even your sister-in-law will visit here, one day—— though, I suppose that has already happened...

I digress.

Fortune's death, and our resulting entrapment, will have allowed the world to fill with darkness since the ancient practice of Healing was destroyed along with it. My wife, my dearest Hazel, was what we once called a Healer, and she was <u>brilliant</u>. To save her life, and the future, I was forced to take Hazel's memories from her. Do not worry, *they are not gone forever; they're alive and well, kept whole in the form of an immortal bluebird.*

I know this explanation may feel strange, confusing, and short, but time is short as well, and you triplets must set our deliverance in motion. Only you can restore the balance and help us come home. Once we return, we can regenerate the Healing practice and eradicate all creatures made of witchcraft. The journey will be long and difficult, made harder yet by everything you've already faced. We are sorry for that. If there was another way, we would design it, but unfortunately there is not.

I know you are asking, why us? The only answer I can give is that Fate foresees you. Without you, the world falls to ruin, darkness will prevail, and the witches will rule the earth.

Your goal is to go north, breach the veil, and retrieve us inside the Wyrd Mountain. The messenger that Death and Fate sent will safely guide and protect you along the way. But before you reach our mountain it's important you obtain Hazel's bluebird from the swamp witch, Baba Yaga. Find something to trade her for it. Something worthy. I know Sparrow is considered a legend in your time, but don't follow in her footsteps, do not try to kill Baba Yaga. Get in and get out, and then head for the mountain.

Good luck. Hopefully I will meet you all soon.

— Time

P.S. Hazel, my love, I know this letter will cause you strife at first, but I can't miss this opportunity. My beautiful wife, my eternal love, I miss you more than you will ever know.

Hazel's voice is a trembling mess when she finishes reading the letter. Her lips are the palest color I've ever seen, and her hands shake like a fall leaf in the wind. She doesn't look good, at all. She's just seen a ghost from her past, one she can't recall. Her husband. *Time.*

Posy and I are stunned too, but at least Poppy and her care-taking instincts give her the wherewithal to guide the Elder Mother to her chair. The woman drops into it, still staring at the letter from her lost love. I try to envision her as this so-called Healer, but I cannot see anyone but the Hazel I know and love. She's somewhere in her early sixties now, her hair more silver than brown with the barest hint of a blooming age spot or two on the back of the hand that yanks the tail of her braid.

"This explains why you can't remember anything other than being the Elder Mother," Poppy says with a soft voice, rubbing at Hazel's back.

Even though I think she knows there's nothing else, Hazel flips the page over, desperate for more answers. "I was in love, I had a whole life––it's all gone... Who was I? Who were *we?*" Her voice cracks.

My chest tightens as I watch the confusion and grief wash over her. It's almost more painful to have only scraps of information. There are too many pieces missing. The Numina? They really exist?

I rub at my breastbone, trying to break past it to loosen the muscles clenching my heart. If I can somehow have faith that these powerful people are real, maybe my sisters and I can give Hazel back her past? I'm not one to jump at believing in fairytales, much like Sparrow and Rush's beloved bedtime stories, but Hazel has lived so long without these pieces of herself. It would be cruel to ignore this chance.

And if it really is true, it sounds like these Numina can take out the witches and erase all the bogeymen from the face of the earth. Not a single soul alive would ever have to live in fear of the creatures that prowl at night again. The marks marring my family's skin would be the only reminder that such things ever existed. I think of Sparrow and the split in her brow, the ragged scars across her chest. Looking at Posy, I see the faint line just at the top of her right cheekbone, the little scar from a graze of iron talons she collected while we sat in a cage.

"We'll figure it out, Hazel," I promise her. "We'll fix all of this."

Meeting my sisters' gazes, I can see it in their eyes, the confusion, the empathy, the resolve. We have a silent conversation, something that comes easy as triplets, and we decide, despite all rationale and reality, that we're going on this ridiculous journey. We'll see the rest of this prophecy through.

—

HAZEL INSISTS we take the journal; she says its knowledge is too much for her to bear. We beg her to walk back to the glade with us, but she refuses, saying she wants to sit in her chair and digest what she's learned, alone. I feel terrible leaving her, but none of us wants to journey back in the dark, salted path or not.

The whole walk home I can't stop thinking about Aspen. I came back from my travels to be here in her final moments, and I don't know how I'll live with myself if I'm gone when she passes. Yet here I am, headed home to pack my bags and leave with my sisters.

It's not until Posy does what Posy does best and flips through the journal while she walks that we stumble across a gold mine of information. Within the recipes and herbal notations, she finds diary-style entries, only less personal, more like this past version of Hazel was telling a story, or recording events for a history book.

Posy reads aloud as we walk. "Time was human once, he died and became one of The Numina, and later fell in love with Hazel." A hum of surprise rumbles through her throat. "Hazel was friends with the other Numina and with Quince, the girl who became the first ever witch. It looks like Hazel even had a little brother named Ellery, she called him Kit."

Reading over Posy's shoulder and tripping on her own feet,

Poppy reads a couple of sentences next. "The first Pooka was created from the dark criminal souls kept in Death's shadow and sculpted into messengers by Fate. They're trapped and forever paying for their past sins by regaling their prophecies."

"Hazel became a Healer after being 'Blessed' by the Sun and Moon," Posy states, then reads on for a moment before she summarizes, "They were the original Numina who, unlike the others, never change, and they have been observing all of us since the beginning of time. Apparently, the art of Healing was lost when these Numina disappeared, and the use of the earth and its magic-based plants were replaced by physicians who concocted chemicals and ridiculous treatments, like experimental surgeries to fix headaches." She holds the journal aloft for me and Poppy to see when she points out a certain underlined sentence: _medicine itself is magic_.

I repeat this phrase to myself before I realize that magic Healing just might be what we need right now. Posy and the Elder Mother have been searching for the answers to Aspen's illness for a long time, but if the art of Healing was lost long ago, then the books they've been reading are useless. Maybe what we need is for Hazel to be a Healer again, but obviously, the only people who can revive the practice are The Numina--_if_ they're real.

Perhaps, if we do recover this bluebird, which according to "Time" himself is made of Hazel's memories, she'll remember him? Then maybe she'll remember her family and her past as a Healer too? But the important question is, will she be able to heal Aspen?

Looking down, I watch my feet move over the salty stone path, listening to the harmonizing buzz of my sisters' continued voices.

All we need to do is go on a wild goose chase to the house of a swamp witch, get the bird, get to the mountain, and make it back home in one piece. I shudder. I never want to be in another witch's lair. Flashes of blue skin and a banner of charcoal hair make my throat feel like it's closing. Is any of this wise?

Poppy, Posy, and I are supposed to trust an old letter, a prophecy, and a Pooka? Who knows what that obsidian, smoky spirit did in its past criminal life. The faerie parading as a cat in Aspen's home could have been a murderer for all we know, and Fate expects my sisters and I to follow it willingly? Though, I suppose the dark creature hasn't steered us wrong, yet--it did give us the message that helped us find Hazel's journal and the letter from Time. The more I think about it, the Pooka was probably a guide, destined by that red thread. And now it's pointing us toward the veil, to The Between in the Wyrd Mountain, where my sisters and I were always "destined" to go.

I rub my temples with a groan. *Moon almighty.*

How Hazel dealt with this Numina stuff before is beyond me... I can't imagine having to meet some sort of mystical beings and learn all of their secrets. My skull is threatening to give me a full-blown migraine with the glimpse we've been given so far. I started out my day an unbeliever, now I'm a forced devotee. And there's no doubt that more than just my beliefs will be changing soon.

THE GOODBYES

*R*eading more on our walk home slows our progress, and by the time we get within sight of the glade it's well past dark. So much for that. The salt infused stone path keeps us safe, but we can still feel the forest rustling around us, things lurking in the night, waiting for a misstep. There are shadows still dancing in the corners of my vision too, but every time I turn to look at them, nothing is there. I've grown used to them over the years, these dark shades that stalk my life. No one else ever sees them and they haven't tried to harm me, so I'm convinced they're not bogeys. But we all catch a glimpse of sulfur-yellow eyes and a smoky tail. The wispy cat is still following us, silently tracking our progress. Knowing what I know about the Pooka's origins now, makes me certain that the one trailing us has to be as bad as any bogeyman. I quicken my pace. My sisters do the same.

When we finally reach the glade and cross the barrier, we see that everything has wound down for the night. The lights in Aspen's house are out and there isn't a peep from Sparrow and Rush's place either; they all must be fast asleep in their beds. The trolls will be snoring, the gnomes burrowed away in their holes, and goblins tucked away with their families. The only sign of nightlife is the soft candlelight glow coming from the barn where the brownies start their chores with only the imps to spy on them.

It's too late to wake anyone and tell them what we've learned, and it's not safe to leave on our journey in the dark, so the only thing left to do is go home to Pop, have a good night's sleep, and wait until the morning.

Most of the goblins live at the outreaches of the glade in little handcrafted houses. Our own small community lives under the cover of willow trees. When Poppy, Posy, and I trudge through the cold winter dark, breath billowing and hands stuffed in pockets, it's hardly a surprise to see that Pop is still out on the porch. What is a surprise is how underdressed he is for this weather. He's in nothing but a thin cotton tunic and trousers, and his green feet are bare as they push at the wood floorboards to rock his precious chair. It appears as though he's watching his daughters approach, but I know better; his gaze is faraway. He's looking right through us.

I sigh, heart squeezing like a fist. "Pop, what are you doing outside? It's late."

The porch groans when we climb the three short stairs. His fingers and toes are a pale seafoam green instead of emerald, which tells me how freezing he is. But in his state of mind, he doesn't feel it. Pop changed after we were rescued from the witch's cave. And it's been a steady decline since. After watching so many faeries be tortured and slaughtered, some close friends and cousins, he has never recovered. He shielded us though-- when we weren't frozen by witchcraft, he made sure my sisters and I didn't see the worst of it. Still, we saw enough. He saw too much. He's broken now, fractured beyond repair inside and out.

That's why the others stepped up to raise us. Feeding us, tending to our scraped knees, playing with us, tucking my sisters and I in, telling us bedtime stories. The responsibilities were split between Rush, Sparrow, Aspen, and Hazel when she visited. But once we got old enough, *we* started taking care of Pop. Most of the time it's a lot like leading a ghost around, putting him to bed and giving him fresh clothes when he can't do it himself.

The surviving goblins of the glade have been a big help too, stepping in to cook him meals and making sure he eats when we girls are out making our own lives. They were the ones who allowed me to explore the world, let Posy work with Hazel, and let Poppy be with the changeling babes.

"I'll go in and build a fire," Poppy says to me with a frown. "Posy, will you make some tea?" she asks.

With a nod, Posy follows her inside while I stand over our father. His rocking chair makes a light squeak with every push of his chill-bitten feet. Crouching to his level, I stop his movement.

"Pop, it's time to go inside." My voice is soft, like I'm speaking to a wild animal.

He blinks, a minimal rouse from his persistent fog. "Hmm?"

"It's cold outside," I prompt, ducking my head to catch his garnet gaze.

"Hello, Posy," he says, lifting a frigid hand to cup my cheek. His fingertips sting my skin.

I try not to let my sadness show, but I feel the edges of my lips pull down anyway. "It's Rose, Pop."

"Oh, I'm sorry, Primrose." He apologizes wistfully. "You girls look so alike."

I sigh. "I know." The most noticeable differences are the color of our eyes, otherwise we all have the same face, emerald skin, long black curly hair, and we stand at the same height too, just two inches shorter than Rush. I share my half-brother's silver eyes while Posy has a citrine shade that comes from somewhere further in our heritage. Poppy has a pinker version of our father's. He'd always been able to tell us apart growing up, could even identify us by the sound of our footsteps, but that was ten years ago.

Standing, I pull on my father's hands. "Come on, it's time to go inside."

He nods, joints popping as he stands. "Okay." He shuffles his way to the open door, my hand on his back as a guide.

Poppy is putting new logs into the hearth while Posy hangs a kettle to boil water for tea. We could all use a warm drink after the day we've had, but Pop needs it most. I bet a handful of shillings he's going to wake up sick tomorrow.

As I lead him to his room, Posy follows, helping me turn down his bed and pick out warmer clothes while he stands in the middle of the room, watching us with near empty eyes. We tug a sweater over his tunic and get him to sit on the edge of the bed to roll on some wool socks. When we're happy with the layers, Posy and I fluff his pillows and get him to lie down. Smoothing the blanket on top of him before adding a quilt Aspen made for extra warmth. He won't go to sleep anytime soon, but maybe a cup of lavender honey tea will at least settle him.

After everything is said and done, and Pop's belly is full of warm tea and his door is closed, my sisters and I sit on the ground in front of the fire drinking steaming cups of our own. We watch the flames and listen to the logs crackle, soaking in the peace and quiet for a time. This might be the last piece of normalcy we get in a while.

—

THAT NIGHT I dream of poison blue, needle teeth, and beetle-black eyes.

–

IN THE MORNING once the glade is bustling, I prepare by taking my travel worn knapsack from my trunk. The scents of my previous trips cling to the bag, dusty desert with a tinge of salt spray and elm. It hasn't been long, but I've missed exploring new places. It's in the *new* that I can let the shell I've developed dissolve, it's where I can embrace joy again and let it know *me*.

Traveling north to the mountains is going to be an arduous trek; we might be well into next year by the time we get back. We'll likely miss Christmastide and some of my nieces' and nephews' birthdays--I can only hope we don't miss Aspen passing into--what did The Numina call it? The After?

Packing with more speed, a childish part of me thinks the sooner we leave, the sooner we'll get back. I store a full water-skin and preserved foods for the mountain in my bag, along with coins to buy fresh meals in any towns we pass. Before getting dressed, I secure a bedroll and furs to the top of my knapsack for warmth at night. Though the weather during the day is manageable, once the sun leaves the sky and the moon appears, the temperature drops by the handful. And the closer we get to the mountain, the more snow we'll encounter. Even I can admit that snow makes my teeth chatter.

I layer double lined leggings at the thought, along with tall woolen socks, and even taller thick brown leather boots with a long sleeve shirt. On top of all that I throw on my favorite traveling sweater—it's midnight black with a hood—and a skirt that hits the backs of my knees. What I love the most about the thick knit tunic is the open panel in the front that lets my legs move freely.

I leave my lengthy curls wild and loose around me like a blanket while I secure a corset-style belt around my waist, one that holds my elder tree dagger. I never travel without it. The gift is beyond precious, and if we are going to face another filthy hag, then I'll need it more than ever before.

The many rings and chains I have studding my rippled ears jingle when I finally make my way to find Poppy and Posy.

The two of them are securing their packs by the front door with coin pouches tied to their hips. They are just as bundled as me. Poppy with her velvet, pomegranate cloak, long split skirt, leggings, sweater, and boots, hair an ornamented mass of curls and braids. And Posy, with her brown cowl scarf, thick blouse, thicker vest, belted trousers, boots, and curly hair tied up like usual. As triplets we're identical, but in truth, we're each so different.

"Ready?" I ask, shouldering my pack and glancing out the front window where I see the back of Pop's head. He's already out on the porch, slowly rocking in his chair. "We've got some explaining to do before we go."

Poppy's berry eyes widen when I peel my gaze away from the window to meet her stare. "No one has a clue we're leaving; the Pooka's message was only about finding a book."

"It'll be a blindside for sure." My stomach sinks at the thought of the many disappointed faces our news will cause.

Posy shifts her feet. "What about Aspen?"

I purse my lips as my stomach turns from a gradual sinking into an outright freefall. We all love Aspen, but my sisters know my connection runs deeper. She's been my mother for the last ten years and it feels like a knife to the spleen leaving her when she's ill.

"She'll be fine. We'll return. And when The Numina are free, they'll reinstate the Healers, Hazel will get her memories and husband back, and then Aspen will be restored too." I open the door as I say this, grabbing Pop's cloak from the hook on the wall before I pass over the threshold quick enough so my sisters can't see the gutted expression on my face. At least, that's what I hope will happen. Reality nags at me though, whispering like a field of tall, dry grass. The blades are sharp, needling as they remind me that even I don't believe my own words.

My sisters follow. I can almost hear the look I know they're exchanging behind my back. It's one of concern mixed with tentative hope, and the same cynicism tiptoeing its way up the knobs of my spine.

I shake off the pesky feeling when I stop at Pop's side. He doesn't even blink at the sound of my boots scuffing against the wooden porch. He doesn't look up at me when I lay a hand on his shoulder, either.

"We're leaving for a bit, Pop."

Only the creak of his rocking chair and the shuffling of my sisters' feet answer me.

With a sigh, I shake out Pop's cloak and drape it over his lap. He's still in the clothes Posy and I put him in last night, but at least he has on an extra sweater and socks, unlike yesterday. Pop will keep warm enough until the rest of the glade wakes. One of our neighbors will be around to check on him and usher him through a daily routine shortly.

"We'll be back before you know it," I say, stooping to drop a kiss on Pop's crown. His movements stall long enough for me to murmur against his head. "I love you. Don't miss us too much, old man."

My heart clenches at the sight of his glassy, faraway eyes as he starts rocking again. But I soak in the slight curve at the corners of his lips and capture the memory of this moment. I take it with me like a token when I turn and descend the porch steps. My sisters' hushed goodbyes and declarations of love for our father are whispers at my back as I trudge forward. Soon, the crunch of dry winter grass overtakes the ghosts of their words and we make our way across the glade.

When we reach Rush and Sparrow's house, we huddle around the festively decorated door and knock. Poppy looks excited to see the child-filled chaos on the other side, but Posy winces at the noise level. After a moment of listening to the laughter and squeals coming from the inside, the door opens. The smile that had been on Sparrow's face slides off as she surveys our clothes and bags.

Without a word, she wheels her chair back and lets us in. The door closes behind as we enter the whirlwind. The family has just finished eating, scraps of fruit rinds and muffin crumbs litter the table, and many faces are smeared with elderberry syrup. It's a warm, happy scene with all the grins, home-baked smells, and the tall pine tree in the corner strung with dried fruit, holly, and berry-studded garlands. I'm tempted to scoop the little changelings in a hug, but think better of it. Their grubby, purple-coated fingers would leave stains. Poppy, however, doesn't think twice, jumping into the rabble with abandon.

When Rush sees us, he stills in his chair at the head of the table. Then, turning to the kids, he says, "All right, go get your cloaks on and go play. Mommy and I need to talk to your aunties."

The flock of children hesitate, but only for a moment before they desert Poppy and scramble for the coats hanging by the door. The younger kiddos struggle with tight, fresh sewn buttons and the older ones help those tiny fingers as Sparrow and Rush clear the table. After a flurry of cheers, the changelings fly outside. Robin and Lark, Kestrel, Starling and Swan all laughing as they go. I'll miss the sticky little things.

Poppy and Posy take off their packs, but I don't bother. I'll have to adjust to this weight, so I might as well start now. Not to mention, I intend to head to Aspen's as soon as our situation is explained and I don't want to take it off twice if she makes me leave it by the door.

"You're leaving," Sparrow states. Not a question, not even an assumption. She says it like a well-known fact.

"We figured this was coming." Rush stands, hip leaning against his wife's wheelchair as he crosses his arms. "I'm guessing you found the book the Pooka spoke of, and it's leading you somewhere?"

A breathy halfhearted laugh leaves me. "Boy, do we have a story for you."

Posy pulls the letter from her vest pocket and hands it to the couple. Sparrow holds it while Rush reads it over her head. Their faces contort in a myriad of emotions, from confusion, to shock, to acceptance and back. I know they both believed in Fate, and Sparrow believes in Death after her brief demise, but now that they have broader knowledge and proof, I'm sure they're amazed.

"Hazel once told me rumors about Fortune, but this—" Sparrow shakes her head. "How do they expect you to bring them back?"

"Maybe our presence in the Wyrd Mountain will be enough." Poppy's voice is full of cheer, but it sounds forced. We have no idea how to recover The Numina. Some kind of balance must be restored to save them from The Between––but that's a lot to consider right now. We just need to get there first.

Rush rubs a hand over his facial hair. "Should we not acknowledge the fact they want you to seek out a witch? I think we've all had enough of *them* for a lifetime."

I shrug. "We don't have a choice. This Baba Yaga character has Hazel's memory bird, and according to Time that's a key part of this mission. It's like he said." Leaning over, I tap on the bottom paragraph of the letter. "Get in, get out."

"We have plenty of salt and Rose has her knife," Poppy offers up. I can tell she's trying to quell our brother's stress.

As Rush argues with her about how that might not be enough, I see Sparrow rereading the letter. When she's done, she looks up at me again, jade eyes searching. "Do you think The Numina could fix my mother?" A tentative hope drips from her words.

I adjust the weight on my back, antsy. "It's a possibility, if they bring back the Healers and restore Hazel's title. If anyone can make her better, it would be her."

Resolute, Sparrow nods and tries handing Posy back the letter. With a shake of her head, my sister pushes it back. "Keep it safe." She takes Hazel's journal from the pack she set on the floor and hands that to Sparrow as well.

"This is the book the Pooka told us to find." I watch Sparrow's scarred brows scrunch together as I continue, "It was Hazel's long before she became the Elder Mother. It'll answer some of the questions you might have."

Sparrow turns it over in her hand and runs her fingers across the cover. She's never lost her love of books, and I can see she wants to dive in right now.

"Keep it until Hazel is ready," I add. "She didn't even want to look at it when she found out what it was. At some point she'll need to read it. It'll help prepare her for what's to come--if we recover the bird and The Numina. More importantly, it'll help her get to know her husband again."

She gives us a wry smile. "I'll keep it somewhere the kids can't reach it."

Her little tiff with Rush complete, Poppy turns to Posy and me. "We should get going soon, we only have so much daylight this time of year."

We say our goodbyes and dole out hugs. Rush narrows his eyes before fixing them on me. "Don't do anything stupid, okay?

Walk past any houses made of candy and don't talk to strangers."

I cross my fingers over my heart.

He laughs.

Bending to the height of her chair, I embrace Sparrow tight. "Watch over her," I whisper in her ear.

She knows exactly who I mean.

—

WE SIT with Aspen in her home by the raging fire. It's a normal visit at first but when we tell her where we're going and how long we'll be gone, she becomes forlorn. I can see it in her frail body, how she's also concerned she might pass away before we get back.

"You're going to wait for us, right?" I ask, throat thick.

She gives us a sad smile, gaze running with love. "I'll do my best."

"I'm not going into a swamp witch's house for you not to be here when I get back. You'll have to hear all about it," I joke, trying to deflect the tears stinging my eyes.

Aspen's face tightens. "Are you sure the three of you should be going alone?"

"We'll be all right. Besides, Rush has all those kids to look after, and Sparrow needs to look after him and the glade." Poppy grasps one of Aspen's trembling hands.

Posy grabs her other hand, voice hushed. "Sparrow also needs to be here for you, and our brother's adventuring days are done."

Aspen squeezes their green hands with weak, pale cream

fingers. "You're right. I'm just worried for you girls. This is a big task."

"We were made to go." I surprise myself with my own certainty. Having gone from being a skeptic to full faith in The Numina overnight makes even my own head spin, but I need to believe it's because I want to save Aspen. I nod. "We're going to retrieve The Numina and they'll bring back the Healers. They'll restore the balance, wipe out the bogeys, and you'll be well again."

Aspen lets out a soft, dreamy breath. "How I'd love to see that world."

"You will," I insist, ribs tightening as I fight back a dam of sobs.

She releases my sisters. "All right, stand up straight, the three of you, and put these inside your boots." She hands us each a stem of dried heather flower. The sprig looks a lot like lavender, but instead of purple, it's a rich pink. In the language of flowers, these symbolize luck and protection, something we taught her when we were children.

We do as we're told, each kicking off a boot and placing the flowers in the heel before shoving our feet back in.

"I want to get a good look at you girls," Aspen says.

My stomach flips at her words. She thinks this is going to be the last time she sees us; she wants to burn us into her memory. I almost don't want to do it, I'd rather walk out the door with a promise of *see you later*, but I can't. So my sisters and I stand shoulder to shoulder looking down at her wrapped-up form, shivering despite the stifling house. Posy clutches at the fabric over my back; I don't know if it's for her own comfort or to keep me on my feet.

"Beautiful girls, so brave." She folds her hands to her heart.

Breaking, I fall to my knees, holding on to Aspen like a child, my arms around her waist and my ear to her chest. "I love you."

"I love you too, darling." She smooths her pale hands over my hair.

"Don't leave, okay? Not until we're ready." I sit up, begging and pleading with my whole heart.

Aspen leans forward and presses her cold lips to my brow. "Of course."

Then we say our final goodbyes, heave our bags up, and walk out the door. We pass the salt barrier and head north, leaving everyone we love behind.

THE BRIDGE

*I*t doesn't take long for the Pooka to appear after we leave the safety of the glade. The creature is in the form of a black fox this time, its pointed ears and long tail trailing off into scentless smoke. It startles us when it breaks from the shadows of the frosted trees to prowl beside me, but after I recover, I can do nothing but grumble.

"Who welcomed you into our adventuring party?" I kick a rock out of my way, watching it skitter with satisfaction when it bounces off the faerie's furry leg.

"You read Time's letter, Primrose." The Pooka's head swivels to side-eye me.

Annoyed at my full name, I kick another stone, but the fox expects it this time and deftly dodges. Then a huff leaves the Pooka's wet nose and it leaps over a log, daring to trod back to my side again. "While you know which cardinal direction the Wyrd Mountain is in, you do not know the right path to get there."

"Then draw us out a map, and we'll be on our way," I huff back.

A smirk finds my lips when little sulfurous eyes glare up at me. The Pooka is a beast, a creature made of tangible darkness, molded and trapped by the hands that formed it. This faerie that was once a criminal human being, and it's forever trapped in the ever-changing skin of an animal. I don't doubt that the punishment fits the crime.

I pull air between my teeth and snap my fingers, my mouth drooping into an exaggerated frown. "Ah, that's right, you don't have opposable thumbs. That's unfortunate."

Poppy shoves her sharp elbow into my ribs as she keeps pace on my other side, bouncing on her toes as she maneuvers over the packed earth. She has a placating smile on her cheery face when she leans forward to address the fox. "But you'll tell us where the Wyrd Mountain is, right?"

Posy's steps pick up on the other side of her, the prospect of finding out where the mythical home of The Numina resides piquing her interest.

The Pooka pads a few steps ahead of me as it turns its snout to speak to the nicer goblins of our trio. "Fate has limited the sizes and shapes I can take, but I've been sent by her to be your guide *and* protector along this journey."

"Protector," I snort, eyeing the slender frame of the faerie. What will The Numina's little puppet do to protect us when we come across Baba Yaga? Turn back into a cat and hiss at her? Scratch her with its tiny claws?

"My inability to take the forms of large beasts does not mean I can't ensure your safety." The ebony fox's ears flatten to its head as its layered, whispery voice turns coarse like gravel. "The Numina's home is a haven, a place that's not meant for any human, faerie, or bogeyman to be. It's difficult to locate if you are not wanted there, and as a result, those who seek it out tend to go missing. They become so hopelessly lost that it takes three times as long to turn back and find their way home. That, or they have a run-in with the mountain's spirits who try to pull them away at any cost." The Pooka's fur rises into spikes, the tips waving along the current of an indetectable breeze. "There are multiple routes the three of you could take to get there, some of which will waste your time and your coin. That's why I'm here to guide you." The shadowy faerie ends its tirade by crossing in front of us and jumping on top of a stump blocking our path, effectively making my sisters and I stop. The fox sits straight spined, looking down its long nose with a narrowed gaze. The forest is darkening as the day wanes. The cloud and tree cover frames the animal's form and highlights its glowing eyes.

Despite the serious picture the Pooka paints, trust isn't my strong suit.

"So..." I begin, crossing my arms under my chest. "What I'm hearing is we could technically find our own way without your help?"

"Rose." Posy hisses out a whisper, reaching around Poppy to thump my shoulder with the back of her hand.

Stepping away, out of elbow and hand's reach, I glare at my sisters and jerk my chin toward the stump. "You guys read the same words I did; you know what Pookas are. We heard its prophecy, and we know which direction to go. We don't need this runt skulking around or possibly leading us astray." I hope Poppy and Posy will see reason.

"You must trust me. I have your best interest in mind," the Pooka's many voices rumble.

"Right, because you want your captors to be free again." I roll my eyes. "That makes complete sense." Fate could throw the thing back into Death's shadow once they're free of The Between and have no need for the faerie again. And in this form, the Pooka is a messenger under Fate's command, but at least it still gets to roam the land. There's no reason this Pooka would want to bring The Numina back, and I don't know how tight Fate's control is upon it.

The fox rises to its feet, ink tail whipping behind it. "I am trying to help you—"

A laugh slips from my throat. "We don't need your help." It's better to be safe than sorry.

The Pooka's yellow eyes look like fuming flames, but it bows its head in a sharp nod. "Very well, suit yourself." With that, the dark faerie leaps from the stump, claws first, toward my face.

I throw up my arms to protect myself as Poppy squeals and Posy gasps. But at the last moment, the fox dissipates into a cloud, its black mist washing over my face before dispersing into the gloomy forest.

"Nice, Rose," Poppy sighs, brows knitted as her raspberry eyes dart around the trees. "We just lost the key to bringing back Hazel's husband and fixing Aspen."

Coughing, I wave a hand in front of my face to clear the slight scent of peat and pine that swept its way up my nostrils along with the Pooka's mist. "We'll be fine." I shrug, then forge past Posy who's shaking her head and issuing a long-suffering breath. I don't give myself time to reconsider what choice I just made for us. I'm too busy rubbing at my nose, paranoid about having breathed in traces of the faerie. My tone is nasally as I speak over my shoulder, double-checking that my sisters are following me, their new guide. "Besides, finding new places is my specialty."

—

THE NEXT TWO hours are long and at moments murderous, at least on my end. I'm accustomed to travel, *alone*, but my sisters aren't used to it at all, especially with heavy bags strapped to their backs. Poppy is quick to complain, and the first to make it on my *"future victim list."* Sometimes she whines about her sore back, other times she fusses about being tired. She even complains that her feet hurt, and she bemoans the heather in her shoe. Posy endures better, never complaining once, but the sound from her constantly shifting knapsack straps nearly drives me up a tree. This makes her second on my list.

Direction, after I refused the Pooka's help, is also a point of contention. Without the faerie or a map, we fight. It isn't until I remind my sisters three more times that *I* am the travel-seasoned one, with a solid sense of direction, that the bickering eases. And later, with her soft, underused voice, Posy asks me to teach her how to tell the cardinal directions apart using our surroundings. I know the question isn't to promote harmony in our little band, but only because I know something she doesn't.

I oblige though. And while Poppy whistles, I show Posy something Rush taught me when we were younger. *"While the Sun hides his face in these colder months and the sky is overcast, you must use the growth of the forest to tell north from south."* I stop my sisters at a nearby tree and have Posy run her fingers over the moss growing on one side of the rough bark. I tell her to stretch her hands out to her sides before I say, "North is where the green stuff grows, so this way is south. Your right hand is pointing west and your left hand east."

New knowledge always gives Posy a second wind, and the remainder of our gray winter day is traveled in companionable silence. Although, it doesn't take long for someone else to fill the third spot on my victim list, someone unseen. The jaunty sounds of a faraway violin slither through the forest as the day darkens. The tune winds around the trees with irritating high-pitched notes that drift in the frosty air, stinging my ears. At first, it's an odd, out-of-place thing to hear, but the novelty wears off after the four-stringed song carries on for an hour.

I'm considering all the ways I can enact my vengeance on whomever has ruined my day with their bow--perhaps the piece of wood and strings of horsehair will hold up as a weapon--but then I hear another, more natural sound. The babbling of water against stone. A river is nearby. Surveying our surroundings, it's apparent by how lush and green the trees are. Even in this cold time of year, they're thriving and well-watered.

When we breach the dense foliage, we see that the forest not only drops into a river, but a ravine as well. And across the ravine is a great stone bridge that connects one side of the forest to the other by a few hundred feet. But nothing surprises me more than the creature sitting on one of the walls, a violin tucked beneath his chin. The culprit who ruined the rest of my day. The annoying, impossibly loud musician looks to be a young man, but appearances can be deceiving. His skin is the color of a lake bottom, and the surface of it moves with the rippling caustic patterns of light shining through water. The ends of his green shoulder-length hair sway around his thin, transparent chest, like he is submerged in the ravine below. I note the tangled halo of seaweed atop his head like a crown when I realize the bogey isn't bubbling away. It's not yet night. If there were any light peeking from behind the slate-colored clouds, the sky would be turning the winter sunset shades of plum and lapis. But there is no purifying sun to splinter the gloom and burn the bogey where he stands. What is he?

Everything in me screams to grab my sisters and run before the musician sees us, but north is across this long cobblestone bridge, and there's no way but forward.

"I don't like this," Poppy whispers at my elbow while the three of us hover hidden in the tree line.

"I don't either, but it doesn't look like we have a choice. I haven't traveled north before, so I've never seen this bridge, but I think we have to walk past this...thing." I murmur all of this while a rotten sensation festers in my stomach. "We don't have time to skirt around the ravine; it looks far too long and wide. And we can't climb down there..." I trail off, staring into the ravine below. Slick walls slope down into a steep, perilous plummet. My best guess is the drop is at least a hundred feet, and who knows what could be down there. Not only could there be sharp rocks to catch our fall, but more bogeys like the one sawing at his violin strings might be waiting too.

"Just stick close and conceal yourselves. We'll make our way across quickly and unseen," I say as I pull on the straps of my bag, bringing it closer to my body like a shield on my back. Sneaking our way across the bridge is much wiser than engaging with the bogey and using our salt, or my blade.

Together my sisters and I use our goblin ancestry to disappear, then we tiptoe from the trees toward the bridge. Poppy has a fist curled into the back of my sweater. Posy's elbow prods into my side while she silently shuffles in my nonexistent shadow. I try not to look at the creature hopping from his perch as he falls deeper into his grating song and train my eyes on the other side of the forest. But his sharp features take up my periphery, and the closer we get, the stronger the stench of brine, underlaid with a metallic tang of blood, grows. We're an arm's length away from him when he lowers his instrument.

My sisters and I freeze.

Slowly, I put my hand over my mouth to stifle my breathing as I stare at the bogey wide-eyed, my heart climbing into my throat. He stands with the neck of his violin choked in one hand and the base of his bow dangling from the other. His haunting *solid* red, glowing eyes glaze over us, peering at the tree line we snuck from. Though his expression betrays little, he must feel a disturbance in the air as he searches the land because neither Poppy, Posy, nor I have made a single sound. If he feels our presence, we need to move before he bumps into one of us.

Bending away, I try to sidestep him. With Poppy still clutching me, I urge my sisters forward. Only the tip of my boot touches a stone of the bridge before the violin bow is held out before my throat, just inches away. I have no choice but to stop before I clothesline myself and stumble back into my sisters.

With this sudden movement, my boot scuffs over the stone and the noise is deafening to my ears.

A jagged grin splits the bogey's face as his eyes dance over the air. "Hello, travelers," he croons. "I can smell your skin; the scent of flowers consumed me the moment you slipped from the trees."

We've been caught. He knows we're here and running would do little more than earn me a bow to the neck. I don't want to find out if the hair it's strung with is sharp enough to open my throat. Which means I need to stall for time while I think of a safer way to cross the bridge. So, with a shuddering breath, I reveal myself and look the bogey in the watery face. My sisters soon appear in my periphery, along with my ever-present shadows.

"Sneaky little things, where do you think you're going?" The creature tuts, pushing the string of his bow against my skin, until the three of us step back from the bridge to face him.

"Uh, across?" I reply, unable to keep the satirical tone from my voice as I rub at my throat.

The bogey points the tip of his bow at each of our chests. "You have to pay to cross."

"Says who?" Poppy pipes up from my shoulder.

I push my arm back into her, a quiet request for silence. Our simple plan is already going sideways, and I don't want her drawing this creature's attention onto her. We just need to get out of here.

"Says me. I'm the River Man." He taps his bow against his clear, bony chest. "This is *my* bridge and *my* water; you must pay my toll."

"We're not paying you to cross the bridge," I say, ignoring how my sweater-covered arms prickle with goosebumps.

"Yes, you will." The River Man tilts his head in a very off-putting, animalistic way. "Or else you'll face the consequences."

His voice makes my blood thicken into icy streams. In this

moment, he reminds me so much of Black Annis. Perhaps it's the way he moves, and how despite his breezy tone, his words feel threatening. It makes me build my wall of bravado higher because I need to hide my discomfort.

"What are you going to do? Play a song to bore us to death?" I force a laugh, herding my sisters to the right with my body as I creep closer to the side of the bridge.

"No." Ever so calm, the River Man puts down his bow and leans his violin against the bridge's wall. His solid, white-less, pupilless eyes rove over us. "I'll drown you, drag your body into the ravine, and eat you." Straight-faced, he folds his hands in front of him. "Then, I'll leave your entrails out on the water's edge to dry and make new strings for my fiddle."

I'm going to pass on that...

If we run, I *think* we can make it across. I don't know if the bogey will follow my sisters and I into the forest or not, but I'm hoping he won't abandon his precious bridge or water. If he does, we have plenty of salt, and I have my knife. And who knows, maybe our little Pooka "protector," the one I hastily sent away, will show its face and get us out of this pinch by scratching the River Man's eyes out.

"Yeah, right," I snort, gesturing forward to my sisters behind my back. Being triplets, I expect them to read my frantic motions. Run. *Now.*

Pushing my way past the River Man to sprint over the bridge, my shoulder goes right through his like liquid. When I turn in surprise, I see my sisters frozen in shock, but I'm the only one with feet on the cobblestone. That's when I see the creature's arm dissipating into a stream of water that twists in the air towards me. The stream lashes toward my face like a serpent and the next thing I know, it's flooding down my nose and mouth. Gasping in panic only shoves the water into my lungs. I'm drowning on dry land. The burn in my airways makes my eyes well as I try to cough out the water. Poppy and Posy are shrieking at the bogey to stop. My body screams for air as my brain grows muzzier. Black dots dance across my vision. I stumble to a knee. Through the haze, I see only a wicked grin and my writhing shadows. They seem angry.

Suddenly, a goblin-green hand wads my sweater in its fist and yanks me off the bridge. As soon as my feet leave the stone, the extra water vacates my body and returns to the River Man. His arm solidifies as I glare up at him, heaving in gulps of dry, painfully cold air. This is most *definitely* worse than inhaling the Pooka's mist; who knows what kind of bogey bacteria makes up the River Man's body. Once my breathing becomes more measured, Posy, my saving grace, pulls me to my feet and cups my face between her hands, turning my chin to face her. Posy's bright eyes are wide, and her eyebrows are pinched as she checks me over.

"Are you okay?" Poppy asks beside her, wiping a teary cheek off on her shoulder. Her lips are pale.

I nod, teeth clenched as I peer back over at the bogey. He looks at us with a smug twist on his dark pointed lips. My skin is flushed with anger and sweat collects on my brow, but beneath that fury is fear. After the cage, one would think my greatest fear would be death by a witch's nails, fillets of flesh peeled from my body until my system gives out. But it's not. I've always feared suffocation, whether by smothering or being trapped somewhere and running out of air. I'd never considered that drowning would be among the list of ways to suffocate. Now I know, and it makes my hands shake. If I were alone, I might shed a tear as my heart races and stomach curdles, but now is not the time or place.

"Have you reconsidered your payment?" the River Man inquires, crossing his arms over his see-through chest with a knowing expression. He has us stuck and afraid.

"Fine," I grit out. "What do you want?"

He nods to my sisters' purses tied at their waists. "Your coin, of course."

With rough, jerky movements, I swing one shoulder of my bag off so I can dig around inside and pull out my pouch of coins. The little leather sack is heavy in my numb hands, making my fingers fumble with the string ties. "How much do you want?" I grouch, fishing past bronze farthings and copper pence for silver shillings.

The River Man shakes his head, his floating hair rising around him. "Oh no, no, it's not that simple. I like to play by wishing well rules."

I glance up at the creature, unimpressed that he continues to toy with us. I'm more than ready to get this encounter over with.

"To pay, you must toss me a coin. If it lands head side up, you get to go across. If it's tails, you must toss another coin until it lands on heads," he explains, glowing eyes crinkled and eager as he rubs his hands together in anticipation of his game. "And if you run out of money before you land on heads, then, well"—he shrugs—"you don't get to cross."

"This is ridiculous." I yank out a halfpence coin and look at my sisters. Poppy's brows have all but disappeared into her curls, and Posy's are furrowed as she whittles her nails down into nubs with her teeth.

"You can't flip for the three of you," he adds with the wave of a passive hand. "For three bodies across the bridge, you must each pay your own toll one at a time."

"Are you making these rules up as you go?" Reshouldering my bag, I glare at the creature. He even plays games like Black Annis did, although his come with *many* more rules. Let's just hope that he honors them and isn't a liar like the dead blue-skinned hag.

The River Man narrows his solid crimson gaze at me. "No sharing your coins either."

"I'll go first, Rose." Poppy, ever the peacemaker, puts a hand on my shoulder and steps forward.

Loosening the ties of her own purse, she pulls out a copper coin and balances it over the nail and knuckle of an emerald thumb. Using her pointer finger as leverage, Poppy flicks her thumb up, and the coin goes flying with a sharp *plink*. The pence lands in the River Man's palm as he claps his hand over it. A slimy, mischievous smile climbs over his face and he leers at my sister. He uncovers his hand slowly, hunching over his arms and peeking into the tunnel of his hands like he's caught a mouse. The bogey clicks his tongue. "Tails," he announces before showing us the coin lying in his palm.

Indeed, it landed on its backside. The full-bodied picture of a woman holding an olive branch in one hand and a trident in the other looks back at us. Once we've seen our fill, the creature *absorbs* the coin. It looks like it's dissolving into his skin as water from his palm laps up over the pence and pulls it into his body. We watch in horrified wonder as it floats up his arm on a current into his chest, where it lazily turns about in the liquid. The metal winks at us every time it catches in the patterns of light rippling through the creature's strange, watery skin.

Without a word, Poppy retrieves another lesser valued coin from her purse and flips it to the River Man. She lands on tails twice more before seeing the portrait of an old monarch in the bogey's hand. Only then does he step aside and gesture with a flourish of his hand down the bridge. My triplet looks between me and Posy, chewing on the thin skin of her inner bottom lip. A terse nod of encouragement from Posy makes Poppy skirt around the River Man and walk down the stone bridge at a brisk pace. She glances over her shoulder multiple times before she makes it to the other side, about three hundred feet away. The only detail I can make out at this distance is her constant shifting feet as she waits.

"Who's next?" the creature asks, brushing away the tendrils

of plant life drifting between his eddying locks and over his hollow cheeks.

"You go," I prompt Posy. "I'm not leaving you here alone after I cross."

My sister frowns at me, but I don't let her argue. One of us has to go next, and by the way her face turns away from the River Man's eerie eyes, I know she's uncomfortable with being left behind. She's better off playing the creature's game so she can join Poppy first, and we both know it. With jittery fingers, Posy takes her glasses from around her neck and slips them over her nose. Digging into her purse, she pulls out a small fistful of coins and one after the other, flips them to the aqueous bogey. She's lost half of her money before she goes to place a shilling on her thumb, and it falls to the ground. The three of us look into the crisp grass where the head of the silver coin shines up at us.

"That's heads!" I point at the engraved face, staring up at the River Man. "It landed on heads. She gets to cross."

"Ah, ah, ah," the creature tuts. "I said you must *toss* me a coin. She dropped it, so it doesn't count."

I throw my hands up. "You've got to be kidding me. How is that fair?"

The edges of his form liquify as he sneers at me. It's a silent but effective threat because I clamp my mouth shut. Balling my hands into fists, I fight the urge to mouth off, refusing to put Posy in further danger because of my tongue. My sister closes a hand over mine and bends to pick up her coin. Her fingers squeeze around my knuckles before she releases me and flips the shilling. Tails.

My nails dig into my palms tighter and tighter with every coin the bogey soaks into his body. Poppy is now pacing the other end of the bridge, helpless and probably unable to see what's happening. I can't decide which is more torturous, Poppy's unknowing, or witnessing every coin land face down.

However, when that shiny head finally lies face up in the River Man's palm, the relief is sweet. My hands relax, color rushing back to my emerald knuckles as I sigh. Posy went through three-fourths of her coin purse trying to buy her way over the bridge, but the sight of her rushing across to Poppy provides more comfort than a perfect slice of oven-warm apple crumble pie. That is until the bogey blocks my view and holds out his hand, again.

"Your turn." He beams.

His needle teeth shimmer like the coins churning through his chest. Bitterness coats my tongue as if I licked every face of the coins strapped to my belt. What will he even do with this much money? I don't think he does anything but inhabit this bridge and play his stupid violin. If I took a good look over the ravine, I'd no doubt see the bottom of the river littered with nothing but coin and bones. I'm not curious enough to test my theory though, so instead, I take a few farthings from my pouch and mutter grumpy curses under my breath as I load one on the top of my thumb. The sound of my nail hitting the metal as I flick the disc is audible and the River Man claps it between his hands to reveal the bronze tails.

Plink. Tails.

Plink. Tails.

Plink. Plink. Plink.

Tails. Tails. Tails.

Over and over again, the coins I flip land on tails. And with each try, the bogey grows richer, and I'm filling with rage. I'm angry at him for impoverishing us. I'm angry at the Pooka, for being right. If I had listened, we may not have ended up here. But I'm most angry at Fate for not weaving this encounter in our favor. I've called her every name in the book by the time I make it to my last three coins. Now, the River Man's chest is so packed with our money that the coins barely move. He's taken years of my sisters' allowances from odd chores around the glade. And months of my earnings from a job I had on my last adventure out west, working at a tea shop. All of it gone, in a matter of minutes.

Looking down the bridge at Poppy and Posy, I see their restless feet and growing concern. If I take any longer, they'll probably come charging back this way, offering more money to haggle. But considering sharing our coins with each other goes directly against his rules, I have a feeling that would only displease this bogey and he'd just drown us all. His game is deadly, I can see it in his hungry crimson eyes.

I waste no time flipping my third to last coin. He catches it, turns it over to reveal the tails, and lets his water take it from his hand and into his chest, again. My heart is in my throat as I flip him my second to last coin. The toe of my boot taps over the grass as the creature shows me the silver tails before adding it to his collection. I pinch my last coin between my fingers and bring it to my lips, gazing hundreds of feet away at my sisters. This is it. I have one more chance to buy my way across the bridge, but after the odds I've faced, this last coin landing on heads would be a miracle. Thus far, I have been nothing short of unlucky, and I could *really* use some luck right now. My thoughts wander to Fortune and how different this situation would be if she still existed. Granted, if she did, we wouldn't even be on this journey for The Numina. I speak directly to them as I mumble against the coin, "If you're real, now is the time to prove it."

Then, I snap my fingers and flip my last hope at crossing the stone bridge into the bogey's awaiting hand.

The Guide

I hold my breath as the River Man stares deep into my eyes. He has his hands clasped one on top of the other like a clamshell, waiting. The watery pattern of light on his skin ripples like a slow glacial tide. The sluggish coins in his chest glitter as they twirl. Around us, the forest falls silent, like it too has lungs to still. My sisters have stopped moving on the other side of the bridge; they must sense the gravity of this moment. If the bogey reveals my last coin to be tails, I'm stuck. There's a slim chance I might make it across the bridge before being drowned again, but there's also a greater chance I'll be thrown into the ravine and become dinner. I might try to find another way over to meet my sisters, but that would waste many hours.

It *has* to be heads.

The River Man lifts the back of his hand to see what the coin landed on before I do. His face gives away nothing. It remains flat and stone-like until he curls back his dirty, turquoise fingers to reveal my fate. The side-profile portrait of a monarch glares up at me. *Heads.* Air comes rushing back to my chest, and I almost keel over with relief. It turns out that The Numina might just be watching over us after all.

"Congratulations," the water bogey says. "You've earned your way across my bridge. I suppose I'll have to make new fiddle strings out of the next traveler I meet." He snaps his teeth in a grotesquely playful manner before absorbing my last coin and turning to retrieve his instrument. The next thing I know, the River Man is climbing atop the bridge's wall and dissipating. His form contorts into a see-through horse with a mane of seaweed as he dives into the ravine. Following his trail of spray to the wall, I peer over to see him leaping through the rapids with his violin suspended inside his stomach. His bloody eyes seem to look up at me. A grating nicker bounces off the sloping walls before he disappears under the water.

I pull away from the wall, a shiver going down my spine. I don't think it's just from the cold, but I try to convince myself it is as I jog my way over the cobblestones to reunite with my sisters. I'm perturbed and still shaking when they pull me back into their fold, asking what transpired between me and the creature. I can't reply right away. I'm too furious at the bogey for taking almost all our money. How will we buy anything suitable for Baba Yaga now? I reprimand myself for being so emotional, for letting myself be unnerved and bested by the River Man. My weakness could've gotten us killed... I need to pull myself together again and suppress the past, especially before we meet the swamp witch.

Crumpling my empty coin pouch in my hand, I shake my head to stop my sisters' incessant questions. "We're skunked." I nudge them forward into the forest.

We walk for several minutes before Posy says, "I think the River Man is a kelpie. Though, I do remember something about the Fossegrim and his music in one of Hazel's books too—"

I block out my sister with the grinding sound of my molars, jaw flexing and facial muscles aching. Then I search for the Pooka amongst my ever-present shadows, but watching them loop through the trees does little to quell my frustration. If anything, the lack of the creature's presence, after I refused its help, and my inability to fully see these invisible figures only makes me feel worse. I resign myself to ignoring my sisters' conversation and focus on burning a trail through the forest. Night is almost upon us.

We stop when the pearl-gray clouds turn black, and the sky appears empty of even the moon and stars. Poppy whines about a blister forming on the back of her heel and I have to bite my tongue. A blister is the least of our worries. Ignoring her, I gather the driest sticks I can find in the dark before kneeling on the forest floor to make a fire for the night. Posy digs around my bag for my flint and iron while Poppy mills around our campsite, being careful to stay within the circle of salt she's created. She's snapping off twigs from the lower branches of the skeletal trees around us, talking, and talking, and talking. It's mindless chatter, something I should be accustomed to by now, but it's been quite a day, and a long while since I've spent so much time in close quarters with my sisters. Only twelve hours have passed since we left home, and my patience is as exhausted as our money. Wonderful.

When Posy finds the fire starters, a noise of triumph sounds in the back of her throat, but I still notice the slight flinch when her fingers touch the iron. Her eyes go wide, reflecting in the dark like a wild animal, switching between discs of yellow and red as she turns her head. Sharp iron scarred her; I know she's remembering the talons as she hands me the metal.

"Thanks, Po," I grumble before getting to work.

Concentrating, I take the iron and flint in each fist, striking them over the tinder. Catching the iron on the sharp edge of the flint and not my fingers is something I've gotten good at over the years, but right now my focus is broken and things don't go smooth. As I try to shave pieces of the metal into crispy combustibles, all I hear is Poppy. Every word she utters is loud and nonsensical. Posy tenses up beside me. She senses my storm brewing. Our triplet telepathy is strong, but it would seem the connection is fritzed with Poppy tonight.

After multiple strikes, sparks finally fly and I watch the embers on my pile of leaves and sticks come to life. Bending down, I blow out a measured breath, encouraging the fire to grow. Poppy passes by in another chatty flurry and the gust of icy wind from her cloak smothers my progress. "What do you guys think they look like? Do you think The Numina have crowns? I think they—"

"For all that is good and holy, will you just *shut up*," I snap, twisting to look at my sister fumbling around with the twigs in her arms.

Her eyes are wide again, surprised by the outburst that sends birds flying into the still night. "I didn't—"

"Do you not know how to be quiet, even for just a second?" I press the back of my fist to my forehead, squeezing my eyes closed. "I can't think when you're always talking."

"Neither can I," Poppy says, her voice devoid of the emotion and curious excitement that was there moments ago.

I open my eyes and gaze up at her. The fronts of her dark brows are turning upwards in a miserable furrow. Her eyes reflect like Posy's, like mine probably are right now, as all goblin eyes do in the dark. She turns and walks toward my pile of sticks with a heavy sigh.

My head is turning. "What?" I ask.

"That's the point. Talking and singing, whistling, humming, it drowns out all the bad." Poppy kneels across from me and snaps the wood pieces she's gathered into smaller sticks. "I can't think about the cage when my mouth is moving, and my thoughts are going at a constant running pace." She looks up at me and shrugs. "It helps."

Without another word she takes up humming again, going back to the edge of the salt to compile more broken branches to feed the fire.

I feel like I've been slapped. Never once did I think my happy-go-lucky sister was struggling *this* much. Granted, we're all blemished by what happened a decade ago, but I didn't know Poppy's main character flaw––according to me––isn't a flaw at all. It's a coping mechanism…

We've never been the sharing type. We don't talk about our emotions and hug it out, we only acknowledge the problems, but then we move on. I'm sure it's not healthy by any means, but it works––or so I thought.

I only survive the lingering trauma by going away for weeks or months at a time, and this makes me unavailable, to every-one. When I'm alone, I don't have to be the strong, protective sister; I don't have to be anything. When I'm alone, there's no one around to remind me of the tortured seven-year-old girl I used to be.

We met evil when we were children; it shaped us into who we are for better or for worse. Perhaps we aren't so healed after all.

My fingers feel numb when I side-eye Posy, who worries at her nails in predictable quiet. "Did you know?" I ask.

She doesn't need further explanation, she just glances at Poppy busying herself and nods. "People say and do a lot when met with silence. You learn so much when you observe."

Growing up, Posy struggled to recognize other people's emotions. It took her a lot of time and studying before she could identify what someone might be feeling. Since then, she's gotten very good at it, almost too good. Guilt gnaws at my insides, making me feel nauseous. I bet Posy knows things she wishes she didn't. Including the more acute misery I missed living inside our triplet. Maybe she even understands why I wield sarcasm like a weapon, and why I wake so frequently at night.

Sometimes, when my night terrors are bloody, I'll get out of bed and walk around the house. I haunt the halls, trying to block out the screams that echo in my head, the sounds of tearing flesh being rend from innocent faerie bodies. Now that I think of it, there were many times I woke up and made my way to the kitchen to see Posy preparing what I thought was a midnight snack. I remember how tired she looked, like she'd forced herself out of bed to butter slices of bread with jam and clotted cream. Had she gotten up because of me--to offer me company in the guise of having already been awake?

The shame hurts, makes my hands shake. But I shove it down too, cramming it all the way down to my toes where it feels like a bumpy rock in my boot. I'll deal with all this another time, not now--now feels too fresh. Too vulnerable.

Taking up the iron and flint, I strike any lingering feelings away. With each hit I feel my protective shell, like a layer of drying mud, adhere back to my skin. And when the embers spark and I breathe onto the tinder, I feel better, emptier. The fire blooms, consuming the leaves and climbing the wood until light blazes and heat flares against my skin. I let my fingers hover, maybe a little too close, but I don't pull away. Posy doesn't say anything, even though I know she notices the way I flirt with the fire, begging it to lick my fingertips.

Poppy joins us, stacking more twigs before leaning into the warmth. Her eyes flutter closed as she defrosts. Watching the flickering light dance across her face for a moment, I see the way the goblin hue we share glitters. The flames dance in Posy's eyes as she stares deep into the flames, losing herself to her thoughts, mesmerized by the fire. I almost laugh.

What broken girls we are.

"I think Death looks like an old woman, more skeleton than person, with spikes for teeth," I blurt, sending a tepid cloud into the nippy air that fades away just as quick as it appeared.

My sisters look at me with confused expressions.

Shifting to sit on the cold ground, I continue, "I mean, that's got to be why she wears that shroud. Sparrow said when she met Death, she was covered from head to toe in black fabric."

"Hazel said in her journal that Death was beautiful," Poppy says, tentative as she accepts my unspoken olive branch.

The ancient Hazel, the one she's forgotten, didn't describe every detail of The Numina in her journal, instead we only got glimpses amidst all the information of what they did for the world.

"I bet the Sun and Moon glow," Posy says, almost inaudible.

"All the threads that Sparrow saw around Fate makes her sound like a spider. She probably has like a million eyes." I let out an exaggerated shudder.

This gets a laugh out of Poppy. "I think Time is a dreamboat, with those curls and copper eyes Hazel wrote about." She smiles.

A long breath eases out of my nose. *There she is.* There's that smile, the same smile that Posy and I have but is seen more often on Poppy's face. I resolve to welcome my sister's incessant chatter now that I understand her better.

"What about Fortune?" I ask, thinking about how Hazel's penmanship had been shakier as she wrote about this Numina's death.

My sisters sit with identical frowns, looking into the fire as they too think about the same journal entry.

"She had pink hair," a layered voice says above us.

We all whip our heads back to find the source as my hand clutches the hilt of the knife on my belt. The sight that greets us is a bat, but not just any bat—one with smoky wings and glowing yellow eyes. The Pooka hangs above us, upside down with little ebony feet clutching a tree branch.

My hand falls from my weapon as I groan, heart still racing. "Oh, so *now* you show up. Some guide and protector you are."

The Pooka shows me its new fangs. "You refused my help."

While this may be true, I'm not willing to admit it. So I take up a twig and poke at the fire. "That's a lousy excuse. Don't you have a job to do? Because last time I checked, I'm not your master; Fate is."

After a moment of charged silence, it says, "I've been following you, you've been safe."

Never once did I catch sight of the Pooka in any form at the bridge. It should bring comfort to know the messenger hadn't abandoned us, but the idea of it lurking without our knowledge and doing nothing to correct our course makes my insides churn instead. "Safe? What about the River Man?" I glare up at the creature and wield my stick, jabbing the smoldering tip at the bat. "Maybe you could've—I don't know—*guided* us to a cheaper route?"

The Pooka only unfolds its membranous wings and flaps them once, twice, three times, before folding them back up to its body.

Whatever. Two can play at the silent game.

I stare at the fire as Poppy speaks. "Pink hair?"

"And four arms," the Pooka adds. "Her real name, when she belonged to a human clan, was Macha."

This piques my curiosity, though I'm obstinate enough to keep looking into the flames. Just because I'm quiet doesn't mean I'm not listening.

"Did you know her?" Poppy asks.

"I never met Lady Luck in this form; she was long gone before I was created. But I knew her when my soul was trapped in Death's shadow. I watched them live and work for many years. Macha was kind, much kinder than my captor." The Pooka's whispers float down and sweep around the campfire. "She was energetic, loved her fellow Numina like they were family. She, Death, and Fate were sisters-in-arms in their first life, warriors with magic like the Elder Mother. Back then, Death went by Morrigan and Fate, Nemain."

Daring to uncover my interest, I peer up.

"What about Time? What was Hazel's husband like?" Poppy's eyes glimmer, eager to learn more about the Elder Mother's forgotten love.

"I heard he was called Icarus long ago. He and his father were captives; it's said they were locked in a tower working as craftsmen for a king," the Pooka continues, small form swaying where it clutches onto the tree. "In an attempt to escape, they made metal wing-like skeletons and collected feathers, attaching them to the frames with wax, and they jumped once they were dry. They glided over the sea to freedom before Time became overzealous, drunk with excitement and freedom."

Further risking my mask of disinterest, I flick my eyes back over to Poppy and see the hope for a sweet love-filled story gutter out of her poor eyes.

"He kept drifting closer and closer to the sun until the wax burned into his skin and the wings fell apart." The Pooka forges on, voice haunting enough that I see my shadows dancing in the dark along to his harrowing tale. "After plunging to his death, he appeared in the Wyrd Mountain in front of the previous Time and he was given a decision. Go into The After or become one of The Numina."

Glancing at Posy this time, I see her gears turning. This kind of knowledge isn't something you can find in any book or scroll. This information is rare and she's lapping it up like a moth to nectar. She'd clamber up in the tree and scoop the Pooka into her hands in its new shape if it would give her more answers faster.

"How did you come to be?" She switches the direction of the conversation to satiate her intrigue.

The Pooka's head cocks to the side, almost twisting to look at her right side up. "I'm sure you read about that in the journal I led you to."

"Yes, but *how*," Posy stresses.

"When Fate needed a new messenger for this moment,

Death searched her shadows for me because I was the one they saw in the visions suspended in Time's pools. I tried to hide behind the darker souls, but she found me, and she ripped me from the seam. With a snip of her shears, I was free of her prison." The Pooka flaps its wings again. "When Fate got her hands on me, she molded me, squished and stretched my soul until I fit her new prison. The body of a faerie compelled to prophecies, confined to varying small or medium animal forms, built to deliver her messages. Built to guide you three goblins of the glade to the Wyrd Mountain."

I look directly up at the Pooka now. "You deserved it though. Hazel wrote that the souls in Death's shadow were terrible. People who committed such heinous crimes that she served just punishment with her eternal entrapment, never allowing you into The After." My gaze narrows. This creature wants us to sympathize, wants us to care, and that makes suspicion turn in my blood. "You make yourself out to be a victim but really, you're a bogey. You're not cut from the same cloth as witches, but you are darkness all the same."

The creature stares at me for a moment. "Perhaps." That's all it says before it wraps its body in a cocoon made of wings. I guess I ruined its chance at deceiving us and hurt its feelings... oh well. When I turn to my sisters, Poppy is giving me a disapproving glare and Posy looks quite annoyed that I cut off her newest source of ancient information.

In a very adult gesture, I stick out my tongue and feed more wood to the fire. "Go to bed. I'm sure we've got a couple days' travel before we hit some sort of town." I untie my bedroll and furs from my knapsack. "You'll want to get all the rest you can because you're going to be on your feet for a long time, sister dears."

Poppy sags at that. But they both follow my advice and lay out their beds next to mine, feet to the fire. I'm not one for snuggling, but it's winter and we are out in the open air and it would be stupid not to scoot in close. Freezing to death would be a terrible end to this quest. I'm glad it's yet to snow, but I think by the time we reach the swamp lands we'll have to find better cover to protect ourselves from the icy flakes.

For now, the three of us can lie close, body heat radiating while the many layers of our bedding insulates the warmth between us. I'm sleepless for a while, watching my breath and my shadows tangle with the dark silhouettes as they creep outside our circle of salt. I also keep an eye on the Pooka. I know it's awake, listening; we've met gazes many times, scrutinizing each other's every breath. Maybe it's protecting us under The Numina's orders, but still, I don't trust it.

Posy's breath becomes even first. I'm jealous at how easily she can fall asleep, how deep and dreamless it is. Poppy drops off next, her forehead pressed between my shoulders, her breath balmy. I draw the line when she tries to put her toes on me though. I absolutely refuse to feel someone's cold, clammy feet on me, even if it's someone I love enough to kill for them.

After a time, my cold-infused exhaustion wins out and my eyes slip closed, pitching me into a saccharine darkness filled with iron bars and the sound of bare footsteps on wet stone.

THE TAVERN

*T*he Pooka stays as we resume our journey North. The first day it silently leads us through the trees, walking ahead of my sisters and me in the form of a prowling onyx lynx. Its fur collects beads of moisture over the course of the foggy day, until it shakes itself off and explodes into a burst of black shapeshifting smoke. Then it watches over us as an owl at night.

On the second day, the Pooka trails behind, skittering around the forest floor as a shrew. I'm pretty sure it brings the dark faerie joy when the frozen leaves rustle, or a twig snaps beneath its tiny claws. The noises make me draw my blade more than once and tweak my neck when I turn too fast. It's infuriating because nothing dark creeps behind us, just our terrible, bogey guide. And each time I swear I hear sniveling squeaks that sound suspiciously like laughter. On this night, I wonder what a magic shrew roasted over a campfire would taste like.

And today, on the third day, the Pooka wakes us up wearing the skin of a fluffy ebony rabbit. The creature's phosphorous yellow eyes do nothing to deter Poppy from melting at the sight of the small animal and its twitching nose.

"Aw, look how precious you are as a bunny," she sighs, her cheek creased from her bedroll and sleep still on her breath.

The Pooka doesn't expect her to reach out and stroke its velvet-looking ears and it stills, paralyzed with what seems like fear before it darts from beneath her hand. Posy and I watch our sister's heart break while she watches the rabbit's chest rapidly rise and fall. Its ears are flattened to its head as she apologizes. "I'm sorry, I wasn't thinking." Poppy cradles her hand to her chest, eyes wide. "I didn't hurt you, did I?"

Its reply takes me aback.

"No." Its multilayered voice comes out as a whisper. "I haven't felt a kind hand in more than six hundred years. My father's touch was the last before Death came for me."

"I'm sure you've missed him and the connection you had with your family." Poppy wears a kind smile when she reaches out an empty hand again, palm facing the slate sky. She's offering a kind hand once more.

Before our eyes, the black rabbit turns into a lanky black wolf. "My father wasn't a good man, and I do not care to be touched," the faerie rumbles. Though its tone is not entirely unkind. It wouldn't have kept its tongue if it had been, but the creature's last words did strike a chord in me, a rusty one, like that of an unused harp.

"Not even when you were alive?" I ask.

The wolf turns its yellow eyes on me. "No, not even then."

The creature pads away, waiting for us to pack our things. While I strap my bag onto my back, the only thing I can think is that the Pooka and I seem to have similar preferences when it comes to physical contact. And now, as we walk on, I can't decide how to feel about it. If the Pooka and I are similar in this way, then that makes it a lonely, wandering faerie. It makes the creature like me, a goblin of the glade who drifts around the earth with only my shadows to keep me company.

I always travel alone, and my adventures rarely have a specific destination. I let myself wander and let my nose take me where it wants to go. I've found treasures, and a few good folk along the way though. In one direction I even came across secluded beaches where no human or faerie feet may have touched. In another, a family-owned art gallery. Then in the opposite way, I found natural rock formations that looked like sculptures, and trees brimming with a kind of hard-shelled, hairy fruit I'd never seen. On my journeys, to pay or trade for lodging, I apprenticed with many different people. I was a baker once, and for a few months, I lost myself, up to my elbows, in flour and dough. It was peaceful, but still lonely.

The sudden pop of pebbles crunch beneath my boots and I'm drawn from my thoughts. Looking up I see that the Pooka has kept to its word, so far, because a village now lies before us. It's an ancient, salty place, but obviously well cared for. Old stone structures stand strong, supported by pristine carved pillars and vaulted arches. The main street, with the most evidence of foot and cart travel in the salt, seems closed down. The permanent buildings that line the other streets are quiet too, but still alive. Along with my mysterious trailing shadows, and the Pooka in the shape of a raccoon, dusk is creeping up from behind us. We traveled a long time while I was immersed in my own thoughts. Oil lamps and candles are springing to life in the windows as we pass. Most of the structures are single homes or community living spaces, but I see some shops sprinkled about too. We try a few doors, but they are locked and each upstairs window lit with candlelight tells me the shop owners, who no doubt live above their workplace, are finished with customers for the day.

"I think we need to find somewhere to stay for the night. We can try shopping for Baba Yaga tomorrow." I yawn as I cross my arms and tuck my hands under my armpits. It's getting more frigid as we wade through this week, crawling closer and closer to Christmastide and the end of the year.

Poppy's teeth chatter as she speaks. "O-okay, sounds like a goo-good i-idea."

Frowning, I take her by the elbow and pull her forward, keeping her close to my side as we walk. Like her inner storm, I wasn't paying attention to how cold she was. When I peer over Poppy's head to check on Posy, I see half of her face is hidden in her scarf, her eyes reflecting in the growing dark. A little shiver goes from her shoulders down her back, but she tries to play it off when we meet eyes. The Pooka, on the other hand, seems unbothered by the cold as it scampers next to us on four small raccoon hands. It looks strange in this form; its all-black coat removes the telltale raccoon marks comprised of a dark mask and ringed tail. It physically pains me not to audibly compare the new shape to a rather pudgier version of the cat we first met.

"Would you care to guide us to shelter?" I ask the Pooka.

"You'll find warmth and safety ahead," it says, lost glowing eyes sweeping the salted street.

Instinctually, my silver gaze dances over the darkened buildings too. I try to see what the shadowy raccoon might've noticed that I didn't. But there's nothing, no sign of life or danger. I realize then it's searching for the shelter to bring us to. That's why it gave me a non-answer. But why doesn't our guide know the exact location?

"How do you know?" I prompt, thoughts of ulterior motives making my left brow quirk.

The Pooka only spares me a single glance before continuing its survey. "Fate let me see pieces of your future. In it, I saw this village."

Posy pops her nose from her scarf long enough to whisper with a tone brighter than the clouded moon hanging above us, "What else did you see?"

Yes, what else did it see? A way to lead us astray? A route that bypasses Baba Yaga's house so we can't retrieve the memory bird? Maybe a way to cut our ties with The Numina, so there's no hope of bringing them back?

84

"Fragments of events that lead to you climbing the Wyrd Mountain," the Pooka answers my sister.

While Posy is excited by this crumb of information, Poppy and I exchange looks. There are things the bogey is keeping from us, and that's making it *very* hard to summon even a shred of trust. But judging by the wince of a smile Poppy gives me, I know the Pooka still has her vote of confidence. Knowing her, it's all about giving Hazel a happily ever after by returning her lost love. It's blinding her.

Poppy leans past me to address the raccoon on its furious search. "Th-then what?"

The twinkle of hope in her voice draws the creature's attention. Its little steps falter before it peers up at her with wide eyes. "I do not know," it says. A low note, something akin to sadness, weighs heavy on its words. The Pooka sounds like it's telling the truth.

And I almost believe it.

Almost.

I must keep my wits about me. At least until I can uncover all the smoky faerie's secrets. So, with a skeptical glare, I gather my sisters closer before stalking down the gritty cobblestone streets in search of this warm safe-place we were promised. A lodging house would be preferable, but I'd take a creepy monastery or even a brothel at this point. Anywhere that might provide some food and shelter for cheap.

Putting my nose to the frigid air, I breathe deep, using my heightened sense of smell to search for––*anything*. Thanks to being a goblin, I catch the scent of cooked apple, seasonal spices, and the sourness of beer mixed with something salty. But it's not the street I'm smelling. Maybe peanuts?

Following the trail, we snake through the street, turning on to a stretch labeled *Parcae Village* where a two-story building stands bright and welcoming. Rowdy voices pour out from an open door and waves of heat waft through to caress us too.

The building is made of sturdy stone with glowing turret windows that bow from the walls, each trimmed in cherry wood. The roof is peaked, covered in layered shingles. It completes the rustic, inviting appearance. But the most intriguing part, hanging right above the giant front door, is a large wooden sign carved with a bird-shaped emblem that reads, "*The Glade — Tavern and Inn.*" When I turn to my sisters with raised brows, they too are staring at the sign. Posy's scarf drops from her nose, revealing her mouth agape. I almost laugh.

"It's a little too on the nose, right?" I ask, amused.

Poppy's feet do a quick dance as she shifts her weight around to generate body heat. "I don't care right now. Can we please go inside?"

Ironic name aside, this place seems to be our only option for finding beds tonight, and staying above a tavern wouldn't be the worst place I've slept. Not to mention, I spotted a few tufts of Queen Anne's lace still growing in the chill winter air under the shelter of an eave on the roof. The flowers represent sanctuary. I can't argue with that, so I wave my arm in a *"go right ahead"* gesture toward the door. Poppy leaps forward, running into *The Glade Tavern and Inn.*

The Pooka looks almost relieved, that is if raccoons can look relieved. Its body is lax as it peers past my legs into the tavern, studying the people and warmth filling the space. But if I was an outside eye and didn't know any better, I would think the creature is about to come inside and scavenge the crumbled peanut shells littering the floor. I'm sure no one will look too kindly upon a wild animal following us inside. Pushing the toe of my boot into its doughy stomach, I catch the Pooka off guard and scoot it backward, a foot away from the open door. Its hands slide easily over the salt strewn stone.

"You'd better get out of here before someone sees you and throws a knife." I hook a thumb over my shoulder, gesturing to the busy wave of bellicose voices behind me. "It is hunting season after all."

Little black claw-tipped hands grasp onto the tip of my boot. "It almost sounds like you care." The Pooka squints its beady eyes, furry head tilting.

With a snort, I shake off the animal's touch. "All I care about is getting to that mountain. Besides, my suggestion was a courtesy, not friendly advice."

The faerie stares up at me, solid gaze boring into my soul. The look makes me uncomfortable, like an itchy wool sweater on wet skin. But before I can use my boot to push it farther back, the raccoon moves out of reach and I take that as my cue to head inside after my sisters. I ignore the Pooka's request for me to leave a window open when we get a room, pretending not to hear as I enter *The Glade.*

The salty beer scent I tracked earlier is tripled by the sticky puddles splashed upon the tavern floor. A group of goblin men lift tankards of the sour hoppy drinks, letting them slosh over the rims as they cheer. There's a handful of tables and a few booths in the far corner of the large room, and it seems that humans and faeries alike drink, play card games, and chatter their night away here. On the far side is the bar, where a lone human man stands wiping the counter, and tucked almost out of sight to the right of him is a set of darkened stairs.

When the man sees the three of us loitering near the doorway, he waves us over, tossing his dirty rag over his shoulder and bracing his hands on the counter with a smile. "Evening, what can I do you for?" He slicks his wavy gray hair back, exposing the few brunette streaks he has left at his temples.

Posy is unable to make eye contact with the stranger. Poppy looks ready to bolt. Apparently, I'll be doing the talking. I nod a greeting at the barkeep before I ask, "Do you have any rooms for the night?"

He looks beneath the counter for a second and produces a

single key, jade-green eyes apologetic. "Looks like I've only got one left. There are two small beds in the room though, should be big enough to fit the three of you. But I'll take two shillings, a third off the price for the inconvenience."

"That'll work for us." I swing one shoulder of my bag off, digging for my coin pouch. When I pull out the empty leather sack, I remember the River Man with a frown. Looking to Posy, she fishes out the silvers from the near-empty purse at her waist. My sister hands them to me before peering down at her feet, kicking at a stray peanut shell. After watching our exchange and pocketing the coins, something akin to sympathy softens the barkeep's eyes. I crack a joke to make it disappear. I hate pity. "We shared a womb once, we can share a bed for a night or two." I smile this time.

The man, who I assume is the owner, laughs and I decide he seems like a nice enough fellow, especially given the discounted price. But I do hope the room is cleaner than the downstairs, or the beds at the very least. A couple stray bugs are fine, but I *will* sleep on the floor if I find any suspicious stains on the mattress.

Just as we're about to head for the stairs, the loud growl of a stomach rings out. Turning to my sisters, they point to each other, placing the blame for the gurgling. I roll my eyes. "That was me. I ate the same amount of hardtack as you, so if I'm hungry I'd bet a toe you are too."

"Do you think they have soup?" Poppy's eyes sparkle at the thought of the first warm food in days.

"I'll ask." I jerk my head towards the noisy part of the room where a lone table sits in the corner, past the card game that's growing sloppier and more aggressive with each drink. "Go find us somewhere to sit."

"Ah." My sister's ears turn dark green, fingers curling into the hood of Posy's scarf. She eyes the men and women, the few tipsy gnomes, and eastern goblins. She's nervous.

Taking the lead, I sit instead at the bar, wriggling onto one of the many empty wooden stools. "Come on, you milksop, hop up." I tap my hand on the counter for her and it also gets the attention of the owner who had gone to refill some drinks.

"Need something else?" he asks.

I'm taken aback when Posy is the one to answer; she never talks to strangers. "Cider, please." Impressed by her bravery, I give her a heavy pat on the shoulder. This is Posy and Poppy's first time out in the world since the attack on the glade. They've only traveled between home and Hazel's cottage, not a step further. And I don't know that they would've ever left the glade had it not been for The Numina planning this rescue hundreds of years ago––for Aspen needing this last shot at survival––for Hazel's memories and lost love. I'm suddenly proud of my sisters. It excites me. I'm glad they'll get to experience the type of things I've been seeing and doing alone over the past few years.

Poppy brushes invisible crumbs off her seat before she sits on my other side. She and Posy let their gazes wander, taking in the tavern with curious eyes. Beneath the nightlife, beer, and peanuts, it's snug. Safe. A warm place that probably smells more like apple after the late-night patrons head to bed and the floors are mopped. When I survey more, I notice decorative swags draped over the walls and a strand of garland wrapping up the handrail of the stairs. Bunches of mistletoe hang above all the doorways too, and in some of the glass bottles shelved on the wall across from us, there's cinnamon sticks, orange slices, and clove buds soaking. It's a charming, albeit travel worn place, but it feels––festive being here.

This pleasant light feeling doesn't last long because a breath later the purpose of our journey hits me in the gut, again. I've heard Aspen's voice in my head every moment since we left, listening to her halfhearted promise to wait for us to get back, to hang on to life. I think about the Pooka's message and the part about the thread to the forgotten unraveling. They say it's the last fated string that ties The Numina to this world and apparently, it's attached to my sisters and I... Then Time's letter comes to mind, but the thought is quickly followed by a tighter squeeze to my gut. We'll be facing another witch––we'll be walking into her home and expecting to walk back out in one piece––how will we manage that?

This sisterly bonding time is weighted by grim circumstances.

I need to get a grip.

It does no good letting the unknown ruin the mood tonight.

My sisters need this rest.

I need this...

The tavern owner places clay mugs of steaming apple cider under our noses. Greedy, we each grab for our cups and pull them in close. The rising condensation washes over my face as the warmth soaks through the pottery into my hands. Poppy is already deep into her cup, frothy foam speckled with allspice coating her pointed upper lip.

"So, what brings you girls through town?" the owner asks.

Shrugging, I try to sound aloof as I set my mug back on the counter. "Business."

The man lifts a brow, looking between my sisters and me. We're young, but we don't look younger than our seventeen years. We could pass for at least twenty. Goblin triplets though? A rare sight, I imagine, so what kind of business could we possibly have?

Posy is smirking at me over the rim of her mug, letting me bury myself in the hole I've dug. Meanwhile, Poppy is still too interested in her cider and watching the tipsier patrons with wary eyes.

"We're, uh, looking for a gift. For Christmastide." I nod to myself as the pieces of my made-up story click together in my brain. "Yeah, for our grandmama."

A GOBLIN OF THE GLADE

Posy chokes on her mouthful of cider as I insinuate that Baba Yaga is our jolly old granny.

"She's a bit of a collector, you see." I shrug again. "Shopping from local stores is futile, we'd never find anything new. Stopping here before we head north, to her house, seemed like a good idea."

"North." The green-eyed owner frowns. "Not too far north, I hope. Between here and the mountains there's only a few towns before you get into swamp territory, and a hag lives there."

This gets Poppy's attention. Baba Yaga must be notorious around these parts if this man is concerned about the distant swamplands. Now I know why the village and its streets are so salty and protected. I wonder how far-reaching this witch's terror is? The rumors about The Changeling Queen and how she slew Black Annis and Jenny Greenteeth had spread far and wide, but it did little to ease people. There are still *many* bogeymen and things of darkness creeping about. Like the new water witches, Peg Powler and Nelly Longarms. Or the resurgence of Allison Gross and Nanny Rutt, and the rise of the newly minted Bloody Mary, to name only a few. And they won't go away, or stop popping up until The Numina get rid of them all...

"We'll be okay," I reassure the man, heart drumming from my untruths.

"All right, in the meantime you'll be safe here. I built this place after passing through a quaint dwelling almost thirty years ago. It was a haven for people and faerie folk of all kinds, and I wanted to invoke that same space here. All are welcome, and no one will bother you. I'll make sure of it." The smile on his pale face is genuine, as is the way his button nose scrunches the slightest bit when he does so.

"I'm Alder, by the way," he adds. "I'll get you girls some complementary grub but let me know if you need anything else."

To Poppy's delight the tavern does have soup, and we fill our bellies with tomato bisque made with soured cream, potatoes, basil, and oil before heading up the creaky stairs to our assigned room. Alder was right, it did have two *small* beds, each no wider than the length of my arm. At least they're long enough to keep our feet from hanging off the ends.

Knowing my aversion to snuggling, my sisters offer to share a bed for the night. Poppy squishes up against the wall since an ardent Posy refuses to be backed up into a corner, preferring to risk a short fall off the edge instead of being trapped. I'm grateful but can't help teasing them as I turn out the oil lamp and settle in. "Careful, Poppy, don't fall in the crack."

A pillow is lobbed at me in the dark, nailing me right in the face.

Sleep takes my sisters fast, and I lie in the dark listening to their soft breaths. The moon is almost covered by clouds, and little light glazes the room, but it's bright enough for me to see the small creature sitting on the windowsill outside, waiting. I know the glass can't stop the Pooka from coming in, it had no issuing phasing through Aspen's window the first time it appeared to us. Yet now it sits there as if asking for my permission before infiltrating this borrowed bedroom. I stare at the ceiling, trying to ignore the Pooka's existence, but the tiny shadow has more patience than I have. My bed groans when I shift my weight to flip the lock on the pane and push the window open wide enough for the mouse to slip inside.

"Now what?" I exhale in a harsh whisper as I pull the window closed, shutting out the cold.

The Pooka sits on the interior ledge, taking note of the bundled, snoozing shapes of my sisters on the other side of the room. "I wanted to ensure you were safe," it says, the hushed layer of its many voices slithering towards me on a lingering breeze that had followed it through the window.

The sensation chills me enough that I shuffle back into the

warm crease I made in the center of my bed, settling back beneath the covers. "Right." I don't think the bogey can see me roll my eyes as I readjust my pillow, but the doubt and sarcasm shine through my words.

"Why are you always so convinced I'm lying to you?" the Pooka asks.

It surprises me that the creature even cares what I think of it. I may have seen myself in its loneliness for a moment, but at the end of the day, we're just a means to an end for each other. That's it.

"Because as far as I'm concerned, you're a prisoner of war turned spy," I answer, thinking of the tangled leash Fate has tied to the faerie. "I don't trust you."

The Pooka lets loose a slip of an exasperated sigh. "Your constant stubbornness confounds me."

The familiarity and sureness in its tone irks me. "You don't know the first thing about my stubbornness." I glare up at the silhouette of the mouse hovering on its perch above my head. The shadowy malfeasant spends less than a week with my sisters and me, and it already thinks it's got me all figured out.

"But I do. I *know* you." The Pooka's claws make scratching noises on the windowsill as it inches closer to my head. "I've known you and every bit of goodness and horror you've seen. And some of what you've yet to see. I also know you think I'll try to betray The Numina, but I won't because that means hurting your family, which in your mind is worse than any betrayal." The creature's sincerity makes my stomach pitch. "We are not enemies, Primrose."

All of my thoughts and suspicions have been laid bare, and while I should feel satisfied that the Pooka knows I've been on to it, I don't. I feel confused, vulnerable even. The Numina let this messenger watch my life play out, every childhood memory and trauma, every milestone and mistake. The Pooka knows why I am the way I am and why my family means so much to me. It wouldn't jeopardize its scheme and try to win me over by telling me all this.

Does this make its words true? Is this dark *thing* really here to just guide and protect us, even if it is little more than Death and Fate's criminal slave? And if so, then why does it care about my thoughts and opinion?

I don't know what to think. Nor do I have the mental or emotional capacity to consider any of this. So I shove it all down as I pull my blanket to my chin like a shell, turning until I face the wall, away from the mouse. Despite the Pooka's small size, I can still feel its raw, looming presence at my back.

"Fate didn't show me what will change your mind or when it happens, but you'll trust me someday soon." The faerie says this like a promise.

I close my eyes against its words. Forcing myself to slow my breathing, I empty my head and clear my conscience of the fear and misplaced guilt I sense starting to build up like pesky piles of sand. But just as they're known to do, grains of sand still find a way to stick in unwanted places.

Eventually by staying silent and pretending to fall asleep, I trick my body into a calm state and succumb to real unconsciousness.

—

I DREAM OF THE CAGE, of Pop holding us tight in his arms when the materializing iron door swings open. Black Annis reaches in and snatches a victim, a honey sticky imp that clings to the bars for dear life. Our horrified eyes meet when its little fingers slip. A howl escapes from its fanged mouth as the witch pulls it away with a laugh.

When the cage door slams closed and the seams melt away

with blue-tinged witchcraft, I know what's coming next. I've heard it happen many times before, to a gnome, a brownie, and a troll. Poppy and Posy cling to Pop with their tiny chubby fists, turning their faces into him. He tries to cover our eyes with his hands, but he only has two. Through the gaps in his stretched hold, I watch in stunned terror.

Black Annis's iron talons and needle teeth flash, she grins ear to ear as she slices into skin. Blood covers her fingers and splashes onto her beautiful nightmarish face. The imp screams and yelps as muscle and tissue tear, creating a prize for the witch to hang out to dry in the banshee trees before going on her belt of skin. She cackles, raising her clawed hand one more time and—

—

I WAKE to someone climbing into my bed. Posy untangles the blankets from my legs as I gasp for air, sweat coating my forehead. My throat is tight, sore. I clear it twice before I can speak.

"Are you okay?" I ask, my pulse thundering like a winter storm. Looking to the windowsill, I find it empty, no yellow-eyed mouse in sight.

Posy nudges me over, sliding in beside me. My back touches the wall as I curl up on my side, stuffing an arm under my pillow to support my head.

"You were thrashing around and flickering out of sight," she whispers as she mirrors my position.

Her reflecting eyes are concerned as she looks at me. The moonlight is brighter now, the clouds shifted enough for it to spill through the gauzy curtains lighting up our faces just enough to see. I hate that I've woken her, no doubt for the umpteenth time since I first started having nightmares.

Glancing over at Poppy across the room, she's mumbling in her sleep, as chatty as she is awake. She's lucky she's a deep sleeper.

I'm grateful to be awake though. Posy pulled me out of the Purgatory I revisit most nights. This time I dreamed of a memory, but sometimes they're different, almost embellished versions of what I saw and heard. The worst one I ever had was watching my sisters get skinned. The scarred scratch Posy received on the cheek was much worse in that dream.

"Was it bad?" she murmurs.

A confirming noise comes from the back of my throat. "It was the imp this time."

Posy pulls the blankets up higher around us, tucking them beneath my chin. "I remember him."

"I wish you didn't," I whisper back. A strange sense of survivor's guilt coats my bones.

My sister's eyes slip closed. "I know."

There's a lot of things I wish didn't happen, but those are wistful hopes. What's done is done. The past has taken its toll and all we can do is move on, grow. Judging by the book we pulled from Hazel's floor, the unforgivable things that happened to us were set in motion hundreds of years ago... This bumpy path was paved for us and it seems we have no choice but to follow it. Hazel has said it many times: *everything happens for a reason.* Even though I feel like we got the short end of the stick, I have to believe, like Hazel, that all the bad stuff was for a reason. I must hope. Hope that the Pooka is being truthful and trustworthy enough to lead us on so we can find a Fortune to bring back The Numina. Who will, in turn, bring back the art of Healing so Hazel can fix Aspen and reunite with her husband. And I must especially hope that, once we save them, The Numina will wipe out every hag and bogey so that no one, no other child, will *ever* have to be a witch's plaything again. I cross my fingers beneath the blankets, hoping it's all true and we'll make it through this cold winter quest to see the day.

The Village Shops

The Glade Tavern and Inn serves an amazing breakfast. While my sisters still sleep in the upstairs room, I sit at the bar and eat, keeping one eye out for any stray mice. Alder blessed me with a beautiful slice of honey-glazed roast, a cup of strong coffee, and the second-best plum pudding I've ever had. Sparrow's is, of course, the first. The palm sized, sugar crusted dome melts in my mouth, flavors of port, stem ginger, orange juice, and molasses reminding me of home.

I don't realize I'm devouring my food with my eyes closed until I hear Alder laugh. "You're finding everything to your liking I hope."

"That's an understatement. My compliments to the cook." I hide a green flush behind my coffee, something we don't get back home. The only time I have the roasted drink is out on my travels, and I've missed the bitter taste and kick of energy.

Alder does a little bow with a hand to his chest, his eyes crinkling at the edges while the wrinkles around his mouth deepen. "Why thank you, I do try my best."

"You made this?" I don't mean to sound surprised. Most would think running a tavern and inn would require employees, but it seems this man is owner, bartender, cook, and maid. That's a lot of work for one person.

Leaning his elbows on the counter, Alder nods. "Food is my passion. When I was making my way to these villages, I had every intention of opening a simple tavern. Though, I found my journey more inspiring than I had ever planned and ended up creating a harbor of sorts instead."

"A port for people," I say around the ball of breakfast in my cheek. He follows the same kind of philosophy Aspen has, creating a home for humans and creatures, whether permanent or temporary.

The older man straightens and picks up my mug to refill my coffee. "A safe place to come and go, or stay awhile," he agrees.

"Speaking of." I swallow the last bite of pudding before continuing, "Depending on how our gift search goes today, will we have a room at the same price for another night?"

"It's yours until you decide it's time to leave." Alder sets the full mug down on the counter with a warm smile.

"Thanks, I appreciate that," I say to him, both for the coffee and the cheap room.

An odd but comfortable silence stretches between us as he wipes down the tables and I all but lick my plate clean. When footsteps pound above us, meaning more patrons are waking up and getting ready for the day, I bemoan the loss of peace and reconcile myself to the upcoming hunt. We have to find something worthy of Baba Yaga, something to trade for Hazel's memory bird--something affordable, at that.

"So, what kind of gift are you looking for?" Alder calls from underneath a booth, picking up stray peanut shells that escaped last night's sweeping.

Letting out a hum, I swirl my new cup of coffee with tiny movements of my wrist. "I'm not sure, but I think my sisters and I will know it when we see it."

Alder groans as he stands, carrying a handful of shells to the trash behind the bar. "Well, if your grandma is a collector, you'll find many one-of-a-kind things here. We have lots of artisans in this town, some who stay, and others who pass through." He cleans his hands off before kneading at his back. "Chances are, you'll find new things every few days."

Part of me wishes we could stay that long. We'd be able to explore so much of this town if we could stay for a week or more. We'd go in every shop, talk to all the locals and creep around all the nooks and crannies. We'd learn all its secrets. Maybe one day we'll come back––if we still have legs to carry us back after traversing the swamp.

"I don't know that we've got that kind of time. We must leave tomorrow morning at the latest," I sigh.

"Timed event, huh?" Alder looks at me with a curious gaze.

I hate lying to the kindhearted man, but there's only so much I can say without sounding like a complete muttonhead. It's best if I stick to the grandma story and move on. By this time tomorrow, we'll just be three of hundreds of customers that have come and gone from his establishment. Our white lie won't really matter in the end.

"Oh, you know, don't want to be late for Christmastide or grandmama will be spitting feathers." Or the very fabric of the world will unravel if we goblins don't find some-long-forgotten-powerful-beings-living-in-a-space-between-life-and-death, a mere bagatelle in the grand scheme of things.

A familiar pair of footsteps thump above us.

When Poppy and Posy reach the bottom of the stairs, they look refreshed and bright-eyed, sleeping in a real bed having done them wonders. After a cheery good morning from one sister and a little wave from the other, they sit and dig into the same breakfast I'd eaten earlier. Once they finish and Alder clears their plates, we brave the chilled morning bustle of the streets.

Locals and visitors to the village meander, greeting their

neighbors and strangers with the same joy and vigor. The sound of life fills me with excitement, the billow of voices, clomp of horse hooves, ringing silver bells, all of it. It's the sounds of a new place full of things I can't wait to discover.

"What do you guys think? Stay together or split up?" I ask, watching the bakery next door that's hung with festive boughs open its yellow shuttered windows.

"I would suggest you split up." The Pooka's voice floats down to me from my left.

When I turn to look up, I find it roosting in the shade of the tavern's eaves. I can't make out anything but its glowing eyes. It's indistinct and almost formless, much like my ever-present shadowy followers.

"The village is protected. You would each be fine off on your own," it adds.

"Can you tell us what we're looking for?" Poppy asks, squinting up at the Pooka just as I did.

The sheen of a glossy feather creates a twinkle in the shade when the faerie replies. "I would if I knew what object The Numina intend for you to find."

I throw my hands up before letting them smack against my legs. "What good are you if you can't help us find what we need?" My own grumpiness catches me off guard. I've eaten enough, I even had multiple cups of coffee, and the only lingering bitterness in my mouth is from a blue-soaked nightmare. Usually, I have more patience to start my day, but I'm already wearing thin. Perhaps a short solo adventure would do me good.

The answering click of a beak sounds distinctly chiding. "I never said I wouldn't help, I said I don't know what you need."

Poppy looks down the vast street around the tavern. "I think the Pooka's right, we'll see more if we split up, better chance of finding something for Baba Yaga."

Posy nods in hesitant agreement as she picks at her fingernails. I know she doesn't want to wander alone, anxious about interacting with all these strangers. No one is forcing her to say yes so I think it's the excitement of seeing and learning about new things that makes her agree.

"Fine," I say to the Pooka. "We'll split up. What are you going to do?"

Sulfurous eyes look off into the distance. "I'll fly overhead first and get a full view of the village. If nothing particularly *destined* catches my eye, I'll take to the streets and listen for chatter; locals always know what's best."

My sisters and I share a look, one that lays out an entire silent conversation in only seconds. I hate to admit that the Pooka's plan is smart. Poppy, Posy, and I can cover a lot of ground by ourselves, but the extra set of shapeshifting eyes is invaluable. Especially with our tight timeline. My sisters know this too, which is why we nod to each other in confirmation and Poppy takes her full coin purse from her belt to loosen the cinching holding it closed. She pulls out coins for me and Posy, divvying them up until my leather pouch is almost half full and Posy has a smidge added to her dwindled fourth. Though I don't like having to use my sister's money, I have little choice after our run-in with the River Man. Depending on what we find we might have enough to make a purchase collectively, if not separately.

"All right, I'll take the main street." I point left. "Poppy, you go that way and cover the brick-and-mortar shops." I gesture to the right. "Posy, you do the same. The four of us will meet back up around lunchtime on the main street."

With a mocking salute, Poppy grins at me. "Yes, sir." She takes off down her side of town with a skip in her step.

"That's ma'am to you!" I call after her, my breath clouding the atmosphere.

We can hear her laughter as we watch her go. The little

rings, coins, and ornaments decorating her wild hair wink in the sunlight, velvet cloak billowing behind.

Before Posy follows, I stop her, a serious undertone to my voice. "Hey, Po?"

Her boots scuff to a sudden stop and she peers at me, expectant.

"Don't talk to strangers," I say with a smirk, reminding her of Rush's warning quip.

She rolls her eyes and turns away, but before her face is hidden from me, I see the little uptick of her lips. She looks like a scholar in her smart clothes, walking down the street with her vest and belted trousers. Her spectacles are hanging from the front of her scarf, her hair high and secure in a ponytail. No one will give her trouble; on the outside she looks confident, like she knows exactly what she's doing, even if her insides are squirming.

I look back at the tavern eaves. "Lunchtime. Don't miss it." I point up at the blob of darkness staring down at me. "It's time to pull your weight around here. This is your chance to earn a scrap of my trust, so don't mess it up."

While I had time to myself this morning, I thought about what the Pooka said last night. I'm still reserving my doubts, but technically, the creature hasn't given us a reason to suspect malintent. I've let my secondhand knowledge of Pookas and their origins lead my judgment. However, the faerie guiding me and my sisters might be nothing like the one that once chased and cornered Sparrow and Rush. My sister-in-law believes in people being able to change just as much as she loves the phrase "innocent until proven guilty." Albeit, she said those things when trusting us triplets alone with a freshly baked cake after the last one had been mysteriously eaten. And again, when trying to figure out where a newly frosted slice had gone from said fresh cake. Though there were only so many times she could overlook the chocolate crumbs on the corners of our lips.

If the bogey is as trustworthy and honest as it professes, this is its time to prove Sparrow right.

"I won't miss it," the Pooka says before bursting from the eaves in a flurry of wings and feathers.

I stroll toward the main street with feigned purpose. I don't know what I'm looking for, at all. Still, I don't feel out of place, I never do when I'm traveling. In fact, most of the time, I feel welcome, especially by the land itself. It's like being embraced, like the streets are saying, *come––come unwind my mysteries, learn my secrets*. And I am more than happy to oblige.

This street overflows with color and scents. At first, it's overwhelming to my heightened sense of smell, but soon my faculties calm and I acclimate. There are vendors selling fire-grilled meats on wooden skewers, tissue-wrapped cherry hand-pies, and paper cones of hot candied pecans. The collapsible stalls, from which the sellers beckon, are tented with brilliant hues of crimson, royal purple, yolk, and sky.

There's a goblin woman with a basket of fresh produce on an elbow and her human child, topped with a fluffy winter hat, on her hip. A young man with an imp close at his heels passes a lumbering troll couple, and a gnome with stacks of letters and small pattern-wrapped parcels to deliver. It's seamless the way they go about their day, the faeries and their human neighbors, not something you see too often. Faeries and humans often stick to their own little communities, not because of prejudice, more out of tradition. Places like this tavern town, or my home in the glade, are exceptions to the rule.

There are even many hybrids here as well. I count more mixes than all of my fingers and toes combined in the first five minutes I've been walking. Another rare sight. I've only met a few in my life, my half-goblin, half-human brother being one. It's a beautiful sight to see. Like Rush, there's many human and goblin offspring here shopping, and surprisingly even gnome and northern dwarf. A couple combinations are hard to pinpoint like imp and something gremlin-esque or a brownie-ish bogle mix, but I find the latter hard to believe considering both are very anti-social creatures. Either way it's fascinating, and refreshing.

Putting my hands in my pockets, I amble over the cobble-stones, looking at each seasonally decorated tent and its wares. I spot a half-nisser man, easily identified by his woolly white beard and round belly. His all-red, fur-trimmed clothes match the vibrancy of his spice cart where each of his wares are sepa-rated into their own sections by shallow wooden walls. There's a metal scoop and little jars to portion out the seasonings, inviting my eyes to rove over the fine milled pickings. Rare shreds of saffron and grains of paradise are so spicy they burn my nose while the black cardamom, that's been smoked and dried over fire, makes it tingle. The fennel pollen smells like licorice, and I'm almost tempted to sift through the grains with my fingers, but I resist.

Putting distance between myself and that temptation, I notice an old half-selkie woman selling bolts of fine fabric, things I can touch. My hands run over mulberry silk made from moth silkworms. The whorls on my fingertips wander over thick linen, and my knuckles sink deep into northern alpaca wool. There's a particular bolt that catches my silver eyes, one that reminds me of Aspen's embroidery—the sight makes my throat grow thick. She would love the deep jewel tones, the hand-stitched flowers, woodland creatures, and threads of accented gold. It's too beautiful, and not something Baba Yaga, with her blackened hag heart, would enjoy. So, after a nod of appreciation to the tent's owner, I move on.

My nose leads me to a cart brimming with coffee beans. Each roast is already portioned out into paper and string wrapped parcels. Rustic and neat. Picking up the first one, I lift it to my nose and inhale, smelling rain and high altitudes, a plantation kept in the shade. The next smells like hot weather and melted chocolate. The owner, a young human girl, hands me a different parcel and tells me how rare the beans are. They smell like flowers and fruit that have grown in a smoke-filled room. But the coffee beans I like best on her shelf are the ones that smell of darkness, like the woods and tart berries roasted under the night sky. The girl ends up giving me a free sample before I leave, a waxed, paper cup big enough to get a taste that will leave me wanting more. But alas I cannot afford it. As I walk on, I sip at the liquid like it's precious, golden ambrosia that'll keep my insides goddess-like and warm.

There are potters and arrow makers, a blacksmith who points to his brick store down the way, a woman with spools of ribbons on her outstretched arms. I even see a soap maker, a goblin hand dipping tallow candles, and a cart stacked with green bottles. They're each tied with shiny red bows and hold infused olive oil that smells of truffle, garlic, and lemon. Again, things a swamp witch has no use for––this quest is proving hard.

My weak sense of self-control makes me stop by a book seller and his tiny cart, the yellowed pages with their muted pastel spines calling to me. They're old, all second- or even thirdhand. If Posy were here, she'd be all over them, and I know she'd love the teal one I'm currently holding. Of course, she's wiser than me and would no doubt advise against spending the money we need for Baba Yaga––I, however, have never claimed to be wise. Street-smart, yes, but wise, no. I count my coins and buy it. The old vendor even wraps the book in butcher paper with a little bow of twine. Then, in the next stall over there's a flash of metal that begs my attention. The table is full of hand-made jewelry, necklaces with thin chains and rings made of bent spoon handles. There's a locket for Poppy that I *can't* leave behind. It's a strange sensation that overwhelms me, a dire need to buy that specific necklace that negates any bit of responsibility I have within me. I lose a few more of my borrowed coins.

The locket gets wrapped up into a square bit of fabric before being hidden in my bag with Posy's book.

It is almost Christmastide after all...

Next, I see a tent draped in rainbow fabric, a swirl of hand-dyed colors urging me forward. When I duck under a low hanging corner I'm met with a peculiar sight. A woman sits ramrod straight on a stool with buckets full of stones surrounding her on the ground. But the eye-catching thing is the moss growing on her bare skin. She's not dressed for winter but that doesn't seem to be bothering her, arms bare in a summer shift. Her eyes are sightless and milky, but I keep returning to the moss, a characteristic common to trolls. Though this woman is no troll; she's pale and human skinned with a perfect upturned nose and soft edges.

"Hello," I say in greeting as I crouch to turn a hand through one of the buckets. My findings are chunks of agate and onyx, turquoise and jasper.

The woman hums, head turned toward me but eyes faraway. "Curious."

"I'm sorry?" The apology spills out before I can stop it. I'm confused and thrown off by her un-greeting.

"Were you born at midnight?" the strange woman asks.

I move to another bucket and paw through it, keeping my eyes on her. Despite being bundled against the cold, a chill settles itself over my back, then like wandering fingers it runs down my arms until my whole body feels on edge. "That's an odd thing to ask a stranger."

The woman slides her thick forest-green hair over her shoulder. It whispers over the moss sprouting from her shoulders. "I've been asked stranger things."

Without replying, I move through the tent and consider leaving, but something imperceptible makes me stay and my fingers pick through another bucket full of geode and hunks of quartz.

"I sense something around you, a veil of shadows." She cocks her head and her body twists on the stool to face me. "I sense Death but not death, not decomposition, but new life."

My brain is telling me to run, to leave and never look back. But like a thread attached to my chest, something pulls me forward, makes me stay in this human-troll hybrid's shop. I dare to sift through the bucket at her bare feet, one hand staying close to the knife sheathed in my belt.

"So tell me, Dark Angel, were you born at midnight?" she asks again.

My fingers snag on a particular stone, latching on, and I'm stuck staring into this woman's blank eyes. "Yes, just two minutes after my sisters. We're triplets."

"Ah," she sighs, body leaning forward. "You're a Chime Child like me."

"A what?" Balling the stone up in my fist, I lean away.

The woman grins. "A Chime Child, a baby born at the start of the Chime Hour, midnight. Some born at that hour have–– abilities, like speaking to animals or healing ailing plants. I've met a Chime Child once who could influence emotions with her musical gifts."

"This is fascinating––" My fingers drift away from my knife as I trail off. There's no danger here; the woman is just feather-headed. Suppressing a snort, I continue, "But what does this have to do with me?"

"I see things, some have called me an oracle. But you, many souls follow you," she breathes, fingers reaching out to dance in the air around me.

A force of habit makes me look over my shoulder. Of course, there is nothing behind me. Nothing except the shadows that dance at the edge of my vision every day, taunting me by disap-pearing when I try to stare at them. This blind woman is insane... unless she somehow senses these so-called souls?

"Do you see them?" she prods.

"I'm afraid not," I say with an eye roll. It's not entirely a lie. I've never been able to fully see the shadows if that's what she's referring to.

"You will, in time." Her tone is full of promise, pure misplaced conviction.

"Okay." A sarcastic clip slips through my voice. "This was very enlightening. I'd better go now."

I'm turning on my heel when the woman calls out, "The stone in your hand."

Oh, that's right. I forgot I grabbed one from the last bucket. It's still folded in my fist, warmed by my skin. Uncurling my knuckles, I see a round tiger's eye stone the size of my eye. The soft luster of its golden stripes, reddish-brown hue, and smudges of inky black-brown sing to me like a lullaby. "I'm so sorry, I swear I wasn't trying to steal it." I apologize, moving to drop it back into the bucket.

The woman stops me with an outstretched hand. "Keep it, you'll need it." I nod, agreeing, but I'm not sure why. Then I blink rapidly as I reach for my coin pouch, but she shakes her head when she hears the jingle of metal discs. "No need, consider it a gift from one Chime Child to another."

"Uh, thanks," I murmur as I stumble back out of the tent. My fingers curl around the stone again, seeking comfort from the small glossy orb that seems oddly heavy in my grip. A cold sweat beads in the dip of my lower back. The woman's ramblings make no sense, her talk about my midnight birthday and the souls that follow me--she's crazy.

Right?

Only a few days ago, I thought The Numina were a myth, but I'm changing my mind about them--but the hybrid woman gave me no reason to trust her. All she gave me was a tiger's eye stone, one that my hand was pulled to like a taut string. Glancing back at the tent as I walk forward, my head feels light and floaty, adrift in a fog of confusion. There's also a curious sensation twining through my ribs that says there are things bigger than me and my sisters happening around us. Things bigger than our quest that even the Pooka isn't allowed to know. Things I can't yet comprehend...

Before I can finish my thought, I bump into someone, the sound of air leaving both of our lungs with an "*oof.*" Hands clamp onto me before I can fall on my face.

"Oh, good, I found you."

GRIM

*P*oppy's shoulders droop with relief. "Posy and I have been looking all over the main street for you."

"I, uh, I got distracted," I mumble, looking back at the oracle's tent one last time before shoving away all thoughts of Chime Children and Death.

"I see that," she laughs, grabbing my arm. "Come on, Posy is just up ahead."

Poppy steers me toward the end of the street where the food vendors are. Tucking the tiger's eye into my pocket, I smooth my hands over my face, rubbing the tense bunch beneath my brows as I try to get my senses in order. I've done a terrible job of shopping. The stone I acquired would be worthless to Baba Yaga, and I don't think she'd care about the book or locket either. Hopefully, my sisters had more luck.

Posy stands off to the side of the street, leaning against the wall of one of the permanent shops. She's people watching. The proof is in her body language, how still she is, how focused she is as her eyes follow those of interest. She looks like a cat watching a mouse and I wonder what's she's learning as she observes. When her gaze catches mine, she lights up with a grin.

Pushing off the wall, she strides to meet us. She's searching my empty hands as she approaches, her smile fading; I guess she didn't find anything for the swamp witch. Which must mean Poppy didn't either.

"How would you guys feel about a little snack?" Poppy asks, jingling her half-full purse while looking at all the choices with delight.

Spending a few more coins won't hurt. I shrug. "I could always go for something sweet."

Posy's palms meet with a smack as she rubs her hands together, eager to make her choice. With a laugh, I hook my arms around my sisters' necks and pull them into the fray. More people mill about at this time of day, grabbing lunch and finishing up their morning errands.

Each of us are drawn to different carts so we divide and conquer, again, deciding to share a little of each thing we buy. The stall of my choosing is selling crisp ginger biscuits by the tin for only one pence. They range in shapes from little men to stars, trees, and candy canes. I can't resist popping one in my mouth as I backtrack to find my sisters. Notes of brown sugar and golden syrup burst over my tongue, the crunchy spiced biscuit reminding me of childhood baking days with Sparrow and Rush at Christmastide.

When I find Posy, she's visited the muffin man in favor of crumpets smothered in loganberry jam and lemon curd. We wander for a little more before we find Poppy. She's shuffling forward, the slowest I've ever seen her, trying to balance three paper cups, steam floating from each one, while humming to herself. The mischievous, teasing sibling in me wants to watch her suffer until it turns into a juggling act, but the scent coming from the cups changes my mind.

"Here," I chuckle as I take one of the drinks from her. "Let's go find somewhere to eat."

We wind our way to the end of the street where the vendors have set out some small foldable tables. There's a few that are empty, but the one that has a coal-black squirrel with yellow eyes sitting on top is the one we go to.

"You made it. How nice of you to join us." I greet the Pooka with a sardonic tone as I take a seat on one of the four freezing metal chairs at the circular table. In the haze of carts and confusion in the oracle's tent, I almost forgot about my deal with the faerie. The creature made it to lunch, so that's one step toward a semblance of trust.

The smoky end of its tail twitches. "I'm so happy to be here," it replies with an equally satirical whisper, though there is no genuine heat behind the words.

My snort is hidden by my cup. Inside is something I've never had before; its thick texture surprises me and leaves a trail on my upper lip. Licking the foamy residue off, I taste the clove, nutmeg, and cinnamon. The custardy drink warms me all the way to my toes, dissolving any trace of the winter chill nipping at my skin.

"Did you see anything while you were in the air?" Poppy asks, mouth full of crumpet.

The Pooka's tiny, tufted squirrel ears swivel. "Unfortunately, no. It seems you were also met with failure, but—"

The word failure sends a sudden zing through my teeth like I've bitten down on a scrap of metal.

"With all due respect"—I pause with a lifted brow—"which is none, sod off." Taking a tree-shaped biscuit, I throw it at the Pooka. "We didn't fail. As long as there's light in the sky and breath in my lungs, there's still time to find something for Baba Yaga."

The faerie dodges the gingery treat, looking from me to the offending sweet and back. "You didn't let me finish."

"Hmm, I wonder why," I retort.

We *didn't* fail.

We *can't* fail.

I can't fail.

"You two are worse than an old married couple," Poppy butts in with a cordial, people-pleasing smile and forced laugh. "Let's play nice, okay?" She's trying to stop the bickering with a joke, just like she does with our nieces and nephews when they fight over toys.

"Your sister is very wise, *Primrose*. You should listen to her more often." The Pooka's mirthful little eyes flick between me and Poppy.

Falling back into my chair with a huff, I slouch down and fight the urge to cross my arms over my chest like a petulant child. Instead, I place the edge of a candy cane shaped biscuit on the table and flick it at the shadowy creature. "Don't call me Primrose, *bogey*. If you know as much about me as you say, then you know I don't like it when people call me that."

"Not unless you're Aspen," Poppy unhelpfully contributes.

"Or it's a holiday," Posy adds as she snatches a few of the treats from the tin before I can use them all as ammunition. She sits with her legs crossed, rocking her body and eating the biscuits while dumping out our coin pouches onto the table to count how much money we have left. The pile is meager. I'm not sure how we're going to pay for another night of lodging *and* something valuable for Baba Yaga. Especially after the treats we just bought and the money I spent on gifts. I can only hope Posy doesn't realize there's a few extra coins missing--

The Pooka's layered hum breaks off my thought. "Then you mustn't call me bogey or *it*. I'd like you to use my name."

I pause, the ginger man I was about to use as a soldier against the squirrel-shaped faerie snapping in two. I hadn't thought about that. This Pooka was a human once, a deviant criminal deemed wicked enough to be captured by Death herself, but a human, nonetheless. Of course the Pooka would've had a name. When the seed of guilt I try to swallow doesn't go down my throat, I shove a biscuit into my mouth, hoping the sweet crumbs will dislodge the sticky feeling. It doesn't.

Nonchalant, I gulp down my pride and shift my way into sitting back up in my chair. My throat is less thick as I slice into one of the crumpets with my elder knife. I cherish this weapon and while I didn't want to use it on a floorboard, I'm content to use it on sweets. Hazel would understand. My gaze stays trained on the swirl of jam and curd covering the blade when I speak. "Very well, you call me Rose and I'll call you by the name you had in your first life. No more patronizing."

Flicking my eyes up, I find the Pooka studying me, black fur shifting in the windless air. Calling this tentative truce doesn't mean I trust the faerie, only that I'm willing to show *some* decency.

"Grim," he finally says, masculine tones reverberating through my every bone. By the sound of the Pooka's ghost-like voice, I know he was a man––maybe even a young man when he was human. I can also tell that his name, that single word that somehow came from his closed mouth and into our ears, hasn't been spoken for centuries.

Poppy offers one of the projectiles I'd launched as a peace offering. "It's nice to meet you, Grim."

He takes the biscuit in his tiny paws and nibbles on the edge. It's sort of cute in a cuddly critter kind of way, which is aggravating. Grim could've been any form of criminal in his previous life; a killer, an arsonist, a thief... He has no right to look cute. Stuffing a wad of crumpet in my mouth, I give in to crossing my arms and grind my teeth, chewing hard.

"Thank you, Poppy," he murmurs.

"Now that we're all friends"—I swallow my food around the lump of sarcasm in my words—"are you going to help us find something for the stingy hag holding Hazel's memories hostage?"

If squirrels had eyebrows, Grim's would be raised at my

word choice. "If you had let me finish earlier, I would've told you that, while my bird's eye search was fruitless, the eaves-dropping I did on the locals was bountiful."

"Quit being so dramatic and tell us what you found," I groan, wiping my knife clean of food before stowing it back in place at my side.

Grim's crocus eyes narrow at me. "I've heard talk around town of a changeling man who frequents the tavern you're staying in. He's a gambler known for possessing rare treasures, and better known for stealing every coin or possession you wager."

With a wave of my hand, I gesture for him to carry on. "And?"

"*And* rumor has it he will be there tonight."

"Do you think he'll have something Baba Yaga would accept?" Poppy asks the Pooka.

The painfully slow pace of our revealing conversation prompts me to take in our surroundings again, and I notice a few patrons giving us funny looks. I can imagine what they're seeing: three identical goblins terrorizing, then talking to a wild animal. We must look like a bunch of nutsy fruitcakes. In response, I glare at anyone who stares a little too long; it's prob-ably not the most polite way to gain privacy, but it works as the tables around begin to clear out one by one.

When I turn back, Grim's head dips. "I've heard the gambler has procured things like ruby-encrusted daggers, and music boxes made for royalty. Even an axe once wielded in the ancient Corvus Clans War fought over inherited magic."

"What war was this?" Posy leans forward, money forgotten.

I pat the arm she braces on the table. "Another time, yeah? We need to focus on the task at hand."

This leaves my sister's gears turning as she cradles her chin in her hands, fingertips tapping a harsh rhythm on her cheek-bones. Her lips are pinched together so tight I fear they'll never part again if she doesn't learn about this war, but now is not the time for a history lesson. We have a big journey ahead of us. She can question the Pooka about anything she wants after we find something for Baba Yaga––and we're a step closer to saving Aspen.

"Overhear any gossip about what this gambler might be bringing tonight?" I inquire.

Grim licks his paws of ginger crumbs. "Something rare, I heard a messenger gnome say it was a stolen item."

"If it's hard to come by it should tempt the witch." Poppy's voice rises in pitch as her spine straightens with renewed hope.

Nodding, I drain the rest of my festive drink. "Something pilfered means the value is already higher than any jeweled blade. If it's good enough to steal and swindle for, it'll probably be good enough for a hag."

"I suppose we'll have to wait for this changeling man to show tonight. What do we do in the meantime?" Poppy peers back down the street at the shops and the people coming in and out of their doors.

Popping the tin lid back on top of the remaining biscuits and tossing my cup into a nearby trash box, I stand up from the table. "We'll bide our time in town. Let's go exploring together. I want to see the brick-and-mortar stores you and Posy looked at."

After scooping the money back into their respective bags, my sisters rise, discarding their cups and papers before they follow. Poppy bounces on her toes, grabbing onto Posy's arm and giving her a little shake, a wild smile brightening her emerald face. A sister excursion while we wait for the gambler sounds like fun, but a little tug in the back of my mind makes me turn back towards the table.

Inwardly, I grumble as a nagging sensation forms in the pit of my stomach. Sure, I've made nice with the Pooka and he's earned *some* trust, but that doesn't mean I want to spend quality, bonding time with him. Still, no one likes to be left out, and I'm sure this applies to enslaved, criminal faeries as well. "Would you like to join us, Grim?" I ask only to appease my conscience.

He pauses for a moment, considering the invitation. "Go on ahead. I'll find you before the evening begins. I'm going to scout the villages and watch for the changeling's arrival." After one last glance, the squirrel-shaped faerie jumps from the table and scampers off.

"That was kind of you," Poppy remarks with a smug grin, dark brows wiggling as she jabs her elbow into my side.

Groaning, I shove her with a heavy hand, making her trip to the side with a laugh. I call over my shoulder as I walk away, "Shut up, I don't do kind."

Poppy jogs to catch up. "Aw, sure you do! You're nice to Aspen and Sparrow all the time, and Hazel for the most part. You're even nice to Rush on holidays!"

My eyes roll so hard I'm afraid one might fall out. "That's because I like them." They are family after all. I might not show affection often, but it doesn't mean it's not there, living deep, *deep* inside.

Posy pops up at my other shoulder, speaking in her soft way. "What about us?"

"You guys are different, you're my sisters." Reaching out, I pinch them each in the meat of their arm. "I get to be mean to you all I want, but we still love each other."

"You *love* us," Poppy singsongs, rubbing at the sore spot I gave her.

"I should have left you at home," I mumble but secretly I'm smiling inside. Although the circumstances are dire, I don't think I'd trade this stupid trip for the world.

Poppy spins in front of me to walk backwards. She's got a cheeky twist to her mouth, curly hair bouncing with each precarious step. "Admit it, Rose, you need us to help find The Numina."

Posy hooks her arm through mine, nodding in exaggerated agreement with our triplet. I fight the urge to tug on her long rippled ear, the same way Hazel does to annoy Rush, ignoring the swell of homesickness. I also tamp down the fear that Aspen is already gone.

"It's an unfortunate oversight," I sigh. "I'm still working on finding a way to solve that problem."

True to fashion, Poppy sticks out her tongue and promptly trips on a frosted patch of stone. I catch her careening arms before she can fall on her butt, cackling at the wide-eyed look on her face. Posy dissolves into laughter with me, pulling Poppy safe to her side as we continue through the streets.

Together we pass by the jolly, decorated shops, peering into the wide glass windows. We watch a young nisser man with a thick orange beard hand carve wooden toys in one, and an old goblin cobble shoes in the other. Poppy forces us into a milliner's shop so she can try on the fancy hats, but I pull her back out when she tries to shove a feathered monstrosity onto my head. My hair ends up decorated anyway once we come across a florist handing out blooms. They tuck a black tulip behind each of our tall ears, the petals tangling with the chains adorning mine. The flower's meaning of rebirth and renewal feels appropriate, not only for the season, but the very purpose of our journey.

When we pass by a barber shop, a young human man getting his hair cut waves at Posy with a charming smile. She ducks her head with a dark green blush and she scuttles away, disappearing out of sight with her goblin ancestry; it's priceless. Almost as priceless as a chubby cheeked babe clapping and squealing while her parents smother her face in kisses under a sprig of mistletoe hanging from an awning. Poppy melts seeing the precious interaction, and I know she misses our nieces and nephews back at the glade.

The last shop we visit is small, hidden between two other

stores and no wider than twice my arm span. There are little baubles and knickknacks, as well as ornaments for Christmas-tide trees. I'm drawn to a statue at the back of the shop; it's a bit dusty and hidden behind some bigger pieces, but I unearth it anyways. It's about a foot tall on a ceramic base depicting three identical hooded women, their heads bent in close together with a length of yarn stretched between them. It reminds me of--

"Rose," Poppy giggles. "Come look at this."

Putting down the statue, I wind through the shop to where my sisters hold a glass figurine of a crowned lady. She sits on something indistinguishable, holding a sword aloft in one hand and what looks like a ball of sticks in the other.

"I think it's supposed to be Sparrow, The Changeling Queen, Slayer of Witches," she wheezes with laughter.

I frown at the peculiar piece of badly molded glass. "What's with the sticks?"

Poppy wipes an amused tear from the corner of her eye. "It's supposed to represent her being a changeling I believe."

"She didn't even have a sword, or a crown for that matter," Posy notes, ever the insightful one.

Patting Poppy's shoulder which still shakes with her giggling, I make my way toward the front door. The afternoon is trickling towards evening, and I want to be at the tavern before the gambler shows up. "Put it back, Poppy."

"Wait, we have to buy this," she exclaims, a whine lifting the tail end of her tone.

It's even colder outside when I swing open the door. "We don't have the money. Besides, it wouldn't survive the trip to the Wyrd Mountain and back, I guarantee it." Sparrow would display it on her mantle for sure, but it's glass. With all the hiking we'll be doing through the swamp and up the mountain, it'll shatter with one hard bump to the knapsack. We'll just have to carry the story of it back to our sister-in-law instead.

With a pout, Poppy sulks, shoulders drooping as we leave the shop, dragging her feet all the way down the street. I swear it's just to bug me. I try to appease her by saying we might be able to buy it on our way back down the mountain, if The Numina reward our good deeds with wealth, but I think we all know that's not going to happen. If everything goes as planned, money won't even matter, it'll be a mad dash back to the glade.

Thoughts of home remind me of the state we left things in, including the revelation we pulled from Hazel's floor. I hope that by the time we make it back, the Elder Mother will have made peace with her past. I don't blame her for not wanting to read the journal; I can't imagine how I'd have felt finding out I had a husband I didn't remember. Still, there's only so long she can avoid it, and there must be a part of her that wants to learn all the answers to the questions she's been asking for hundreds of years.

Her love story is pressed between those pages, her dream of being the best Healer is immortalized in that purple ink, her past is waiting for her. Time is waiting for her, loving her for over six hundred years from The Between––

Picking up the pace, I push away all thoughts of Hazel, Aspen, or the future. First and foremost, we need to find out what the gambler is putting on the table tonight. It won't matter where the object came from, even if it is stolen, as long as it's worthy.

When we arrive at the tavern there are small groups sitting for dinner, but no one crowds around any specific table. He must not be here yet. We head to the bar, greeting Alder with a smile before requesting cider, sipping while we wait. My attention is focused, and nothing breaks my gaze from my surroundings, not even the pest that keeps buzzing through the air in front of my face. My annoyance grows. Bugs usually die off in the cold weather, and it's rare that one can cheat Death this time of year, especially as the skies start to darken with the anticipation of snow. But I'm sure the pest that snuck into *The Glade* will succumb to the chill soon. That is, if my palm doesn't kill it first. I keep swatting the black blur away. But eventually when I fall back into an oblivious state of concentration waiting for the gambler, the bug lands on my hand and I feel a sharp, pinprick pain.

"Ow," I mumble, looking down for the source of the discomfort.

The culprit is a beetle the size of my thumb with large pincer-like horns and a pattern that looks suspiciously like gold eyes on its black shelled wings. "Quit trying to hit me."

"You bit me!" I hiss at the Pooka sitting on my knuckles, gaze darting upward to see if anyone is watching me scold the insect. My sisters give me sideways looks, but they don't say anything once they see the shapeshifting faerie.

"I didn't bite you." I can hear the eye roll in Grim's impossible voice as it finds its way up to my ear.

I point to the small green welt forming on my skin. "My hand looks bitten to me."

"You'll live." The beetle starts to work its way over my sweater and up my arm. I fight the urge to flick the bug off me in fear of retaliation or accidentally crushing it. Instead, I watch with a wrinkled nose and doubled chin as Grim climbs to my shoulder. "Be quiet and pay attention. I heard that the gambler will be here any minute now, he's late." He scuttles to the flat space above my heart and clings to my sweater like a brooch. Grim falls quiet and becomes unmoving.

I guess we're watching the room together then.

Every time someone comes through the front door I scan them, looking for a bag over their shoulder or playing cards poking from a pocket. There's no telltale sign of being a changeling—it's not like their twig heart, glowing gold with a troll charm, peeks from their chest. They look like any other human, which means I just have to give each male patron an uncomfortable and detailed look.

There is a particular man I find myself glaring at many times. He sits in the furthest corner, slouching in his chair with a lazy ankle over his knee. We keep making eye contact because every time I look in his direction he's already looking at me, a smirk on his face as he picks his teeth with a shaving of wood. I'm about to storm over and punch him in the nose when he winks at me, but that's before I see the bag he grabs from under his chair and drops on top of the table. Piles of coins spill out before an ornate wood box, as well as various jewelry pieces and three gold gilded cups with a matching gold ball.

The gambler has been lying in wait, furtively tucked away in the corner of the tavern all along.

THIMBLERIG

*P*oppy gapes. "Is that—"

"Yep, the son of a hag's been sitting there the whole time," I grind out.

Grim's wings flutter and click in tandem with my frustration.

The gambler stacks up his coins in neat towers, fingers steady as he shuffles them off to the side and lines up the wood box and jewelry. He's showing off the prizes he has up for grabs tonight. Patrons watch him set up, patting their pockets for coins and family heirlooms, things to offer as a wager.

An air of arrogance exudes from the gambler's relaxed shoulders and lazy grin. The way the right side of his lips quirk upwards makes me want to do something irrational, like throw the stool I'm sitting on. But the travel-savvy part of my brain holds me back. He's a gambler, he'll have tricks up his sleeve, things that make people feel confident before he cleans them out. All my sisters and I have to offer is what little there is left of their coin purses. And we still have to pay for lodgings for another night, so we can't fritter it away, no matter how much we need a bauble for Baba Yaga.

"Should we go over there?" Poppy asks, eyeing the changeling man, legs crossing and uncrossing as she wiggles in her seat.

Shaking my head, I take the tulip from my ear and make my home on the stool more permanent, leaning back until my elbows rest on the bar. "No, not yet. We need to wait and watch, see what we're up against." It's best not to go in blind, not before we know our odds.

I've watched a few betting games before; most dealers used cards, but I don't see any on this gambler's table, only the golden cups and matching ball. In the past, I've seen other games like throwing dice, or racing. On one of my trips to the east I watched people race their chickens, of all things; granted, a lot of the people were deep into their drinks, but I did end up placing a winning bet. This game though, whatever it is, is new.

"Okay, folks." The gambler claps, the boom from his hands echoing around the tavern. "Who's ready to play a little Thimblerig?"

Poppy leans into me with a whisper. "What did he say?"

"I don't know, I've never heard of it." I glance down at the beetle still clinging to my sweater. "Grim?"

"I was never the gambling type," he replies.

I turn and look at Posy next. "How about you?"

She shakes her head in reply, eyes narrowing in concentration as she watches the first player slip into the seat across from the changeling man. His angular eyes light up, like a predator catching its prey, as he shakes hands with the beer-bellied man now sitting across from him. The gambler tucks his raven, shoulder-length hair behind his ears, rolls the sleeves of his shirt to his elbows, and cracks his knuckles.

"This is how the game works. I'm going to place this gold ball here." The ball goes onto the center of the table in plain view of the crowd that's begun to gather, my sisters and I included. "Then, I'm going to take these cups and turn them upside down, but here's the catch, one cup goes over the ball." We all watch as he covers the ball with the middle cup, leaving a perfect straight line of overturned vessels. "I'll mix up the cups and your job is to keep your eye on the ball. Track it down and you get the prize of your choice." He slides a tower of coins forward. "Lose it and I keep your wager." The crowd nods in understanding. The stout man with sausage fingers is already doling out his hefty wager and pointing out the prize he wants in return.

"Ready?" the gambler asks. He lifts the middle cup to prove the gold ball is still underneath before replacing it. Like a crack of lightning, his hands move, shuffling the cups and swapping their places. The third cup to where the first one was, the second cup trading places with the first. His movements are a blur. The golden cups mix round and round and I misplace the ball just by blinking too long.

When he's done shuffling, the gambler sits back in his chair and gestures to the cups. "Now tell me, good sir, where is the ball?"

The larger man looks unsure as he points to the middle cup. The changeling lifts the chosen vessel and just like that, the other man's wager is lost. Grumbles and groans fill the air along with a series of claps and cheers. The gambler scoops his winnings into towers and stacks them off to the side with the prizes to be won.

"It's a simple game but also one of skill," he tells the crowd. "Who's willing to try their hand?"

Next, a woman in simpler clothes sits down, eyes downcast. She only puts three coins on the table as a wager, but points to the pile of money the last man lost as her prize. It seems like an unfair wager to me, but the gambler accepts it. He smiles his arrogant smile again, but there's a hint of softness to the edges of his mouth as he makes a show of putting the ball beneath the first cup this time. With the woman's go-ahead he begins his quick mix of the cups, my head spinning like a top as he does.

By the time the cups stop I can't be sure if the ball is under the second or the third, but I know it's one of them. The woman playing looks as unsure as I. She takes a deep breath and chooses the third cup. To my relief, the ball is underneath. The gambler claps for her along with the crowd, returning her three coins along with the tower that she won. She leaves the table with tears of joy in her eyes.

We watch the game continue for another hour, most patrons losing their wagers and only a couple more people winning. One sooty man walks away with a sapphire ring, and a too thin goblin boy gets away with two towers of coins. The gambler gains seven more stacks of coin though. As well as an engraved hand mirror, a wing-shaped hairpin, and a set of silver-plated spoons.

Night is well upon us by the time Grim suggests it's time my sisters and I play. But I'm baffled. There is no way this is a game of skill, not even one of chance. The gambler has been swindling every person who's sat down except for a chosen few. I just can't figure out how he's doing it. He's no witch, so it's not witchcraft hiding up his sleeve. Perhaps he has a certain kind of dexterity that I'm not quick enough to catch––but maybe, just maybe there's one person here who is quick enough?

Turning to Posy, I put my hands on her shoulder. "I know that clever head of yours must have picked up something by now. It's your time to shine, sister dear." Without warning, I push her down into the chair across from the gambler. She is his next player.

He cracks his knuckles. "Ah, I was wondering when one of you pretty ladies would sit in my chair."

Standing behind Posy, I hold back my scoff and try to look

like her imposing shadow. My hands land on my hips with one grasping the rose-engraved hilt of my knife, feet apart and planted firm as I burrow my silver gaze into him. Poppy is a little too twitchy to be imposing so I leave her off to the side as she wrinkles her nose at the man. The three of us look at him, silent and waiting. The moment stretches on long enough that I can see him getting uncomfortable. Good.

"Well?" I tilt my chin to his pile of prizes. "Would you mind sharing what you have up for grabs?"

The man searches through his stack of goods and holds up a gaudy necklace. "How about something lovely to adorn one of your even lovelier necks?"

My lips turn down at his attempt at a compliment. "Pass."

"How about the winged hairpin for the cherub?" He gestures a breezy hand towards Poppy.

I'm proud of her when she looks at him with a blank face, not even blinking until she turns to examine her nails. She appears bored but I know on the inside she's buzzing, holding back her incessant hums.

The gambler lifts a brow. "Hard to please, huh?"

Placing my hands on the back of Posy's chair, I loom forward. "We're looking for something one of a kind. Not costume jewelry." Angling my body to the side, I make it seem as if I'll walk away. "If you don't have anything better than coins or things that look to be raided from old fogies' nightstands, we'll go."

"Wait." He readjusts his rolled sleeves, dark eyes flicking over his pile before he reaches for the ornate box, a tightness to his face. The way he stalls tells me he's apprehensive about giving up the object inside. "This will be an offer you can't refuse."

He opens the lid of the box and turns it around to face Posy and me. I swear my blood stops pumping for a second when I see what's within. Even Poppy gasps and huddles in towards us to get a better look. Inside, nestled upon a bed of crushed velvet, is a heart made of gray elder tree twigs. A changeling heart.

"Where did you get this?" I demand, skin prickled with goosebumps when I think of the same hearts that sit in many chests back home. Robin and Lark, Kestrel and Starling, Swan and Sparrow.

Despite early hesitance, the gambler's face is pleased as he leans back in his chair with an easy grin. He knows he has us hooked. "I took it years ago before I left home. The trolls were crafting all these hearts, but their human daughter kept locking them away before they could be used." He shrugs. "So I took one and saved it for a rainy day."

The heart hasn't been imbued with a troll charm so there is no golden glow of life in it. Without a doubt, this is a rare object, something that should pique Baba Yaga's interest. She would have no use for it; only trolls can bring a changeling to life, and she'd never be able to convince one of the old mossy creatures to make a body for the heart. Hopefully, there would be no harm in trading this to her.

My sisters and I communicate with our eyes, weighing our decision. We all come to the same conclusion--we need this heart. It might be the only thing interesting enough to trade for the bluebird housing Hazel's memories. And moreover, it's not like we have money to buy anything else this valuable.

Taking in a deep breath, I face the changeling man in front of us, my sisters following my lead. "Fine, we'll wager our coin for the heart."

As my sisters go to untie their coin purses from their waists, the changeling holds up his hand to stop them. "This prize is worth more than any coin you're carrying. I want something of greater value to you." He points at my chest. "How about that brooch of yours?"

Frowning at the strange suggestion, I look down only to meet the yellow eye-like pattern on the Pooka's beetle back.

Grim would bite me again if I tried to gamble him away, and while it pains me to admit it, we need him. All I can do is choke out a laugh. "Yeah, that's not for sale. Besides, it's cursed."

I feel a deliberate pinch through my sweater as I try to think of anything we have in our room or on our persons that's worth more than our money. Rush made Poppy's prized cloak, but the fabric was second-hand. Posy's blue-tinted glasses cost less than my pure leather boots, but even they aren't worth much with all their scratches and years of use. The chains looping from my ear are as cheap as the locket and book I bought for my sisters in town. All in all, we're not worth much. Although, when I put my hands on my hips as I fall into deeper thought, I find my answer. With a gut-wrenching sigh, I pull my knife from my belt.

"Rose––" Poppy begins.

I speak over her, leaning past Posy to place the blade on the table. "A knife made from the same trees as your heart. It was crafted by the Elder Mother herself for me personally. I received it as a gift from her and my—" I choke on my breath as my throat grows tighter. "My mother."

Grim releases an almost imperceptible sound that sounds like a whisper of sympathy. My lurking shadows writhe in disapproval. And I don't dare look at my sisters. I can already picture their sorrowful, pitying faces.

Thick, raven brows rising, the gambler takes the gift Hazel and Aspen had given me before I became a traveler. He turns it over in his hands, fingers running over the curling hilt and rose filigree down the smooth blade to the pointed wood tip. A small bead of blood sprouts from his fingertip when he tests its sharpness. The man sucks the blood from his finger and then places my knife beside the box containing the elder twig heart.

He nods, gaze running between Posy and me. "This will do just fine."

A sense of bitterness makes my tongue feel like it's been

dipped in poison. Logically, I know I can always ask Hazel to make me another knife when I get home, but it was a special gift from two of the most important women in my life at one of the most important times. And the fact that if we lose, my sisters and I will have to carry on the rest of our journey without a weapon concerns me. Time said not to provoke Baba Yaga, to get in and out, but it never hurts to be prepared for the worst.

Shoving down the roiling feeling in my gut, I cross my arms and press my forearms against my sternum. "Are you going to play your game or not?" I say to the changeling.

He looks between me and Posy again. "She didn't tell me to start."

I tilt my head toward his golden cups. "I'm fluent in silence, she said go."

The gambler looks at Posy, expectant.

The curls in her ponytail bounce as she bobs her head in confirmation, putting on her spectacles to give him the go-ahead. He shows the ball beneath the third cup and once it's covered again, his movements are a flurry, cups switching places faster than they have all night. I lose the ball in no time and when I glance over at Poppy, I can see she's lost it too. It's all up to Posy now. I've put a lot of trust in her; if she didn't figure out the trick to this game earlier tonight, then we're going to lose my knife and any shot at the heart or an enticing offering for Baba Yaga. And that means no bluebird, no Numina, and no Healers. No Aspen.

When the cups comes to a smooth sliding stop, the gambler beams at us, his cocky demeanor making my fists ball. He doesn't want us to win and if we were any other players, we'd walk away empty-handed. But Posy is a borderline genius, she'll sweep *him* under the table… I hope.

"So," he drawls, "which cup is the ball under?"

Posy stares at the cups for a moment, and then two. Long

enough that I start to get nervous and shift my feet like Poppy has been doing for the last three minutes. My sister's mouth becomes a thin line as she squints at the gilded vessels, readjusting her glasses. Her back curves inward, and she points to the middle cup with a shaky finger. When the changeling lifts the cup and there is no ball underneath, our reactions fall like a line of dominoes. Posy deflates in her chair. Poppy gasps. Grim nearly slips from my sweater. I put my face in my hand to rub at my forehead. We lost. All hope of finishing this quest is gone, and we are empty-handed.

"Again," Posy requests.

Looking back up at the table, the gambler shakes his head and snaps the top of the ornate box closed. "I'm sorry, ladies, but you had your chance."

"Please," Poppy jumps in. "You don't understand our situation. We might not be starving or without a home like the others who won, but this mess my sisters and I are in is dire." The gambler doesn't say anything, but we all see that rare softness returning to his eyes. "Please," Poppy pleads again.

He lets out a long exhale before he speaks. "I'll let you wager your coin as long as I get to keep the blade."

Poppy glances at me, and Posy twists in her chair. The gambler cheated, I know he did, but we all know better than to snub our noses at a second chance. Especially when you have goblin senses like us. And while I might not smell deceit or honesty, I have a feeling this changeling will give us a fair shot now. There's *some* decency in the swindler.

I toss my pitiful pouch of borrowed money on the table and let my sisters do the same.

Then we're shown the ball hiding beneath the first cup, and just like the first time, they move in a flurry. The cups are switched around so much that I lose track of the ball and end up watching Posy instead. When the gambler's hands slow, my sister's back is straighter. When the cups stop, she takes off her spectacles, folding them with a calm, half smile as she hangs one of the wire arms from her scarf. She points to the third cup; Poppy and I freeze.

The gambler's face is composed as he lifts the cup. The ball is underneath. "Congratulations, you've won yourself a heart," he says to us. "You had much better luck this time."

"I figured out how we lost." Posy's voice is quiet. "The first time you removed the ball with sleight of hand after you showed me where it was, right before the switching commenced." She reaches out and overturns the other cups before taking the gold ball between her fingers. "It was never on the table when the cups were moving and whenever someone lost earlier tonight you never revealed where the ball truly was." Posy slips the ball into the cuff of her sleeve. With a slight flick of her wrist, the ball rolls from the fabric and into her palm. "While everyone was distracted, jeering about the loss and searching their purses for a wager, you snuck it back under a cup before the next player sat down."

The changeling's eyes are wide as he stacks up his cups and pulls them to his chest. "You're forgetting that three people won tonight."

Posy reaches across the table and slides the ornate box holding the heart off the table, giving it to Poppy. "You let them win. You placed the ball under the cup they chose so they could go home with money to survive." Next, she scoops up our coin pouches and hands mine over her shoulder to me.

The gambler packs up his things with slow movements and wide eyes. I stare at my precious dagger sitting on the table, knowing I'll never hold it again. The sheath at my waist feels depressingly empty. "I'm impressed," he says. "You're the first person that's caught on in the twelve years I've been drifting around doing this."

"My sister is a bit of a genius." I shrug, trying to release my sadness with a smug smile.

Posy stands from her chair, sharing a look of triumph with Poppy as they walk towards the bar. This reminds me that Alder has been present throughout this whole ordeal, and when I peek over my shoulder, I find him watching the table while he leans on the counter. The jig is up for the gambler. I don't imagine the kind tavern owner will welcome him back into *The Glade Tavern and Inn* to continue taking advantage of his patrons.

Turning back to the changeling, I hook a thumb towards Alder. "I think it's time for you to move to another town and consider a new career path."

Once the gambler has all his heisted winnings in his bag, he slings it over his shoulder and tucks my knife into his belt. *Goodbye, beautiful blade. I miss you already, my sweet, sweet child.*

"Perhaps." The lazy grin returns to his face as he gives the room a two-finger salute and glides out the tavern door into the frosty night.

"You three are quite the team," Alder says later, placing dinner plates on the bar top for us.

We each sit on a stool humming and hawing our agreement. The ornate box sits before us like a trophy as we dig into the red potatoes, green beans, and roast beef. Who knew playing a conman could work up such an appetite?

"So, you ended up picking out a faerie heart for your grandma?" he asks, dusting some shelved tankards.

Poppy looks at me wide eyed with a green bean hanging from her mouth.

I wipe my greased lips, scrambling to come up with a believable answer. "I'm pretty sure she has nothing like it in her collection. She'll be thrilled."

"Seems like an odd gift," Alder laughs.

Waving my fork in the air, I try to twirl the right words onto it. "She's…eccentric like that."

Posy chokes on a potato.

Eccentric is one word for the witch we're about to tempt, using the same kind of heart that sits in our sister-in-law's, nieces', and nephews' chests. It feels wrong to give a hag such a thing; it puts all ethics and morals beneath a magnifying glass. If the twigs were imbued with a troll charm it could give life to a faerie body. But without magic, does it make it any less a piece of a potential person? Weaving a heart made of cedar or elm would be nothing but a sculpture. So does this one being woven from an elder tree not make it a ball of twigs too? What would Sparrow, Rush, and Hazel do if this was something they had to do to free us from the cage? I'm not sure what to think, but there's no doubt my sisters are on the same page.

Baba Yaga had better find it worthy.

Dusting done, Alder moves on to cleaning the bar. We pick up our plates so he can wipe under them as he makes his way down the counter. "Well, I'm sure she'll appreciate it considering how much you've gone through to get it."

"Oh, she'd better," I chuckle. I'll force the heart down Baba Yaga's throat if I must because we need that bluebird. We'll get it from her one way or another, I just hope it's as peaceful and quick of an exchange as Time wrote about in his letter. Get in, get out.

After we finish eating, we say our goodnights to Alder, pay two more shillings, and head toward the squeaky stairs to our room. My sisters start their climb, but when my boot hits the first step, I remember my suspiciously quiet tagalong.

"Why are you still here?" I ask the Pooka in the shelter of the dark hall.

"I wanted to make sure you're okay, I know how much that knife meant to you." Grim crawls his way over my collarbone to my shoulder and down to the back of my forearm. "If I remember the vision Fate showed me correctly, you cried after you unwrapped it."

I hold my arm up in front of my nose and summon the fiery pits of Purgatory with my glare. "You mention that again and I'll *squish* you," I hiss.

The Pooka's shell parts into fluttering wings as he marches his way to my wrist, horns first. "There's nothing wrong with being vulnerable, Primrose."

"Oh, buzz off." I flick the beetle just hard enough to make him fall from my hand but unfortunately, his wings catch his fall.

"I'll see you in the morning." Grim zips around my head, the amusement more than apparent in his whispery voices. "Get some rest."

The faerie then flies past me through the tavern, out the front door, and into the chilly night. My footsteps are quiet when I turn and ascend the stairs, so quiet that I can hear my sisters' voices halfway down the hall through the door they left ajar. I catch only the last half of their conversation as I hesitate, pausing near the closest wall.

" still talking to Grim." Posy's murmuring is soft but still loud enough for me hear.

"What do they have to talk about—don't they hate each other?" Poppy remarks with a laugh.

The gentle hum of Posy's next words makes the tip of my jagged ears hot. "It might look like they do, but they don't, not really. And especially not Grim."

It doesn't take a genius to use the context clues given to me to know Posy has been observing the Pooka and dissecting his interactions with me. But I don't want my sister and her big brain and watchful eyes to know I overheard her and Poppy. So I back away on silent feet down the hall before stomping my way forward to make my presence known. I enter the room more aggressively than I need to, though neither Poppy nor Posy comment on it. Nor do they mention the conversation they just had. They're both too busy getting ready to fall onto their bed and into peaceful dreams.

Our journey continues tomorrow, so we need to leave bright and early to make decent progress. According to the conversation we had with Alder yesterday, there's a few towns before we reach the swamp. It could take us a good week to arrive. With any luck, Grim will find us the fastest route.

Not that I *completely* trust the Pooka now, but I did see a glimmer of humanity in him today––I think. Either way, beneath the shadowy soul there used to be a person, someone who had a life, maybe even friends and family. I'm not sure what he did to be gleaned and captured by Death herself, but she was his judge and jury. Not me. I don't have to like him; he doesn't need to be my friend, but we do need a guide to the Wyrd Mountain. For the sake of The Numina and all the things they'll make right, I can at least tolerate him.

As I lie in bed, rolling the tiger's eye stone from the self-proclaimed oracle between my fingers, I listen to Poppy and Posy sleep again. My mind drifts to Aspen. I feel like a part of me would know if her soul has already left this earth. I'm imagining her tethered, hanging on, waiting for us to get back. It makes me wince thinking of Sparrow watching her mother suffer and Rush watching his wife prepare to mourn. Then my thoughts float on to Hazel again. Has she read about her husband and past yet? This leads me to musings about the Sun and Moon, Death and Time, Fate and Fortune. I'm wondering if they can reward me for bringing about their return by getting my blade back from the gambler. When I finally drift off, the stone is still clutched in my fist.

—

I DREAM OF BLACK ANNIS.

It's filled with visions of the cramped cage we were all stuffed into and the imp I watched the witch skin, of the screams and cries from the faeries. My head is pounding with images of the blood, the metallic smell that hung in the air and the taste of salt.

I dream of agony.

CHILDHOOD TRAUMA CLUB

The stars are still out when my sisters and I finish our breakfast. Alder was kind enough to wake up early and prepare us for our journey with a hearty meal, and many cups of coffee. He even packs us food for lunch and dinner. The hospitality and pure kindness that the owner of *The Glade* shows us reminds me so much of Aspen, of how she loved and cared for us growing up. It's almost a little hard to say goodbye.

"Now here are a few pouches of salt to use at night. You girls stay safe and be smart, okay?" The concern in Alder's eyes makes me question whether or not he even believed my story about buying a gift for our granny who lives way up north in swamp land.

"We will," I answer.

He raises a brow at us.

Taking my finger, I make an *X* over my heart. "I promise, we'll be safe." I look at my sisters. "Won't we?"

With sleepy smiles, they cross their hearts too. Posy has a brain big enough for the three of us, but I know how to traverse the land. We'll watch out for each other, and Grim will have our back too. Speaking of which, it's time we find him so he can lead us out.

Alder leads us to the door, the morning air seeping in through the wood. "If you ever find yourselves traveling this way again, the three of you are always welcome."

I turn back and look at him. His jade-green eyes and pale skin, gray hair dark brown at the temples, already familiar to me now. He offers out a hand for a shake and I clasp it between both of my own. "Thank you, Alder." *Thank you for being kind, for giving us a warm place to stay and for making us feel safe.* I don't say these things, but he knows, I can see it in his soft smile and fretful gaze.

Then, we steal into the wintry air, pulling our layers closer to ourselves for warmth. The sun hasn't risen yet, but there's a hint of gray light on the horizon and the winter's morning birds are beginning to wake. We hasten our steps through the salted streets, hoping to find Grim and get out before we get caught in the daybreak rush.

We're heading the opposite way we came into town when I spot a messenger gnome setting up his stall early. Gnomes collect letters and packages throughout the day and usually, in the afternoon, deliver them to the people who live in any town. Yesterday I saw this same fellow with a bunch of parcels that I guessed would be passed on to another gnome in the underground tunnels for delivery.

This gives me an idea.

My sisters continue a ways down the road before they realize I've stopped walking and I'm not with them anymore.

"Rose?" Poppy prompts before she and Posy walk back to me.

"We should write a letter," I suggest. "We could let everyone back home know we're okay so far. It would give Aspen a little something to hold on to."

Posy nods, almost a little bleak as she approaches the stall and grabs a sheet of paper and pen from the allotted boxes. Her forehead is scrunched as she writes her own greeting to our family first, her words perfect, straight loops over the page. She finishes her paragraph with words for Hazel, wise healing words that urge her to read the journal Sparrow is keeping for her.

Poppy is next. She writes her hello and then jots down little notes for each of the tiny changelings, letting them know their aunties are having a grand adventure. She also asks about Pop, even though she knows we won't be getting an answering letter back. Her letters are like cheery bubbles compared to Posy's pristine handwriting.

Never having cared much for penmanship, my words are quick, harsh edged and messy, but they get the point across. They tell everyone where we've stayed and how we've collected a changeling heart in hopes of recovering Hazel's memory bird from Baba Yaga. My light tone tells them not to worry, that we've made a truce with the Pooka named Grim and we'll be okay. But most important, I remind Aspen to hang on, to rest when she can and wait for us. I promise that we'll have so much to tell her and how I will require a hug from her when I get back. I'm hoping my message will encourage her to keep fighting, just a little longer.

We each sign our name at the bottom before Posy takes the paper and folds it with careful hands into long thirds. The gnome manning the stall melts a chunk of frosty blue wax inside a spoon over a candle flame before pressing his messenger's mark into it, sealing the letter closed. Poppy tells him the whereabouts of the glade and the gnome's face brightens.

"I know that place! My second cousin, Fern, and his brothers, live there. I haven't seen them in a decade, not long after that witch attack when his arm got skinned." He holds the letter we've given him close, like it's a precious stone. "I'll hand deliver this myself. I'll be speedy about it too, you have my word."

Thanking the gnome, we continue.

When we reach the edge of town where the salt-dusted

roads turn from cobblestone to packed dirt, there's a long trail heading out into the open before it fades back into the forest ahead. I can see my ever-present shadows waiting for us there.

Once we step foot onto the dirt, Grim materializes. He's in the form of a small, lean buck this time, his coat a deeper shadow than I've ever seen, and the tips of his thin antlers disappear into wisps of smoke. His eyes glow like sunlight on a gold coin, and the ruff of his neck waves as if in a strong breeze.

"Morning!" Poppy waves at him.

Grim dips his heavy head in greeting. "Rose, Poppy, Posy. Are you ready to go? We have a long journey ahead of us."

A minuscule sigh slips from under Posy's breath, but Poppy is raring and ready as she hops from foot to foot. I think they've figured out that despite the exhaustion, when they keep moving, they keep warm. This will make for less complaining the remainder of our trip, and I am thankful.

"As we'll ever be." I give Grim a good-natured pat on his flank and start walking.

The pat startles the Pooka, making me laugh and show him my palms in surrender. "Right, sorry. You don't care to be touched."

A cold puff of air rolls from the Pooka's nose. "Nor do you."

"I don't like to be smothered." I shrug, watching my boots as I walk through the dirt, but I still feel the small buck's heavy stare. "Don't give me that look. It has nothing to do with *vulnerability*." I glare at Grim, remembering what he said in the dark hall before I climbed the stairs. "I love my family to death. I just don't like feeling people's breath on my neck when they hug me. And the moisture of my nieces' and nephews' palms when they hold my hand drives me crazy." A shudder rolls down my back. "I like my personal space to be dry. My bubble is sacred, thank you very much."

The faerie releases a deep, rumbling hum. "Yet you still reach out to those who care about you and allow them to show you affection."

"Well, if my bubble is going to be popped, I'd prefer it be on my terms," I snort. His words and my actions connect, making me look at Grim's smoky-antlered head sideways. "Did you just imply that I care about you?"

He stares straight ahead down the path. "No, but you don't hate me as much as you think you do."

Shaken, I turn my face forward. I've seen a version of the same unkind past that broke Grim when I look in the mirror daily. He had a beating heart once, ambitions, family, trauma, and feelings. He was human. But here, amongst the trees and other monstrous things that may be lurking about, he is a part of our group. I'm familiar with the dark and seclusion; my shadows are my only friends besides my sisters and my family. But when I look at Grim now, I see less of a shadow and more of the ghost of a man who knew a life of misfortune just like we did.

After watching my sisters' knapsacks bump against their backs for several long, thoughtful moments, I give him a quiet reply. "No, no, I don't."

—

IT'S BEEN A WEEK. A miserable, cold week. We've walked until we can't feel our toes, and our bones are weeping with exhaustion. Poppy's heels have become raw from the inside of her boots and Posy's back is bruised from sleeping on uneven ground. I'm not faring much better; the dead of winter weather has gotten to me, and I can't pretend it doesn't bother me anymore. I can almost feel the impending snow every time I shiver.

All of us are tired and dirty, except Grim. It seems that being made more of darkness than soul protects him from the elements somehow. He's left us only once, three days ago, when we passed through the last town to restock our food and salt with the remainder of our money. Our meager funds were turned away, deemed too pitiful for the town's prices, so the Pooka had taken action. He scavenged for discarded scraps, scouring the streets and back alleys for stale offerings from the previous day. All he found was biscuit dust, muffin crumbles, a half-eaten apple, and a singular hot cross bun that had been frozen in the night. My sisters and I were desperate though, eating every crumb and tiny morsel after I stuffed the bun under my sweater to defrost it against my skin.

Later, we'd tried to find somewhere free, like a church where we could rest and bathe, but the stingy town was too small, comprised of only homes and family stores, no place for charity and strangers.

So we kept moving. Most of the time, my head feels a little *off*, but when we stop to rest for the night, and my stomach growls, I chalk it up to hunger. Grim leaves us once more to hunt for small animals in the form of a hawk. When night falls, we gorge ourselves on burnt rodents as we sit around a campfire. But even after eating my fill, a muzzy fog still compresses my head. When I mention this to the Pooka, he reminds me of what he said about the journey to the Wyrd Mountain. "It's difficult to locate if you are not wanted there, and as a result, those who seek it out tend to go missing. They become so hopelessly lost that it takes three times as long to turn back and find their way home."

I didn't realize how truthful he'd been and I decided to be the bigger person, apologizing to Grim because, despite me being travel savvy, we wouldn't have made it this far without him.

Today the woods have dissolved into frosted flatlands, and my head is feeling less like it's been filled with cotton and more like trickling sand. Grim says we're only days away from the swamps now and the magical haze of confusion will fade soon. Apparently, the things inside the swamp are what tend to keep most of the people and creatures who try to reach The Numina's home at bay. But this does not sound encouraging, not one bit. Especially knowing that when we exit the swamp, the spirits living on the Wyrd Mountain will be the next—and last—wall of tortuous protection we'll have to endure. Grim's proclamation catches Posy's attention, which leads to a geography lesson about the surrounding flatland's shrubs and meadows. The Pooka tells all this with gusto and warns us many times over to avoid the submergent areas of the swamp that might be covered with thin ice, saying that cracking that layer is like falling into a lake you'll never climb out of.

This of course reminds me of Sparrow's battle with Jenny Greenteeth. Her scar, the one just missing her eye and running from her brow up to her hairline, fascinated me as a child. I still remember the time she let my little fingers run over it because I'd wondered what it felt like. Though what I really wanted to know was what it was like to survive a fight with a witch, to bring one to Death's door like a storybook hero.

I'd fantasized about killing that blue-skinned hag for years, pictured myself as the one to run her through with Hazel's elder wood blade instead of Sparrow. I watched it happen--all of it--the tar bubbling from the witch's mouth as she died. But I also saw her cleave open Sparrow's chest, baring her twig heart. Those memories still make me feel like I'm spiraling at times. I hate the color cerulean blue, refuse to eat blueberries because they look too much like belladonna berries, and, like my sisters, I try to avoid touching anything made of iron when I can.

I'm afraid to meet Baba Yaga. I'm scared to see how similar to my last tormentor she might be. Even worse, I'm afraid of how my sisters might react to meeting her. Knowing that we're traveling to her home and anticipating going inside is one thing, but seeing her face-to-face will be another. I don't think any of us are ready, but we have no choice.

"What are you thinking about?" Geography lesson over, Grim's lowered, whispery voice interrupts my roving thoughts.

Blinking and gazing around at my surroundings, I notice Poppy talking to Posy, having their usual one-sided conversation. Grim is in the form of a small reindeer now as he strolls beside me, an odd gauzy, tepid warmth radiating from his side. Our positions give me a sense of déjà vu.

"My past," I answer him, blunt and simple. Trying to make it clear that I don't want to talk about it. Grim already knows everything about my sisters and I, about our whole family. His soul is over six hundred years old, and he's been aware every second, even during the time he spent jailed inside Death's shadow. He's seen much of the past and present, and Fate has shown him bits of the future too. It's infuriating, but he probably knows me about as well as I know myself.

He hums. "I was alive well before Quince became the first witch and murdered Fortune, but I still saw wickedness."

Looking at him from the side of my shadow-filled eyes, I see he still faces forward, hooves clomping over the dead, frozen grass. Somehow, he knows the exact directions my thoughts had been taking me.

"Darkness existed long before it was shaped into witchcraft and spread," he continues. "It lived like little shelled seeds inside the hearts of man and faerie alike. It remained dormant in most, but some people watered it, let it grow and fester, even back then."

Sounds to me like a garden of weeds. And I know weeds from gardening in the glade. They're stubborn, and given the opportunity they'll grow tall and wide, choking out all other plant life. "Is that what happened to you?" I ask.

Heavy puffs issue from Grim's nose, curling into the biting air like a cloud. "My darkness was shaped by hate and injustice, not by an evil nature."

"Death was convinced you were evil since she personally cleaved your soul from your body and made you a prisoner." I point out the obvious, recalling his words from the night he hung above us in the form of a bat. Honestly, his punishment sounds worse than Purgatory.

"Many may think what I did was wrong, but in the end, I believe it was justified."

I spare a glance at my sisters to find them still occupied before narrowing my eyes at the Pooka. I don't want them to be privy to any of the horrible things our guide has done. "What did you do?" I almost whisper the question.

"I killed my father." Grim meets my gaze, yellow eyes fiery, scrutinizing me for my reaction. "I was eighteen."

Swallowing, I keep my face neutral. Part of me wants to scream at my sisters to run, but I can't. The Numina wouldn't have sent someone who would hurt us, would they? They *need* us. Grim must have had a reason for committing such a violent crime. My voice is even quieter now. "What did *he* do?"

"He was a monster, but where I saw a vulture, others saw a dove. My father was a revered member of society, but if anyone had looked close enough, they would've seen the truth." A weight settles over the Pooka's furry back; I can see it in the way he moves. "He was a terrible father and even worse husband, but only my mother, myself, and the walls of our house saw his cruelty."

My heart aches and my ever-present shadows also seem to bend in sympathy.

"One day his wrath was so vicious, so unholy that he killed my mother in a fit of rage. So, I tore him apart." Grim's voice echoes throughout my body. I feel his words all the way down my throat, winding through my ribs. They pull and they tug until I can't breathe.

"You...you tore him apart?" I sputter.

"Piece by bloody piece. I started with his fingers so he couldn't even think about raising another hand to anyone again."

For a moment I can't speak. We still walk next to each other with Poppy and Posy ahead, but the silence is heavy, weighed down by his brutal admission. He took justice into his own hands. While it seemed like an eye for an eye, in truth all he did was match his father's brutality. I wonder if maybe I wouldn't have just done the same? After all, I'd thought about killing Black Annis in many violent ways...

When I find my voice, it sounds resigned to the punishment that was doled out. "And Death trapped you for murder, but not him for his wife's?"

A rumble comes from his broad chest. "Oh, no, Death jailed him too. She shoved him into the deepest recesses of her shadow so that he couldn't claw at the edges with the rest of us. Fate won't even make him into a Pooka."

Grim has blood on his hands, but technically so does Sparrow, my half-brother, and Hazel. They killed Black Annis and Jenny Greenteeth, for the good of everyone. Still, it's strange how similar crimes can be weighed differently like two sides of a scale, just and unjust.

This image reminds me that supposedly, life had many paths when Fortune was still alive. There was still pure, dumb luck and chance encounters. There was still free choice, an opportunity to choose what direction your life took. So, if Fortune was still alive when Grim was, there must have been a path where Grim controlled his rage after his mother's death and left before he killed his father. There could've been a path where the law took its course, enacted justice against the murderous husband,

and left his son alone to live his life. There had to have been more paths than the one where Grim decided to shed more blood. Perhaps there was even a path where his mother never died. There had to have been at least *one* peaceful path. "If you had been given a second chance, a moment to cool off, would you have still tried to kill your father?"

Grim hesitates, but I can see it's not because he's unsure of his answer, it's because his answer makes him sound good-- more human. And by the way he avoids my silver gaze, I can see he doesn't believe there's much good left in him anymore. "No. My mother would've wanted me to bring her justice through the Council," he sighs.

I let out a breath of relief. If Fate and Fortune had given him the chance to make the right decision, he might've chosen the path of peace. There's good in this creature still. "So, you're not a bogeyman after all," I tease.

His neck cranes at the sound of my ease. "Make no mistake, Rose, I'm still a monster in Death's eyes. I'm one of the dangerous ones, and when The Numina are back on earth, Fate will no longer have need of prophetic messengers and I'll be wiped out of existence with all the other dark things."

I'm not sure what to say to this, or if I'm even able to provide words of comfort. Should I comfort him? Ethically speaking, what he did was wrong, but morally, he put an end to a merci- less man. If I were in the same position he was, I may have done the same thing. Which makes me a monster too, I suppose. We are who we are because of the darkness we've survived, two sides to the same unfortunate coin. He doesn't deserve to disap- pear with the witches, but I have no say in that. All I can do now is offer him the first fellowship he's had in a long, *long* time.

"I think this earns you a potential spot in my childhood trauma club." I give one of his large fuzzy ears a tug. "Get my sisters and I out of Baba Yaga's swamp in one piece and I'll make you an honorary member."

He bumps his antlers into me. I take that as a yes.

After a few moments of companionable silence, I glance at the Pooka now comfortably strolling beside me. He's near enough that the tepid warmth of his side radiates toward my arm. I can't even force myself to smirk; the tilt of my closed lips simmers down to a soft grin. "Careful, Grim, walk any closer to me and someone might think we're friends."

An animalistic bellow that sounds like it might've been a laugh slips from the creature before he trots ahead to my sisters. Following behind, I admit that we have a long way to go yet, but at least the Pooka and I have a solid alliance now.

"Grim," Poppy crows. She welcomes him into the fold, allowing him to walk between her and Posy as she chatters away. "You have to help us settle something. What's the most important gift in life, love or knowledge?"

The Pooka's multi-layered voice sounds off-kilter as he speaks. "I'm not sure how to answer that. Both love and knowledge have the power to build or tear someone apart."

"But isn't love more fulfilling?" Poppy prompts, shooting a pointed look at our sister on the other side of the ebony reindeer.

"I don't know." Grim turns his head back to look at me, glowing, doe-like eyes pleading for help.

I stick my hands into my sweater pockets and pretend to find the barren flatlands *very* interesting.

"Haven't you ever been in love?" Poppy asks.

The answering silence is loud.

When the Pooka doesn't answer her, I hear my sister's tone droop like a wilting flower. "Not even when you were alive?"

"I've never loved in the ways that are considered *normal*." After a sound that seems like the clearing of a throat reverberates from the animal's chest, his words come out strained. "I find fulfillment in a companionship with someone as like-minded and devoted as me. Someone to *'love'* unconditionally more than any earthly object, friend, or family member. Someone whose soul matches mine and touches my heart and mind rather than my body."

Poppy groans at his poetic answer. "Ugh, you sound like Rose."

That he does. It's like he stole the words I never got to speak straight from my tongue. It catches me so off guard I can't help giving up my façade to watch the trio as I follow from a short distance.

"Looks like knowledge wins." Posy's quiet yet musical laugh rings out as she shoves a finger in Poppy's direction. "I told you so."

Amusement replaces my surprise as Poppy tries to reach over Grim's back to pull or pinch any piece of Posy's body she can reach. The Pooka tilts his head and gently pushes Poppy to the side with his antlers to further separate my sisters as if they were children. My sister sticks her tongue out at Grim, and when Posy laughs at her expense, he nudges her forward with a headbutt to her knapsack.

Fellowship indeed.

The Swamp

Grim was right, it took days to see the flatlands morph from winter's bare shrubbery and frosted meadows to softer ground glazed in delicate frozen layers. I notice now how thick the trees have gotten since we first walked into them, how unpredictable the earth is beneath my boots. Fresh snow dusts the branches of the droopy cypress trees like a rain of powdered sugar, something I've seen Sparrow do in the kitchen over baked sweets many times.

But this place is nothing like home, it's haunting, and too quiet to feel safe. There are no birds chirping, and no bugs clicking. Our crunching feet make the only sound as we walk further into the dense, icy swamp, the gloomy snow-laden clouds blanketing the skies providing little light. Especially under the cover of all these trees.

"How are we supposed to find Baba Yaga's house through all this muck?" I ask Grim, nose wrinkling as I stare at the brownish-green swamp soup trapped beneath a film of ice and drifts of snow. Our sickly colored surroundings stretch on and on, growing darker the further in we go.

"In all the visions I was privy to, I never saw specifics like this. I don't even know how your story ends, I only know what happens if you don't bring The Numina back." I smell some untruth as Grim turns his head away. It's suspicious, but it's worry in his tone, not mischief or the ulterior motives I once accused him of. "The best I can do now is go ahead and scout in a different form," he suggests. "The land is going to suck you down and slow your progress if you're not careful about where and how hard you step. And anyway, I can cover more ground on my own."

Posy gives him a worried look. "Do you think that's safe?" Always the sound of reason, my sister is.

Though I think she's right. This place gives me a bad feeling and we have no clue what else resides here besides the witch. And as if on cue, a spectral kind of groan echoes through the swamp, rattling the tree branches enough that piles of sticky snow fall to the earth below. There's either something very large or a large group of many somethings haunting this place. And, like a cherry on top of one of Sparrow's fancy cakes, I'm reminded we're weaponless.

"For me, yes. For you three..." Grim trails off, glaring into the distance for the source of that sound. "Not so much."

"Aren't you supposed to protect us?" Poppy squeaks, berry eyes sweeping through the trees.

The Pooka looks out into the gloom. "Technically, I could do my job better if I knew what to protect you from as well as where I need to be taking you. I can solve both of those problems by scouting ahead, finding the hag's house, and coming back to guide you safely."

He has a point. While we don't have a map, we do have a shapeshifting faerie, and it's better than nothing. I just wish I still had my knife.

"Don't boggle about, okay? The longer we talk about this, the longer it'll take to find this stupid house." I sigh, bone-tired and admittedly nervous about running into who or whatever just made that ghastly noise. "I don't want to be in this swamp any longer than I have to be."

"Agreed," Grim says with a nod. Then, his body rearranges itself in a gust of smoke, swirling and writhing towards the ground until he shrinks into the shape of a toad. He's a warty little thing with tough onyx skin and sulfurous glowing eyes. In this body he'll be able to hop his way near weightless over the iced marshland to find the witch and look out for any other bogeys. Not to mention he can search the freezing murk below the surface for any unseen swimming dangers...like Nelly Longarms or Peg Powler.

Poppy crouches down to poke at the bumps along his back. "Aw, look at how cute you are." She winks up at me with brows wiggling, "Say, Rose, do you think if you kissed Grim, he'd come back to life and become a prince?" It seems like my sister still has love on the brain.

I snort, irked by her jab, but glad she's trying to split the thick layer of fear in the air. "Witches will rule the world before that'll happen. These lips of mine will never touch another being." I circle the air in front of my mouth with a finger. "This is a no touching zone, only for me and the cutlery that delivers me delicious desserts."

"You'll fall in love someday," Poppy teases me, albeit a bit halfheartedly.

Pulling the hood of my sweater up, I try to ward off the chill that runs up my skin when the swamp releases another guttural sound. Perhaps the spirits that Grim told us about have also branched out to haunt the swamp? Everyone likes a change of scenery; maybe these mysterious things got tired of the Wyrd Mountain and its high altitude. But something tells me that's not the case as we all freeze for a moment, listening. The four of us wait and watch for several moments, but nothing appears. The noises we hear are coming from far enough away that I can tamp my emotions down like I do on the daily and crack a joke.

"Who needs love when you have sweets and the whole world to travel?"

Posy looks at me not only with thanks for being the constant comic relief, but also with acceptance. Her face is open as she nods with a half-smile, although her fearful gaze still darts around. She's always listened to my preferences, but Poppy is the one to roll her eyes like she's saying, *"You just haven't found the right one yet."* She believes everyone will find true love like Sparrow and Rush did, all tied up with a pretty red string and wedding bells. But what she doesn't realize is I don't want that; I don't want to be kissed and caressed. Sure, a romantic committed companion like Grim spoke of would be nice but the physical aspect that comes along with the love that Poppy dreams of has never appealed to me. And there's absolutely nothing wrong with that. My adventures are enough. No one expects me to court someone when I'm in new places. There's no expectations at all, just simple discovery and experiences to last a lifetime. When I look down at Grim, his tiny eyes are understanding, familiar even, as if he knows my exact thoughts and feelings. Of course he does. However, now is not the time for any of this, especially as a hissing, like the sound of water being thrown on a fire, seeps from deep inside the marsh.

Gulping, I nudge the Pooka with the toe of my boot. "What are you still doing here? The witch isn't going to come to us. Get a move on."

Grim shoots his gross sticky tongue out at me, leaving a mark on my boot before he leaps away into the swamp. We lose sight of him and his smoky toes in mere seconds, the chilly damp air swallowing him whole.

"We might as well follow, shorten the distance he'll have to make to come back and get us," I say against all better judgment. But something about standing still out here makes me uncomfortable. All I can think about is a little fuzzy duckling bobbing on top of a lake as something with razor sharp teeth watches it from below. I don't want to have the same future as that duck, not today.

I hear my sisters' squeaking steps behind me as the spongy bottom of their boots make contact with the ice we tread on. "What do you think we'll find when we get to Baba Yaga's?" Poppy asks, voice high-pitched and shaky.

"A witch," I deadpan, tense because of the unknowns that might be creeping around us in the cold shadows. There's a lapse of silence, a heavy feeling coming from my sister, radiating toward my back. It makes my neck itchy. Even more so when something like a thunderclap sounds in the far distance. That cannot be a mountain spirit, no way.

Poppy's voice is rough. "I may have Pop's eyes but I'm not oblivious, Rose."

Carefully, I turn around, surprised by her dour words. "Of course you're not." After I check the land behind my sisters, I really look at Poppy's face. Deep inside her red raspberry eyes, I see the truth behind her statement. She's afraid. She's scared of the things we hear and terrified to go into another witch's home. I know Posy is too because she's chewing at the skin around her nails again. "I know you're not, Poppy," I soothe.

With gentle hands I tug her forward, the hem of her Rush-made cloak sweeping over the ground and becoming stained by the layer of moisture lying over the frozen swamp. The three of us walk closer together this time, our boots getting more slippery the farther we go. I spot velvet foot mushrooms topped with snow growing from the side of the trees and resilient hairy stemmed azalea flowers in their dormant stage. Azaleas are in the rhododendron family––they represent danger. A ghostlike moan somewhere in the swamp makes me struggle past the half-drowned bushes faster, hoping my sisters don't catch sight of the flowers because they'll know exactly what they mean too.

This does *not* bode well.

I distract from the flowers and the noises, but my voice is

still wobbly. "I think we'll find a creature much like a dragon from Sparrow's stories. Baba Yaga is known for being a collector; I bet she'll be sitting on a hoard of treasure, keeping it warm like an overgrown, fire-breathing bird."

"I'd put money down on her having a forked tongue," Posy says, pulling the cowl of her scarf up over her head to block out some of the frost and fright.

A wet, strangled laugh escapes from Poppy's throat.

"I doubt we have anything to worry about, sister dear." I lightly nudge her with my elbow, but I don't sound convincing, even to my long ears. "Baba Yaga is a collector of things, not people. We'll get in and get out, just like Time said in his letter."

"You really think so?" she asks, a glimmer of hope widening her innocent eyes.

My gaze flits to a line of icicles hanging from a nearby tree and back. "Yeah."

"Okay." Poppy nods, a small smile growing on her face as she soaks up my mistruth like a blossom to sunlight. Though it's quick to be smothered when a crunch like thousands of cracking bones peals through the fragile bog.

Glancing at Posy, I find her already looking at me, lips pressed thin. Poppy disregards this exchange and hums to block out her inner noise. She looks up to the obscured sky, letting the few flakes of snow that fall collect on her lashes, and I consider it a win. Even if she is deluding herself, at least I've minimized her fear, for now. On the other hand, convincing Posy we're not in danger is something I don't think anyone is capable of; she's far too clever for that. She's logical too, and there's no doubt she's calculating our chances of getting out of this swamp alive. And besides the eerie, unknown ruckus around us, there's Baba Yaga to face yet. A witch is a witch, someone who let themselves become corrupted and malignant for the sake of power. Witchcraft changes a person into poison personified, and it makes them crave toxic things. They're always on the hunt for more. It's hard for me to imagine that Baba Yaga satisfies those cravings with only trinkets, but I suppose people wouldn't trade with her if she didn't let them leave her house. I do wonder if she keeps a visitor every now and then to stay satiated. It wouldn't be hard to believe.

Black Annis had her belladonna and skinned her victims. Jenny Greenteeth had an unknown poison that polluted a lake and the surrounding plant life, but she drowned her victims before she ate them. Though I've heard rumors about Peg Powler and her oleanders, Allison Gross and her bloodroot, as well as Nanny Rutt and her wolf's bane. I'm sure Baba Yaga has her personal pick of poison. I'm just not very excited to find out what it is.

I almost fall on my face when my foot suddenly breaks through a parchment thin patch of ice and sinks down to my ankle, pulling me from my witch-glazed thoughts. The three of us stop moving, waiting to see if this small hole will splinter. We're in the thick of the swamp now. I need to be more careful and keep a closer eye out for those stupid submergent areas Grim talked about. We could be walking on a solid surface one moment and tripping into disgusting icy water the next if we're not more observant. I don't really feel like going for a swim today.

"All right, single file now," I instruct my sisters as a shiver slides down my back. My constant shadows are nowhere in sight. That's concerning. "Step where I step, or risk becoming one with the swamp."

My sisters fall in line behind me after I lift my foot from the hole and steer us toward thicker, more opaque ice. Their feet land where mine land. They follow the muddy print of my right boot and align their toes and heels with mine, matching like a pair of perfect gloves, a small perk of being identical triplets. We all keep our steps light and tentative, but I still hear Poppy scuffle and slip every now and then. I blame her cloak.

"You know," Poppy starts with a weak voice, "that doesn't sound too bad, becoming one with the swamp, I mean. I bet it's nicer here in the spring."

A huff of a laugh slips through my nose. "When moss grows from your toes and the leeches become your best friends, I think you'll change your mind."

As if the swamp agreed, it lets out a gurgling bellow. More snowflakes fall from the sky.

Poppy squeaks. "On second thought..."

I throw a quick glance over my shoulder to check behind us again. Poppy is toddling directly behind me, and Posy is almost skating behind her. "When we get home and The Numina fix Aspen, I'm taking you all to the beach. Sand in every crevice is preferable to this," I promise, cringing with every tentative step. Our voices and the sound of the ice groaning beneath our combined weight no doubt alerts anything living in the swamp of our presence.

"I've always wanted to see the ocean." Posy's faint voice rings out as she tries to help me lighten the foreboding mood.

Her statement is news to me. Posy has never spoken about wanting to see anything outside the glade. Still, she always listens to the tales of my journeys with rapt attention. I figured she was happy seeing the whole world through her books and research, but maybe the glade isn't big enough for her after all.

"Oh yeah?" I ask, surveying the landscape of solidified muck slowly getting covered with white powder, knowing my half-hearted question will lead to some story about her research.

Posy speaks just a touch louder, a tentative excitement in her tone despite our current situation. "Did you know there are stories about an ancient city that got swallowed by a storm and sank to the bottom of the sea? Coincidentally, it happened about six hundred years ago. Do you think The Numina being sucked into The Between caused that? Perhaps the sudden imbalance and the Sun and Moon being forced apart into the sky? Do you think they could bring the city back? Imagine all that forgotten knowledge, the architecture--"

She continues with her tangent, speaking more than I've heard since the time she told me about a fire razing down some sort of Great Library. As I listen to her, I'm picturing the conversations she might have with The Numina if we spring them from the veil in the Wyrd Mountain. She would talk off their ears if they allowed it, with all that knowledge ripe for picking. Posy would also be the first to write the complete history of The Numina so they would never be forgotten again. Maybe besides bringing them back, that's part of her purpose in life? Maybe she'll create a library just of all they've seen and done over the millennia.

"What about you, Poppy?" I hear Posy ask when I tune back in. "Do you want to see the ocean?"

Another violent rumble makes the trees tremble. Piles of snow and sharp icicles rain from the trees, the latter smashing to the ice below and exploding into shards. We wait, one breath, two, three, and when the swamp's surface stays sturdy, we continue.

My bubblier sister hums, hand clenching the hem of my sweater that peeks from under my knapsack like a child clutches a blanket. "I've never thought about it," she answers Posy.

"You never pictured yourself outside of the glade?" I take my next step farther to the left to avoid a scattering of large icicle pieces, eyes roving the horizon. Between her and Posy, I would've guessed Poppy would be the one to think of adventure. Especially considering she's wanted to fall in love and start a family ever since she was a kid.

"No," Poppy grunts as she slips and yanks on my bag to gain purchase again. "I have everything I need at home; everyone I love is there."

"What about your *true love*? How are you going to find him?"

Once I know I can keep steady, I listlessly tease her, not unlike the way she always does to me.

There's a gap of hushed hesitance when a flock of what looks to be vultures flee from the trees in the distance and disappear into the snowy air. "I don't know. I always figured he'd stumble into the glade somehow, and that's how I'd know he's the one."

I bring us to a quiet halt, listening for any movement besides ours. As we wait, I think about the part of me that prefers the idea of us all being strong and independent—not traumatized young goblins fighting for emotional survival—in my heart, Poppy isn't a damsel in distress, but a girl who can find her own knight whenever she pleases. Perhaps he's the one in distress and in need of saving. "What if he's out there waiting for you to stumble upon him?" I say this softly as I search the sky for any more disturbances.

A sort of muted *harumph* comes from Poppy's throat. "I hadn't thought about that."

It's hard to believe it's never occurred to her, especially with all the thoughts she keeps at a constant spinning pace. She does hold a rosy hue over things that concern love, but there's got to be more to her than being a caregiver, future wife, and mother. She must have other hopes and dreams.

I gingerly turn to face her under the guise of a distracting conversation, but I'm really triple-checking the near arctic swampland we've already passed. "If you could do anything, what would you do? It must be something that doesn't involve us or helping care for Sparrow and Rush's flock—or finding a prospective husband."

"I don't know, Rose," she mumbles, thrown off balance by the question, searching my gaze. She turns to look past Posy, eyes wide and forehead lined.

"Come on." I touch her shoulder to keep her facing me. "There's got to be something."

Poppy pushes her mass of curls off the sides of her chill-bitten face. The rings and coins dangling from the sprinkling of braids jingle with the frustrated movement. The noise makes me cringe as an odd silence overtakes the swamp. "It doesn't really matter. I can't leave Pop, and Sparrow has her hands full with the kids, and Aspen and––"

"Poppy. It's a hypothetical question, no one's feelings will be hurt by your daydreams." I pivot and resume our walk forward, mindful of the frost we pick our way through. My stomach turns with anxiety and something akin to anticipation because now, after my scan of the swamp, I'm fairly certain we're not alone. I continue speaking anyway, not wanting to scare my sisters more. "And besides, we're only seventeen. You have so much time to decide where life will take you."

Who knows what our lives will be like once The Numina are back. The resurgence of Healers will open many opportunities; I could even see Posy becoming one with her big brains. We all have a Floriography background, which taught us a thing or two about a flower's medicinal properties. The three of us could all be Healers if we're deemed worthy enough to be Blessed, whatever that means––but we need to survive this place first. A cold sweat breaks across my skin and beads at my temples. What chance do we have since we're weaponless? We have salt in our bags, although the grains can only do so much when you're on the move...

A tense minute goes by before Poppy blurts, "A floristry shop. I want to open a little place where people down on their luck can come in and smile because of all the colors. It would smell like a whole garden, and the shop sign would have beautiful gold lettering. But I only have two hands, so I'd have to hire help. And one day, I'd end up working side by side with the love of my life."

I'm stunned into a handful of silence when I spot what might be a human skull poking from the frozen mud at the base of a tree. I would've thought it was an alabaster rock protruding from the ice if it weren't for the empty eye sockets staring back at me with a grin full of missing teeth. My gut flops, and I hope my sisters don't notice.

"You've put real thought into this, this isn't made up on the spot, is it?" I say with a grimace, leading us away from the skull. Our steps make popping sounds as the stiff rime coating of the swamp strains; I try to lighten my feet to no avail.

"I've thought about it for years," Poppy admits, blissfully unaware of my gruesome discovery.

"Why didn't you ever tell me?" I can't bear to turn around. Beneath the fear, there's a certain kind of burning shame gnawing at me, and it makes me curl my fingers into my pale green palms. I should've known all this or asked these kinds of questions sooner. Obviously, I'm a poor sister most of the time. I've always taken Poppy and Posy at face value and pushed their dreams and needs right down alongside my own battered emotions.

There's a wince to Poppy's voice when she answers me. "You were always gone on your adventures."

When I open my mouth to respond, a rattle like that of a western snake splits the atmosphere. I don't like the sound, not one bit, but I forge onward as if I didn't hear it. You can't fear the things that aren't there, right? "You could have come with me and apprenticed somewhere for a while." Poppy could have learned a menagerie of floral skills in the time I spent at that one bakery. The number of arrangements she could've made would have filled this whole Timeforsaken wintry swamp.

She lets out a tiny peep of a sigh. "We had to stay behind and help out so you could follow your dreams."

I spin around to gape at my sisters—maybe a little quicker than I should—feeling like I've been shot by a bow. "What?"

"The glade couldn't afford to lose two of us, and definitely not all three." Poppy looks guilty, having said this aloud. She would've gone on the rest of our lives without talking about this to not hurt me. But I'm not hurt, I feel sick. I thought my sisters chose to stay home because they wanted to, not because they were picking up the slack my absence created.

My stomach hurts. "So, you guys stayed behind, miserable, because you wanted *me* to be *happy?*"

"I'm happy," my sister scrambles to reassure me, wiping away the snowflakes melting on her cheeks as she whips her head to look at our quiet triplet. "I'm sure Posy is too."

Posy nods her head in aggressive agreement, though her citrus eyes are trained on something behind me. My guess is she caught sight of our unlucky headless friend abandoned beneath that one hoar frosted tree.

"Besides," Poppy continues, "I don't like to be alone. It's too quiet for me, and when my thoughts get too loud, I go numb, and I'll do anything to feel something. Even if it's painful." Her eyes are fraught as they look away from my gaze. "I do better when I keep busy and have a purpose. A flower shop would be wonderful for a while, but I want to do something more, something grand."

My ignorance is painful. And my sister status is crumbling even further. I always cared for Poppy and Posy and ensured they were safe before I left. I've loved them more than anything else, but I've been so blind. My sisters are so much more than the single-layered girls I thought they were... Their dreams reach far, and despite their broken, shattered edges, they've found ways to hold themselves together. Without me.

They don't realize that the glade doesn't depend on them to survive, and while our home is better with my sisters in it, they deserve greater. They are greater.

The fine hairs on the back of my neck stand on end.

Unsure of what's prickling my senses, I clear the emotion from my throat, stamping it down like the muck trapped beneath the ice under my boots. "Well, I suppose we're doing something now. And together, at that. We're out here saving the world. How much grander can it get?"

Wary, Poppy gives me a close-lipped smile and reaches out to squeeze my hand. I look at Posy, who shares the same expression. But when she tries to walk closer to Poppy and me, the grin melts off her face and the verglas over the submergent pocket she stepped on gives. She looks down at her foot lodged in the syrupy mud she's uncovered. Posy wiggles her leg, trying to pull her foot free, but her boot is stuck and by the looks of it, well suctioned.

Over her struggle, I hear something new echo through the swamp.

"Posy, stop moving." I shush her, holding my hands out for silence and balance. She's hunched over with wide eyes while Poppy transforms into a statue. Their visible breath rolling from their nostrils is the only thing that lets me know my sisters' hearts are still beating.

There's a haunting sound coming through the shadows growing from the nearby trees, a lulling sound that dances along the softly falling snow. The stillness surrounding us seems to break apart as I feel life stirring. Poppy flickers in and out of sight as a result of trying to stay quiet and still.

Closer and closer the sounds float toward us. It's like Sparrow's storybooks described, a siren song, but only if sirens were ghosts with razor-sharp teeth. By the time I realize it's singing that we hear, the voices are dangerously close. Too close. And they already know we're here. I search the land around us for somewhere to hide. But there's nothing but bare snowy trees, none of them wide enough for one of us to stand behind. We can't wait for Grim to retrieve us, because he could be on the other end of the swamp by now. We're out of viable options.

Staring at my sisters, I breathe out a single whisper. "Run."

Water-Wyrms and Their Pets

With both hands, I grab on to the leg of Posy's boot and heave. The answering slurp of mud, and the pop of her shoe coming free is deafening in the snow-scattered swamp. But not as deafening as the ice spiderwebbing around us. I push my sisters forward and shatter the frozen surface under our boots before throwing a quick glance behind us, gazing at the approaching figures. The singing is drawing closer, coming from the low-hanging trees to the right. But I feel something moving through the deepest pits of the marsh and creeping in from the left as well, ever so slow. My sense of smell is polluted. All I catch is a whiff of mildew, wetland gases from uncovered decomposing plants, and fresh snow.

We sprint, or attempt to, slogging over the soft earth that's been revealed, our bags bumping along our backs as we try to stifle our gasps and heaving. But the way we fumble about as we head further into the swamp, makes it impossible to be quiet. It's pointless to use our goblin ancestry to try to sneak away unseen. We're a beacon of noise with the horribly cold muck and chunks of floating ice up to our calves and pouring into our boot tops. The swamp is like frost-thickened molasses, the underwater plants grabbing at our ankles and twisting around our boots, pulling us down like we're its last meal. Every step creates waves of sloshing, making a rippling icy trail that leads right to us, *X* marks the snack.

Falling is something we cannot afford right now. So, whenever Posy or Poppy missteps and lurches forward, I grab them by the knapsack and yank them up, then urge them to go faster. I can feel splashes of filthy water getting into the tops of my high boots. It's biting from the snow that's melted into it and now the snow that's dusting it, making my toes numb. We need to find Grim and Baba Yaga's house before we become crystallized bogey food. And fast.

"Does anyone see the house?" I pant out thick clouds, skin prickling with sweat and fear.

Poppy keens, "I don't see it anywhere!"

The tree cover and gray snow-filled skies make for dim surroundings. For all we know, the witch's house could be tucked further into the deeper marshes. The only thing we can do is keep running and hope whatever is trying to lure us with its wraith-like songs doesn't like the taste of goblins.

Poppy's soaking wet cloak keeps trying to trip me. I throw it aside, grunting as I try not to eat a face full of mud and tiny icecaps. "Keep looking," I gasp.

The eerie voices are at the edge of the trees now. I can feel the creatures lurking, watching us run. Why they aren't racing into the snow and attacking us is a mystery, but I don't intend on sticking around to solve it. Catching sight of numerous pairs of briny, glowing eyes is enough to make my stomach swoop and make me push my sisters even faster. They're waiting for something while they sing their dastardly songs.

Posy cranes her neck to see what's hiding in the dark.

"Don't turn around," I bark. "Just go!"

The swamp churns to the left of us; something is swimming beneath the water and bobbing ice and it's growing closer by the second. We've attracted something else with all our noise, and a large something by the looks of it. Not good, not good, at all.

That's when the first crooning bogey comes out of the woodwork. I catch sight of a grayish-green-colored woman before seeing the long tail where her legs should be. She's serpent-like with scales, long forest hair covering her bare chest, and hands tipped with claws. *Big* claws. Her dark lips split at the edges, making her wicked smile wide, then she changes her tune, the grating sound emitting from her throat in harmony with the other snakes still in the frigid shadows.

Posy falters. Even though I told her not to, my bookish sister turns to look at the singing serpents. Her firefly eyes widen before she latches on to my hand for balance, and pulls me forward. "Nixie," she chokes.

"What?" Poppy turns now too, face speckled with mud like freckles.

Gasping for breath, Posy reaches out and turns Poppy's chin forward before shoving her into another run through the cold wetland. "They're water-wyrms!"

"She didn't look like a worm to me," Poppy puffs, head turning side to side as she searches past the snowfall for Baba Yaga's elusive house.

We are forced to slow our painful running when we come across natural debris. There's a massive fallen tree lying on its side covered in both new and old drifts of snow. The trunk is half sunk into the water with frost slick algae growing along it, turning the tree into countless shades of brown and green. The sheer size of the obstacle forces us to scramble over it instead of trudging all the way around its towering, rooted end.

"No, not a *worm*. Wyrm, like a mermaid," Posy explains between deep lungfuls of air as she helps Poppy over the tree's thick corpse with shaky hands.

With my own lungs burning from the winter weather and pure exertion, I help Posy over by using my hands as a foothold to boost her. Poppy's on the other side, making sure she doesn't slip over the iced grime and snow piles. And once Posy is over, I glance back at the nixie, only to find her kin have breached the trees as well. Their long, viper tails curl through the water, propelling them smooth and languid through the once frozen swamp. "Those are *not* mermaids, Po." I swallow, cleaning the chilly muck from Posy's boots off my increasingly numb hands by dragging them over my mud-spotted thighs.

"Of course not," she huffs as I clamber up my side of the tree. My foot glides over the algae, making me lose purchase for a moment as my graceless body falls into the same path my sisters' bellies already made for me. "Nixie lure creatures, not people. Specifically, other water beasts to capture and rend their chosen victims into pieces before they eat them. So hurry up," Posy pleads.

"Wonderful," I grunt.

Poppy lets out a squeak as she grabs my hands, helping me over the frosty, goo-covered bark until my feet are back on uneven ground. We step backward as we watch a snow-sprinkled nixie slither ahead of her kin, her hand outstretched, palm facing upward. It's like she's offering us the choice to come to her before she sends something else to do her dirty work. Posy and Poppy turn to resume their clumsy, bogged-down run.

Shaking my head, I follow my sisters into the knee-deep swamp water and call over my shoulder to the serpent lady, "No thank you, we choose to live!"

The nixie's bogeyman song increases in volume, voices rough and beautiful. It's a horrible, enchanting melody, like a lullaby played by a symphony of serrated knives. And it doesn't take long for us to figure out what they're summoning when a spine-dotted hide emerges from the patches of broken ice mere feet away. The rugged rounded snout and slits for eyes are unmistakable. The nixie are unleashing a congregation of alligators upon us, and the dinner bell is ringing.

"What in the world is that?" Poppy wheezes beside me. Her pace has slowed enough that I'm no longer the only one trying to hang back. I can't be a buffer for her against the bogeys with the way she's slacking.

"The butchers for today's meal." I heft my bag. Not only does it hold the changeling heart we won at the tavern but my traveling supplies as well, and the weight isn't making this soupy escape any easier. It's also a constant fight to keep pushing through the burning in my freezing calves and the muddy liquid swishing around inside my boots. Stupid, son of a siren swamp. "It's a meal we will not be attending, so swerve right and run faster," I grit out, hand on Poppy's lower back, urging her closer to Posy in the lead.

With Poppy on her tail, Posy cranes her head enough to see our new, hungry pursuers and gasps, "It's winter! Alligators should be brumating and near frozen to keep warm beneath the ice. They should be slow if not sleeping!"

"Apparently, they didn't get that message," I puff. "Pay attention to where you're going, Po; veer left."

Posy huffs in reply, but she listens and charges onward. Any other time I would've laughed at her frustration over nature not following its own rules, but if the nixie's song is strong enough to shake the overgrown lizard's cold blood to life, I'd hate to see what other irritable beasts they could summon.

The three of us shift our desperate route on a diagonal, though we still run in the direction Grim disappeared instead of trying for the choking cluster of trees beside us. There could be more nixie in there. And from the looks of it, it's too dense to have built a house inside, so Baba Yaga probably isn't in there. Forward is the only option. We'll come across either Grim returning, or the witch's home, eventually. I only hope Death plans on keeping her hands off us a little longer so we can escape these swamp creatures first.

"Rose, I can't—I can't go any faster," Poppy says, tears thickening her throat. She's tired and cold, we all are, but my sisters have less endurance than me. I can tell she wants to stop and catch her breath, but I can't allow it.

Even Posy has slowed down, but I see the hardness in her jaw, the way she's gritting her teeth to push past the pain. Her breath is coming out ragged through her nose, her scarf hood thrown back, and her ponytail messy. She goes to grab Poppy's hand, guiding her onward through waves of ice lapping at our legs when Poppy is yanked back with a choking sound.

Pivoting, I see one of the nixie's alligators has caught my sister by the end of her cloak. I always told Rush the garment was too long, and now she's being choked by it. The ribbons around her neck strain as she claws at them, but her fumbling sage-tipped fingers can't grip the silky ties. The alligator is pulling her closer with every whip of its head and Poppy's wide eyes look blood red with panic. With no thought to my own safety, I kick the gator in the nose.

Its teeth hold strong, chomping down, swallowing more of her cloak. The heel of my sister's boot is so close to its sludge-infested mouth that I decide it's time to sacrifice Poppy's warmth. Wishing I had my knife, I latch onto her throat with both hands and her brows raise in breathless confusion before I release the ribbons from her neck with deft fingers.

She flies forward into my arms, her precious velvet cloak hanging from the creature's large, stained teeth. Poppy scrambles toward Posy, who's slowly backing away into the mire with pale seafoam lips. That's when I notice all the eyes watching us. The nixie leer with ravenous gazes as the alligators' slitted eyes hover above the murky water, hunks of frozen mud bouncing off their hide as snow collects on their scaled backs. Everything swims closer and closer, trying to box us in.

Putting myself in front of my sisters, I walk them backward with an empty hand out in a stopping motion. Salt will do little against wildlife, but my palm trying to ward them off does even less. One of my sisters grips the shoulder strap of my bag, guiding me so I don't trip in the dirty slush as I glare at the creatures and their slow descent. They're building our fear, letting our flesh tenderize with anxiety.

"I think I see it," Posy whispers. "There's a huge, peaked shadow further ahead. I think it's the house."

I don't risk turning my head to look, but I imagine she's gazing in the direction we're moving. My foot slips on something slick under the water. I stumble. But as I've had Poppy and Posy's backs, they have mine, catching me under my armpits. One of the gators twitches forward, eager to catch me with its teeth if I fall again.

"On the count of three, run to it. Don't turn around, and don't look back. Just run," I whisper to my sisters, letting my words sneak out of the corner of my mouth. "One."

The nixie smile their split grins, needle teeth at the ready.
"Two."

The alligators' tails stir the thickened water.
"*Three.*"

My sisters' feet are loud as they take off towards Baba Yaga's house, but I stall for several moments, letting them get a head start. Vulnerable, I stare down the grinning bogeys and their armored lap dogs with my fists clenched, snow sticking to my lashes. Only when the splashing of Poppy and Posy's footsteps sound farther away do I turn and run after them. A burst of nightmarish noise erupts as the alligators lunge after me. The serpent women, no doubt, are close behind. The bellows and hisses from all the beasts make the terror I've been trying to suppress crash into me like a tidal wave. My eyes burn with tears.

My lungs feel like they're going to explode, the winter's boggy ground makes each submerged footfall heavier, slower. I see breath clouds billowing closer in my periphery. The monsters are too near, and the house is too far. The structure's shadow is looming, but it's not close enough...not for me at least. Forcing myself to go faster, I try again to make it, but all I manage is a frustrated yell when my legs fail me.

My war cry catches my sister's attention. They look back. I try to scream at them to keep going, but my breath is lost when a smooth, cold-blooded tail curls around my waist and wrenches me off my feet, my arms trapped at my sides. I'm twisted around against my will, the tips of my toes half a foot away from the swamp's watery surface. The tail holding me curls tighter, constricting. My ribs protest the squeezing as I face the nixie that's captured me. She holds me close enough to see the gray speckles across her nose and the cheekbones poking from beneath her skin. Her long, pointed tongue pokes from her mouth to lick her teeth as moisture strings across them. The bogey's mouth is watering at the sight of me.

Poppy and Posy scream my name in terror while I shriek in pain. My hands are stuck, knuckles grinding together. The air is coerced out of my lungs even more as the nixie crushes me in her grasp. I let my thoughts stray toward home. To Aspen, Sparrow and Rush, the kids, and Hazel. Toward the people I love in case these are the last thoughts I'll ever have.

As blackened stars dance across my vision, something crashes into the nixie and me.

Head spinning, I drop back to my feet, teetering as my legs sink back into the viscous bitter swamp. A long black alligator rears up in front of me, gaping smoky maw blocking most of my lower body from the nixie's view. Its stature isn't large enough to cover all of me, although it could still tear me limb from limb if it wanted to. But it doesn't turn its teeth in my direction, it just cuts off the rest of the women and their pet alligators from advancing further. And then with a croaking hiss, the dark alligator turns its head my way, yellow eyes fuming.

"*Go*, Rose," Grim commands, his echoing voice shaking the

snow from the cypress trees and sending a shockwave through my frozen bones.

Not needing to be told twice, I race for my sisters. They wave at me to hurry, identical faces a pallid green as they watch the fight between the Pooka and the nixie commence behind my back. There's a high-pitched cacophony vibrating from the serpent women's throats. I don't dare turn around to look at what's happening because I can still hear moving water, the sound of things with sharp teeth swimming towards me. Grim is more than capable of taking care of himself, but we goblins are not impervious to being eaten alive by giant reptiles.

Once I'm within reach, Poppy and Posy pull me forward by the elbows and we sprint side by side. Finally, Baba Yaga's house comes into clear view. It's startling how normal it appears with its weather-worn porch, wood-shingled peaked roof, and chimney, almost all covered in snow. The dwelling doesn't look like a witch's home, but it sure doesn't look like safety either. We'll just have to cross our fingers that the alligators aren't determined enough to climb onto that porch before we can get inside.

The gnashing of teeth and rumbling at our heels spurs us forward until we're in spitting distance of the house. I hadn't seen it before, but it hovers over the swamp like it's held up from the muck by short stilts. Posy jumps onto the porch first, mud and water sluicing from the leather of her boots as she clutches the banister. She holds out a hand to Poppy and drags her to safety while I grab the other side of the banister to lug myself up. I've just cleared the step up to the porch when the house shudders. Snow falls from every nook and cranny like an avalanche. The next thing I know, we're clinging to the white-powdered floorboards as the whole structure begins to rise, saving us from the swamp but trapping us with the witch on the other side of the door.

Baba Yaga

*I*n our panicked state, it's easy to think we'll continue surging into the snowflake strewn sky, lying on our bellies with fingernails digging into the warped porch wood. But the house stops with a series of creaks and groans. We're well over the treetop, looking down at the hostile arctic swamp below. Daring to look over the railing and following the slow falling snow, I hope to see what's happening fifty feet below between Grim and the nixie, if the alligators are circling the house's…legs.

"What in the Sun and Moon's green earth are those?" Poppy asks beside me. Her pointed nose is peering over the edge while Posy flops onto her back, squishing her bag beneath her as she gazes at the gray clouds above us.

"They're, uh—they're legs." An incredulous laugh bubbles from my chest. "They're chicken legs."

This catches Posy's attention. After a few more deep breaths, she climbs onto her hands and knees. Her limbs are shaky as she peeks at the legs sprouting from beneath the house.

They're ugly, wiry things, each as thick as a tree and coated in a faint pumpkin glow. They look bumpy like bark too. Knots and ridges cover the legs all the way down to the feet submerged in the green-tinged water below that now swims with teeny tiny icebergs. Each frosty mud-covered toe is tipped with a claw the size of a well-fed cow speckled with spots of lichen growing over the surface. I expected more growth since a house that's roosting like a hen, in a swamp for years on end, would be furry with moss and other plant life. If it weren't for the solid layer that topped the marsh being a whole frozen sheet before we broke it, I would've thought that maybe Baba Yaga's house gets up and stretches its legs.

Snorting to myself, I use the handrail to stand and look around as I dump the liquid from my boots and scrape what mud I can from my body. My sisters follow suit. From this vantage point, I see a white-capped mountain, perhaps the Wyrd Mountain, considering how close Grim said we were. It's in the near distance and a shallow wall of fog is crawling its way across the land. It's colder up here; a snowy breeze unencumbered by trees blows all three of our heaping curls away from our faces. The sweat I worked up during our frantic run through the swamp cools against my already nippy skin.

Poppy, who is now cloak-less and as unsoiled as she can get, shivers as she wraps her arms around herself in a hug. "Why does the house have chicken legs?"

"Witchcraft," Posy explains simply.

The orange glow around the creepy limbs makes more sense, though why a witch would use her tainted magic to give her house bird legs is beyond me. I suppose it keeps unwanted people and creatures out, which must mean the hag wanted us on her porch. She probably knew we were in the swamp the whole time, and just waited to pull us to safety. *Safety.* We may have been rescued from becoming a meal, but Baba Yaga being our hero is *not* a comforting thought.

Once Posy and I deem ourselves cleanish, the three of us turn to face the simple front door. The windows on either side of the door flare to life, the warm light glaring at us like a pair of eyes. What a welcome. Taking a second to glance at the side of the house, I see the porch wraps around both sides to the back. I also note the edge of a rocking chair peeking out. It reminds me of Pop and the mindless rocking he does nowadays. When he was more present, before the glade was terrorized, he used to bring his breakfast out on our porch to watch us play in the grass. Picturing Baba Yaga sitting out here with a morning cup of tea like he once did makes me want to laugh again. My nerves must be muddled because this kind of unstable humor is coming too easily. If the hag drinks tea or coffee, I'm sure she takes it with a splash of blood instead of cream, and a sprinkle of crushed bones instead of sugar.

Dark musings aside, I realize the three of us have stood here huddled together, staring at the door for well over a minute, stalling. It's been ten years since we faced a witch, and despite the memories that haunt us, we volunteered to face another. I'm not ready to go inside, but would I ever be? Would my sisters ever be?

"Should we knock?" I ask, heartbeat thrumming in my throat.

My hands are so sweaty.

Poppy swallows as she fiddles with a silver ring looped through one of her many braids. "That would be the polite thing to do."

Posy nods in agreement, sticking the side of her fingers in her mouth to chew on the pruney skin while she rocks on her feet.

"Good idea." I drum my fingers on my cold, damp thigh.

A new kind of numbness blooms in the tip of my toes. The rippled edges of my pierced ears tingle with the slow loss of feeling. Or maybe it's the buildup of feeling, old mental injuries fizzling beneath the surface, trying to clamber up from the blue-tinged shadows I've buried them in.

We stand motionless, boots rooted in place. It's like we're

growing into one of the wood planks under us or becoming tall green topiary statues to decorate the witch's covered porch. At least my sisters and my shadows are here to keep me company. The latter has finally reappeared and now become unruly in the presence of the house. So much so that I think one of them is daring to move from my periphery for the first time. That's before I realize the shadow is made of contorting smoke.

Grim drops onto my shoulder in the form of a black sugar glider and almost makes me jump out of my skin.

"*Sun on a scone,*" I gasp. "A little warning next time?"

"*Hello, Grim.* So nice to see you made it out of that den of vipers, Grim," the Pooka gripes.

Poppy half raises her hand in the air. "I'm glad you're okay."

Posy nods in quiet agreement as Grim peers at me with expectant brimstone eyes. The palm-sized marsupial clings to me with creepy little four-fingered baby hands, the end of his twitchy tail fading into a wisp. The faerie looks shaken but intact. If something in my chest loosens at this thought, I don't acknowledge it. Instead, I just poke at the strange skin that stretches from the creature's forelegs to hindlegs and allowed him to drop in on me.

"The nixie can't kill what's already dead." I gaze at Grim looking for confirmation. "Right?"

His head cocks at the poorly disguised concern beneath my sarcasm, glazing my words like a piece of shoddy pottery. "No, no, they can't."

"Good." With a firm nod, I turn back to the hag's door, accepting the Pooka's light touch.

"You got here just in time, Grim," Poppy squeaks. "I think we're about due to say our hellos."

I take a deep breath. She's right.

We can't stand out here much longer; the time for stalling is over. I bounce on my squelching toes and shake out my hands, my bag and its contents jangling as I gather the energy I need to move forward.

"Okay." Blowing out my breath, I stride to the front door, pulling a mass of hair over my shoulder to cover Grim. My fist knocks firm and loud, a confident sound when, in reality, my hands are extra heavy and losing all sensation.

Not even a second passes before the door swings open. "It took you long enough," a lurid female voice purrs.

Baba Yaga leans up against the doorjamb, posture lounging and lazy. The curl in her dark lips might be categorized as sultry, but to me, it's almost cat-like. A feral grin that makes me feel like we're a trio of mice caught in her claws. Luckily, she can't see the Pooka. Her youthful skin is the vibrant orange of an overripe persimmon, just a few shades darker than the haze of witchcraft coating her house's legs. My heart stutters when I meet her feline eyes. They're a solid shade of slate gray, not beetle black like the ones in my nightmares, but the deep color-less pools still invoke horrible memories all the same.

I feel the nails at the tips of Grim's glider fingers through my sweater while Poppy fists the tail of it, constricting my breathing even more than it already is as I stare at the witch. Posy must be holding her breath too, judging by her still silence.

The hag has the tell-tale body type of a witch, a gauntness that swallows them whole, and causes sharp, sunken cheek-bones. Her ribs are outlined under her skin up to her collar-bones, and her long, knobby fingers are tipped with talons. Only the shock of white hair against her painfully beautiful face and matching silk shift helps me remind myself I'm no longer in that old iron cage. Baba Yaga's hair is long and straight like a blanket of clean cotton, contrasting the features of a woman in her twenties. I know her appearance is misleading though. Despite living for hundreds of years, witches stay young with their poisons and witchcraft, but their insides are rotting and decrepit.

One of Baba Yaga's snowy brows arch. "Well? Aren't you going to say hello?"

I awkwardly cough against the dryness in my throat. The numbness is almost agonizing, as if an army of ants is crawling across my skin, burning me as my limbs get heavier. My tongue falls from the roof of my mouth, feeling like a block of sandpaper. "We're here to make a trade."

"You don't say." The witch's tone is snide, her face cavalier. She watches her silver talon drag down the wood of her doorway, almost bored by how still and quiet we are. I'm not sure if she expected us to wet our already swamp-moistened trousers or fall to our knees in praise, but the stoicism we present her with is not it. Little does she know we're all reliving the nightmares of our childhood. I can feel those shackles of upheaval and suffering living inside of me, and at the sight of another witch, they grow tighter still.

"According to the surrounding villages, you're quite the collector. We're looking for--" I pause and look at my shivering sisters. Should we show our hand and tell her that the three of us are here for the bluebird? Maybe we should hide our desperation? If she knew we were here for one thing and one thing alone, would it give her too much leverage? We need Hazel's memories back, but we should probably be shrewd. I wonder if Baba Yaga even knows what's hidden inside the bird? "--Something one of a kind. I'm sure a connoisseur such as yourself has many a treasure," I finish, trying to play towards the vanity I smell she possesses; it's like the stink of gaudy perfume.

She perks up, the sly slinky line composing her body curving as she leans toward us, one hip still against the door frame. Here, under the cover of her roof's eave, she doesn't have to worry about the overcast sun and the purifying light that would burn her to death. "I have the best collection, things you couldn't dream up," she brags. "Tokens from a golden king with a lavish touch, and a witch's cup that turns men into pigs. A lyre that's song once moved Death so much that a man's true love returned from the earth."

Truthfully, those all sounded interesting, but my eyes are drawn to where Baba Yaga now rests her hand. Slung over her hips is a large belt made of well-loved leather. On one side is a satchel with the hilt of a small knife protruding from behind it, and on the other is a row of vials. Some of the tiny glass vessels are filled with liquid, while others have powder and dried flowers, one of them being chamomile. I recognize this belt. I remember a sketch of it inside the journal we pulled from Hazel's floor. It's her herbalist belt from her past life as a Healer. And Baba Yaga is wearing it. So, not only has the witch obtained all the Elder Mother's memories from more than six hundred years ago, but she also has what used to be her prized possession.

Son of a Lich.

We *need* the bird, but now I *want* to return the belt to Hazel too. It might make her feel more in touch with her husband when we return to the glade with her memories––if we return. It could also even help her cure Aspen. But we only have the heart to trade... There's nothing else of value on our persons. The coins braided into Poppy's hair are cheap, and Posy's spectacles are the most expensive she owns. I'm sure a hag would have no use for the locket or book I purchased in the villages for my sisters, nor the tiger's eye stone the hybrid human-troll gave me. I couldn't even joke about trading Grim at this point; I'm beginning to value him as more than just a guide.

But maybe, just maybe, a changeling heart is worth two objects? It's wishful thinking, but a rare item might put Baba Yaga in a good enough mood that we can test our luck. I have to try. I can't imagine leaving this relic from Hazel's past behind.

Peeling my eyes away from the herbalist belt, I meet the witch's pupilless stare. "That sounds like quite the trove." I nod, turning towards my sisters with a pointed look. They nod in stilted tandem.

Baba Yaga preens.

Gritting my teeth before I step toward her, I crowd the doorway. But that's when I get a whiff of foxglove, a deadly flower that means secrecy. It's a bitter scent, one that feels *off*. It's almost as if you could smell the word "hot," but it's not like a smoky fire or spicy cayenne. It smells of poison.

I remember the smell of belladonna berries was cloying, almost choking and saccharine. Like rotten treacle and crystal-lized sugar being shoved down your throat. Thank the Sun and Moon, Baba Yaga doesn't smell like *her*, though the over-whelming wave of foxglove is enough to make my sensitive nose crinkle.

"Let's go inside so we can look around," I suggest to the witch.

Grim shifts on my shoulder, reminding me of his near weightless, yet comforting presence. I can only hope my heap of curls is thick enough to keep him hidden with the movement.

"We?" Baba Yaga's puffed up, metaphorical feathers seem to be ruffled. She plants her feet, using her body and arms to block any of us from going inside. "Only *one* is allowed to enter." The silk of her voice hardens to steel, and I catch the first glimpse of wickedness beneath her smooth mask.

My sisters use timid hands on my elbows to pull me back a step, out of teeth and silver-clawed reach. With sweat pooling in my palms, I gaze down at the witch. Her eyes are lined up with my nose, but her presence makes her feel larger as she gives me a sharp-toothed smile.

"Those who have looted pay the price. However, my punish-ments took too many customers away, so the rules have adapted. Only one is allowed to enter, no salt or weapons of any kind, and you *must* have something worthy to trade." Baba Yaga tilts her head. "Understand?"

My molars grind at the thought of either Poppy or Posy going inside with the hag alone. I once again mourn the loss of my knife, probably cities away on the belt of the gambler by now, though I do have multiple pouches of salt. If this bogey is anything like the last witch I met, I could become a part of her collection at any time. But we need that bluebird, so going in "alone," with Grim stashed away on my person, is a risk I must take.

"Yes," I grit out.

Baba Yaga's posture softens as she slinks back into her house with an orange hand on the door. "Decide amongst yourselves and once you're ready, come inside," she says, her sharp grin widening before she closes the door with a click.

I almost double over, letting loose now that's she's gone. When I catch my breath and look at my sisters, I see that Posy's lips have now gone sage green, and Poppy is wiping at her cheeks, tears escaping her jittery fingers. None of us are okay.

"She was wearing Hazel's belt," Posy whispers past her pale lips.

If anyone was going to notice that detail and recognize it from the centuries-old sketch by Time, it was Posy.

"I thought that looked familiar." Poppy glances back at the closed door as if she can still see the witch and the bulky leather belt hanging around her bony waist. "What are we going to do? Only one of us can go in, and we have only one item to trade."

I bite back a groan. "Trust me, I've already been thinking about that." Flicking my hair over my shoulder, I reveal a simmering Grim. "Do you know what we're supposed to do?" I ask him.

"No," the Pooka sighs. "Death was cagey, and Fate would only show me flashes of the house's interior. I saw nothing but the lock of the back door and a walkway tossed with strewn items."

"So, what? We have to pick one thing or the other, the

memory bird, or the belt?" Posy asks, quiet voice coated with dread. Some color is returning to her face though.

"Obviously, we have to pick the bluebird," Poppy chimes in.

"But we can't just leave Hazel's belt behind." Posy's brows dip low. "That's a Healer's belt, everything that stands against creatures like Baba Yaga."

Poppy worries at one of the tiny braids hidden amongst her curls as the breeze blows fresh snow under the cover of the porch.

"I have an idea, but it might be really stupid," I sigh.

My sisters look at me with familiar trepidation while the sugar glider on my shoulder looks to the heavily clouded sky toward Wyrd Mountain. The Sun and Moon can't help us now.

Many of my ideas as kids got us into trouble. Like the summer I convinced Poppy that the chicory popping up throughout the glade were good to eat. We'd just learned that they meant unconditional love and endless waiting, and Poppy was in the early stages of believing her soulmate would be a prince. I told her the flowering weed would make him show up faster and recognize her as his princess. She got violently ill, and her mouth was stained blue for days. Sparrow took my dessert privileges away for a month.

But this idea--it's a *little* worse than childhood mischief.

WORTHY OF A TRADE

I open Baba Yaga's door with a surreptitious look back at my sisters. They nod at me in return as my lips press together. Then, I enter the house and seal myself inside with the witch. The plan is set and there's no going back now.

The inside of the chicken-legged house is deceiving. It's impossibly large compared to the outside and reminiscent of a greenhouse with the way variegated foxglove crawls the walls and ceiling. There are smudges of pumpkin-tinted witchcraft in the corners of the inner roof like a cloud of dust motes. Somehow, the hag is using her magic to alter her house in more ways than massive functioning legs. It seems purposeful too, considering the stacks and piles of treasure before me. Baba Yaga's trove snakes throughout the house, creating a literal maze of coveted possessions. The towers are twice my height, precarious as some of the items jut out like a tilting pillar of children's building blocks. If something were to shift, the whole structure would come crumbling down.

The collection reminds me of a hoard, but not one of trash, one of memories and keepsakes. Things of sentimental value traded away and filed into these odd formations for the next person to find. It's almost like the dragon lairs from Sparrow's gilded storybooks with all the shiny bits and bobs sprinkled about. Part of me wonders if the witch has a roost somewhere where she's hiding some of her most precious items.

Envisioning Baba Yaga sitting atop a favored golden egg helps me move forward into the fray, as does Grim's hidden presence in my hair. I am not entirely alone. The gaunt witch is nowhere in sight now, and all I hear is the occasional clink of glass from hanging bottles and groaning floorboards. Almost like the house is breathing, the objects inside settle into new places with each inhale and exhale. It makes me eye the towers with even more suspicion as I pass through the aisles, the shadows of the traded items flitting over me. There's a presence all around me, and it's not coming from the witch or the Pooka, it's coming from all the abandoned paraphernalia. Like the ghosts of the items' old life haunt the stacks, creating an amalgamation of sadness and forgotten pieces. My ever-present shadows double in number and writhe with this thought.

My heart starts pounding as I recall the labyrinth, the one we fled through after Black Annis was slain. Using the sheet that had covered our cage, Sparrow's blood-soaked and haphazardly stitched body was carried in the makeshift sling by Rush and Bramwell. My half-brother had taken the lead, carrying the end where Sparrow's head lay as he guided our haggard group into the first sunlight we'd seen in almost a week.

Crouching where I stand, I put my head between my knees as an anxiety attack settles in my chest. Grim scrambles to perch on the back of my neck, the sudden change of posture nearly sending him flying from my shoulder.

"Rose?" he whispers, confused.

"It's getting harder for me to breathe in here," I reply between silent gasps.

When I squeeze my eyes closed, I accidentally summon the same pitch-black from the cave all those years ago. It was no longer lit by blue witchcraft when we left the center of the labyrinth where we were held. We had to stumble through blind, my sisters and I holding hands while our Pop's shaky fingers fluttered over our shoulders. I remember Aspen holding him by the elbow as the absent look settled in his ruby eyes. She was really the one who helped us follow the rest of the faeries in our sightless escape. The tower of treasure surrounding me here reminds me of those stone walls, of that cold, wet maze.

"Breathe, Rose," Grim soothes.

Imaginary drops of water echo, mimicking the ice-cold water that dripped from that cave ceiling. I thought it was blood raining down upon us until we breached the darkness and tripped into the light.

"Use your senses to ground yourself," he prompts. "Feel your surroundings."

Slapping my palm onto the ground beneath me now, I let myself feel the shabby wood floorboards.

Grim's multilayered voice caresses the shell of my ear. "Good. Now tell me what you smell."

"Foxglove," I choke out. "Dust and rusted metal."

The Pooka hums in approval. "What do you hear and see?"

I trace the whorls in the floor's grain until I don't hear the faint *drip-drop* anymore, until I have the courage to open my eyes again. I'm not trapped in that dark cave. "The home of a witch," I answer.

"Yes, but you're free. There are no bars, and you are not frozen." Grim's voice in my ear and his light weight on my neck is soothing. He knows what the source of this attack is. He has seen the horrors I witnessed; he has felt their darkness. And yet, despite the weakness I feel, he calms my soul like a soft, cooling balm. "You're *free*," he repeats.

Technically, he's right, I'm not caged, but I will be if my hurried plan falls through. I need to get up. I need to find that bird. Legs prickling with pins and needles, I drag my body up and let Grim settle himself back on my shoulder before we move through the pathways.

I center myself with deep, shuddering breaths until I feel calm enough to speak. "I'm sorry you had to see that." I wince, glad the faerie can't see my face past my curtain of hair.

Grim sighs. "You don't have to apologize for being vulnerable, Rose, not with me."

Feeling too raw and suspicious about where Baba Yaga could be lurking, my words are so quiet it's hard for even me to hear them. "Thank you."

We carry on in silence, each row feeling a bit like a different graveyard. I distract myself by replacing my darker, panic ridden thoughts. How old are some of these treasures? How long has it been since the previous owner has died? Will anyone come for the sword that looks like it belonged to a king before it was given to the bottom of a lake? Or the perfectly preserved golden apple fit for a goddess? What about the silver scythe or winged sandals? I can see the rabbit's foot hanging from the tip of a bronzed trident and perhaps the bottle of sea glass labeled "mermaid tears" being forgotten. They're never leaving this bewitched house.

All memory of The Numina might die here too...

I shake my head.

Seeing this vortex of lost wonders reminds me how important this quest is. The earth has been tipping more and more towards the edge of unbalanced. Not only do bogeys haunt our nightmares and daydreams, they steal and destroy all that is good and whole. The world grows bleak in their terror. We need heroes who can tip the scales back to where they need to be. The Numina must return. And my sisters and I are the last thread to them. We cannot let them be forgotten, nor can we let Hazel's memory bird, or her belt, wither another day in this tomb of relics.

So Grim and I will do precisely what we shouldn't. We will loot.

Is robbing a witch a terrible, stupid idea? Yes, yes, it is. But it's the best plan we've got. And if any faerie race is well suited to thievery, it's goblins. Grim will find and unlock the back door so Poppy and Posy can use our goblin ancestry to conceal themselves, become invisible. They'll sneak around the back of the porch and steal inside once the Pooka opens their way, all while I barter for the belt. I just need to find where Baba Yaga is keeping the bluebird first, then I can distract her with my offer and give my sisters a chance to steal it.

After more wandering, Grim and I come across a large unit of shelves intertwined with poisonous, bell-shaped blooms growing along a far-reaching wall. My head is down, looking at some of the larger items on the floor, and I'm peering under cloth-covered boxes attempting to find a birdcage when I see the table under the shelves. On top is dish upon dish of coins of all shapes, sizes, and metals.

I sift through them, the bits of copper, bronze, silver, and gold clinking around the ceramic dishes. There's Grecian drachma printed with faces of a gorgon and some coins with the body of a bee. Along with denarius featuring their wreathed emperors, daric coins depicting their warrior king, groat and florin coins, even pennigar from the north. There's even a strange coin that looks like it's been stamped with the likeness of a wonky unicorn. I almost pocket it just to show Poppy, who would've loved to tie it in her hair, but I don't dare test my luck––yet. I'm already planning on stealing one thing, it's best not to add something else in case we get caught and pay the price, as Baba Yaga had warned.

Grim peeks his face through my hair with a grave tone. "Rose, look up."

My blood runs cold when my gaze lifts to the shelves above the table full of coins. Jars ranging from short and squat to tall and skinny line up in neat rows, each filled with a thick, yellow-tinged liquid. Suspended in every glass vessel is a specimen labeled with a square of parchment and cramped, slanted handwriting. A pair of eyeballs stares back at me, the deep brown orbs preserved to perfection. Their label reads, *"Eye of Newt Culpepper."*

Then, I see the human tongue. *"Tongue of Dogwood Graham."*

A goblin-green toe with a lacquered nail. *"Toe of Frogge Oakley."*

The jar full of teeth. *"Tooth of Wolfgang Eaton."*

Row after row, I find body parts from humans and faeries alike. Fingers and ears, tails, wings and horns, each marked with the first and last name of their reluctant donors.

I now know how this witch punishes thieves. The collection stems from her dark, malevolent spirit. The last witch I met tore pieces of flesh from her victims. She laid the skin out to dry in the wailing banshee trees outside her cave like cowhide. Afterward, she hung them on the belt around her waist as trophies. But Baba Yaga? She rends whole pieces from her unlucky victims. I can only hope, for their sake, she leaves the rest of the person intact.

My lip trembles in disgust at the macabre snow globes before I lurch away from the horrid sight and down another aisle. I'm stopped short when I come face-to-face with Baba Yaga herself. In my haste I almost plow into her, catching myself with only a hairsbreadth between us. Before the witch can spot him, Grim burrows himself away against the side of my neck where the fall of my curls is most dense. Her grin is lascivious as she soaks in the unease rolling off me in waves. The hag has caught me in a moment of panic, and I know my wide eyes show it.

"Find everything you're looking for?" she purrs.

No, I think to myself. We still haven't found the bluebird, but I thank the Sun, the Moon, and *all* their stars that it wasn't dead inside one of those horrid jars. "Nothing lights my fire just yet." Somehow, I keep my voice steady.

Baba Yaga hums. "Well, why don't we find something to spark your interest? Let me show you to the potions section. I have one of the last bottles of ambrosia known to man and a few drams of water from the Lake of Fire."

I'm opening my mouth to say no, but she scares me into silence when she wraps her thin arm around mine and pulls me forward. Grim climbs to the opposite side of my neck to put distance between him and her teeth. I can feel the quick pace of his furry chest rising and falling against my skin. One would think the ex-criminal and deathless faerie would feel no fear towards a witch. Though, part of me thinks his rapid breaths might be a result from fearing Baba Yaga *for* me. I'd imagine she'd skin a goblin ear from my head if she found out I smuggled the Pooka in her house.

"Might you be interested in a coat made from a selkie's skin? Or perhaps a golden fleece from a winged ram?" the witch continues, glancing at my stricken face. I can feel my lips gape like an emerald trout. "No, you don't need something material; you're not the type. There is a bow that used to make someone fall in love somewhere in the area, but then again, I don't think you're one for that either."

I try to pull away from her. The horror of feeling her hands on me makes my heart falter while a dull, numbed ringing keens in my ears. She tightens her hold. The threat of her silver talons poke at my skin through my sweater. They remind me of cold iron.

"The seed of a fruit that can send someone to Purgatory sounds a bit more like it." Baba Yaga nods to herself, padding forward on her near-silent bare feet. My steps sound clunky in comparison. Grim had the right idea. I'm trying to keep as much distance from the witch as physically possible while she holds me, but my boots feel leaden.

When I speak, my voice is no longer solid, it sounds like the last leaf on a tree during a winter storm. "I'm looking for something a little more, uh, practical."

She says nothing, leading me on through the maze of *things*. We walk up and down the paths, around every corner and bend, until we reach the back of the witchcraft-enhanced house. The items here are a lot older, and much dustier than what I'd seen earlier. Even the unconventional foxglove garden is fuller here, some of the objects disappearing behind the wall of flowers. I think I spot the curved side of a shield peeking through, and the dainty hand of a sculpted marble statue reaching towards us. There's an upside-down helmet with a red feather plume trying to roll its way out from under the growth too.

The window and the door out to the back of the porch are the only things not blocked by either plant life or the witch's collection. She must go out there to sit in that rocking chair I saw and admire her swampy home. It's not the kind of view I'd enjoy, but to each their own. And I suppose it's to be expected from the hag considering her insides match her land.

Baba Yaga strokes my arm. "There's a chest of books under the window. I have a grimoire or two that belong to my sister, and preserved scrolls saved from the Great Library. There's also many journals full of tasty secrets." She strokes my arm again. "Do any of those sound practical enough for you?"

I want to crawl out of my skin, but the tips of her nails anchor me to my spot. I feel like a frightened fawn. The tiny scar running along Posy's cheekbone comes to mind. My thoughts roll toward those same claws that ran over her, flaying the flesh of friends and family before my seven-year-old eyes. It's been ten years, and I still keep my fingernails cut to the skin. Posy would chew hers to the bone if we let her, and Poppy never lets hers go too long past her fingertips. I try to push the feeling of the cold points grazing my skin to the back of my mind. "What about something more...lively?"

The witch gives me an odd look, her depthless eyes studying me before she nods. "I have just the thing." A blessed moment later, she frees me from her grasp to step away, striding past the door and frosted fern window.

Only when her back is turned and the glass is out of her view do I see my sisters appear. They stare at me through the pane covered in a pattern of ice crystals with worry-tight eyes before concealing themselves again. That was a signal to let me know they're ready. Glancing at the round doorknob, I see the button-shaped lock in the middle is flipped down, meaning it's locked for their forbidden entry just as Fate showed Grim. I give my invisible sisters a short nod before I hold my arm out towards the door. With Baba Yaga still distracted, Grim breaks free from his spot against my neck and runs from my shoulder and down to my wrist before he jumps. His arms and legs extend out and the skin stretched between his limbs flares out, catching a draft and letting him glide through the air. He lands on the doorknob, curling his whole body around it to hold on tight.

Baba Yaga motions to what I thought was a curved floor lantern in the corner without looking back. The base is over-taken by vines that crawl upwards to wrap around the shade-like covering. "This thing has been here for hundreds of years. It doesn't need a sip of water or a single worm. So it's impossible to kill."

Glancing at the Pooka, I see him using his tiny four-fingered hands to grip the lock. It doesn't budge.

The witch turns to me with a sharp smile as I step in front of her to block her view of the animal trying to unlock the back door. "Trust me, I've tried," she laughs. And, with no further flair, she rips the shade away, tearing the vines that had grown onto it. This startles the creature that seemed to have been sleeping under it.

Inside a tall domed cage is the bluebird. It sits on its metal perch, flapping its vivid, sky-colored wings in displeasure, puffing its orange throat feathers. The bird's bleary eyes blink at the sudden awakening, taking in its surroundings for the first time in who knows how long. When it sees me and hops along the perch a little closer to the bars, I see the intelligence behind its gaze. This has to be Hazel's memory bird.

"It's the perfect pet," Baba Yaga muses, nails tapping the cage making a high tinny sound as she studies the bird.

In the back of my head, I hear deep clangs of iron. But the only metal that's important now is the doorknob and its lock. I catch a glimpse of Grim heaving at the button with all his tiny might.

Despite the bad memories and desperation rising, I try to look passive when I fix my gaze back on the witch, relaxing my lips and shoulders. I don't want to seem too eager, especially when it's not the item I'm going to try to swindle. "I don't know if I'm ready for a lifelong commitment like that." I force my eyes to wander toward the ceiling as if there might be a better option where the highest collectibles are stacked.

"Then what do you want?" The witch's voice is sharp, annoyed that I'm not finding her unique, prized items desirable.

I rub my hands for show, but deep down, I'm getting nervous that none of this will work. That is until I hear the muffled metallic click of the lock flicking up. I clear my throat, hoping to cover the tail end of the noise, so it escapes Baba Yaga's notice. My terrible plan is officially in action, and it could go downhill at any time. "I don't know if it's available."

"Oh?" The hag goes to lean into me.

Playing down my nerves, I move, shuffling back the way we came, putting distance between us and the back door while drawing all attention to my movements. Through the window where they're concealed, my sisters can see the birdcage hanging from the arched stand now that it's uncovered. They'll know what to do. I let an apprehensive curve bow my shoulders as I peek back at the witch, an invitation to stroll while we make a deal. And as I hoped, Baba Yaga bypasses Grim and follows me down the closest aisle where the back door is out of sight, but still close enough for me to run to if things go awry.

"I quite like the belt you're wearing," I admit, running my hands over the knife-less corset belt around my waist for show. "It's my style, and I'd get good use out of it."

The hag's storm-gray eyes narrow at me. "I thought you wanted something *lively*."

Shrugging, I pull my lips into the imitation of a half-smile. "I decided I want something practical after all."

She considers this, claws gliding over her dark bottom lip as she thinks. I see the moment she decides it's for sale when her walk changes, almost going liquid before my eyes. "I've held this belt for a long time," she moons.

"But I have something I think will be worth the trade." Stopping halfway down the aisle, I swing my bag over my shoulder where I can reach inside. "I didn't see anything like it in your collection."

Baba Yaga lets out a *humph*, coming to a halt in front of me. As I dig inside the bag, she unclasps the herbalist belt from around her waist, waiting to hand it over for inspection while she considers my offer in return.

This is the moment. Poppy and Posy will open the back door slower than cold honey and creep into the house any minute now.

When I present the witch with the ornate wooden box, her eyes light up with curiosity and something akin to lust. We switch items, her running her thin hands over the lid while I scan Hazel's belt for any damage or sign of witchcraft tampering.

My sisters should be inside now, grabbing the shapeshifting faerie from his spot balanced on the doorknob and approaching the bird on silent feet. Posy will do most of the sneaking since it's hard for Poppy to stay quiet. I'm sure she's been having a tough time keeping her nervous humming at bay while they waited outside the door.

For a moment, the witch fumbles with her long nails and the latch before she gets the lid open. After I find the belt, its vials, and knife in perfect condition, I look up to watch the hag's face fall. Panic floods my body, making my fingers and toes go colder than they already were. I can't feel the leather under my fingertips, and I lose track of the steps to my plan. I can feel my stupid scheme sliding towards the edge of a metaphorical hill.

"It's a changeling heart. Authentic and everything, made by a troll from elder tree twigs," I explain, tone rising and voice shaky.

"It's not alive," Baba Yaga deadpans.

Scrambling now, I struggle to come up with anything that will make the heart appealing to her. "Well, no––"

"I like the anatomy pieces I collect to be *fresh*." She closes the lid of the box with a snap. "There is no life in this wood, not without a troll charm."

I pull Hazel's belt closer, holding it tight against my chest. "But––"

The witch's dark lips curl as she bares her needle teeth and snarls, "No deal. What you've brought me is not worthy of a trade."

Thus begins the tumble my plan takes down the hill.

THIEVES

*T*he house shudders, piles swaying, and wood creaking. The tinny clanking of the birdcage rings out an aisle over, along with a tiny squeak that sounds suspiciously like Poppy. It takes me a moment to realize that we're starting to make a slow descent. The chicken legs growing beneath the house are bending their knees to place us back inside the swamp.

"If you have nothing else to trade, you must leave." Baba Yaga holds out an orange hand, reaching for Hazel's belt with an icy look. *"Empty-handed."*

I strain to hold it closer. But the belt is already tight to my skin, the buckle pressing through my mud-stained sweater hard enough to leave a mark on my chest. If only I could burrow it inside my ribs to keep it safe but alas...

"I—I would really like to keep this. I don't have much else, but I'm willing to give you anything you want." A mantra of *stupid, stupid, stupid* circles its way through my head. It brings back memories of Sparrow giving a different witch a similar offer in exchange for Aspen's release all those years ago. She was trying to set us all free, and to do that, she almost died. Or I suppose she did die, considering Time backed up Sparrow's story about when she met Death and Fate in The Between. I, however, would like to avoid meeting with them until The Numina are back in the physical world, thank you very much.

"That's a dangerous offer." A cutthroat smile slices through the witch's mouth. "I have a very specific taste and not just anything will do."

A cold sweat coats the small of my back as I sway on my feet. The house is lowering further. "I have a few trinkets in my bag, some coins, a tiger's eye stone, and—"

"Oh, no, you've wasted much of my time. And not to mention, you made my poor house stretch its legs. It had just gotten comfortable for the first time in years." Baba Yaga walks a slow, sinuous circle around me, depositing the ornate box holding the changeling heart back in my open bag. She runs a wandering hand from my shoulder where Grim had hidden to the fingers clenching Hazel's belt. "Nevertheless, I'll accept something a little more personal," Baba Yaga singsongs.

She pulls her hand away with a sharp swipe, purposely nicking one of my knuckles to draw blood. A bead of it sits on her shiny claw, a bright gem against the metallic nail. She eyes the spot before her sharp tongue flicks out to lick the blood clean off. My gut flips in the most unpleasant way when her words and what I just witnessed match up. Now I realize what she's saying.

"I saw your collection of"—I swallow—"parts."

The witch bats her glossy white hair behind her shoulder with a coy look before aimlessly picking at the items stacked to the right of us. She drags a finger over a dull cutlass sticking out of a pile before she unearths a leather eyepatch that smells salted by ocean air. "Ah, my leftovers," the hag chuckles. "I'm saving those for a rainy day."

I'd been joking earlier when I was thinking of the ways Baba Yaga might take her coffee with blood and bones. Turns out it didn't end up being a joke after all. The witch has eaten the entirety of poor Newt Culpepper, and apparently left his eyes for a midnight snack. It makes me cringe to think about her using Wolfgang Eaton's teeth in a salad like croutons.

I peer down at the littlest finger on my left hand as the house comes to a grinding stop, the disturbed swamp water lapping against the bottom of the house. I've decided that I can function without my pinkie, seeing as it's not a piece of me I depend on or use very often. Losing it will only hurt for a little while; at least, that's what I try to convince myself. Grim and my sisters are in the next aisle over with nothing but material memories separating them from a monster. I need to give them enough time to get the memory bird out of here, and if that means losing my pinkie as a distraction, it'll be worth it. I won't let Baba Yaga lay a hand on them. They just need to unhook the ring connected to the top of the birdcage from the stand and run. Grim will keep Poppy and Posy safe once they make it back out into the swamp.

"You have a deal," I croak, the sting of bile rising in my throat. I'm nauseous thinking about what the witch will do with the small piece of me.

My left hand shakes as my fingers unlatch from the belt. I'm second-guessing how much Hazel will need this belt... Maybe she can live without it? Still, against my better judgment, I hold my hand out to the hag, almost as if she were a gentleman waiting to kiss my knuckles. It's too late to back out now. Part of me expects Baba Yaga to chomp down on my fingers, but I didn't foresee her clamping on to my hand with her own and pulling me forward. She traps me flush against her gaunt frame. The scent of foxglove petals on her breath chokes me more than her other arm does as she wheedles it underneath my knapsack to crush my waist. Baba Yaga is deceptively strong, like a trap of steel biting into my body. This house and these arms are just as bad as iron bars; no matter how hard I try to slip from them, I can't get free.

Grim was wrong, I'm a prisoner once more.

"What are you doing?" I gasp, squirming to get free. But the witch tightens her arm, releasing her crippling grip from my hand to slip the leather band of the eyepatch over my head. It hangs like a noose around my neck. My mistake dawns on me then: I never specified our deal before I gave her confirmation. I just held out my hand like a mooncalf, expecting her to understand the offer and take a single digit. But of course that's not the case.

Baba Yaga's poison-darkened tongue darts from her mouth and licks a slimy stripe up my cheek, stopping over my left eye. I'm too stunned to speak. Even my flailing limbs come to a halt. Beads of moisture stick to my tightly shut lashes, and my skin burns like lemon in an open wound where her bitter trail of spit sits.

The hag's melodic laugh sounds like a cello strung with catgut strings. "It's the dealer's choice now and I taste midnight on your delicious skin." The witch peels my left eye open with her thumb, her metallic nail grazing my black brow. I don't dare move and risk gaining a scar like the one Sparrow got from Jenny Greenteeth. "These peepers of yours look like silver bells on a rainy day." Baba Yaga nods to herself. "And they are worthy indeed."

The next thing I know, there is a talon in my eye. Pure agony sets my nerves on fire, making me want to thrash, but a clawed hand clasps the back of my head to lock me in place. My teeth chomp onto my lower lip to keep my cries inside. I can't alert my sisters or the Pooka that something is wrong. They need to get out with the bird. *Now.*

The herbalist belt falls between our bodies to the floor when I start to scratch at any part of the witch I can reach with my short stubby nails. I shove her shoulders, strike her neck, and force her face back, but I can't get loose. Blood and tears pour out of my eyes. Tiny trinkets tumble around our feet as Baba

Yaga pushes her finger in deeper. She curls it like a hook to pierce the tissue, anchoring her claw inside my skull before ripping it free from the socket. The sound it makes is like tearing a piece of parchment in half.

Falling out of her arms with an ear-splitting wail, I land on my tailbone and slam my hands over the empty hole in my head. Through the stream of tears cascading out of my remaining eye, I see Baba Yaga holding her bloody hand aloft. My silver eye is skewered on the tip of her pointed nail.

"The patch is free of charge," Baba Yaga cackles before she pops my eye between her teeth and slurps the dangling optic nerve past her full lips. In a moment of excruciating delirium, it reminds me of my travels East where they make vibrant red pasta from rice and flavor it with turmeric and coconut. I'll never eat noodles again.

"Rose?" Grim yells from the aisle over, waves of his voices crashing through the pathway like a tidal wave.

My sisters' echoing calls sound like a storm.

Their worried shouts shake me out of my pained stupor. Fueled by the fear coursing through my body, I find the strength to get on my knees. My fingers, slippery with blood, smear the floor with stamps of my hands as I latch back onto Hazel's belt and clamber to my feet. I scream an unintelligible warning until I can muster up actual words. *"Get out!"*

Behind me, Baba Yaga lets out a screech of fury. She knows now. We fooled her for a time, but we weren't as successful as we hoped. Poppy and Posy were supposed to slip inside, grab Grim, take the birdcage from the hook, and slip back out undetected. All the while, I was supposed to trade the changeling heart for the belt without a hitch, but my plan not only went downhill, it keeps on rolling.

Baba Yaga's hands are glowing with witchcraft now. The house shakes and groans, and I can feel the enchanted chicken legs preparing to stretch again. We need to get out of here before we start moving again. Plus, the house is inescapable if we get too high. I don't know that we would walk away without serious injuries after a fifty-foot fall once the house reaches its full height. Although, I think I might prefer chancing the plummet rather than having any more of me eaten.

Little songbird squawks of surprise mixed with the panicked pounding of heavy winter boots on the floorboards sound throughout the house. My sisters are jumping into action. I stumble forward too, half blind and groaning at the sharp ache in my orbital bone. I sweep a hand through the weed-like foxglove, knocking down stacks of traded items, trying to turn them into obstacles for the witch. It's a feeble attempt to slow down the angered bogeyman hot on my heels, but it might be enough to get me out of here. The tongue of the belt I traded my eye for is crushed in my bloody fist while the rest of it swings wild. It bangs into my legs and sends more of the witch's collectibles crashing down. I leave a tossed mess of strewn items in my wake.

The house rises.

After I trip my way around the corner, the back door is in my damaged sight. An unveiled Posy runs outside and into the swamp with the domed birdcage in her arms. A wavering Poppy waits for me by the open door, bouncing on anxious toes as she appears, disappears, and reappears again. But I don't see Grim, *where is he?* My sister's jaw goes slack when she sees my face, then her eyes grow wider as she notices the witch barreling around the corner after me, shrieking like a banshee.

"*Thieves,*" Baba Yaga howls. "Thieves!"

It's a bit too late and rather pointless to hide now; the witch knows we've taken from her, and she'll hunt us down, concealed or not. So, with my knapsack rubbing against my spine, I launch my sister through the doorway with my tremoring body, depth perception thrown off now that I have one eye to see out of. "Go, go, go!"

Past my tears, I note the house is a few feet out of the swamp now and getting higher every second Baba Yaga wills it to stand. The snow-covered land that makes up the witch's backyard is a little rockier than what we waded through earlier. Even with a single eye, I can see where the bleak swamp ends, and more mountainous land begins. There are sharp stalagmite-like formations creating a border between the two and that's where we need to go. Quick.

In my urgency, I almost take a spill when my boot catches the edge of the rocking chair that I would've otherwise seen in the periphery of my missing left eye. Blessedly, Poppy hauls me upright. Whispers of, *"we're going to die,"* spill from beneath her cloudy breath over and over like a mantra.

By the time she pulls me to the porch railing, Posy is at least a hundred feet away on the ground. She's keeping herself and the memory bird at a safe distance while Grim's raven form makes nervous circles above her head, keeping her safe like I would've wanted. His smoky wings skip a flap when he sees us. Poppy is attempting to hold me upright while I crumple in pain, a palm suctioned to my face and belt loose in my other hand. I imagine the picture we paint isn't pretty. But the furious hag is in the doorway at our backs now and that might have some-thing to do with his surprise and horror.

When a Witch Has a Temper Tantrum

"We need to jump," Poppy pants.

The house is still rising, but with my bleary eye I can't tell if we're ten feet up or a whole world away. All I can focus on is how my empty eye socket throbs with every heartbeat. The only thing that pulls me back to the gravity of our situation is Grim diving towards us. I'm too numbed by pain and shock to react or duck like Poppy, so I watch his approach like I'm standing outside of my body, waiting for his black beak to drive into my chest. Then, just as he's about to ram his feathery frame into me, he tilts enough that he only skims the top of my head. The Pooka flies, clawed feet first, into Baba Yaga's face, scratching and beating his wings to blind her. She howls as she tries to pry him away, stumbling backward into her home. That's when the house shudders, powdery snow falling from the shingles as its chicken legs waver from the witch momentarily losing control of her magic.

Poppy locks her arm around mine. "Now, Primrose. We need to go *now!*" She pulls me closer to the edge of the porch, but I dig my heels in.

"I can't—I can't see. I'm going to break a leg or something." I shake my throbbing head. My sister's use of my full name doesn't even phase me, I'm more focused on my newfound fear of heights that I can't fully see. "You jump down with the belt, and I'll lower myself down by hanging––"

I don't get the chance to finish my sentence because I'm vaulted off the porch by a body of shapeshifting darkness hitting me in the back. Grim's shadows seem to envelop Poppy and me, wrapping us in a protective hug that feels like a luke-warm breeze as we fall back into the half-frozen swamp below. My teeth knock together when my feet hit the packed mud, causing a stab of pain to rattle through my skull. But other than that, my sister and I are unharmed from the surprisingly short drop.

A green hand reaches through the Pooka's peat-and-pine-tinged mist and yanks us through. Posy's haunted face is on the other side. She watches the witch's house rise to its full height while the birdcage is wrapped tight in her arm, the bottom of it digging into her hip for leverage. The bluebird inside looks a little ruffled though fine otherwise.

Grim solidifies, this time appearing in the form of a shaggy dog whose back just hits my hip. The curls of his ebony fur end in little wisps of smoke. "Rose, what did you do?"

"What did *I* do?" I bleat, pressing the back of my wrist against the gaping hole in my face; the pressure seems to help the pain despite the agony-fueled tears pouring from my face. "What do you mean, what did I do?"

Posy tugs on the cuff of Poppy's long sleeve as she takes a step back in the direction of the mountains, urging us all to follow. "Now is not the time for this," she hisses in a whisper.

The Pooka doesn't notice this, he's too busy studying what a disaster I am. Bloody and incomplete with Hazel's belt in my hand and the box holding the changeling heart peeking from my bag. He's upset, furious even as his muzzle pulls back into a snarl, baring his sharp canine teeth. One might mistake his anger as part of his duty towards The Numina, but if you squint, you can see it's pure, unadulterated concern.

"You could have gotten yourself killed," he huffs, sulfurous eyes fuming. "I can't protect you if you're dead, Primrose--"

"Hi." Poppy waves a hand between us. "Do I need to remind you that there is a very hostile witch in control of a house with legs that wants to kill us?"

"What was I supposed to do with myself if I lost you? I couldn't stand it, it would've killed--" Grim begins, outright ignoring my sister.

But Poppy is right. Baba Yaga is standing on her shaded porch staring down at us from fifty feet above like we're roaches. Her clawed hands are bubbling as they clutch onto the railing where the barest hint of sun pierces through the gray winter clouds and lightly falling snow to hit the wood. Even from down here, through the blood, tears, and sobs, I can see she's scratched up rage and white-hot fire, and she's about to explode. Orbs of orange glow from beneath her burning hands while she lifts them into the air back under the cover of her roof. One of the chicken legs picks up a foot—she's commanding them to move.

"Less talking, more running," I gasp.

"Conceal yourselves," Grim urges us.

"What about you?" Poppy and I say in unison, though my voice sounds more like a cry.

"I can't die, you can." The hound jerks his head forward, silently commanding us to run. "Now do it!"

Soon after this, I discover I don't have the coordination to run, hold Hazel's belt, cover my empty socket, *and* keep myself concealed. It's hard enough adjusting to my new way of sight and I find myself wishing that Fate didn't limit what shape and size Grim can take. If he could become a giant bird, one big enough to rival Baba Yaga's house, he could carry me and my sisters away from here to Wyrd Mountain. But as pain splits my head like an axe to a tree stump, I lose hold of wits and the gift my goblin ancestry gave me, making me flicker in and out of sight. So I remove my hand and let the blood seep slowly from beneath my swollen lids while I splash through the unforgiving wintry swamp, hoping I look less like a guttering candle every time I disappear and reappear.

Eventually, I can conceal myself no longer, the pain is too much. Having the ability to be invisible is pretty useless when you're not in the right condition or setting to use it.

Grim produces a deep, resounding bark when he sees this. "Primrose!"

"I can't," I shout, though, to my ears, it sounds like a pitiful wail. "I can't hold it!"

Poppy and Posy reappear, much to my dismay.

I can't help the groan that slips from my bloodied lips. "What are you doing?"

"Making more targets," Poppy answers, her face a hardened stone as she throws a quick look back at the pursuing house.

"Are you stupid?" I stumble but Poppy, bless her, is there in a heartbeat to catch me.

She takes the bulky herbalist belt from me to ease my struggle. "Baba Yaga can see the murk and ice moving with each of our steps. Besides, she knows where you are, concealed or not, because Grim wouldn't leave you behind." Then, she continues her sprint with a skip in her step, stained split skirt flying around her legs now that she doesn't have her cloak weighing it down. Posy is hot on her trail with arms wrapped around the cage, murmuring her apologies to the bluebird inside for all the jostling. Clumsy, I follow the tracks in the thickening swamp mud and soft layer of snow left by Grim's paws as he tries to forge me a path.

It doesn't take long for me to fall back. I find myself growing unsteady as the mire gets rockier, tripping on frozen sunken stones that are a bit too far left for me to see with my narrowed vision. The frustration, combined with the fear and agony bubbling inside me, makes me sick to my stomach. And when I spare a glance over my right shoulder, which has quickly become my good side, I almost lose my stomach contents. The tall house is following us with monstrous strides; there is no way I'm going to outrun this thing.

As if he can sense my thoughts, Grim stalls to let his side brush up against my left hip. "Hold on to me."

"What?" I have to crane my head farther sideways to see him with my remaining eye.

"We're going to get trampled at the pace you're going," he rumbles as he takes a glimpse at the gaining house.

I can't make myself turn around this time, I'm too afraid of seeing a giant scaled foot about to descend on my head. He's better served protecting Poppy and Posy and getting them to the Wyrd Mountain in one un-squashed piece.

"You are more than welcome to go ahead and catch up with my sisters," I grunt. The toe of my boot hits something in the shallowing ice-cold water as I scamper forward, making me slow to a pitiful jog. My sisters are way up ahead. I pray they don't turn around and see how I'm lagging because I know they would either stop or double back.

A vibrating growl comes from deep within the dark faerie's chest. "I'm not leaving you behind, Rose. Stop acting like you're disposable and let me guide you."

My roiling gut sinks like an anchor. My unspoken job is to keep Poppy and Posy safe when I was home; it's always been that way––ever since *then*. When that hag scratched Posy's cheek, leaving that little scar, I swore to never let any harm come to my sisters again, if I could prevent it. I trusted Sparrow and Rush to look after them when I was traveling as a nomadic adventurer, but when I was home as just a goblin of the glade, a scared, broken girl, that meant throwing myself into the fray, becoming the dry, emotionless, tough sister. The one to give up an eye to ensure their safety. But then I think of Aspen, Rush, Sparrow, Hazel, the kids, and even Pop. They might not forgive me if I don't at least try to fight for myself. Not to mention, Time's letter said the *three* of us goblins need to be the ones to bring them back. I imagine Death would give me a good wallop if I don't heed Time's words and let the last thread to them unravel.

Perhaps I do need to work on my self-preservation skills… but still, old habits die hard, and I hesitate. As my blood-slick hand hovers over the space between the Pooka's snow-dusted shoulder blades, my slow ambling pace stutters because of a stick.

Grim huffs. "Do you trust me?"

I taste iron on my sandpaper tongue when I nod, surprised by my own conviction. "With my life."

"Then hold on."

Curling my fingers into his smoke-tipped fur, I hold tight, but not tight enough to hurt Grim as he lopes forward faster than I can run. It's easier for me to keep up now that he's covering my blind side and maneuvering us. Grim steers me to the right by leaning into me and tugs to the left until I can feel his body against mine again. He guides me forward with my full confidence, bonding to me and becoming my other half, helping me function as a whole. He is my sight and he's furthering the gap between us and Baba Yaga's terrifying advance. I can feel the ground reverberating beneath my feet, but the shaking is nothing compared to the sound the house's enchanted footfalls make. First, there's the slap of the massive claw hitting the frosted surface and then the boom of it contacting the earth. The disgusting squelch of the marsh squishing over its giant talons is unnaturally loud too.

Over the deafening creaks and groans of the wood structure atop the freakish legs, I hear the witch yelling. It's all gibberish to me, but I don't think it's anything nice. I'd bet my good eye it's a *very* colorful tirade. Baba Yaga won't stop pursuing us until we're flattened into little green goblin-meat pancakes. Our only chance at escape is to make it as close to the mountain as possible.

After blinking the tears from my healthy eye, I see that the stalagmites in the distance are *big*. Much bigger than my sisters and I stacked up if we stood on each other's shoulders, and quite pointy as well. We'll be able to seek cover amongst the rocks, but we just need to make it there first. Which might be a problem considering we're catching up to my tiring sisters and I see broad white-topped slate stones protruding from the ground ahead. These flat stones are bad news because they're large enough that we can't avoid them, and they have gaps between that must be hurtled. It's going to take forever to get through them. Yet in some ways they're a good sign because they mean we're making the final transition between the swamp, the mountain area, and its rocky border.

A gust of wind buffets my back as a witchcraft-powered footstep hits a little too close for comfort. Grim bounds faster, pulling me behind him as snowflakes assault my throbbing face. When we reach my sisters, he nips at their heels with his pointed teeth, something I've seen a dog do to herd sheep in a pasture. It's effective and spurs my wheezing sisters onward while the memory bird chirrups. Grim continues to push us hard until we reach the first stone.

It's the length and width of a garden shed, and each gap between the slates is a bit wider than a tall man, requiring a leap instead of a simple step. They're like behemoth versions of the steppingstones the gnomes use back at the glade to decorate the garden. But they're a smidge more precarious and swampier with a fresh powdery blanket and old drifts of dirty snow.

Posy goes first, taking a running start before pushing off her toes, hopping onto the next stone with a loud metallic rattle and indignant bird chirping. Her boots hold her steady and don't sweep her legs out from under her; hopefully that means there's no ice beneath us.

Poppy lets out a long breath, securing the pilfered belt over her shoulder like a sash. She shakes out her hands and rolls her neck. "Think of it like Leaptoad," she whispers to herself before she hums a tune and takes off, landing the jump. The part of the song I heard rumble through her throat sounded like an old nursery rhyme Pop used to sing to us as kids. It's been a long time since I heard it. I might have laughed at Poppy's timing for reviving that song if it weren't for the walking house and its bogeyman puppeteer still chasing after us.

Baba Yaga's shouts sound frantic now. Peeking over my good side, I see the glow of her hands is a brighter salamander orange as she drives her cursed home onward. Part of me hopes the slates might be a slippery obstacle for the chicken legs. But I'm not sticking around to find out.

"Jump with one foot first," Grim says as he leads me to the edge of the rock. The snow is disturbed here, almost wiped clear from my sisters' launching steps.

After a few clumsy attempts over the following stones, we find our rhythm. A long, running stride before each leap keeps my long legs in line with his paws.

Run, run, run, jump. Run, run, run, jump.

To my surprise, Poppy doesn't falter once despite being clumsy on a day-to-day basis, along with the added precipitation. She's more sure-footed than she was in the swamp when the nixie and their alligators had been on our tails. Even the bookish Posy bounces her way closer to the mountains like she's part rabbit. The Numina must be looking out for us.

I think this until I catch something careening toward us from the corner of my remaining eye. The old red-plumed helmet I'd spotted inside the witch's house rolls off the rock Grim and I just landed on. As I spin around, I keep a hand on Grim's back to steady myself, and I see Baba Yaga lob the golden apple next. The fruit plummets fifty feet down and explodes all over the slate in a spray of glittery flecks and ambrosia. It covers my face and clothes, making the stale, travel-worn fabric and flaking swamp mud smell like apple juice. Without a doubt, my skin is going to be sticky later.

"Seriously?" I scream up at the hag. "You didn't even like the bird anyway!"

She answers me by throwing a jewel-encrusted chalice.

I duck to avoid a concussion. Picking up the overturned helmet she threw first, I brush off the snow and stuff it on my head before throwing a rude gesture behind me. "You're not getting this back, you wretch!"

Grim lets out a bark that sounds a lot like a laugh before guiding us back on track. Joining the white flurry, a hailstorm of collected objects rains down on our heads as we all run, getting closer and closer to the pointed stacks ahead. Baba Yaga will regret using her treasures as ammunition once she recovers from her temper tantrum, but I haven't seen the witch toss any of her more valuable assets, like her sister's books or her precious body part collection. I did see an expensive-looking timepiece ricochet off my helmet at some point though.

We're only two large stones away from disappearing into the spike-like stalagmites when a spear whizzes past my head toward Posy. Grim and I are making our second-to-last jump when she goes down. I slip on the landing as I watch her fall, knees banging into the rock and trousers tearing. There is blood painting the thin sheet of snow in garnet. I've skinned my leg, though Grim saved me from a worse fall. The shoulder of my sweater is clenched in his jaws to hold my weight up, but I don't care to say thank you. My sister is hunched over on her knees with her arms wrapped around herself. The birdcage with its very distressed occupant is lying on the cold ground on its side.

Poppy is rooted in her spot, staring at where the red-tipped weapon disappeared into the tall stacks.

Scrambling past her, I rip my sweater from the Pooka's mouth to get to Posy. "Po?" I ask, placing a shaky hand on her back. I don't know where she's hit, but I know the spear got her; I saw the spray of blood.

She lets out a loud groan as she sits up. "Son of a selkie, that hurt." She peels her hand from her bicep to uncover the cut slicing through her thick blouse down to her green arm. It's only a surface wound.

Before I can stop myself, I flick her long jagged ear, relief flooding through me. "I hate you so much right now."

Still concerned and a touch meek, Poppy steps closer to us with watery eyes. "You're okay?" she asks our triplet, tone soft as she wrings her hands.

Posy nods, wiping the small trail of blood from her arm onto her torn, damp trousers.

Then, a rusty dagger lands inches away from Poppy's foot, metal tip lodging deep into the stone from the force and height of the throw. I flinch, eyelids closing over nothing but an empty hole and making my eye socket throb. Gritting my teeth, I haul Posy up while Poppy retrieves the birdcage with gentle hands, cooing to the snow-drenched bluebird inside.

"We're still in danger. It's time to go." Grim's voice winds around me like a lasso.

He gathers us like sheep and pushes us forward until we make the final jump and dash into the safety of the sharp stacks. They're packed together tight enough for the four of us to walk single file through them, my hand latching on to the Pooka's long tail. And when we feel safe enough, we turn around to squint at the dark billowing sky. Baba Yaga rages, a blast of witchcraft bursting like an unruly bonfire. If she were to try to coerce her house to follow us, it would impale its foot on the stalagmites. We are free from the hag. I discard my helmet, skull aching as I ignore the familiar shadows peeking from behind the rocks in my single-eyed periphery.

On the way back home from the Wyrd Mountain, I'll find us another path to return. I refuse to step foot in another swamp ever again, including this one. But maybe this journey will earn us a favor. Maybe the Sun, Moon, and Time can transport themselves to the glade to restore Hazel's memories so she can heal Aspen before we return. That way, me and my sisters can take the safe, long way around.

We are so close to bringing back The Numina. From where we stand, surrounded by these enormous stacks, we see the beginning of the Wyrd Mountain. Now we just have to find a way inside. According to Hazel's old journal, The Numina made it very hard for anyone to reach their home, and from here it looks like she was right because the only way we'll find any kind of entry is by scaling the snowcapped mountainside. As our appointed guide, I pray that Grim knows where he's going. And hopefully he can lead us far away from the spirits that he warned us of, and into the mountain before we freeze to death in the snowstorm brewing above us.

The Climb

*J*t's been a week. At least, I think it's been. I lost count once we circled the first third of the blizzarding mountain and the cold started to bloom like frosted roses in my bones. We should've packed thicker clothes, more furs, more food––I feel like a novice traveler, but nothing makes me feel more ill-prepared than encountering the mountain's spirits.

Get closer; I can help you.

Some of them are tricksters, and I can barely catch a glimpse of the wretched things in this storm, only seeing darts of varying colors against all the white. But they're terrifying... and persuasive. Poppy hums her songs louder than ever and sticks her index fingers into her ear canals while Posy rips the hem of her blouse, wadding the fabric into balls to stuff them into her ears. I can see my sisters struggling, I know the horrible things they hear because the spirit's harsh whispers burrow into my skin like a wire fishing hook too. The resulting fear makes me *want* to listen to them, makes me want to do as they say. It's backward and strange; I know it is. But I crave safety, and their words are tempting. Grim, the only one not affected, distracts my sisters and me with incessant conversation and storytelling to try to block out the noise. I'm relieved to find that talking over the spirits to answer him does help. Most of the time.

This is not where you belong. Let me show you back down our mountain.

So we talk and talk and talk and talk. But no matter how much I nag Grim—still in the shape of a black hound—about finding the entrance to the mountain and what we need to do next, he can't propose a plan on how to recover The Numina from The Between. He doesn't even try to make a guess, no doubt worried about the fact that he knows little of how our story ends. Or perhaps it's the wicked wisps trying to encroach on our temporary camp that he's concerned with. Either way, our guide and protector is leading us half-blind up this miserable mountain. If I had more energy, I'd be mad about Fate's secrets, about the turmoil she's creating for Grim, for us. But I can only muster up so much before Poppy releases a high-pitched sneeze that rattles us all.

"Bless you," I mumble as my eye tracks the muddy, purple-hued spirit dancing around the lip of the overhang we're camped beneath. My molars grind together when I hear another one of its hoarse whispers.

Follow me. I can bring you refuge if you just step over the—

"Have you ever wondered where that saying came from?" Grim rumbles, urging us to ignore the spirit by providing more distraction.

When none of us answer, his glowing eyes don't look surprised. "It comes from The Numina."

"Really?" Poppy sniffles. Her gaze flits toward our sister, who switches between folding her arms over her head and clamping her palms over her stuffed ears to block out the voices.

"Think about it." Grim shifts, so his lanky body leans against our curled-up legs. Being a faerie made up of shadows, he's not very warm, more of a tepid temperature, but out here on the snowy Wyrd Mountain, his odd body heat thaws our lower limbs out just a bit. "Back when The Numina were still on this earth," he continues, "who would they send when someone was sick?"

"The Healers." Posy's quiet voice drifts out and almost gets lost in a curl of wind. But Grim hears it.

"And how does someone become a Healer?" A low hum vibrates his chest and ripples down his side, buzzing along my shins.

"They get Blessed…" I trail off, noticing that Poppy's attention wasn't on Posy but past her head to the other side of our shelter. That's where I see a flicker of near imperceptible color.

I can help you find the way if you leave the rest of your companions.

My hand clamps down on Poppy's knee when I notice the muscles in her thigh bunch, preparing to shuffle her feet beneath her and move toward the icy edge of the mountain. Poppy strains against my hand for a moment. I know from experience that her body is telling her to disregard the dangers of the freezing temperature making us cold and sluggish. Just as I was tempted by the spirits to let my own blood and grime overtake me to find warmth when we first started climbing the mountain. Because besides the winter weather and the spirits trying to lead us off this mountain in rather violent ways, infection is my biggest enemy. Cleaning my wound as thoroughly as possible has been the best we can do to prevent a fever from forming. We don't have medicines up here, and the herbs, tinctures, and powders in Hazel's belt are over six hundred years old. They'd most likely do more harm than good at this point. Possibly even more harm than these haunting spirits could cause.

It seems like Grim's combating the testing of that theory when he further explains the role of the Healers, attempting to capture Poppy's attention again. "Even though the human and faerie races have forgotten The Numina and Healers existed, traces remain. They've been subconscious, buried in your lives every day."

My sister shakes her head as she shivers and turns back to me. Patting her leg, I try to ground her. When our eyes meet, I recognize the same instinct to flee that's rattled my mind for days, but we didn't come this far just to be led astray. And, as a rude reminder, a pale-colored breeze flies past us, bypassing the rocks that block us from the worst of the blustery, snow-laden air.

You are weak.

With a frown, Poppy leans against the bag strapped to her back and adds to Grim's efforts by humming. She trails her fingers gently over the bars of the cage beside her, holding the unbothered, sleeping memory bird.

The Pooka's side expands as he breathes in deep, outlining his ribs even through his wispy fur. "But if you three can't bring them back, they'll disappear forever, and all balance will be lost. It won't happen overnight, but this world will devolve into profound darkness, and evil will rise to infect future generations."

Poppy's song pauses, and a momentary silence descends over our vulnerable camp. It's just long enough that the eerie sound from a moldy green flash speeding by fills the wavering gaps between the four of us.

You have been lied to; you are going the wrong way.

I'm hoping that if I pretend that I can't hear the newcomer fluttering around and focus on the wailing song of the blizzard outside this overhang, it will leave us alone. But I know better than that. Not even a deep growl from Grim will chase these spirits away. All I can do is take off Baba Yaga's parting gift to give the sore skin covering my face a rest and distract myself. "Well, Merry Christmastide to you too, grumpy bear," I grumble, loosening the eyepatch hanging around my neck like an unfashionable necklace. It's a similar brown leather to the corset belt I'm wearing, a warm chestnut kind of shade that's been softened by the sun and its original owner. The part that goes against the eye is formed to fit like a comfortable glove, curving over the top of the cheekbone and front of the brow bone. I'm thumbing the soft material of the inside of the patch when the next spirit speaks.

You will die out here, but I can help you get home. Just crawl out of your cocoon and see what safety waits for you below over the edge of our moun—

The sudden echo of Poppy's voice bounces off the rock wall behind and above us, erasing the tail end of its dangerous offer. "Is it really Christmastide already?" she asks.

"It's either today or tomorrow." I shrug, numb toes curling in my boots, fighting the urge to follow the spirit's convincing instruction. The metal jewelry looping through my tall ears that swing against my cheek feels icy enough to burn my skin. "I lost track a while ago."

We both look at Posy for confirmation the moment I hear the heel of her boot scrape over the ground. I can see the tattered ends of the white blouse stuffed into her ears, loose threads hanging down from the rippled edges like the chains of my earrings do. But packing her ears with thin fabric does little to escape the noise. There's this faraway look in my sister's bright eyes when she moves to climb to her feet as Poppy did earlier. Grim stops her by flopping his upper body into her lap until his front paws weigh down her legs, forcing her to stay seated. She blinks at him.

With shaky windburned hands, I dig through my knapsack until I reach the bottom where I stashed away my irresponsible purchases from the villages. My cold, clumsy fingers fumble around the parcels before I give my sisters their gifts. Posy gets the hefty paper-wrapped rectangle, and Poppy gets the small cloth-wrapped oval. It's a desperate attempt to pull our focus away from the horrible whisperings. Still, I'm hopeful it will work, for a little while at least.

You are but lambs being led to the slaughter.

The helplessness and devastation I feel must be written all over my face, because Poppy embodies a mask of holiday excitement, forcing cheery bubbles to form in her tired voice. "What's this?" she gasps.

You will never find your way.

"It's Christmastide…maybe. I figured I'd get you guys something in case we fall off the side of the mountain," I sigh, glancing back with a wince at the Pooka resting on Posy. Over the week, I've been noticing something odd surrounding Grim after I managed to settle into seeing through a singular eye. Even through a snowstorm, I keep seeing brief flashes of another image when I look at him. It's like opening a book and seeing the letters on the next page beneath the one you're reading. If I focus, I see the ghost of a young man hiking beside me. It's such a short glimpse, so quick it's difficult to make out the finer details, but I see him, and I know it's Grim. Who he used to be before he became a shadowed messenger faerie.

You are already lost. Hopeless.

Feeling scraped raw from the Wyrd Mountain's spirits, I pat the Pooka's flank. My fingers sink into the misty ebony wisps curling from the tips of his fur. "I'm sorry, Grim, I didn't get you anything; I didn't like you when I bought these gifts." I catch the specter of a smooth, easy, almost human smile at this.

Despite my aversion to anything past familial physicality, I admit this transparent version of Grim is beautiful. He's someone Poppy might even call a prince, and in Sparrow's books, the tall, dark-haired, and handsome type. He's all cheekbones and strong jaw with jet furrowed brows. He might have had light-colored eyes when he was human, but it's hard to tell. Almost all the color is leeched from him though; only the barest hint of a flush sits deep, deep beneath his skin. Most of the time, Grim's ghost looks melancholic, broody even. We've grown closer this week, especially since he's joined my shadows and become an ever-present guide through my partial blindness. He and I are two sides of the same rusted coin, we're each a little roughed up in our own ways, but together we've found we're worth more than we thought. We've even discovered we have similar, albeit strange views, and that makes me feel less alone than I have in a long time. I trust Grim and rely on the bond we've created. He's been with us every day now, and I can't imagine the life I have now without him.

Move along, and I will show you to a paradise, somewhere warm and far away from here.

"No offense, my friend," I add after the evil coaxing spirit makes me realize I've been staring at the air, searching for a longer glimpse of the Pooka's ghost.

"Only some taken." A fan of lukewarm air wafts from Grim's nose as he stares at me, surprised and somewhat...fond? His solid eyes glow like two candle flames, and I'm fixated on him like a gnat. I'm desperate to hold on to his light to keep me from the tundra of plummeting darkness the spirits are trying to drag my sisters and me down into. The Pooka's head drops to his paw, still constraining my sister, keeping one yellow eye on the dozing bluebird and another on the different sweeps of color taunting us.

I prod his side with the tip of my boot. "Get us inside the mountain, and I'll gift you whatever you want." I don't know what I could buy for a ghostly creature made of smoke and shadows. Maybe some incense sticks?

If you continue to climb our mountain, you will cease to exist. Go back.

The new spirit presents me with the sad reveal of my disillusionment. Grim once said after The Numina are back, Fate will no longer require messengers, and he'll be wiped out of existence with all the other dark things that roam this earth. He's a self-proclaimed monster, and I know Death and Fate agree. After we unlock The Between, he won't survive, and I'll never be able to buy him a Christmastide gift. This fills me with a kind of bottomless grief I can't explain; it makes my throat hurt and my chest feel hollow.

Turning my head, I see a flash of the human ghost inside the Pooka. He wears an asymmetrical grin, one of sad under-standing and mournful peace, like he knows exactly what I'm thinking. And I don't think he wants to leave. Perhaps I can petition Fate to keep him around after we get them out of The Between? The Numina will owe us something, right? Plus, that would make a really great Christmastide gift.

Reverting my focus back to my sisters, I find Poppy glancing between Posy and the trace of an anemic yellow spirit whizzing toward the hail of snowfall in front of us. Her stare is pulled to the latter like a fish to live bait. "Go on ahead, open your gifts," I prompt them.

Your time is up.

Posy slowly resurfaces from the delirium the mountain throws at us in waves. At the same time, my coin-bejeweled sister's brows unravel like the threads of a worn sweater. Surprisingly, Posy moves first, tearing the butcher paper from the book I bought her, pulling me from my morose reverie. She lets out a tiny breath when she sees the teal cover and gilded gold title in a language foreign to me. Posy traces her stiff fingers from the cover to the beaten spine in awe.

"I couldn't read the cover. I think it's Latin, so I thought you might have fun translating it." My sister flips through the book while I speak. "I know Hazel's been having you transcribing some Latin scrolls and—"

Posy releases a waif of a laugh. "It's a Floriography book." Her fingertips reverently run over the yellowed pages.

This journey is a fool's errand; our mountain has nothing to offer you.

"What?" I ask her, numbly speaking over one of the many messages trying to erode our minds as I strain to read the pages she flips past. I didn't even look at the book's contents to see if there was art inside that would clue me into its subject. Instead, I was drawn to the pretty textile cover and thought Posy might like exploring whatever secrets it held.

The Numina must have a sense of humor.

Poppy has more of her wits about her when she unwraps her gift with trembling hands. The cloth falls from the necklace, and she lets out a dreamy, "Oh." It's a copper locket with a moth in flight engraved on the front. When I was pulled to the locket, it brought up one of the first good childhood memories I had after returning from the cave.

It was around the time Pop fully lapsed. Rush would come home from doing Sparrow's chores around the glade--she was still recovering, so he did what he could to help--and he'd find us dirty and hungry. Pop just sitting in his rocking chair, empty-eyed, no longer able to be a doting father. Hazel was planning to return to her home and the elder trees the day she deemed Sparrow's twig heart fully healed. So Aspen and Rush decided it'd be good for me and my sisters to spend a few nights with the Elder Mother while they tried to help Pop.

After everything that happened those weeks before, the three of us weren't happy about being separated from our family. But Hazel made it fun by introducing us to Floriography. The best part of our stay with her was the night she took us outside when her magic was at its peak. She made the trees dance for us. The branches swayed, and twisted limbs came down to brush our cheeks and play with our hair. We ran squealing into the tall grass with giggles spilling from our lips, and the moths flew. They rose from their hiding spots in the blades, rising into the air like a swirl of magic, their wings powdery and butter soft as they tickled our skin. One landed on Poppy's nose, making her go cross-eyed. We laughed and laughed. Hazel helped us heal a little bit of our childhood that night, and this locket reminded me of that moment. The softness amidst the storm.

Poppy presses the necklace to her chest as her other hand absently twists the braids almost hidden within the mass of her curls. "Thank you, Rose. I love it so much." There's a little cringe in her teeth when we meet eyes. "I'm sorry I didn't get you anything. I was planning on making you something special last month. But then Grim came to the glade, and we found the journal and Time's letter and—"

Leave this place. Jump, and I will carry you back home.

Poppy frantically clasps onto Posy, crushing her fingers into a tight grip. Then, she lays a bruising hand on my knee. Grim side-eyes us like he's considering sprawling over all three of our laps to keep us here firmly on the mountainside. I don't know how we'll last much longer out here. I'm terrified our resolve will be whittled down until we are nothing more than complacent slivers willing to do anything to escape our fear.

Clenching my teeth, I brush away my cloudy, morbid thoughts and place my chilly hand over Poppy's. "Hey, I didn't expect anything in return. I'm just glad you and Po are here with me." I let my palms rest over her ice-cold knuckles until her death grip eases. "Even though you're annoying," I add, hoping to see a little smile as she traces over the engraving. Posy is already so immersed in the book, covering one ear with her palm and the other with her scrunched-up shoulder. I don't think she even heard our exchange. Nor does she see my eye stray elsewhere to a maroon-hued spirit.

You must follow me.

Maybe I should follow this spirit and let it take me where it pleases? It might end up bringing me where I need to go, and that might be worth it, no matter how long it takes. All I have to do is get up, and it wouldn't be that hard to move, even half blind. One foot in front of the other. Maybe it's really not that bad of a spirit. Perhaps it's just misunderstood…

No. That's a horrible, hazardous, idiotic idea.

The sooner we can find the entrance to this mountain on our own, the sooner we can return home. But at this glacial pace, we'll be too late to get Aspen help.

Another stupid idea occurs to me. However, this one isn't *too* bad or dangerous.

I clear my throat. "So, before you guys say anything, hear me out."

My sisters both look up at me with glassy, narrowed eyes full of disapproval. They already know from experience that nothing good happens when I end a sentence like that.

"What would you say to letting the bluebird out of its cage and following where it goes?" I close my eye, expecting an eruption of disagreement. It's silent besides the faint whispering.

Look over the edge. You will find your answers at the bottom of our mountain.

Peeking at my sisters' faces while doing my best to ignore the spirits, I find consideration written over their pursed lips and wrinkled chins. Grim's eyes dart away, looking at anything but me when I raise a brow at him. He's nervous about something and it's not the persistent tricksters. He insists he hasn't seen the full picture, and that he doesn't know how our story ends, but now I'm positive there are things Grim's been shown that he's not saying. Or maybe he's unable to say? I stare at him, letting him feel the weight of my gaze pressing against his muzzle. His ear twitches, and when he lifts his head, I can sense that he's picked up my trail of thought.

"I saw a vision of the storm and the bird in flight, for only a few short moments. But that was it." Grim chokes out a grumbling sigh.

Nothing but mistakes lie ahead. Go back home where you belong.

"How do you know it wouldn't fly away and disappear into the snow forever?" Poppy asks after a hesitant beat, head turning away from the spirit's voice.

"We don't," I grunt as I lean over and reach a grabby hand toward the cage on the other side of Poppy. My berry-eyed sister hefts it up and over, passing it to me by the ring. We all inspect the waking creature inside. "This isn't just any bird though, it's a version of Hazel."

Poppy taps out a song on her thigh while she thinks. "Then wouldn't it leave and fly back towards home?"

"I think it'll fly towards something important, someone only it can remember." I smile weakly at the intelligent eyes now looking at me through the cold cage bars. This bird has every moment of Hazel's first life stored inside it, remembering her old family and being the best, most knowledgeable Healer. It also remembers The Numina, one of which is her husband.

"Time," Poppy supplies, her tapping speeding up.

Posy hums in quiet though distracted agreement.

Give up.

"It's worth a shot." My fingers trace the door of the cage. The spirit is wrong, we need to keep going. This bird has been trapped for so long, and because I'm no stranger to being captive, I know it wants to be free. Just as I want to be free from the things living on this ogre of a mountain. "We're not having much luck on our own," I note.

The tapping comes to a crescendo as Poppy nods. "All right, let's do it."

We prepare to brave the blizzard again, rising to our weary feet. My legs already miss that smidge of heat Grim provided. I try to keep my quivering to a minimum as I hold the birdcage aloft. The bluebird chirps and beats its wings, filling me with a different kind of warmth.

Do not do it. Turn back while you still have a chance.

I don't care what the spirits say. The memory bird is ready, and so are we. When I unlock the cage door and let it swing open, I release a long breath. The memory bird springs free from its confines for the first time in almost six hundred years. It's a beautiful picture. The creature's vibrant wings spread wide against our bleak, monotone surroundings. It's a vision of freedom. The blur of blue darting out from under the overhang and through the sky in pure glee before disappearing around the side of the mountain is breathtaking. Even more so when I realize we're meant to be chasing the bird.

"Follow it!" I drop the cage with a clatter and herd my sisters forward, shuffling into the squall as quickly as I can without risking a fatal tumble down the mountain.

Near blinded by the wind and snow, we climb, skirt around boulders, and follow icy trails, all the while dodging the licks of color that yell in our ears. A glimpse of a blue wing or orange throat in the whiteout every so often is our only guide. Grim lopes behind us without so much as a single word. It makes me worried for my traveling partner and my sisters.

After about an hour of agonizing frigid chase, with the spirits' voices growing louder, we lose the bluebird.

YOU ARE NOT WELCOME HERE.

I knew this was a risk, but after Grim mentioned Fate's brief vision, I'm still convinced that the bird is trying to find a way. It's just a little too quick for us in this heavy of a storm. Poppy, Posy, and I try to use our heightened smell to track down the herb scent attached to the memory bird, but the strong gales blowing snowflakes directly into our faces are either covering it up or carrying it away before we can catch it. Part of me hopes the tiny creature got inside the mountain, that somehow it breached The Between, and made it to Time. The other part of me is exhausted, frustrated, and near frostbitten. So, when I come to a sudden stop, Poppy bumps into my back. "Now what?" I throw my hands up as our situation weighs down on me heavier than my knapsack.

LEAVE.

The Pooka tailing us speaks up over the wind, "I'll go after it."

I spin around to peer into his sulfurous eyes; he can't meet my singular, narrowed stare. The fact that he's hiding something big is wearing on me too. "Grim, do you know where the door is?" I press.

"Not technically, no." His head hangs between his shoulders, spilling the snow that collected on his fur. "After Fate made me, I materialized my way out through the walls and into open air. I couldn't get you three in that way if I tried."

Stalking closer to him ankle deep in the actively piling snow, I poke at his wet nose with my finger. "But you'll find the bird, how it got in, and come back for us?"

Grim's edges get smokier under my scrutiny.

"Right?" I prompt again, almost yelling over the moans of the wind.

He squints in the direction we last saw the bluebird. He shakes his head, though I believe it's more at himself than at me. My shivering sisters crowd at my back. The tension and worry coming off them in waves makes my head itch.

YOU ARE BEING LIED TO.

I weakly kick the top layer of snow at his legs and shout over the spirit, "What aren't you telling me?"

The Pooka lets out a long, growling breath before facing my sisters and me. "My knowledge of your futures stops here. I know something important is about to occur, but The Numina wouldn't let me see it. They didn't want me to influence you-- because they knew my loyalties would inevitably--" Grim pauses, both his ghost and his canine form looking directly at me. "Change."

"Well, that sounds ominous." I let out a loud pained laugh as my stomach bottoms out. I can't think of anything monumental enough to prevent Grim from being privy to what's waiting for us inside the Wyrd Mountain. My mind wanders to Sparrow's stories of minotaurs and three-headed dogs, making me think something might be loose inside the mountain. Or perhaps it's the key to opening The Between? Is he not supposed to know for fear of him betraying his makers and somehow destroying their way out? Either way, this makes me nervous.

"Fine, go after the bird, but be careful, okay?" I press our guide.

A tremor ripples across my skin as Grim falls quiet, and the blizzard wails in his silence. Multiple spirits take this as their cue to speak.

TURN AROUND.

Turn around before it's too late.

You will freeze out here. Return to the comfort from which you came.

Nothing but peril lies before you.

GO AWAY.

Some of the tricksters could be right. It's frigid up here, and it will only get worse the higher we go. But worst of all, we're running out of time. Aspen is running out of time; I can feel her hanging on, and her thread is pulled taut. I'm stretched thin between her and the fraying ends of The Numina, this mountain, and its inhabitants. Both of my hands are holding on as tight as they can. But I'm afraid that at any moment, my grip on one of them will slip and tumble down past the point of no return.

When I focus again, Grim's ghost has his brows furrowed, the fronts dipping upwards in agonized concern. His expression in this form makes me think of the oracle woman who gave me the tiger's eye stone. In addition to telling me that I have a veil of shadows around me, she said Chime Children born at midnight had certain abilities––was she referring to this? To my ability to see Grim's shaded Pooka form?

TURN BACK OR FACE YOUR DEATH.

I remember reading an underlined sentence in Hazel's journal, right around the passage of Fortune's death, it was something Fate said once. *One must lose their sight to truly see.* How poetic is that? Realizing I can see literal ghosts after a witch plucks out one of my eyes? The irony isn't lost on me, but I wish I could've discovered this without the drama and pain. Though it does seem like Fate had other plans for me, including climbing around this ridiculous spirit-ridden mountain in the dead of winter. I can only hope that Grim, quickly locating the memory bird and ushering us inside, is another one of her grand schemes.

Soon, the Pooka relents and dips his thick furry head. "Just... please don't do something that I can't protect you from. I need you to be as whole as you can be before--before I go." His raised voice falters on the thought of dying for a second time, yet his distress is for me. Once he sees that I recognize this in him, he tags on warnings for my sisters. "You two as well. Keep your eyes on Primrose; you know how she is with her self-sacrificing heroics."

Before I have time to be offended by his words, or beg him not to go, he's a cloud of black peat-and-pine mist. The form of a crow bursts from the cloud. A tail of smoke trails through the snowy tempest and flies off past a peak in the mountain. Though a cry from his black beak cuts through the storm and echoes off the stones around us even though he's out of sight. And just like that, my sisters and I are alone, lost and freezing. We've been left to find our way to The Numina on a raging, wintry haunted mountain without our guide and protector.

CRACKS

*W*ith little choice, my sisters and I head in the direction the bluebird and the Pooka flew. It's mind-numbingly cold now, and the snow pelting our faces feels like tiny knives to my skin. This has me taking back everything I have ever said about not minding chilly weather. I hate it. I hate it so much. But perhaps not as much as the increasingly volatile spirits whipping past us like colorful shards of glass. The higher we climb the more they make themselves known. Even with my limited sight being worsened by the weather, I catch faint glimpses of their fiery faces and sharp teeth as they yell at us. Poppy attempts to use her goblin ancestry to disappear from the spirits sight so they won't attack her, but she doesn't consider the fact that we can't see her either. In seconds, Posy knocks into her and the petrified squeak that Poppy lets loose makes my stomach flop to my feet and my heart soar into my mouth. My displaced organs is reason enough to make me call out and force my sisters to walk where me—and the spirits —can see them. Then I say, "Did I ever tell you guys about my favorite beach?" My teeth chatter through these words as I dodge an angry orange wisp.

Poppy, who's wearing my sweater with the hood pulled tight

around her face like the visor of an armored helmet, shakes her head. Or maybe that was a full-body shiver, I can't really tell.

"It had sand so black it looked like ground-up obsidian. *Oh man*, the water," I groan at the memory of that perfect toasty ocean. "It was clear and so warm it felt like bathwater. And the seafoam, *gosh*, it looked like candy floss."

An audible grumble spills from Posy at the mention of the fluffy treat. Looking at her now, she's hunched over with only her citrine eyes showing through her snow-engulfed scarf. Her hands are tucked under her armpits, and I know she's beyond frozen. The cut on her arm from Baba Yaga's spear is bare to the volatile air because of the tear in her blouse, and the snowflakes slipping their way through it surely doesn't help.

My distracting observations are cut short when a ragged, mauve spirit flies at my face, its scream blaring to my nippy ears.

IF YOU CONTINUE ON, YOU ARE EMBRACING YOUR DOOM.

When I jolt back to avoid the trickster going up my nose, my boot finds a hidden patch of ice. Thick piles of snow and rubble skitter over the edge of the mountain first before I slide after them like an avalanche, arms pinwheeling. Panic alights in my chest, and I swear to Time my soul leaves my body when my right foot leaves the side of the Wyrd Mountain. The spirits finally got what they wanted.

Before I know it, Poppy's painfully cold hand is wrapping around mine and Posy's is fisted at the front of my shirt. My sisters pull me back to safety and drag my frame closer to the rocky wall where we can all catch our breath. The side of my neck is pulsing from the speed of my pounding heart, its rapid pace making me queasy. Posy and Poppy look as terrified as I feel. One bends to brace her hands on her knees while the other hugs the wall with her cheek pressed to the frozen stone.

Do you not want to know what it is to fly like the creature you released? Do you not want to return to your home?

That was a close one. Too close for my liking, but not for the voices stirring around us, who seem to be taking another approach to making us leave the mountain. We need to be more careful.

"I have this little jar at home full of sea glass I found at all the beaches I've visited," I project, shaky as I continue my tale in hopes of dispelling the fright when we resume our climb. My feet are much more tentative now that I'm without my other seeing half. The snow is piling up to our shins in some spots now, and it's only going to get worse if we don't escape these worsening conditions soon. "The salt from the sea tumbles these weathered chips of forgotten glass, making them all frosty with smooth, rounded edges. I've hunted down a lot of pieces from bottles and broken ceramics, but the rarer fragments are from old shipwrecks."

I can help you begin anew and change your shape like tumbling rocks down our frosty mountain.

Like a snowdrop, I feel myself folding inward, pulling the long sleeve I had on under my sweater over my shaky hands. All I can do is ignore the chartreuse spirit's creative threat and ball the material into my fists, sealing off any air that could come in to freeze my arms. "Most of the ones I've found are various shades of green, some white, browns, and the occasional blue. Purple and red are hard to find, but I have a couple in my jar."

Prattling on with increasing volume, I try to comfort and warm us all with my words. The stone wall to our left feels jagged under my hand, but we continue on now, cautiously climbing up and over the sizable boulder blocking our path through the side of the mountain. I concentrate on what I can see out of my right eye to avoid a repeat of my almost trickster-induced plunge while we trudge forward with little direction.

"There was this lady living in that town on the beach who

combed the sand like I did. But she turns her finds into pieces of jewelry and things like wind chimes or ornamented dream catchers." My trailing fingers dip into a tiny crack that runs along the wall, making me pause my story. I turn my head until I can narrow my eyes and use my lashes for cover to see where it's crumbling in some places, splitting like a fragile eggshell. It appears to have been damaged by an earthquake or something else cataclysmic, maybe something Numina related?

It must be dreams you seek, not our mountain. Make your plunge, and I can show you visions of sand and sun as you fall.

A flare of lilac slices through the couple inches of space between my sisters' shoulders. And when my boot rolls over an unseen rock beneath the snow again, I turn my attention back to the blustering hike ahead and my tale of safer times. "It was neat to see broken things thrown out by people get recycled by the sea. The glass comes out beautiful and new, then gets turned into breathtaking art. Kind of made me feel like I could do the same thing if I took a dip in the water. Just let all the bad memories wash off and come back out with my sharp edges filed down. I never tried it, though," I admit, my words fading into the howling wind. The tips of my fingers feel sore from sliding them over the broken wall. If I drag them harder over the rock to keep myself from acknowledging the multicolored flames begging for our attention, my sisters don't say a single thing about it. Poppy takes to tugging on her damp braids—perhaps more firmly than needed—to noisily jingle the charms adorning her hair and deflect her attention. Posy has removed the fabric from her ears and replaced them with her fingers. Any other time I'd probably be concerned about how deep she tries to push them into her canals.

Clouds of frost come from Poppy's tremoring mouth when she shouts, "I'd li-like to do that someday, ma-make my own j-jar."

You can. Turn back, and you can escape the horrors of this mountain and throw yourselves into the se—

"Did you know sea glass is thought to be mermaid tears?" Posy's small, shaken voice erupts, muffled by her thick scarf and the gust that burns my eye sockets, both good and bad.

A noise of surprise slips from my chest as I secure my patch over the hole on the left side of my face. I'm honestly shocked she can hear me considering how desperately she's attempting to touch her fingertips to her own brain. "I saw a bottle of sea glass labeled with that in Baba Yaga's house. The owner of the shop on the beach mentioned a story that said each chip is a tear shed for a drowned sailor," I add, peering past the storm and the spirits that batter our faces with cold weather and lies. They'll keep trying to force us off the edge if we don't find a way to slip into the mountain soon. And I realize now that the higher we climb, dragging our sore bodies through the snow, we won't magically find some sort of gilded door. Even Grim said he merged through the solid stone walls in his smoky form when he was sent out to deliver us The Numina's prophecy. Distracted by these thoughts, I continue, "I heard from another person in town that mermaids were said to be guides for ships. And sometimes, they fall in love with sailors or even the ship's captain, which is forbidden. Those mermaids were banished to the bottom of the sea to forever cry for their lost love," I muse, my throat growing hoarse trying to speak loud enough for my sisters. It hurts almost as much as the jagged ice that sprouts from the cracked mountainside and bites into my fingertips. "Sea glass washes up as tokens for their lovers to keep and—"

A harsh sting on the pad of my index finger makes me stop in my tracks, surprised. A fat drop of blood stains the whorls of my green fingerprints a deep ruby red. Looking for the culprit of the tiny nick, I see the icicles growing like a geode between the splits in the mountainside where the precipitation snuck into the crevices and bloomed into razor spikes.

Popping my finger into my mouth, I glare at the frozen little daggers. The way they glint at me in almost icy defiance makes them look like cold crystal guards. They're even all lined up in a neat row like soldiers meant to keep something or someone out...

"Rose?" Poppy's footslogging pauses as she turns to make sure I didn't actually fall off the mountain this time.

A cloud of white rolls from my mouth when I murmur, "The cracks." My blood-tipped finger follows the rough edges cutting into the mountain. A cracked egg splits because it's been broken, and broken means the egg has been opened. "The cracks!" I jab my finger at the wall, excitement slipping into my shout.

TURN AROUND.

My sisters look to where I point, their faces a mask of squinty, furrowed confusion as they wipe at the snow flying at their faces. But I don't wait for them to understand what my crazed exclamation means. I just trudge past them, listening to the crunch of the piling snow beneath my boots with a smile on my face. I don't even care when I trip twice in my haste; all that matters is my sisters follow.

GO THIS WAY.

Dodging an oncoming spirit that reminds me of the color of Baba Yaga's foxgloves, I press on with my palms dragging against the wall. The cracks are widening, and the spirits are getting louder, more urgent. They don't want us here for a reason.

DO NOT FALL PREY.
IT IS NOT TOO LATE TO JUMP.
STOP!
YOU WILL BE YOUR OWN UNMAKING!

It's a fight to keep going. To fight against the spirits hurling their lies and transparent bodies at us, to push against the wind that makes tears and snot stream from our faces. The snow is on its way to knee-height, and taking each step is harder and harder.

YOU HAVE FAILED!
THIS IS NOT THE WAY!
TURN AROUND NOW!

But eventually, after desperate persistence and what feels like ages, we come to the craggiest part of the mountain we've seen yet. And when my sisters and I see the giant crack running through the face of the mountain, gasping for air so cold it makes my insides sting…the spirits fall quiet. They've lost. We found the gash bisecting the stone, and it fades into a dark, tall hole. A way into the Wyrd Mountain.

The broken opening is tight, but I think we can squeeze through if we turn sideways. I test this by almost crawling to the entrance in exhaustion, where I first push away layers of snow and flimsy ice blocking my foot space. Then, I stick my head inside, and all I see is darkness. "I think this is it." My statement echoes, multiplying as it ricochets off the stone. The hole sounds hollow as my voice travels farther into the space before I can barely hear it fading out. "I can't see anything, but it seems like a tunnel."

Pulling my head back, I see Poppy bouncing on her toes with a delighted grin, even with the blizzard beating at her back. Posy, on the other hand, is now a different story. I have never seen her turn such a pale green, not even when she had the flu a few years ago and couldn't keep anything down for a week. She's almost the same color as the whiteout surrounding us while she whittles her fingernails down to bloody nubs.

"Everything all right there, Po?" I tighten the straps of my knapsack, bringing it closer to my body. I'll need all the room I can get when I shimmy my way through that hole.

Posy's eyes are wide as she continues to pull what's left of her thumbnail from her raw skin, making her words come out garbled. "Maybe the spirits are right," she says.

"This is it, Po. It's dark down there, but I think this is the only way." Since she makes no effort to move, I reach out and tighten the straps under her arms too. "No biggie," I shout over the storm with a shrug and an easy smile, trying hard to calm her.

I can only read her lips as she whispers, "That's fine." She shifts her feet, making a well around her legs where the snow has started to bury her.

On the outside, Poppy is vibrating with excitement, ready to leave this blizzard behind and dive through that crack to get into the Wyrd Mountain. Although, I do see her rubbing her thumb over the locket in her fist, the chain dangling between her fingers as she hums. She's nervous too. But I don't think it's the same nerves our quiet triplet is experiencing. Posy is crippled with fear.

Wasting no time, Poppy is first to turn sideways and squeeze into the hole. She keeps her head turned to the left facing the tunnel to fit. I step up next, ready to push my body through, but Posy is still standing frozen in the snowstorm, so I stop. I've never known my sister to be afraid of the dark. What is this about?

"I can't," she wheezes. "I can't go in."

"Of course you can. Come on." I tug at the straps of her bag again, trying to pull her closer to the wall. But Posy digs her heels in.

"No. It's too small in there," she stammers, staring blankly at the crack. "I'll—I'll get stuck, and then we'll be trapped, and I'll run out of air and—"

Putting my hands on my sister's shoulders, I bend my knees to catch her lowered eyes. "Hey, slow down. You'll exceed your daily thousand-word limit." I laugh loudly in an effort to ease her as fragmented memories surface.

Posy finally looks at me, petrified eyes wide. The wind

delivers her gut-wrenching whisper to me. "You don't understand."

My heart squeezes. "I do, Posy. I get it now," I shout. "All the times you sat in a seat where your back was to the door, you never had a solid wall behind you. You even made Poppy sleep against the wall when we stayed in the tavern." It feels like a palm to the face realizing for the first time after the cage that Posy is claustrophobic. "I didn't recognize it because you dole out hugs and kisses freely with no qualms about personal space. But I get it now."

Gently, I take her hand and urge her towards me, sticking one foot through the crack. Unlike Poppy, I keep my head turned toward my sister instead of the tunnel. "I'm right here," I assure her. "I'm sure the walls open up further in, so we just have to get through this first part." Posy meets my eye. "I won't let go, I promise."

Shimmying my body farther into the opening, I understand how Posy might feel the mountain walls are pressing in on us. It's a tight fit, not painful by any means, but it does take some maneuvering. Posy's steps grow hesitant the closer she gets to the hole, so I encourage her with a smile and a nod. Her palm is clammy now, and her breath ragged, especially when she turns her body to make her first slide sideways. Tears pool in her reflective eyes. I squeeze her hand before tugging her out of the cold winter elements and toward Poppy's echoing hums.

"Go through your catalogs and make me a mental bouquet. Fill it with flowers made for forgetting." I distract my sister as we scoot farther into the pitch black, our feet scuffling over small rocks while our locked fingers graze the cracked walls. The pace I set helps us catch up to Poppy. The slow, melodic song coming from her on one side, mixed with the whispers beneath Posy's breath on the other, is like my own personal symphony.

"Rosemary and forget-me-nots, rue and anemone,

columbine and marigold." Posy puts together bundles meaning remembrance and regret, forsaken love, foolishness, and grief. A very fitting bouquet for things forgotten.

I squeeze her frosty hand again. "Don't forget the garland. You can't have a bouquet without greenery."

"If I had my own shop, I would call that arrangement The Ballad of Hazel and Icarus," Poppy remarks, the sound of her humming still reverberating down the tunnel.

"Now that is dreadfully sad," I snort, shivering from the snow that's soaked my clothes. "You'd better throw in lilac for first love and maybe orange blossom to make it of the eternal variety. They'll be reunited once we free The Numina, and Hazel will get her memories back."

"In that case, adding a few roses and camellia for longing wouldn't hurt," Poppy says. Her ornamented hair chimes when she seemingly stumbles out from the crack.

Posy gasps in relief when we pop free after our sister, but our threaded fingers don't loosen. For her sake, I keep the comforting hold as I feel my way around, fully blind and single-handed. It seems we're in a tunnel just a hair wider than my long arm span.

There's a metallic clink followed by Poppy letting out a sudden whine. "Oh, crumb!"

"What's wrong?" I ask her, patting around and using the toes of my boots to feel the walls for any other openings.

Misery drips from my sister's voice. "I dropped my locket. I heard it skitter forward, so I think I might have kicked it."

Her words make me grumble, "This is why we can't have anything nice." Now, instead of a way through this tunnel, I pull Posy into a crouch with our conjoined hands to scour the pebble-strewn floor for the necklace. "Why didn't you just put it around your neck where it's supposed to go?"

"Don't judge me," Poppy sulks with a pitiful tone.

"Chances of finding it in here are slim." Despite my words, I still hunch down with Posy firmly glued to my hand. We fumble our way around in a blind crouch like crabs as we hunt for the stupid moth locket. I'll never hear the end of it from Poppy if I don't try.

Minutes go by with the three of us abrading our hands on the sharp pebbles and unforgiving stone floor. But just when I'm about to call it quits and label the stupid necklace as a lost cause, the sound of scraping metal bounds off our rocky confines.

"Hey! I think I found it," Poppy exclaims from what sounds like multiple feet away from Posy and me.

A loud snap splits the tunnel in half.

Then, there's a splintering sound, and a faint light pours in through the fissures. I can see my sisters now, just as I can see the fissures expanding and running through the ground like ice, spidering out from under Poppy's feet and back toward Posy and me. More illuminated cracks consume the walls as the ground starts to shift beneath our boots. None of us have time to scream before a deep thunderous rumble comes from below, and the floor falls out from beneath us.

INSIDE THE WYRD MOUNTAIN

*T*he wind is knocked out of me when I land on slick stone. The edges of the wood box with the changeling heart cuts into my back with the impact. I can't catch my breath, and there's a constant flow of water rushing around me as I slide ever downward. Once my brain has time to get past the shock, I gasp for air around another passing wave of water. We've fallen into some sort of underground passage made of florescent, glittering stone, and it's propelling us through the mountain like a chute. Surprisingly, the glowing stone and water is warm instead of arctic. Poppy and Posy are shrieking at the top of their lungs, screaming for this harrowing ride to stop.

"Hang on," I yell, throwing my arms out to the sides, trying to stop myself by catching the gilt walls. I'm only rewarded with scraped palms. And from the little momentum I lost, Posy catches up to me, crashing into my back before her legs slot around me. Poppy is way ahead of us, learning the same lesson I just did as she claws at the slippery walls.

We're tossed and turned, flipped this way and that, even thrown against the bright stone when we career around sharp bends. And I've almost swallowed a gallon of this ancient flume water now. This incremental drowning feels a lot like my experience with the River Man. Of course, the mat of soaked hair creating a net over my face doesn't help with the panic either.

Peering through wet curls, I see a harsh corner coming, and Poppy gets flipped onto her stomach facing me. When Posy and I hit it too, my body is thrown sideways, and my head hits the low earthen ceiling. Judging by the sound that gets knocked from Posy, I know she didn't fare much better.

The eyepatch has fallen from my left eye and hangs around my neck, knotted in my hair as water slips through my bruised eyelid and into the empty cavity behind. It's painful, to say the least. But the worst feeling is seeing the sheer terror in Poppy's eyes now that she faces me. All I see is the water bashing her in the face as she coughs, her nails trying to dig into the bottom of the chute as her face pleads for help.

Soon, a speck of growing, blue-tinged light appears behind her, widening as we lunge closer. This slide is coming to an end, and the chute looks like it opens into the inside of the Wyrd Mountain. The roaring of what sounds like a waterfall makes my stomach lurch. How far will we drop?

I reach out a futile hand. "Poppy!"

It's too late. The only thing left for me to do is clamp on to Posy's ankle as our sister goes spilling out of the opening. We join Poppy moments later for the near fifty-foot fall past a giant statue stepping out of the waterfall. The empty stone eyes of a woman I saw in Hazel's journal, sketched with her husband's red ink and labeled *"The Last Time Before Me,"* watch us plummet.

The banshee-like screams that rip from our throats are the thing of nightmares. Except what haunts me most, is making eye contact with Poppy. It's slow motion. I hear the twinkle of trinkets braided into her hair and see the tears slipping down her emerald cheeks. Her arms and legs pinwheel through the air as she bypasses the alabaster statue, heading toward the shallow, slow-moving river below.

Somewhere along the fall, I lose hold of Posy's leg, but I see her now. We hurtle together toward the outstretched hand of the old statue of Lady Time. And as I clip the edge of the carved hourglass she's holding, I catch a glimpse of Posy hitting it dead on. Her spine folds back over the top lip of the hourglass with a sickening crack before her limp body flips head over heels and we freefall the remaining twenty feet.

I don't remember hitting the ground.

All I know is *pain*.

My ribs burn when I manage a tiny gasp. For reasons unknown, I can't fill my lungs without a blinding, white-hot stabbing in my chest. I sound like a gasping fish, and black dots dance along the vision of my remaining eye. Peering up at the golden rock ceiling hundreds of feet above me, I see a massive tree whose roots have spread down inside the mountain and opened it to the outside world. It looks primordial with how big it is. Over time the limbs widened the cracks in the stone where the falls splash into the narrow river, causing chunks of florescent rock to fall. This must've weakened the structure of the mountain, which is why the floor collapsed beneath us, and dumped us into the channel that crests with the waterfall and the colossal statue.

Lady Time is beautiful; I can admit that even in breathtaking pain. She looks like she's emerging from the water with an hourglass, now splashed with blood, held aloft in her left hand. Her right holds the end of her dress while one sandal-clad foot steps forward. Her soft marble features are like nothing I've ever seen, bone structure lost in long bloodlines never to be seen again. Forgotten, one might say.

I can't tell how long it takes me to remember the quest we're on. Or to notice that I'm partially submerged in the strangely warm river, enough that my ears are underwater and I can't hear anything but my own heartbeat. It's lulled me into this hazy-minded space where one second, I feel like I'm being tortured, and the next, nothing at all. When I can finally pull in normal-sized breaths, I drag myself to a sitting position while holding a hand pressed to what seems like broken ribs. Sound surges back to me after the water has dripped out of my ears, and the first thing I hear is my name.

"Rose?"

Blinking away any lingering disorientation, I search the shallow water brightened by the smooth gilded stones lining the bottom.

"Poppy?" Posy sobs.

My sister is mere feet away, lying still in the water as she cries. Soggy pages from the book I gave her drift along the top of the water, surrounding her like a sea of pulpy words. From here, I can't tell what's wrong with Posy. Shifting onto my knees with a moan, I discard my crushed knapsack and its contents before I try crawling to her. My palms are torn raw, and one elbow is scraped down to Purgatory. I think a knot is blooming on my head above the blood trail leaking down the side of my face. That goes without mentioning that it feels like the whole backside of my body has been beaten black and blue.

My fuzzy senses begin to clear. Where is Poppy?

At first, I don't see her with my limited sight, but after my second scan, I find her. Scrambling to my feet, I push past the pain, stumbling and falling, clutching at my side as I attempt to run to her.

"Poppy!" I stand over her, looking into her eyes.

"Poppy, look at me."

She doesn't even blink.

"*Poppy?*"

She stares at the ceiling.

I sink to my knees in the water. All I can do is let my hands hover above my sister. I don't know how to fix her. Her chest is still, and her neck...her neck doesn't look right.

She's gone, and I don't know what to do.

Hearing Posy howl shatters my soul like a dinner plate falling from a broken shelf. "Rose, Poppy, please! Somebody," she weeps. "*Please* be alive."

Hesitating for a moment longer, I stare at my triplet, dead in the water. Poppy's usually bright gaze is vacant. Her skin is a sick shade of death green, and her long hair is a cloud of black, splayed out in the water around her. She's the quietest I've heard her in ten years, too quiet. We'll never hear her annoying humming or constant talking again, no more bouncing legs that shake the table, no more incessant finger tapping to drive me nuts.

A glint of copper catches my eye.

The chain of the necklace I gave Poppy waves at me from under the shining water, the locket still clasped tight in her fist. She found it in the tunnel after all, and by some miracle, she didn't let it go once she got it back. Even when she fell into the chute and to her death.

With my stomach in my throat, I pry her stiffening fingers open and grab the locket, placing it around her neck where it was meant to be. The moth sits over her still heart.

A numbness starts to spread from the Poppy-shaped hole in my chest as I climb back to my feet and hunker my way over to Posy's side. She still needs me. I can still help her. And when she sees me standing above her, she cries harder. But she doesn't try to sit up from where she lies in the river. Something must be broken, maybe a leg?

"Rose, I thought you were dead. No one was answering me, and I've been lying here for *so long*." Her face screws up, though not in pain, but in complete and utter fear. "You have to help me, Rose; I can't get up. I don't want to be in the water anymore. Please—"

I hush her by putting a hand under her head and lifting it from the river, water pouring from her ears. She's so scared, more afraid than when we were kids and cold iron talons cut her cheek. I haven't heard her babble on like this, *ever*. I've never heard her speak this many consecutive sentences unless she's talking about her studies. She's always been the opposite of Poppy after our capture, sometimes frustrating with her silence. Now it seems she's making up for all the words Poppy can no longer say.

"What hurts?" My voice cracks as I blink away tears.

Posy stares up at me, her eyes shifting between my empty socket and my silver eye. "I—I don't—" She shakes her head. "Nothing."

Frowning, I look beneath the clear glittering water at her prone body. I don't see anything that looks apparent in its brokenness. The knees of her trousers are ripped, and the wound on her arm from Baba Yaga has reopened. Blood leaks from many little cuts, garnet trails floating away down the slow stream. Other than a missing button on her vest and the fact that her spectacles are nowhere to be seen, she looks relatively unharmed.

"What do you mean nothing? I can see you bleeding," I say, voice nearing despondent and devoid of emotion from grief and harmful events.

New tears well up in Posy's eyes. "Rose, I can't feel anything. I can't *move.*"

It's as if I'm falling all over again. The numbness has surpassed my chest, and my ribs are just cold now. My head is buzzing when I let it fall against my sister's to hook my arm under her armpits, and pull her closer to me as she cries. "It's okay. Everything is going to be okay." My lies come out as a faint murmur.

"Where's Poppy?" she whimpers.

My forehead rocks over hers as I shake my head. I can't

bring myself to tell Posy that she's gone; I don't want to say those words out loud. I think it might kill me if I do.

"Where is she?" Posy bawls.

My unspoken answer is enough for her to understand.

"No. *No*," she yells. "*Poppy!*"

Posy continues to call out for our sister, refusing to believe she's dead. She can't turn her head to search for her to see if I'm lying. I'm not. Poppy is dead, and Posy is paralyzed.

"I'm sorry, Po. I'm so, so, so sorry." I repeatedly apologize, whispering empty words as I hold my only sister close. That's when the dam inside me breaks loose for the first time in so many years, when everything I've tried to push down rushes out. I cry until I feel sick. There's nothing I can do to fix my sister, and if I could trade my injuries for hers, I would in a heartbeat. But it's impossible.

I don't know what to do now. We're inside the Wyrd Mountain like The Numina wanted, but we are not whole. The *three* of us were supposed to bring them back into this world, yet one of my sisters has perished. They had to have known; The Numina can see the future. With no Fortune, we don't know more than one path in life, which means Fate designed this to happen. She pulled our threads like puppets until we landed in this very moment.

This is senseless.

How are we meant to retrieve them from The Between now? The Numina let their last chance at being free and restoring this world die. And where is Grim? He was supposed to protect us and be our guide. Fate has him on some kind of a leash though––is that why he acted the way he did, abandoning us in the snow, because he was told to? He knew something was going to happen, but he wasn't allowed to know what. If he had, he would've prevented us from going into that tunnel in the first place. I'm sure of it. He wouldn't have let my sisters meet this end. He wouldn't have let *me* get hurt, not with the bond of vulnerability we've forged. Over the last month, we've come to understand and trust each other. And though I called him my friend for the first time today, he knows my past and my mind in a way that exceeds a normal friendship.

Which means this is some kind of cruel joke his captor is playing on us all. Fate must be corrupt, but it makes no sense as to why she would let darkness reign.

Without the other Numina, the world will fall out of balance, running rampant with bogeymen and ruled by witches. The art of Healing will forever vanish, and no good will be left on this earth. Which means no more Aspen. And at some point, Posy and I will die inside this mountain. If Rush, our travel-savvy half-brother, were to ever make the trek to come find us, he'll never be able to get inside the mountain. The tunnel that we entered is nothing but shambles now. Even if Rush has some mysterious magic I don't know about, and he does breech the mountain's walls, we'll be gone by then. Any food we had left in our bags was squandered or swept away by the river. All Posy and I have now is a splintered box with broken elder twigs and the stupid stone the oracle gave me in my pocket.

We've failed...or perhaps, The Numina failed us.

The Moor, the Moon, and the Sun

"*R*ose," Posy whispers, "I don't want to be in the water anymore."

Hearing my sister repeat this shatters me in a whole new way. She sounds so defeated, so *broken*. I'm almost afraid to move her, not knowing what's damaged. It could be anywhere along the vertebrae of her spine, or the cord connecting them all. I'm afraid that moving her will kill her. But we can't stay in the river forever, so I'll just have to be gentle.

"Yeah, okay." I don't recognize my softened voice when it slips out; I feel disconnected from my body. Even pulling Posy out of the water by her underarms is like being in a dream. I've disassociated from my pain so much that I don't register being on dry land until I've taken the bag off her back and sit with her head in my lap.

Tears trail from her eyes, sliding sideways over her cheeks and pooling in the ripples of her long ears. Loose wet curls are pasted to the sides of her face and forehead. I find myself smoothing them back, raking the strands into her sopping ponytail with my stubby nails. Studying the darker green freckles over the bridge of her nose, I trace my eye over the round tip. When she closes her eyes, it's like looking at Poppy.

She has the same dip in her chin under her bottom lip and the swooping corners, the same almond-shaped eyes, and full ebony brows. We both do. I'll never be able to stomach looking at a reflective surface again.

Painfully, I realize I need to talk, to open the parts of myself that I've closed off to everyone around me. To be vulnerable. Because it seems I might not have a lot of time left to express this, to say the things that need to be said. There is so much more to life than cramming everything down and convincing myself that I'm fine. I'm more than the "strong," sarcastic sister that everything bounces off of. I'm more fragile than I admit. I care so deeply about my family, and though I'm late, it's time to show it. Show Posy who I truly am beneath the layers of hurt, stress, and fear.

"Can I tell you a secret?" I carry on without waiting for an answer as Posy peels her watery citrine eyes open to peer up at me. "I did something on my trip to the east that I never told anyone. I thought you and Poppy would've snitched or made fun of me. Or maybe both. So I never said a word..." I wipe my face on my damp shoulder to soak up some of my tears.

"I came across this ancient village where people were still living the way their ancestors did. Their huts were made of more natural foraged materials like mud and clay with grass thatched roofs instead of the smooth planks of wood and manufactured brick we use." Pausing, I take in a deep, shuddering breath. "Anyway, the village welcomed me, and I learned things like making terracotta bowls that got hardened by the sun, and stripping sugar cane stocks. We would all sit around the fire at night and chew the sugar cane like it was dessert while they taught me about their heritage." Posy's gaze looks between my silver eye and socket, trying to gauge where this story is going. "Almost everyone but the children were covered in rich, colorful tattoos. If I remember correctly, they made their black ink from burned pine soot and the blue from a certain kind of leaf."

Posy's eyes close when I smooth her hair again. Neither of us have run out of tears yet.

"Well, one night, they invited me to see how the tattooing was done. The newly appointed chieftain was getting a tattoo over his heart. It was a painful process for him, but it was so mesmerizing. They used a large needle made of bone and they dipped it in ink and stabbed it in and out of the skin to make the design." Clearing my throat past a wad of emotion, I continue. "Hours later, when it was done, they would rub more ink into all the tiny open wounds to ensure the image stayed. It was such an amazing thing to witness that when they offered to put a new needle to my skin, I couldn't refuse."

My sister snaps her eyes open at this.

"I never believed in the red thread of Fate that Rush and Sparrow always told us about as kids. I didn't care to learn about it and rolled my eyes at their silly bedtime stories about the string around their pinkies. You know this. But I'll never forget the three of us lying in that tiny bed smooshed together when they tried to lull us to sleep with their own fairytale. Some nights, after the two of you fell asleep, I thought about the dumb *romantic* string for hours. I hoped that if it was real, that it was more than Rush and Sparrow's kind of love, and a thread of our own made of sisterly love would tie us together." Posy's forehead wrinkles as she chokes back a sob at the reminder of Poppy, but I forge on. "And when we were younger, before the cage, Pop always used to say we were attached at the hip. So I did something I was too prideful to admit, especially since I made such a big fuss about not believing it. I got a long line made with ink of red ochre trailing down my hip and thigh." I shrug to myself. "I knew no one would ever see it; it was just for me. A way to keep you and Poppy with me on all my travels."

Damp eyes stare up at me in surprise, a dam of water on her

lash line waiting to break. A moment of silence lapses before she speaks in her familiar soft tone. "Rush is going to kill you when he finds out."

A wet, painful laugh chokes its way out of my chest and sends my damaged bones aflame. Of course that's what Posy would say. A sad smile finds my lips knowing she's right, my half-brother would have a lot to say about me having a tattoo. I would never hear the end of it from him. Sparrow would secretly like it while acting like she's supporting her husband. Aspen would probably sigh, pat my leg, and say, "Whatever makes you happy." If I caught Hazel in the morning, she'd fawn over it and want a tattoo of her own. But the nighttime Elder Mother would roll her eyes and talk about the consequences of permanency.

My family will never find out though, not unless our bodies are recovered from the Wyrd Mountain somehow. Even then, we would most likely be long decomposed. From knowledge I've gained on my travels, I know that without food, Posy and I will only make it three to five days. A week at most. It's been six hundred plus years since someone has lived here; I doubt there's food in this mountain. Of course, that is if The Numina even ate food. And let's not forget, it almost took us a month to make it to the mountain. If someone got inside and found us, we'd be skeletons by then because of the damp conditions. I also don't see Grim coming to our rescue anytime soon, not with Fate's evil hold on him.

So essentially, we're skunked.

Posy and I will be stuck here with Poppy's body until we too succumb to The Between and go to meet Death and Fate ourselves. I can't wait to punch the weaver in the eye.

With a long-suffering sigh, I throw my head back and breathe through my nose, trying to calm my rising fury. When I look back down, something dark catches in the periphery of my good eye. My head whips to the side so fast I feel a little crick and twinge in my neck. What I see isn't my usual shadow friends, instead it's the unlit, yawning entry of what looks like a tucked-away hall.

"Son of a Trow! You've got to be kidding me," I mutter, annoyed beyond belief at the sight of another blackened tunnel. I can only imagine whose death this one would lead us to.

"What?" Posy's paralysis allows her head to twitch the barest amount. "What is it?"

Because of her spinal injury, she can't turn her head, but part of me is glad for that. I don't want her to see Poppy lying broken in the water.

I glare at the hall across the way, my stomach bubbling with acidic anger. "It's another tunnel," I spit.

The upside-down look Posy gives me communicates, "*Well, where does it go, you muttonhead?*" She doesn't even have to say it out loud for me to know she wants more information.

"It's just a tall, shadowed, structured opening. It's not natural, it's carved into a perfect arch and trimmed in filigree etchings," I huff, wiping my snot and tears with a moist sleeve. Surveying the rest of our surroundings, I find that the only other opening in this large portion of the mountain is an arch connected to a platform about a hundred feet up, to which there are no stairs. I'm sure the river would lead us somewhere, but I refuse to go back in that water. Posy and I would have to go through the hall across from us to access more of The Numina's home.

However, walking blindly into a tunnel is what got us in this predicament in the first place. That dark hole led us into this mess of misfortune. Maybe The Numina should stay forgotten at this point, because apparently, all they do is cause insurmountable pain.

"We should go through it," Posy whispers.

I'm pretty sure I get whiplash this time when I meet my sister's bloodshot gaze. I scoff. "First of all, no. Second of all, also no. Did you forget what the last one led us into--what happened to Poppy, to you--"

Fresh tears sluice down her face. "No, Rose, I didn't forget. But this isn't over, it *can't* be."

"Posy, The Numina wanted Poppy to die, they knew this would all happen! And for what? They took your own body from you, and now you want to see what's on the other side of that tunnel?" Wrath heats my skin, and the pain in my ribs returns with a stabbing vengeance. The Numina played us all like pawns, dooming us to lives of horrific predestination. It wasn't supposed to end this way in my book.

"Please," my sister whimpers. "Don't make this all worthless. Maybe the entry to The Between is in there, and Death can bring Poppy back like she did Sparrow once we get The Numina out."

I hate to let any little bit of hope in, but she's right--there's a chance...

Letting out an exhale that makes my side burn, I shift Posy's head. "Fine, I'll run ahead and check it out. Once I come back--"

"*No!*"

I almost let her head thud to the ground in shock at the force of my sister's exclamation.

"No, take me with you." Posy's eyes are wide, her lip trembling. "I want to go."

My body sags with sorrow, which makes me hold on to my ribs for support when they flare again at the movement. It would be a new shade of agony to try to hoist her limp body up. "Po, I don't think I can carry you."

Her eyes are pleading, a torrent of saltwater pouring out. "Drag me if you have to."

It's not hard to understand why she wouldn't want to stay behind. Not only would she risk me getting lost, trapped, or worse, but she would be left alone with the body of our triplet lying in the river. She'd have nothing but the sounds of the waterfall that killed her to listen to. I don't know why I suggested she stay in the first place; her body losing feeling is trauma enough. This all leads me to wonder how much more Posy and I can survive before we fall apart like Pop.

While I figure out how to maneuver around my ribs to carry Posy, I think about the many storybooks Sparrow has on her shelves at home. Once we were old enough to read her gilded books, she let us use her collection as a library. I'd noticed a lot of her stories revolved around characters who had to save their whole kingdom or the entire world from an evil entity. Sometimes it was simpler, like saving a princess or two, but they all ended with said character becoming a hero. But even then, being a hero wasn't appealing; they almost always had to make tough sacrifices. They all lost something or someone to gain the title, and it never seemed fair to me.

It's less than fair now as I hunch over lopsided and grit my teeth, hauling my limp, damaged sister toward the dark hall.

If Fate is less twisted than I believe, then maybe she's trying to use our pain to make us into heroes? Poppy is already a martyr, she sacrificed the most. Posy is still alive, but she's an entirely broken hero. And what am I? Are The Numina trying to make me into the world's most begrudging hero by taking one of my sisters from me and hurting the other? This is not the story I want, and I'm going to find these beings and make them change it. And if they don't want to do the right thing and restore my sisters, then I'll show them how they turned their would-be hero into a villain. I'll find a way to wreak so much havoc they'll wish they never wrote me into their story. The red threads of Fate that pulled us here will drip with blood when I find a way to seal them in The Between forever.

The grunts and groans I make while having these thoughts aren't pretty. I haven't even made it to the entry of the hall, and I'm already covered in sweat. My teeth are about to crack in half from gritting them so hard. Once we're back far enough and the river is in full view, I prompt Posy to shut her eyes. She obeys. The way I'm pulling her, her top half almost sitting up with her heels and lower boot-covered legs dragging on the ground, she'd get an eyeful of our sister's body. I don't want her to have nightmares like me.

When we make it into the entrance, I take in as deep of a breath as my ribs will allow and toddle backward. About halfway through I stumble on a rock and lose my firm grasp on my sister. Her butt hits the ground with a thud. "Son of a witch, I'm sorry, Po."

"It's okay," Posy laughs through her tears. "I couldn't feel it anyway."

With a wince, I continue our awkward, painful journey through the dark. My breaths come out rough and sharp through my teeth. I'd yell if I knew it wouldn't make Posy feel bad. But contrary to the thoughts she likely is spinning about her head, she's not a burden to me. If we could get out of the mountain, I would drag her the whole way home, broken ribs and all. Though The Numina *will* fix this before that ever happens.

Soon, the hall becomes lighter and lighter with each grueling step and before I know it, it spits us out into a part of the mountain that's open to the sky. It's like a hidden grotto captured within a peaceful moment of time that occurred many centuries ago. No snow falls here, and even with the blustery weather outside the mountain, it's not cold either. Instead, it feels like we're in a bubble of perpetual spring. The lingering moisture in my clothes feels warm against my skin, and all the mature trees around us bloom with pink blossoms. It smells like the garden in the glade during spring, where fat honey-drunk bees laze in the berries and blossoms.

I see a temple when I look over my shoulder. The open circular structure has cracked stone stairs leading up through vine-snaked pillars that are topped with a stone ring to crown the dais.

Shifting Posy to sit on the ground and face the temple, I crouch beside her and support her back. "Open your eyes," I whisper.

Her tears turn into those of hope when she sees the view.

"The steps are too steep to drag you up." I grimace. "I'm going to have to carry you."

Posy looks at me with doubt. I'd respond with a funny, sarcastic quip if this were under better circumstances. I grew up slinging large wheat sheaves in the barn and working and paying for my travels with hard labor. I'm not exactly weak. If I can lift my own body weight, I can lift my identical triplet.

Taking a long, pinching breath in and out, I lift my sister like a princess. And I curse like a sailor as rotten Purgatory burns its way up my side. I feel each of my ribs screaming bloody murder. Every stone step I climb earns a name colorful enough to make a hag blush. By the time I reach the top, I'm gasping for breath and shaking. My legs buckle in the middle of the dais, and before I can stop, I collapse in pain, aggravating my body further and sprawling Posy's limp frame beside me.

We lie next to a dusty mat and a lone wooden chair, and not too far away from this is a spinning wheel with stray pieces of lifeless string sprinkled about. But no Numina, no tapestry, and no red thread. This temple and this whole Timeforsaken mountain are an empty husk. There is no veil to The Between to part and no door either. The Numina abandoned us in here to rot, leaving us and this world completely high and dry. *If only Grim were here.*

When I roll my body sideways to lessen the pressure on my ribs, I become level with dips in the stone surface of the dais. I trace them with my eye until I recognize how uniform they are; these marks are purposeful and laid out in a pattern. Pushing myself up to my knees with a groan, I fold an arm across my ribs and study the shapes.

"Posy, I think there's something written on the dais." My gasping words sound delirious to my ears, but I can't find it in me to care right now.

My sister strains her eyes to the side, trying and failing to catch a glimpse of the marks I can see surrounding us. "What is it?" she asks, her voice breaking as she attempts to muster up a crumb of hope, just one last time.

With clenched teeth, I force my feet under me to get a full view of the chiseled inscriptions. The dais is expansive, and I can't see all the markings from where I stand, but I can see enough to know it's in a different language.

"Well, I think I'm looking at Latin, but I'm not entirely sure." I squint as if it will help me magically decode these mysterious words. "It's definitely something I don't know how to speak."

Posy's face is a calm, collected mask when I peer down at her. The look in her eyes gives her true emotions away, but she's slipped into her bookish self to help me identify what's carved before me. "Does the writing look like symbols or our alphabet?" she asks.

Cocking my head, I follow the curve of words by her head. "Our alphabet. I recognize the letters, just not the combination they're in."

"Good, I can work with that." Posy lets out a long, soothing breath to steel herself. "Read it to me."

From where I stand at the top of her head, she's upside down. But it wouldn't take a genius to notice the exasperation in my raised brow. "Po, have you forgotten I don't know how to read ancient languages?"

My sister mirrors my expression. "Sound it out."

With a long-suffering sigh, I locate the capitalized letter signaling the beginning of the script by my sister's foot and follow the ring of letters around the dais. "Tran-sire ve-lum, mortu-o-rum?" I sound like the eldest of Sparrow and Rush's kids when they first learned how to read. My slow pace and utter discombobulation frustrate me. When I glance at Posy's prone body, her eyes are shut in concentration. She doesn't seem as perturbed as I am.

"Keep going," she encourages, her face smooth and patient.

I'm on the other side of the circle now, and my voice raises in volume. "Okay, uh, let's see. Manibus qu-qua—" My stuttering collapses into a groan. "I really wish I would've taken up Hazel's offer to learn Latin with you. She only asked me *a million* times." Pulling in a deep breath that sets my ribs aflame, I try again. "Mani-bus qua-ere."

"Manibus quaere," Posy echoes, though the end of her words rises like the tail end of a question.

I hum in confirmation, but as I open my mouth to continue reading, I notice half of the lettering appears to be cut off. At first, my heart flies into my throat thinking The Numina may have left this likely clue unfinished. But relief calms me when my boots hit the woven mat where the spinning wheel sits. Peeling back the thick material, I reveal the last six letters. "Mor-tem. Does that make a lick of sense to you?"

Posy's brows are furrowed when I approach her. "Are you sure it says manibus? Not manus or manis?"

Tracing back my steps, I hunt down the word she's looking for to see if my remaining eye betrayed me. "Yep, manibus." Comforted that my eye served me well, I double back to where my sister lies. "What's the difference?"

"That translation can be tricky. Manus could mean hand, and manis could mean shade or ghosts of the dead." Posy squeezes her eyes closed harder until her skin creases. "But manibus…it's all of those meanings at once."

Hands and ghosts? The only thing of the dead that has hands in this mountain is lying in the river we fell into. What would Poppy's hands do in this situation? Act as a key to The Between?

The Numina wouldn't want us to cut— *No.* Absolutely not. I refuse to even think of such a thing.

"You've always been a genius, Po," I say, shaking my head with a grimace to rid myself of such macabre thoughts. *"Please tell me the years of studying were worth it."*

"Transire velum, mortuorum manibus quaere mortem." She pieces together the Latin phrase before she translates. "To pass through the veil, seek Death with the hands of the dead."

My left eyelid twitches, sending a burst of pain through my head and making me rest my forehead in my palm. "For all that's good and holy," I whisper. My insides feel hot, my hands are shaking, and I feel like a kettle about ready to boil over into a fire. The more I think of the cryptic words The Numina left behind, and their possible implications, the more hostile I become. And steadily, I reach my tipping point and break. "What is that supposed to mean?" I snap. Though not at Posy, more to myself and the empty air where Death, Fate, and Fortune once worked.

And my sister knows this. That's why all she does is sigh and gaze up at the stone ring above us, crowning the dais.

With whirling thoughts, I walk the dais again. And again. And again, and again, until I lose track of how many times my boots have scuffed over the words etched in the stone. My footsteps don't wear down the carvings or magically reveal my answer. But my hands are busy wringing themselves until my emerald skin turns sage from the lack of circulation. My ever-present shadows do little to calm my anxiety as they writhe in the far reaches of my limited vision like snakes on hot stones. The ghosts' movements are wild, wholly untamed to the point they look like black flames. I want to scream at them to stop.

That's when I realize something. My shadows have always been there, hovering just out of sight. I've acknowledged their existence and tried to catch glimpses of the elusive things. But not once have I ever spoken to them. Not even in my darkest, most lonely moments when no one else was around to hear me. And if they are true ghosts or shades or whatever Death might call them, and they were once human or faerie...then they must have hands. Right? They *should* be able to return to their source. My sisters and I were meant to bring The Numina back. Surely my strange, lingering friends are no coincidence.

I spin on my heel so fast I hear something in my side pop. Ignoring the pain, I rush to Posy and stand over her with a crazed grin. "Po, I think I got it."

Her eyes are weary. The hope is trying to spark in them like iron against flint, but the flame just won't catch. Sinking back to my knees, I sit back on my heels and lift her head to rest on my thighs. I hope and pray for the both of us and give my shadows everything I've got.

Posy peers up at me in confusion when I speak, but I keep my eyes trained on the pieces of the Latin inscription closest to us. "I see you. I've *always* seen you." My voice echoes through the grotto, and my shadows pause.

"You've followed me since I was a little girl, but I never understood why."

A shadowy wisp inches the slightest bit out of my periphery.

"The oracle told me I was a Chime Child and said she could sense Death around me. I figured it was Grim, a shadow and a ghost in his own right."

A billow of black makes a small advance.

"He traveled from The Between as a creation of Death and Fate. I believe you can too, but you were never asked to do so. Nor was it ever the right time."

My vision is dark on either side of my silver eye, but still, I keep my gaze fixed on the stone words.

"This is me asking you to leave me, my friends. It's time to go do your job and make yourselves useful."

My vision narrows into a pinprick as my shadows swarm me.

"Bring. The Numina. Back."

All I see is pitch black, a bottomless sky without stars.

But then, a beacon of light peeks through. Posy gasps as my shadows move into my line of sight and make themselves known to both of us. They're a tangible swirl of dusk, like silk sewn with flecks of magic dancing and twirling through the air. Slowly, it changes shape as figures emerge from the dark plume and sink into the dais one at a time.

Some of the ghosts are featureless, little more than people-shaped forms. And others have the silhouettes of hunchbacked trolls and small bat-eared imps. With each ghost that fades into the stone, the ebony mass gets smaller, and a letter of the inscription lights up like a candle flame. Brighter and brighter the temple grows, and more and more my shadowy ghosts look like people.

Distant childhood memories tug at the back of my head, but most are overlaid horrific events, rendering them blurry and unreachable. Something inside tells me I should recognize my shadows, but I don't, or rather, I can't. However, the more they dissipate, the lighter my soul feels. It's almost like letting go of a subconscious pain, sweeping away repressed splinters that scraped against my insides for years.

Posy is laughing, tears spilling down her salt-crusted cheeks. Hope flares to life in her once more as the dais floods our skin with golden light. The only time she falls quiet is when my last shadow stops to smile at us. She's the clearest out of all the forms we saw, with crisp-edged goblin ears and wild, dark corkscrew curls. The woman looks peaceful and accepting when she steps onto the last dull letter. As she dissolves into the stone, it illuminates, and the circle is complete. There's a brilliant burst of light that blows my hair off my shoulders and sends a cloud of dust into the air. Then, like the fall of sunset turning into twilight, the glorious luminescence disappears, and Posy and I hold our breath.

We hold it until we gasp for air with burning lungs. We watch, and we wait, but as the seconds tick by and not even a breeze stirs, I die a little more inside. Minutes pass, and Posy's hopeful tears become bitter sobs. My plan should've worked, and it seemed like it would. Now, not only is the memory bird and the one shadow I wished were with me and Posy missing, but the ones I've known since childhood are presumably gone forever.

"*No*. No, *please*," I whisper as one of my hands leaves my sister and numbly falls to the stone. "What happened? What did I do wrong?"

Posy's sobs become wails.

My heart crumbles at her cry as devastation ripples down my arm. My veins bubble and the muscles of my forearm burn before my palm slaps against the dais floor in frustration. My scream echoes the painful sound of my raw skin weeping on impact. "Please!" And just as I expected, I get no answer and all fight leaves my withering body. "Please," I quietly beg. "We did everything you asked of us." A dull ringing takes over my ears and I can do nothing but look down at my sister falling apart. "Wasn't what we've already gone through enough for you?" My final words fall from my lips with a quiet breath. "Weren't we enough?"

When the temple stays still and silent, I get my resounding answer. The Numina aren't here, and they're not coming.

My sister realizes we're on our own the moment I do. I peel my hand from the floor and reach for hers to squeeze it, but it's more for myself than for her, a silent apology that the faith we harbored is being shattered like glass, again. I decide then that we need to make the most of whatever time we have left, and I need to be a better sister while I still can. First, I'll find a place to give Poppy a proper burial, and then I want to tell Posy *everything*. Everything I have seen or done on my travels, all the little thoughts I've had, the feelings I've felt, the lies I've told, and secrets I kept. It will be just like when we were little, whispering beneath the covers way past our bedtime, talking and giggling.

"I need to go get Poppy out of the water," I murmur, my voice wavering like shredded ribbon.

"Don't go." Posy's breath quickens with her plea. The expression on her face reminds me of a deer caught in a hunter's path, petrified.

"I need to get Poppy; she deserves a proper rest." I look out at our surroundings, picturing how starry-eyed she would've been. She would've fawned over seeing Fortune's old wheel and where Fate used to sit in her chair with Death at her feet. Poppy would've adored all these trees flourishing in spite of the Christmastide season. She would've loved to see my shadows and the stupid candlelight show they put on. "Maybe somewhere around the temple--"

Posy is hyperventilating now. "Please don't leave me."

I've only seen this kind of anxiety twice: the first time was Sparrow consoling Poppy after the cage, and the second from Sparrow herself. It was supposed to be a private moment between her and Rush, but I saw the way he hugged her to keep all her cracked pieces together. And the way she gasped for air as her rosy lips went white and her body shook like an earthquake.

"Rose, I'm scared," Posy whispers between wheezes. "I can't feel my body past my head, yet I feel fear climbing around my insides, and it hurts so much." She sobs harder than she ever has. "Will you hold me? *Please.*"

"Okay, okay, Po. I'm here." Scooping her head from my thighs and her upper body off the floor, I fold her into my arms. I stroke the tiny, dried curls framing her face while I re-drench the top of her head with my tears. "I'm so sorry. We deserved better."

To calm Posy, I move us in a slight rocking motion akin to her self-soothing habit. After a while, I see why she likes it; it's like being on a boat or a babe in its mother's arms. Unfortunately, she can't do this for herself anymore, and she'll never be able to again.

A bitter laugh escapes me. "What broken girls we are. We should've grown up happy and without an ounce of fear, instead of scars marring us from these threads sewn before our birth. We shouldn't have had to be The Numina's little martyrs." I let out a heavy sigh as I press my cheek to my sister's head. "What do we do now?"

My rhetorical question sets Posy in a downward spiral. I should've known better. She'll try searching through every bit of information she has ever saved inside her head for the answer. "I should know, I-I've read so many books, and memorized Time's letter. I should know what we need to do." She lets out a keening sound that makes my eyes sting. "I can't think, Rose, I can't feel anything, but my brain is fine. Why can't I think?"

"Shh." Gentle, I keep rocking her side to side like the imaginary waves that seemed to comfort her in the past as she settles into a panic attack. "You don't have to do everything, all the time," I say, my voice nearing a whisper.

Posy gets hiccups from crying so hard. "That's what I'm for, I'm supposed to know."

"You're more than your mind, sister dear," I tut, chest heavy and ribs molten. "You are my moor, the steady planet to my moon. I orbit around you and Poppy." I swallow around the soreness in my throat—it feels like ingesting rocks. "Poppy was our sun, bright and unbearably, annoyingly shiny. I think she kept you and I alive. She kept us whole, she was the string that tied us all together, she--"

My lament is interrupted by a familiar bird-like voice. "You know, it takes three strands to make a rope."

The Numina

The world shifts beneath us, and a feeling of rightness clicks into place. Looking in the direction of Poppy's voice, I find something unexpected. My sister's features are the same, a perfect match to Posy and me, and despite her ears being the same, she no longer resembles a goblin. Instead of our signature emerald skin, I find a vibrant lavender hue. Her eyes are still a pinkish red though, and her curly hair is still blacker than coal and decorated with all her little charms, coins, and braids. The only other difference is the flowery, deer-like antlers sprouting from her head––those are *very* new.

"Poppy?" Posy fights to pick up her head, needing to see if the voice she hears is truly who she hopes it is. But in her immobilized state, she can't turn. Dumbfounded, I move Posy, swinging her around to see the miracle before us.

"How?" I gape. "You're dead. How is this possible?" The last I saw her, her neck was broken, and her eyes were beginning to look like they were dipped in milk.

Poppy glides across the dais in her new champagne-colored gown, threads of golden luck cascading from the epaulets on her shoulders. When she crouches in front of us, I smell spring blossoms. The fresh flowers crowning her head tell a story.

Irises mean wisdom, fern sprigs mean magic, and the most surprising of them all, dandelions. Those fuzzy white puffballs represent fortune telling.

Poppy reaches out and cups our faces.

Posy weeps, "Is it you, are––are you real?"

"Alive and in the flesh." Poppy beams. The moth-engraved locket I gave her swings over her chest as she laughs like her old bubbly self. "Though I suppose you might have to start calling me Fortune."

Tears of pure elation spill from my eye. I don't even know how to express the range of emotion exploding inside me. The best I can do is use my tried-and-true love language, satire. "That's not going to happen, you're the purple sheep of the family now. I'll spend the rest of my life coming up with nick-names for you."

Poppy's grin widens. "I love you too." She pulls Posy and me into a hug.

The hole in my heart fills with her arms around me, the three of us fitting like pieces of a puzzle. Not an ounce of numbness is left in my system, just complete and perfect joy... and a little pain, but that's just my ribs.

This. This is what balance feels like.

"How did this happen?" Posy mumbles from beneath the pile of our clinging limbs.

I feel a hum in Poppy's throat where my face is buried. "After I died, I woke up in The Between sitting with Death and Fate. It was exactly how Sparrow described it. They explained to me why our path had to be the way it was and how much you would hate it, Rose." She pulls back so I can see her wry smile. It falls the slightest bit. "I couldn't survive that fall, I had to be the one to cross the veil by death because there was never a physical door that we could've opened without this happening first. Since I was born to be Fortune after Macha, it had to be this way."

"So my shadows…" I start, though my voice trails off, still too stunned to string coherent thoughts together.

"They were the last of their kind, shades that hadn't become Pooka. Solving the riddle and sending them back to Death allowed them to unlock the doors leading to The Between, The After, and, well, here." Poppy laughs and squeezes Posy and me again. "It was like opening the floodgates. The balance is on its way to being fully restored, and fraying threads have been strengthened. Forgotten magic has even been returned to the soil."

My jaw is slack when I find the words to respond. "All from those ghosts?"

"We were the last thread to The Numina for many reasons. I was the lock, you were the key, and Posy—" Poppy grins at our sister. "You were the one to forge it. Our locksmith, if you will."

"So, we did it?" Posy breathes. "We brought The Numina back?"

Poppy places a gentle hand on one of her debilitated legs. The sympathetic compassion I see on her face tells me she knows everything that happened after she died. She saw every bone that was broken and every tear that was shed. Once she became Fortune, she might've known or seen Posy was paralyzed with whatever magic she has now.

"We did," Poppy confirms. "They'll be here soon, but Time figured a private reunion was in order first."

"But why did you get saddled with this responsibility? Don't get me wrong, the antlers look great on you." I shake my head, baffled. "Why couldn't they have chosen someone else? Maybe, I don't know, six hundred years ago to be the next Fortune so the world didn't run rampant with bogeymen?"

My Numina sister sighs. "There were certain things that needed to fall into place first. Lost magic returned to the earth through Hazel's bloodline. In the villages, Grim mentioned a war fought over inherited magic called the Corvus Clan Wars.

This was her mother's northern clan and she fought alongside Morrigan, Nemain, and Macha. But Hazel's mother didn't have magic, so it skipped a generation like it was known to do sometimes, and later lived in Hazel and her brother. Hazel's fate, once she became the Elder Mother, was to carry magic through the earth once again. It seeped into the elder trees she grew, and it spread. It even crept into a chosen few, Chime Children as you learned without telling us." Poppy gives me a pointed look. "For the most part, it stayed in the trees and helped birth a new race of faerie, changelings. That way, Sparrow could come to be, and the dominoes would fall the way they had to since The Numina became trapped."

I notice as my sister speaks that there's a stillness to her that I haven't seen in a long, *long* time. It's like a blanket of calm has come to rest on her shoulders. Poppy doesn't shift or fiddle with her hair, nor does she try to fill the brief silence between us with a song. She's at peace now.

"We experienced the things we did in that cave, ten years ago, to become who we needed to be for this journey," she continues. "Learning about the dark things in this world and knowing what it's like to be at their malicious mercy allowed me to be *good*. To love without constraint. There's bravery in being soft, and to be Fortune, I needed to understand these things."

Trauma has never been a simple thing to have to overcome. There is no quest anyone could ever set upon that would make the horrific things we've experienced magically better. We could never just "*get over it*." But we did learn from the darkness, and we grew because of our hardships. We accomplished the things we have because of our childhood. Not despite it. We grew the teeth we needed to bare back at the snapping fangs. My sisters and I strengthened the bones that would keep us standing when we started to lose Pop before our eyes. When the dark smudges grew under Aspen's eyes, and she became increasingly tired, we transformed into snowdrops to survive all the heavy things that would suffocate us.

The things we saw and heard in that witch's cave were awful, something no one should endure. But we lived. And now Poppy's transformation has brought back the beings this earth has been suffering without. But why did Posy and I go through it all as well? Just so she could become paralyzed from the neck down, and I could watch her suffer? Knowing now that Death and Fate aren't corrupt, it still seems brutal.

I relay this oddity to Poppy. "I can see why you might have had to learn those lessons, but what does this have to do with Po and me?"

"That isn't for me to tell." The gold coating the tips of her antlers glints when she stands.

Then, a blaze of light blinds me, leaving black dots to dance along my good eye. When I blink them away, I gasp. Five people stand behind my sister, each glittering and gleaming in their own way. They're so beautiful that they can only be the other Numina. The Sun and Moon aren't hard to pick out with their fingers interlaced; the couple's contrasting skin tones look like Sparrow and Rush. The Sun shimmers with gold, highlighting his long white snowy shoulder-length coils and glowing palms. While the Moon has silver-flecked skin and three shining eyes, one of which is in the middle of her forehead, and they're all boring into me.

Death stands unshrouded, unlike Sparrow's story, with feather-capped shoulders, blood-red eyes, and storm cloud skin. Time is next to her, as handsome as Hazel's journal described him to be. He has shiny chestnut curls brightening his copper eyes, and large wings made of dripping candle wax that brush over the ground behind him. The memory bird sits on his shoulder, looking proud of her perch. And Fate, the woman I'll hold a forever grudge against, has a metal filigree mask covering her eyes. Her red threads twine around her halo, weave through her honey hair, and hang from her ivory fingers. *And Grim.* Grim is on her shoulder in his crow form, head hanging low with guilt. I see a flash of his human ghost standing behind Fate, and he seems ready to fall to his knees in repentance. But to whom is the real question.

"Uh," I gulp. "Hello."

Posy, propped up in my arms, remains characteristically silent.

Time is the first to step forward, kneeling at our level with a dazzling smile. "Primrose, Posy, it is so good to finally meet you after all these years. Waiting for the day you would find my letter felt like an eternity." The bluebird makes a little chirp. "And thank you for recovering Hazel's memories. I swear, sometimes this bird is so much like her it drives me crazy. I knew it would get stuck doing something it shouldn't, but I couldn't bear cooping it up." He takes a finger and ruffles its orange throat feathers.

"It was no problem," I say with a half-shrug and uncomfortable squint. It's awkward having Time use my full name. But after a moment of consideration, I throw off my breezy awestruck exterior and risk getting smote. "Actually, no. It *was* a bit of a problem. One, I lost all my money to a kelpie and my favorite knife to a changeling. Two, we got chased by snake women with pet alligators and trapped up in the sky by a house with literal giant chicken legs. Not to mention, number three, a witch *ate* my left eye in front of me."

The look on Time's youthful face can only be described as boyish, and the look of sheepish regret leaves him rubbing at the back of his neck with a blush on his high cheekbones. "I am really sorry about that..." He looks over his shoulder at the other Numina for help.

Death snorts at his expense.

He stands and points an accusatory finger at her. "That last part was your idea. I believe you said it would help her *realize her abilities*' by losing part of her sight."

"Don't you point at me, I got that page out of Fate's book." Death hooks a gray thumb in the masked Numina's direction.

If I could see Fate's brows, I'd imagine one of them would be raised with how her mouth pinches into a stern, unimpressed line. The childish part of me refrains from sticking my tongue out at her, just in case she takes my other eye in punishment. My anger aside, I can tell she's the most logical and meticulous out of all The Numina. Hazel's journal described her as cold, but maybe she's become even harder since *her* Fortune's death? I remember seeing somewhere in those old writings that Nemain and Macha were close.

"I think that is enough," the Sun chuckles. It's a warm, summery laugh that I can feel all the way down to my toes. "Everything has already fallen into place, and now we fix what has been broken."

When he parts from his wife and strides toward Posy and me, I don't know what I expect. But him stooping with a tender hand closing over Posy's and pulling her to her feet, isn't it. There isn't a crack of bones snapping into place or a spongy click of her spinal cord coming back together. Instead, Posy lets out a gasp and a sigh when their skin meets. It's like a ripple of sunshine goes through her body, an instantaneous transformation that heals her right before my eyes.

"How do you feel?" the Sun asks her.

Posy's brows crease as she stills, trying to gauge how her once paralyzed body feels now. "I ache." My sister shifts her weight from foot to foot with a wince. The corners of her eyes are tight as she gazes up at the Sun. "There's this compression in my back and a strain in my hips—they almost feel inflamed when I move. But *I can move*." Regardless of her discomfort, there's still a little smile on Posy's lips.

The Sun squeezes her hand. "All magic comes with a price

and ours is the inability to achieve perfection. While I repaired your spine and lessened your suffering, I am unable to take it all away. Unfortunately, with your type of injury you might experience pain that is chronic, but I can supply you with an aid to help." The Sun releases Posy's hand to cup his glowing palms together. As he pulls them apart, his light grows, stretching into a bright ray half our height. His fingers twirl through the air and the light follows his movement. And when he's happy with his creation, the Numina reveals to us a golden cane that resembles the style of Sparrow's enchanted elder tree wheelchair. Though instead of black lacquered limbs, the cane's twisting branches and knots are pure metallic sunlight.

After the Sun hands it to Posy, she marvels at the way the curved handle fits perfectly in her hand and molds itself to the shape of her fingers. She holds the cane in her right hand to take the weight and stress off her left side. The slight flutter of her eyelids and the way her shoulders drop tells me she's found some relief. At this point, I can't hold myself back any longer.

Stumbling to my feet, I throw myself at Posy. The impact makes me groan, and her suck air in through her teeth. But before I can pull away, she squeezes me back with her arms strong and tight once again. We hug for several moments until Posy's cane puts pressure on my ribs and I pull myself from her with a hiss, and dissolve into laughter. "Oh, I am so glad I don't have to tote you around for the rest of our lives. You're heavy."

Posy snickers as she tugs at my ringed ear before wiping away tears of joy and entering Poppy's awaiting arms.

Suddenly, the Moon stands before me. "May I?" she asks, hand held out toward my side.

After exchanging glances with a grinning Poppy over Posy's shoulder, I nod, and her cool touch seeps through my shirt into my skin. It's like wading into moonlight-chilled water after a hot summer's day. The pressure from my bones being cracked by the statue of Lady Time lifts, and a wave of goosebumps grow over my skin. With her brief touch, the Moon knits together my deeper cuts and scrapes until they're only red lines in their last stages of healing. My ribs still feel tender, but I think because my injuries were less extensive than Posy's, my body will fully mend itself with time.

When the Moon steps back to her husband's side, I reach a tentative hand up to my left eye. It's the one thing that she didn't fix; the socket still sits empty. Everyone is watching me. Shoving down my disappointment, I default to nervous snark. "Why didn't you fix my eye? It's not like you don't have one to spare."

Death lets out a loud cough that sounds a lot like a smothered laugh.

The Moon lifts her sharp ebony brows at me.

"Look, I'm sorry. It's just--" I press my fingers into the bridge of my nose to ease my growing headache. "You all put my whole family through the mill. And although you gave my sisters back to me in one piece, that doesn't negate the fact that you made us your last chance at returning. Strings were proverbially pulled to get us here. I'm not going to thank you, and say all is forgiven." I put a hand on Posy's shoulder. "You put us through Purgatory."

Poppy holds our quiet sister's hand like she has something to apologize for. Her death wasn't her fault. Seeing her unnatural, contorted body was mentally scarring, but she isn't the one to blame here.

"The lionhearted do not have to be grateful for their trials and tribulations. Your anguish through the years was not a gift," the Sun says in a deep baritone. His black, gold-ringed irises appear sincere. His gaze is also heavy, and wise beyond comprehension. He and his wife have been alive since the beginning of the world, making these sorts of decisions, but this accord does seem to weigh upon him.

I shake my head as flashes of bitter blue witchcraft and iron talons cross my mind. "So, what, it was all some lesson?" I gesture to Posy and the scar on her cheek. "What was *so* important we had to be tortured at seven years old?" My hands flail toward my purple-skinned, antler-crowned sister. "Or brutally killing my sister only to yank her back into your fold?"

"We needed you to understand why we made the hard decisions we did. Fortune was gone, luck and chance no longer existed," Fate reasons with a slight frown. "We did the best we could designing your fates given the circumstances."

"But why? You higher beings don't need our forgiveness. We're but one string in your grand design, even if we were the very last one leading to you." My throat gets tighter trying not to give away my emotions, but with a quick glance at Grim all I hear is his voice. *It's okay to be vulnerable.* "One day Posy and I will die, but now that you're back on this earth, you'll keep on living and start weaving again. All life will relearn what they've lost, and *we*"—I gesture to Posy before stabbing a finger at my own chest, tears pooling in my eye at the thought of Poppy being the next one to watch her sisters die—"we won't really matter anymore. So why do you need to rectify your choices with Posy and me?"

"Humans and faeries are our greatest creation," the Moon says. "Our purpose has always been to watch over them, and care for every life that is woven into the tapestry. When we watch your present and future unfold, we develop a bond, and through the thousands of years of observing, even if we never meet every being, they become friends and family to us." The Moon looks at Time with a knowing glance. "We even fall in love."

His wings drag over the dais floor as he shifts his feet, sandals crunching over the sand that trails behind him. Now I see why we get the saying, *"the sands of time"*; the stuff is everywhere.

Death steps a little closer to me. I can't help looking at her shadow, the one that I've heard so much about. It's empty, and exclusively the outline of her body now, but I know it used to be a prison. Her dark red eyes fill with awareness; somehow she knows that I know. "The paths we sew aren't always easy, and sometimes they break our hearts." She lets out a dour laugh. "It's not pleasant for me to cut the threads I do, especially when we know each soul so well. But being trapped in The Between has meant I couldn't be at anyone's bedside, it means I wasn't there to comfort anyone. They passed into The After all on their own, afraid, alone with no guide."

Grim was afraid too, being trapped in shadowy darkness with his murderous father and many other evil, immoral criminals; he was trapped for hundreds of years. Looking at his ghost right now, I can see he's afraid even now. Fate will wipe him from existence soon, and he's not ready to go.

I don't want him to go.

The all-high and mighty Fate clears her throat. "I tried my best to create threads like Fortune's, but creating luck is not my job. I don't make chance, I make destiny. Still, I attempted to make events that seemed like fortuity, even though it was all façades. And that is unforgivable." It's obvious that she's uncomfortable admitting that. It's plain in the way she tilts up her chin, looking down her nose through her metal mask. If I didn't know any better, I'd think she was even about to cry.

"Are you asking for our forgiveness?" I meet each of The Numina's weighty stares, excluding Poppy. She has already absolved them of their wrongdoings by becoming Fortune. I don't know how long her time in The Between was for her, but I can tell she understands more than Posy and I do.

Time peers over at Death and Fate before turning back to us, copper eyes wide with hope. "No, we're asking for another favor."

Haven't we done enough? *They* should owe *us* a favor. The

Numina should be whisking their way over to the glade to give Hazel back her memories and fix Aspen.

"What would that be?" Posy murmurs, gazing at Poppy with down turned lips and squinting firefly eyes.

Our revived sister beams. "For you and Rose to become one of The Numina yourselves."

Deathly Duties

a strangled laugh makes its way out of my throat, a tired, hysterical sound that's spurred by the absurdity of Poppy's words. And yet, no one else is laughing. Posy appears as bewildered as I am, standing frozen, leaning on her cane with a parted mouth. But everyone else is sober.

Oh.

"You're serious?" I look to the other Numina for answers.

Death speaks up first. "I've been around long enough to know when it's time to hang up my shroud. I would've retired years ago if I could have." The hilt of the dagger-like shears at her hip catches my eye. From Sparrow's stories and Hazel's journal, I know she uses them to sever people's threads from the tapestry of life. And Death wants me or Posy to inherit those shears?

Fate expands on all of this while I continue to gape at the dark Numina. "That wasn't as eloquent as I would've put it, but it's time for Morrigan and I to move on. If these last six hundred years have taught me anything, it's that there is room for improvement. I am not the best Fate there could be." Her shoulders droop. "And I want nothing more than to be reunited with Macha in The After."

"You want to give us your roles?" I stutter out.

Death nods, her onyx, painted lips curling soft at the edges. "Unbeknownst to you, you've been prepped for this your whole life. And we cannot retire without someone to take our place, or this will happen all over again, and we can't afford that. The world might not survive an imbalance a second time."

I'm picturing the earth splitting in two from earthquakes as contorted creatures worse than my nightmares crawl from the depths by witches' calls. There's massacres, torture, disease, and things too vulgar to even continue imagining. I wouldn't want to subject my family to that, or anyone else for that matter.

"You are both young, fresh." Fate removes her mask, revealing smooth skin where her eyes should've been. She has no eyelashes, no lids, nothing. The smoothness is unsettling and impossible, but I can't look away. Is she blind? The irony of the woman who oversees everyone's fate being sightless is not lost on me.

Thankfully, Grim distracts me by flying from her shoulder, landing on the abandoned spinning wheel behind her as she continues. "And you have lived, breathed, and endured a world of witches and the bogeymen. You've made a family with humans, changelings, and trolls. You know what this new world needs better than we do, and we know the three of you can restore it to what it once was. As Numina, you'll even be able to improve upon it."

When I glance at Posy through the side of my eye, she's contemplative. I can tell she's turned this information over in her mind at least twice, and judging by the dip of her head, she's ready to agree with Fate now. I told her we deserved better when I cradled her on the ground not long ago—maybe this is better?

Poppy smiles at Posy and me, soft and hopeful. "Together, we could help cleanse this earth and ensure no one would ever have to endure the horrors we did. As Numina, we could repair the things the bogeys have infected, like the waters Sparrow almost drowned in ten years ago--and we could prevent worldly fractures like the ones that web through our Pop's brain."

Posy nods, her voice just as soft and just as hopeful. "We could spend centuries together turning, weaving, and snipping the earth into a place better to inhabit."

"Somewhere I'm not afraid for our nieces and nephews to grow up in," Poppy adds.

That kind of world sounds idyllic, safe. It's compelling and I'm tempted to agree with my sisters up until I think about the rest of our family, and the revelation I have breaks my heart. "But we'll also outlive everyone in the glade..."

Time must see a change in my face because he speaks up with a gentle, comforting voice. "Remember, my letter said it would take all three of you to accomplish this. Poppy was supposed to be the one to breech the veil from The Between, but you, Rose—" A familiar broken wooden box materializes in his hands. Before my eyes, I watch him turn time back on the object. All the splintered pieces reaffix themselves, and the cracks seep away until it's whole again. Time opens the ornate box to show me the restoration of the changeling heart. "You've always had the ability to see the lingering shadows of ghosts, it just took a few extra nudges for you to realize that and use your gift. Those souls clung to you not just because it was fate, but because they sense Death's presence. They knew you would one day become her."

With shaky hands, I take the proffered box.

"And Posy," he carries on, now with a pile of waterlogged pulp in his palms. "The quiet, clever girl who watches and listens. You see beneath people's masks, making astute and kind choices." He reverses time again, and the pulp turns into the crisp yellowed pages of the dry Latin Floriography book. "The knowledge you have gleaned is remarkable, close enough to rival Fate's, but you can learn *everything* when you step into her shoes." Time holds the book out to Posy as another offering.

She takes it from him with ginger hands and presses it against her chest. In Posy's eyes, a damaged book is a lot like kicking a puppy. So to see her Christmastide present restored almost brings her to tears for the umpteenth time today.

"Yes." She accepts the Numina's offer with a whisper.

Fate sags in relief, posture bowing like a willow tree as she lowers her tilted chin. The crow sitting on the spinning wheel and the ghost of the young man standing beside it sag in defeat. His sadness makes my stomach drop and my heart clench. This can't be it for him; I'm not ready to let my guide go.

Death stares at me, hopeful and expectant with her close-lipped smile and tapping foot.

If I take her mantle, I will watch everyone I love perish—Aspen, Rush, Sparrow, and all the kids—and the strangers whose lives I'll end daily. There would be so much sorrow at my hand. I don't know that I can do it. Then again, I would also be with my sisters for a small eternity—I would never have to watch them suffer or die ever again.

"You'll have access to The After," Death says in a soft tone, like she knows exactly what I'm thinking. "You can even go down to Time's cavern whenever you want to look at the pools of the past. And you won't have to sleep again...so no more nightmares." She gives me an olive branch of a smile. "That was my favorite part when I first became Death. I didn't have to relive the war every time I closed my eyes."

If I can go into The After, I'll never truly lose my family... And in the future, if I retired from being a Numina, I would get to be there with them all *forever*. I'd never be haunted by darkness again, and I'd become something that witches fear. My face will fill their dreams and give them nightmares instead. I like the thought of never being fearful again.

"I can visit The After whenever and for however long I

want?" I ask Death.

"Absolutely," she answers.

My mind is turning with all the possibilities this opportunity might provide. As Death, I could go visit the friends and family we lost to Black Annis. I would even have say over who lives and dies, and when it is someone's time to rest...I could be the one to spare Aspen with help from a Healer. And now that I know how badly Morrigan and Nemain want to move on, I know they're willing to gift my sisters and me a little grace. So I test their leniency for me. "Will I be able to form ghosts into shadows and shadows into ghosts?"

Death blinks at me before her brows pull together. "I'm not entirely sure what you mean, but as Death, I suppose so."

"Does that mean I can call on them?" My eye darts toward Grim, catching a flicker of his near-colorless human self before looking to his smoky crow body. "Including the shadows that already exist?"

Following my line of sight, Death looks upon the Pooka, and her features soften. Her garnet eyes are understanding when she nods. "I don't see why not."

"You and Fate will leave your authority over all the Pooka to me right now?" I stare directly at Fate's eyeless face. "You won't touch them before you move on?"

Somehow, she must see this because she presses her lips together before she turns to the dark Numina. The two women seem to have a well-practiced, silent conversation before Death again meets my gaze.

"Yes." She says this like a promise.

"Okay." I nod.

Solace settles over Death like a new shroud, but not one of shadows, one of gratitude and freedom. Poppy reaches behind Posy to squeeze my arm. My sister is shining and I can't help giving her a dopey grin. My chest feels lighter, fresh; this will be a new beginning for us––

My eye narrows, and I survey Death. "How does this transaction work? Do we have to die now?"

"No," she chuckles. "That's a method saved for more dire circumstances. This will be a simple transference of magic."

Death turns to her fellow Numina, folding Poppy in a brief hug while Fate chooses to shake my sister's hand. Together, Morrigan and Nemain say goodbye to their centuries old family. Death ruffles Time's hair like he's her little brother, and to my surprise, Fate pulls him into a tender, sisterly hug. When they give their last greetings to the Sun and Moon, it's like they're approaching their elders. Death and Fate lay a peck on the celestial husband and wife's cheeks as they clutch their hands. The Sun is beaming with pride, and the Moon's smile wobbles with bittersweet mourning. It makes me want to ask Death and Fate if they're sure they want to move on, but when the women turn back to face us, they seem so *free*. Their bodies are light, their features tranquil as the weight of duty and yearning for rest lifts from them. It's not hard to see that they've been ready for a long time coming.

From where I stand, I watch Fate offer Posy a hand, her palm upturned and waiting. At the same time Posy takes it, I'm pulled into a sudden one-armed hug. My unsteady balance makes me brace my hands on the gray shoulder blades I identify as Death's and return her embrace. There's a quick hand at my hip dipping into my pocket before it comes to rest over my missing eye. Morrigan's palm presses against my skin until I feel the pressure of something slipping past my lids and into my skull. The surprise intrusion makes me gasp.

"Thank you," Death whispers in my ear before I sense the power. It's a tiny spark at first, but then it explodes. The magic casts a cloak that feels like cool, star-speckled treacle dripping over my head, past my chest, and knees, down to my toes. It's like breathing in a crisp lungful of winter air after warming in front of a fire, it's peppermint tinged and refreshing. My eyelids fall closed when it recedes past my skin into every muscle, coating the fibers of my being all the way down to the bone. The more and more magic I receive, the lighter the woman in my arms is until she is nothing more than a wisp.

Opening my eyes, my vision is anew. The flashes of Grim I saw on occasion are stable now; he doesn't flicker away. And I can see the spirit-like forms of the human-looking Morrigan and Nemain walking away and down the inscribed dais towards a waiting strawberry blonde woman. Grim said their Fortune had pink hair and four arms, but it looks like they've all returned to who they used to be before they became Numina. When the three young women fought on a battlefield in the north with Hazel's mother at their side.

Macha throws her hands around her sisters-in-arms with the biggest smile I have ever seen before she looks up at me and waves. This leads the other two to gaze at me as well. Morrigan still has her long black hair, but now her skin is alabaster instead of gray, and her eyes are a brilliant green-blue instead of garnet. Nemain has the same blonde hair but now a pair of stunning hazel eyes where her skin used to be smooth. Morrigan gives me a final pearly grin before the three ghosts walk into The After, disappearing from my sight.

Remembering the pressure I had felt in my head, my fingers reach for the socket that was empty minutes ago. There's something orb-like and smooth filling the emptiness. It's cold to the touch and definitely not an eye made of flesh and blood, but I can see out of it, very well in fact. My new sight as Death is like looking at a second layer over the world, an astral layer full of ghosts and the threads that make up the universe. When I pat at my pockets, I realize I'm not in my dirty, travel-worn clothes. A starry, gossamer gown drapes over me like a gloom-filled night, and a corset depicting a silver ribcage hugs my torso. The leather eyepatch is still around my neck, but there's also a new accessory holstered at my hip. Death's shears, or I suppose *my* shears. Morrigan took the tiger's eye stone that was in my pocket and placed it inside my head to help me see this new layer.

Spinning towards my sisters and away from the dais stairs, I find Posy transformed. The goblin-green shade is gone from her skin, replaced with rich teal. Cursive golden words, matching the color of her cane, dance over her bared limbs, shifting like turning book pages. My sister is clothed in a dress of ruby red, fated threads creating a long train to trail behind her. Atop her black curls is a haloed crown of gold embedded with precious red gemstones. Posy rightfully looks like one of The Numina—she's Fate, through and through.

Still, I can't help but point at the words on her skin and laugh. "Who's Rush going to kill by berating now?" Although the ever-changing script is beautiful, it gives the same impression as full-body tattoos.

That's when my own hand startles me. I look like I've been dipped in snow as my skin is now pure white and flecked with pearl. Pulling my hair over my shoulder, I note that it's still black like my sisters'. It might be the only thing that looks identical when you first glance at us. But if we were to stand in a line, you'd see our facial features remain the same, still triplets though now leaning towards the fraternal side. At least Pop might be able to tell us apart, that's if he recognizes us at all.

"You have a rock in your head," Posy taunts. Her voice is crystal clear, but her mouth doesn't move. That's new. "Did you know in the Central East, the tiger's eye is said to be an all-seeing and knowing stone? I believe I read something about it 'expressing divine vision' and helping find balance." Her voice comes from nowhere and everywhere at the same time. Posy sounds more confident than she used to be despite not using her lips to speak.

"You have a crown of shadows as well," Poppy points out.

I don't feel anything on my head, but I suppose that's the

point.

Speaking of shadows, I peek at Grim still sitting on the spinning wheel in his crow form. Through the tiger's eye stone, I see his ghost standing beside the wheel with his hands in his shadowy pockets.

The Sun looks at me while he gestures to the crow. "Consider this your first act as Death. As you know, Nemain created the Pookas, but Morrigan was the one who turned them into shades. Now that we are free from The Between, we have no need for messengers." The gold band around his brow winks as he nods toward my shears. "Since you brokered a deal, it is your job to do what you will, but I suggest you dispatch them before they realize they are free of their makers."

"Is this an order?" I ask, trying to get a feel for the hierarchy of The Numina.

"No," he says with a soft upwards tilt to his full lips. "We are equals here, balance incarnate. I trust you to handle the Pookas as you see fit." He loops the Moon's arm over his. "Now, if you will excuse us, my wife and I have much work to do after being trapped in our respective places in the sky. We will be in the observatory beginning our search for every witch and evil seedling."

They disappear in a blaze of light.

"I can't wait to be that dramatic," I snort.

My sisters roll their eyes at me, but I at least get a chuckle out of Time. Though now is the moment for more serious matters. He glances from Grim to me. "So, Death, what's your verdict?"

My new name sounds foreign––this is gonna take time.

I stride towards the spinning wheel where the Pooka is perched, but I don't stop in front of the bird. Instead, I stop in front of his color-leached ghost. His pale eyes widen when he realizes I can see him. I'm not sure if what I'm about to do will work, so I'm acting on instinct as I reach out for his hand and pull him back into existence. The crow-shaped shadow dissipates into a whirl of mist that seeps its way into Grim's chest, leaving me with a fully formed, handsome young man. The scent of peat and pine is wonderfully strong now. He's still a bit colorless with only a faint flush beneath his skin, but his hair is a dark shock. And *his eyes*—his eyes are a bright sulfurous yellow reminiscent of his time as a Pooka.

Grim's not human, nor is he ghost, or Pooka––I don't know what he is, but I know I've made a new sort of faerie. The shadows are attached to his back, the smoky writhing tendrils evidence of his magic. He's a creature that has walked through life into death, through the deep dark, and back again. He's my creature.

Despite this new life, the fronts of Grim's brows are swooping with devastation. "Primrose, I'm so sorry. I couldn't tell you––"

I hold up a hand to stop him, not even bothered by his use of my full name. Not even that can ruin this moment. "I know. It's okay."

"I wanted to warn you." His voice is no longer an accumulation of male voices, it's just him. Dark and husky with smoke. "I would've gone to stop you, but Fate's hold was––"

"Grim, I know," I soothe him with a soft, close-lipped smile.

He had been acting odd before he left after the bluebird. I knew something was off, but I also knew there was something he wanted to say, but couldn't. It was all a part of the twisted design.

Grim looks down at this new version of his old body. "What is this? I was supposed to be wiped off the map."

"This is freedom." I huff out a laugh. "Consider your sins absolved. You can go anywhere you want, there are no orders to follow, no messages to carry."

His perpetual furrow pulls tighter. "But––"

"You can live again," I cut him off while his protests are still on his tongue. "Go out on your own and live the life you wanted before your father destroyed it. Find love and settle down. Get a job and make money. Heck, make money and gamble it all away, I don't care. I just want you to *live*."

Time makes his way to my sisters then. Everyone in this room knows the crime Grim committed as a human, the monster that his father was. If his father hadn't been a murderer and Grim didn't put an end to him, he could have lived a normal life. He might have been a scholar or an artist, traveled the world, or discovered lost cities. He deserved a second chance.

Voice rough, Grim dips his head in closer to me. "I don't want to go out on my own."

"Then what do you want?" My brows rise.

"I want to be where you are." He throws his hands up in frustration, like this is obvious.

Shaking my head, I take a step back from him. "I'm not Morrigan. I'm not your jailer." I don't want him to associate me with her just because I carry Death's mantle. All I want is for Grim to be happy.

"Of course you're not. I've known you, Primrose. I know you and I think you've come to know me too." He takes a step forward. "Maybe I can help you still. I can try being a better guide, I can protect you from the other Pooka you'll have to hunt down. Or perhaps I can assist you with your deathly duties somehow."

This makes my heart stutter with joy and amusement. "Are you offering to be a reaper of souls, Grim?"

A smidge of color rises to his cheeks, but even then, his pallor is still colorless. "I'm offering to be your companion, in life or death." The ex-Pooka clears his throat as I've been rendered speechless. "Or maybe just until you settle into your role. But I'll gladly follow you to The After, The Between, even Purgatory. Wherever you'll allow me."

Oh.

Grim was paying attention to all my remarks about what I want in life. Where I stand with my aversion to certain forms of affection, while still wanting a companion for all my days. He shares the same sentiment, wanting to love someone's mind, heart, and soul. That kind of bond and commitment is a rare gem meant to be cherished. Just like how he taught me, we're not broken after all. Grim saw through me and the emotions I ignored in every moment of my life Fate had ever shown him. He was there to get me through my most vulnerable moment when I entered Baba Yaga's house and again as he led me through the swamp. We built a special understanding during this journey, especially after I lost my eye, and now I can't imagine a tomorrow without him at my side. I've grown so used to Grim being there beneath my hand and trusting him to be my other half as I stumble on, partially blind. Now I can grow used to the man he was always supposed to be and trust him to walk confidently with me into this new phase of life. We're partners in defiance of the dislike I used to carry for him. Two sides of a newly minted coin.

A forever with him beside me, guiding each other along, wouldn't be so bad.

"Yeah, okay," I accept. A cloak of safety and comfort from finding someone like me, someone who accepts me, dons my shoulders.

Grim's answering smile is so fragile, so wholesome.

"Don't go soft on me, Reaper." I punch him in the shoulder to not only punctuate the moment but break the spell of mushy feelings in the air.

Grim flicks the chains still hanging from my long ears. "Never."

The memory bird behind us lets out a trill. Turning, I see it pick up a scrap of string from the ground, hanging from its beak like a worm. This is a clear signal that there's still a thread that needs following. And that thread leads us back home.

HOME

$\mathcal{U}$sing our newly obtained magic to transport ourselves to the glade is just as dramatic as I hoped. It takes only a single thought to focus the energy needed to bring my body home. The process is painless and happens in a blink of an eye. It's a lot like being dismantled in one place and put back together seconds later in another, all with a showy burst of luminescence. And I'm more than thankful that we didn't have to make the month-long trek back home.

It's morning, the air is still, and the glade is dusted with fresh, gleaming snow. The quiet is off-putting at first, but when I notice the children's shoes, all lined up outside Aspen's front door with gifts from the trolls tucked inside, I realize it's Christmastide morn. The smoke wafting from the chimney smells like caramelized sugar and cinnamon. And the closer my sisters, Grim, and I get to the door, the more we hear the excited chatter from within.

Time has given us yet another kind moment of consideration before he comes to deliver his wife's memories; he's allowing us to see our family and explain everything first. Part of me is grateful. The other part of me wants him to hurry up so the Sun and Moon can get down here to work their magic. They could re-Bless Hazel as a Healer so she gets to Aspen faster, or even if they could Heal her themselves--I don't know or care how they'll fix her, as long as it gets done. I want the woman who's been a mother to me to be at peace inside her body again. These desperate thoughts make me glance back to where the four of us materialized, hoping I'll catch a glimpse of the other Numina following. All I see is the trail of our feet in the snow and the holes from Posy's cane. There's no Time and certainly no Sun or Moon.

When we reach Aspen's doorstep, we all pause. Being here, especially this way, isn't something I thought would happen after enduring the Wyrd Mountain's waterfall. I'd accepted that I would never see my family again. I was convinced they'd live out their lives wondering what happened to us. But here we are, lingering like timid children outside the door. Poppy is quiet, hand reaching up to touch the root of her antler before dropping her fingers to tap against her thigh. Posy's teal fingers squeeze the handle of her cane in a death grip as the words on her skin move quicker.

Will our family even recognize us? What will they think of who we've become, or the roles we'll have for the next millennium or so?

I feel Grim's shadows extending from him, reaching out toward me, prodding and searching with curiosity. Glancing over my shoulder, I watch him search between my silver eye and the stone I've covered with my eyepatch. When he sees the nervousness behind my gaze, he places a firm hand on my shoulder. His anchoring touch gives me the confidence to knock on the wreathed door.

Starling, Sparrow and Rush's eldest son, is the one to open the door. He blinks at us in confusion until his seafoam eyes widen with recognition. "Whoa." He gapes.

Their oldest daughter and first child, Swan, pulls the door open wider. "Who's at the door?" The words trail from her lips as she peers up at us. She looks like the perfect mix of her parents, from her complexion to her hair. The changeling squints, tilting her head as she follows Poppy's antlers down to Posy's cane and up to the wispy crown of gloaming on my head. When she catches the abnormality of my covered left eye, her brows pull together. "Auntie Rose?"

A sigh of relief leaves me. The kids still recognize us. "Hey, chickadee, merry Christmastide."

The rest of the kids barrel towards the door after hearing my name and voice. Robin and Lark don't hesitate to throw their arms around Poppy's legs. It's as if her lavender hue and adorning flowers have always been there. Kestrel trips at the sight of us at first. But he's quick to eagerly greet Posy, asking every question imaginable about her gold cane and the script crawling across her skin.

It's Rush who's in total shock. He pulls his oven mitts off at a snail's pace as he emerges in the doorway, just staring at us. His scruffy face reminds me of a fish out of water the way his mouth opens and closes, at a complete loss for words.

"I know you said not to do anything stupid," I start, "but I swear this wasn't my fault."

Rush's chest stutters and then stops moving. He's so dumbfounded I'm afraid he might not take in another breath. Posy shifts her weight further onto her cane as Poppy toddles forward. The children are clinging to her legs and the glowing threads hanging from her shoulders like a bunch of gremlins.

I give my half-brother a wince of a smile. "On the bright side, we brought The Numina back."

Next thing I know, Rush strides forward and pulls the three of us into a hug by our necks. Poppy's antlers whack Posy and me in the back of the head as we clash together.

"I'm so happy you're safe," he breathes.

"You're not even going to comment on all of this?" I gesture between our bodies to the changes my sisters and I have gone through.

Rush pulls back with a soft smile. "Sparrow and I considered many scenarios, but this wasn't one that crossed my mind." He smiles wider. "It's much better than the other possibilities that kept me up at night."

He reaches out to thumb where the leather band of my eyepatch crosses through my crown of shadows. Rush then palms Posy's cheek, which still has that decade old scar. And finally, he cups the side of Poppy's head where her antlers grow. Rush looks relieved, proud even, as he soaks in these changes with bright silver eyes. Though our faces are the same, we each look like our own person now. No longer are we an amalgamation of identical girls with the same sad story. We are Death, Fate, and Fortune, one half of The Numina.

Like the protective older brother he is, Rush acknowledges Grim who stands like a guard at my back. "And you are?" he asks, sticking his arm out to shake the former Pooka's hand.

Grim leans forward, pressing into my shoulder when he gives Rush's hand a firm shake. "Grim. We never formally met, but your wife and mother-in-law might have told you about me. I was the cat that gave your sisters the prophecy."

Rush's grip loosens in confusion, looking into Grim's yellow eyes and studying the tendrils of smoky shadows curling around him.

"Grim is reformed," I blurt out. "He's uh, he's...mine?"

This earns me a raised brow from Rush and a snort from Grim. My sisters unsuccessfully stifle their laughter behind their hands.

"Consider me Rose's Familiar. I'll accompany her in this new life and keep her from doing anything else stupid," he says, bumping the side of his arm into mine.

Peering from Grim to my burning snowy face, and back, Rush nods with a grin. "Well then, welcome to the family."

Robin lets go of Poppy's right leg to tug on the sleeve of her father's sweater. "Can we go inside now? My socks are wet."

My half-brother's face melts with endearment as he chuckles. "Go on in and dry off by the fire; we'll be there in a second." He ushers all the children back inside the warmth of the house, ruffling the tops of their heads as they go. Some duck just in time while others end up with mussed hair. Slowly, the smile falls from Rush's face when he turns back to us. "Before you go in, I want you to know that Aspen isn't doing well. She's taken a steep decline since you left." He expels a sorrowful sigh. "Sparrow and Hazel have been trying to keep her comfortable, but it's good that you showed up when you did. I don't think she has much time left––"

My stomach drops. Without hesitation, I dart past Rush and through the door. I knew the other Numina should've just come down with us. Aspen needs to be Healed. We can't waste another moment.

When I burst inside, I first notice how the furniture has shifted. Her bed has been moved out of her room to sit in front of the fire. The kitchen table and armchairs have been shifted towards the wall, making space for it and the decorated tree in the corner. The second thing I note is Pop sitting in a chair beside the tree. He has that mindless look on his face as some of the kids play a newly gifted game of jacks by his feet.

Sparrow is sitting in her wheelchair beside the bed, holding Aspen's hand. Her mother looks like death, to be straightforward. She's lost a considerable amount of weight, making her face sallow and gaunt. Her collarbones poke from the neck of her nightgown, and her willowy arms look frail. The hair Aspen always keeps in a low bun has been brushed out to lie over her bony shoulders; it's almost as lackluster as her skin and the hollows beneath her eyes. She looks so, *so* tired.

Stunned, I slow my all-out dash and shuffle to the end of her bed. Sparrow is surprised when she gazes up at me, but Aspen doesn't bat an eye. Her cracked lips just split into a sleepy grin as my sisters make their way to my side.

"Look at you three," she croaks. "I always knew you were meant for great things."

Sparrow shakes her head, mystified. "What happened?"

"I'll tell you what happened. Our girls restored the earth." Aspen lifts a feeble, shaky hand and points to each of us. "Posy is now Fate with her train of red threads, and Poppy must be Fortune with all that life blooming above her. And Primrose…" Her finger trembles harder. "That makes you our pure-hearted Death."

My sister-in-law takes her mother's hand again and rubs soothing circles over it. That movement and little bit of speech took up all of Aspen's energy. She wilts into the bed like a fading flower.

"We tried to complete the trip as fast as we could," Posy whispers, her voice floating through the air without physically speaking. This oddity raises some brows but now is not the time for trivial questions.

Aspen lets out a wheeze that sounds like it might have been an attempt at a laugh. "You made perfect timing, darlings."

I hear the old words she's said since she first got sick: *"When it's my time, darling, it's my time."* She thinks we're going to let her go, just like that? We made it back home in time, and I'm Death now. I have a say in who stays in this world and who goes to The After, and for all our sakes I want Aspen to stay.

"Don't say it like that," I say, misery creating a knot at the base of my throat.

"Like what?" Sparrow asks with a small crack in her voice. She knows what I meant; I can see the irritation of past tears in her green eyes.

It would be pointless to spare her from hearing the reality she can't admit. "Like we got here in perfect time to watch her die," I say, tears collecting in my lashes. "We're here now, and we're going to fix this. Time is going to give Hazel back her memories, and she'll Heal you and—"

"Primrose—" Aspen starts.

I speak over her. "Or I'll drag the Sun and Moon down here, and they'll fix you themselves."

"Primrose, enough," she rasps, her lips stern and white.

Her tone freezes me in my spot. It's been a long time since I've been scolded like that; it makes me feel like that lost little kid again. The one made up of shattered pieces that took cover under Aspen's wing when I needed someone the most. But I'm not that girl anymore, am I? I'm no longer just a goblin of the glade, I'm Death incarnate, and I'm not afraid of loss, but that doesn't make me any less stubborn.

"Come here." She pats the other side of her bed, opposite where Sparrow sits. "It's my time, and I'm almost ready to go."

"*No*, we can help you," I choke out, taking my seat as softly as possible, so I don't jostle her.

"Listen to me, look at me." She reaches for my face. I meet her halfway by leaning down until her hand connects with my cheek. Her fingers shake over my eyepatch, wanting to uncover what wound I might be hiding.

It's been overwhelming for me to see the world through the tiger's eye stone. The new layer of threads connecting to everyone, and everything, only go away when I cover that eye. From what little I've glimpsed, The Numina's threads are binding, stronger than any rope or cord. But peering into my family's chests to examine their threads without permission feels wrong, too private. However, I follow Aspen's wish to see what's beneath the leather by reaching behind my head to loosen the ties. The eyepatch hangs around my neck.

What I see is heartbreaking. Aspen's soul is worn, her thread blackening and fraying along the edges with only one string hanging on. She may be too far gone for a Healer's medicine to work. But maybe the Sun and Moon can repair her thread. They fixed what was severed in Posy's body, giving her back the use of her limbs and taking as much pain as they could. My ribs were mostly fixed with a single touch. Surely they could fix this. Whatever *this* is that's ailing Aspen.

When I look deeper into the older woman to try to find the cause, I dive into the center of her soul where her light flickers. There I find happiness. Her body is filled with tranquility, love, and a wave of peace so overwhelming that I sense almost no pain under the credence. Her life has given her so much satisfaction and joy that she doesn't feel the need to negotiate a second chance. I can identify her fulfillment as a mother, as a daughter, protector, and caretaker. She's proud of who she is and what she's done in her lifetime. Aspen is ready for the next generation to step up into her place. She doesn't want a Blessed miracle or old medicine. Nor does she want a crafted body that the trolls, who are like her parents, offered to make for her. She's ready for rest and what lies beyond in The After.

The air shudders out of me. I cannot be selfish, I cannot deny Aspen what she wants. Looking at Sparrow and the strong, gold and red glowing threads that wind around her twig heart, I see she has already started grieving. She's known for a while now that Aspen would pass. After all, she inherited her strong will and compassion from her mother. She's also accepting that the time has come. And I suppose I must accept this too. At least I know as a perk of my new deathly duties, I can visit her in The After whenever I please. This thought acts as a calming bandage to my own heart and allows me to nod.

When Aspen has seen her fill of my new eye and I get the closure I need, I put the patch back in place. "Okay," I murmur, wiping away my tears before they fall. "I have one request."

Even though she doesn't know what I just saw, a smile of gratitude graces Aspen's face. "What would that be, darling?"

I wrap my hand into hers. "Hang on a little longer today. Let us have this Christmastide with you, and then I'll aide you into The After."

"Of course." She squeezes my hand.

Not long after that, Hazel arrives with the trolls in tow. At this morning hour, she's my age, and she lays her hand over Bramwell's green craggy skin. Hazel guides the big old troll into the fire-warmed house. Dirt clods and bits of moss fall to the floor when he settles into the armchair beside Pop.

After that, Rush goes into the kitchen where Sparrow's yeasted Christmastide sticky buns have been rising. He's putting them into the clay oven to bake while Grim reintroduces himself to Sparrow and Aspen. With Hazel's onslaught of questions about him, our journey, and how we became three of The Numina, we decide it's story time.

My sisters and I tell our story as our hodgepodge family listens in earnest. The changeling children's eyes are bright, and every inch of the house is decorated, setting up our winter tale to perfection. Potted poinsettias sit on every flat surface, while the ceiling is lined with swags of greenery and holly. The candlesticks tinted with vanilla are lit, and the whole room smells of sweets.

Poppy and Posy stand at the forefront of the room, regaling everything from the River Man to finding the tavern. They recall our shopping trip through the villages where we found that terrible statue of Sparrow as The Changeling Queen, Slayer of Witches. I tell everyone how I acquired my eye when it was a simple stone, and how I tried to nail Grim with biscuits as a squirrel. Things get tense when we talk about the swamp. Our family sits on the edge of their seats when we mention the chase with the nixie and their pets. The children cuddle up to Sparrow and Rush out of fear when we start talking about Baba Yaga. But I get them to laugh when I tell them about the house's chicken legs.

By the time I recall some of the treasures inside her house, the sticky buns are done, and we take a break to eat. I find out that as one of The Numina, eating isn't necessary to stay alive. But I am never one to turn down a daytime dessert. The toffee-like brown sugar and cinnamon coats my mouth in glorious sweetness. The bun is soft and airy, and the notes of maple in the pecan topping make me even happier that we survived the Wyrd Mountain. I try not to think about this being Aspen's last meal, but Sparrow's sticky buns have always been her favorite. And unfortunately, I can tell she hasn't been able to eat much since her illness progressed. However, she still takes tiny savoring bites when we continue our story.

Rush makes a round of cocoa for the kids and tea for the faeries who drink it, as I glaze over how I lost my eye. I don't want to scare the kids. I describe grabbing the memory bird and the big stones we leaped over on our way to freedom, and the bit about wearing that old helmet makes my nieces and nephews giggle so hard their cheeks turn red. The tone turns somber when we tell them about freeing the bluebird and how Grim had to leave us. He looks very uncomfortable when the kids pout at him, but Aspen pats his arm where he leans against her bedpost, listening.

Once everyone learns about the cracked tunnel and what followed, things get a little too quiet. I don't describe what it was like to see Poppy dead when she runs out of her side of the story to tell. But Posy does talk about her temporary paralysis and how I brought her to the temple where we solved the Latin riddle with my shadows. Next, Poppy tells what it was like to be in The Between, and Sparrow recollects her time there, sharing how similar their experiences were. Posy and I explain what it felt like to get her back as Fortune and becoming Fate and Death.

The logs burn low when we wrap our adventure up in a bow. Much like the ones scattered about the floor with the balls of paper. Grim retrieves the ornate wooden box I had him carry from inside his shadows, and we give it to my sister-in-law and half-brother as a special Christmastide gift. Rush is sitting on the arm of Sparrow's enchanted elder chair when we hand it to them, and Sparrow gasps when she opens the lid.

"What is it?" the children cry, scrambling to get a peek of the changeling heart nestled amongst the velvet lining.

Rush wipes away happy tears as he laughs, "It looks like we're having a baby!"

Bramwell rises from his chair to look at the heart he or one of his kin made many years ago. He pats Rush's shoulder in congratulations as Sparrow passes the box to Aspen to see.

"Will you name them, Mother?" she asks, a torrent of tears pouring from her eyes.

Aspen hums a fragile note. "How about Raven if it's a girl and Crow if it's a boy."

"I think that's a wonderful idea," Rush agrees.

A silence falls.

We all know it's time. Aspen is having a harder time speaking more than a sentence now, and her body is getting too weak for her to even move. Everyone, even Grim and Pop, stand around the bed. When I come back to sit at Aspen's side, Sparrow and Rush are at her head. They all say their I-love-you's as Sparrow hugs her mother, exchanging words that make my throat tight. My sister-in-law nods when she's ready, stroking Aspen's hair as she makes room for me.

"I'm glad you were the one to see me off," Aspen heaves out when I take her hand.

Sniffling, I take the shears from my hip. I don't feel ready for this moment, but I don't think anyone could ever be. "It was always meant to be me," I say. The truth and conviction of my own words provide some comfort.

"I wanted to give you girls carnations before I went, but they aren't in season." She takes in a slow inhale. "Promise me you'll plant some."

Carnations represent a mother's eternal love.

I cry as I nod, my heart breaking in two and stitching itself back up simultaneously. "I promise. I love you...Mom."

When Aspen lets out her last exhale, she's smiling. This was the first time I have ever called her that. She became my mom ten years ago, but I think she knew that without me ever having to say it. I remove my patch to wipe at my eyes and see the shred of string holding her soul in place. Once again acting on instinct, I pinch my fingers together and pull the black thread from Aspen's still chest. The room gasps. Taking my shears from my hip, they slide through the thread with a snip, and I feel the gates to The After open.

Grim must feel it too, because his posture straightens while he stares at me with the ghost of Aspen standing behind him. She appears as healthy as the day she led me out of the maze. When Grim turns he sees her there and follows in my instinctual footsteps. He wraps her hand over his arm and leads her where she's meant to go. Aspen blows me a kiss and mouths the words, "*I love you too, darling,*" over her shoulder as she goes into The After with my Reaper as her ferrier.

"She's in good hands," I tell Sparrow when everyone notices Grim's sudden but temporary disappearance. Then, I take Sparrow's hand over the bed and wrap Aspen's darkened thread around her pinkie. With a bit of focus and magic, it sinks into her skin, creating a black band like a tattooed ring on her finger. "She'll always be with you," I promise my sister-in-law.

And just like that, peace descends on all of us. Aspen is gone, but with that thread, she will never be forgotten.

ime refrains from coming to the glade until the hour of Aspen's burial. No doubt he was watching his pools in the Wyrd Mountain because, like his namesake, his timing is impeccable. The lone Numina is already waiting for us at the burial plot, the small graveyard that became a memorial after the slaughter that occurred here a decade ago.

I remember concealing myself as a child and sneaking around to watch the adults dig the graves. The trolls scooped the soft summer earth with their giant hands. The surviving goblins used shovels until we had a complete cemetery near the garden at the edge of the property. Rush, Hazel, and Aspen had been too busy waiting for Sparrow to wake from her death-like sleep after getting her chest cleaved open. That made it easy for me to sneak away unnoticed.

Headstones were created for the identifiable bodies, hand chiseled with looping names and words of memoriam. But the grisliest thing was watching the trolls try to put the body parts that had been ripped from their owners back together. It was a miserable, macabre puzzle that sometimes ended with missing pieces or a couple extra that didn't seem to fit anywhere. A special headstone had to be made for those who weren't identified or lost their lives and bodies inside the cave. And we'll have to make a special one for Aspen now. It needs to be beautiful so the kids can visit their grandmother. And peaceful, a place where Sparrow can come to talk to her mother, or the trolls their adoptive daughter.

With it being the dead of winter, we know the ground is frozen with snow and ice, so we have a couple of the trolls take the kids and Pop to watch them back at their respective houses. Bramwell volunteers to be the one to watch over his daughter's body. Now, my sisters, Rush, Sparrow, the Elder Mother, and I will bear the cold and start digging. Though now that Time is here, he seems to have solved that problem for us.

He stands there with his back to us, feather-shaped burn scars on his back on full display, his wings nowhere in sight. His head is bowed, and the bluebird perches on his shoulder. The cemetery is free of snow, trapped in a bubble of spring where the grass is fresh and green, and the dirt is warm. A plot is already dug, and an empty space is waiting for a headstone.

"Is that…" Hazel's footsteps falter when she sees Time.

"Your husband?" I can't quite read her face as she looks upon Time's tall frame. Her gaze is roving over him too quickly for me to capture what emotion might be rolling through her. "Yes, it is."

"I've come to terms with the reason why I can't recall my past, not that it was too long ago but because my memories were removed," Hazel murmurs. "Sparrow gave me the journal when I was ready and sat with me while I read through it multiple times. I felt so much grief because of the detachment that echoed through me. But this…" She shakes her head. "It makes it worse seeing him and feeling *nothing*."

"I can only imagine what it was like for you to read your past thoughts, feelings, and experiences without remembering," I soothe. "It would be a lot like experiencing someone else's words and not your own. Reading about your old passion, to meeting The Numina, being betrayed by your best friend, falling in love, and getting married. It would've been so painful knowing you should still feel the emotions that came from those experiences but can't." The Elder Mother looks up at me and I give her an encouraging, close-lipped smile. "It's not your fault, Hazel; your feelings, or lack thereof, are completely valid right now."

Looking into her wrinkled wide duo-toned eyes now, I finally see that the steadily aging woman recognizes and accepts she had once upon a time loved the man waiting for us. She had read everything they went through together over and over again to try to jog her missing memory, but to no avail.

"This is a moment over six hundred years in the making," I say, reaching down to squeeze her hand, letting her know that we're all here for support.

Hand in hand, we follow my sisters who trail Rush and Sparrow down the shoveled stone paths. My sister-in-law's wheelchair crunching over lingering chips of Christmastide ice, and the *tip-tap* of Posy's cane are the only sounds made.

When Time turns, I somehow hear the skip in Hazel's heart and her sharp intake of breath. Time's youthful copper gaze goes right to her with the softest, most tender expression on his face.

"All these years he's waited," I whisper to Hazel. "He's loved you from the farthest place no one could ever reach until my sisters and I came along. And now, you're at arm's length with your memories perched and waiting atop your husband's shoulder."

Hazel squeezes my hand as she gulps.

"Hello." He gives her a tentative smile when we all stand before him.

Hazel releases her death grip on my hand to tug at the end of her gray-threaded braid, glancing from him to the bird excitedly hopping and flapping its wings. "Hello."

They stare at each other with curious and doting eyes for a long moment before Time clears his throat and turns to Sparrow. "I hope this is okay." He gestures to the defrosted plot. "I accelerated the time in this area and stopped it, so it'll always be a shade between spring and summer."

"Thank you, it's perfect," Sparrow says, her voice thick with emotion.

Rush puts one hand on his wife's shoulder. She reaches up and loops her black-ringed pinkie around his. It's a sickeningly endearing habit they've had ever since Sparrow told him about the fated red thread attached to them.

"I wanted to give you all my condolences, but I'm also here to return something." Time holds out his pointer finger, and the bluebird hops onto it. With slow sandaled feet leaving a trail of sand in the grass, he approaches Hazel. "I believe this belongs to you."

Everyone's muscles tense in anticipation; we know what's coming next. Rush fully holds Sparrow's hand, and she clutches onto Posy's hand holding her cane beside her. Poppy slaps at my shoulder as if I wasn't already watching this exchange with rapt attention.

Hazel gazes up at her husband, appearing as a woman in her fifties as the afternoon rolls toward the evening. Only a hint of her youth lies beneath the surface of her creasing skin. I can tell she's nervous, maybe even scared as she glances back at us before she turns and reaches a jittery finger out for her memories. In excitement, the bluebird bypasses her finger altogether and flies straight into her chest, dissolving into her with a flash of light. Hazel's eyes slip closed as she gasps, the missing pieces of her first life pouring over her like rain. We all watch as she ages backward, her wrinkles receding and the silver hairs disappearing from her tawny braid. Once she reaches a point where she's just older than my seventeen years, but younger than Sparrow's twenty-eight, she opens her eyes. Knowledge and recognition fill her brown and blue eyes as she looks upon Time.

"Hello, Icarus." Hazel grins, pure adoration making her face glow. "I told you in another life we'd have a happily ever after. Didn't I, my love?"

Time's body relaxes as he lets out a hopeful sigh. "Please tell me it's this one."

Hazel barrels into his much taller frame and throws her arms around him. Time picks his wife up off her feet, spinning her around in a hug with a spray of sand and a rich laugh. When he puts her down, she steps back and smacks his chest with the back of her hand. He looks at her, surprised but amused.

"That was for not letting me say I love you back before you took my memories." Abruptly, she grabs his chin and pulls his face down to her level. We all hold our breath with Time as we watch the rest of their unfinished story unfold. "And this is to make up for every kiss we've missed." She lays her lips petal soft over his, and Time melts as his waxy wings unfold from his scarred skin to wrap about Hazel.

Poppy holds back a cheer behind her hand while Posy beams. Rush bends to kiss the top of Sparrow's head as she cries again, though these are happy tears this time.

That's when I sense Grim's return, and I pivot to meet him. To my silver eye, it looks like he materializes from nowhere. But I know if I uncovered my other, I'd see him coming from the gates of The After. I walk away from the group to where he strolls down the path.

"How is she?" I ask.

"Aspen is settled. She's happy," he answers with a small smile, no doubt pleased with himself and the turn his life has taken.

I feel guilty that I didn't usher Aspen into eternal peace myself. But I know my family needed me here and Aspen would have wanted me to stay with them. "Thank you for guiding her."

I glance back at the precious reunion over my shoulder as I speak. "I couldn't leave everyone."

"Primrose, this is why I'm here for you." Grim shakes his head at my gratitude underlaid with an apology. "I would guide every soul down the river to the gates for the rest of time if you asked me to."

Grim's use of my full name doesn't even bother me as I study the earnestness on his face. There's care and admiration, maybe the seedling of something that could eventually grow into a thing akin to love. Or our own different version of it. His yellow eyes burn for me and me alone, the girl who hated his very being and held no trust for him. The girl who made a tentative truce when she saw his humanity and realized how much he truly knew her. And the girl who became his friend and depended on him, choosing to trust him when Fate made it so she shouldn't. I can't help brushing the lock of his dark hair that had fallen on his forehead back in place.

His surprise makes me smile.

"I know," I say as I fold my arm into his. Then, I lead him back to the family where they look like they're making plans for Aspen's grave. By the sounds of it, life will soon bloom where she'll lay.

—

WE PLANTED carnations around Aspen's headstone in her honor, as she requested. One of my distant goblin cousins made the curved stone that crowns her burial place. It's a beautiful thing of marbled stone with her name in swirling cursive at the top, bordered by filigree. Underneath, it says, *"Daughter and Mother, a safe haven and stronghold, a harbor for all."* Over the short time that's passed, the flowers have flourished under Time's bubble of warmth. They've even spread to the neighboring stone, teeming with soft moss and chiseled with the name "*Copsewood.*"

Since we laid Aspen to rest, my sisters and I have been learning how to be half of The Numina. We transported ourselves with Grim in tow to the Wyrd Mountain to learn the ropes, and back home to be with our family. We've spent many of our days in Time's caverns with his pools, to understand how the past, present, and future flow together. This triggered some of Poppy and Posy's first visions as Fortune and Fate. Poppy has practiced spinning her gold threads of chance while Posy weaves, picking out red fated moments when needed.

The world is balanced again, but it will take a while for human- and faerie-kind to readjust. We'll have to gradually reintroduce ourselves to the world and remind them of what this earth used to be, long ago. According to one of Posy's destined visions, getting everyone used to having Death make personal visits again will take decades. So Grim and I have been visiting the Sun and Moon in their observatory. There they've been following the threads to where every witch is hiding. We've learned that people who have corrupted themselves into hags no longer have threads attached to their bodies. But their darkness hides beneath the threads of the people they've encountered like a trail of breadcrumbs. I've convinced the celestial husband and wife not to just wipe the witches off the face of the earth with a wave of their hand once they find them all. If Grim has taught me anything, it's that not every shadow wants to be a part of the dark. Maybe there's a witch or two that became one against their will. Maybe there's not, but even the bogeymen deserve a trial. Thus, the cleansing began with one witch at a time. Baba Yaga was the first at my request. Later, when the Sun and Moon came back covered in ash, I found out that she was a willing malignancy. Poppy had a vision after that that told us it might be a common pattern we come across as we face the possibility of some dark, poisonous times many years from now. She even said more bogeymen will pop up like tangled cornflowers and burrow their invasive roots in neighboring territories, making some foot travel more dangerous when or if the resurgence happens. And amongst those clouded visions of pestilence, and the gaps blackened with strange blind spots, there might be uncertainty surrounding friends and foe. However, Poppy also saw a couple different paths where bogeys like old Nanny Rutt might reform and turn new leaves to become a Healer. That was something hopeful to note.

After Aspen's funeral, the Sun and Moon visited Hazel. I thought it was to reinstate her as a Healer. But it turns out, she never lost her Blessing when she lost her memories. It had just gone to sleep, like an ember that needed to be stoked. It was awakened the moment she set eyes on the Sun, since he was the one to bestow the Blessing upon her brow so many years ago. She was beyond ecstatic when we found her belt washed up in the mountain from our fall and returned it to her. Hazel and Time then disappeared to her cottage for a while. They needed to restart her herb garden and figure out how to go about restoring the Healer practice to the world. Hazel promised her first act as a returning Healer will be to help Pop in whatever way possible. She said it would take time, but she'll try to concoct a medicine of the mind to help him rise from the fog Black Annis's actions created.

I also learned that when Hazel regained her memories and her age reversed, her body froze as well. Time took back the part of his gift that originally made the Elder Mother age back and forth and kept a cap on her magic...under one stipulation. The way her age fluctuated kept her power in balance. Hence, she had to give up her tree magic in exchange for an immortal life with her husband and the ability to spread the knowledge of Healers by traveling with him. She agreed in a heartbeat.

However, this left a lot of loose ends. Hazel's magic flowed into the trees and gave the Elder Mother a responsibility, and there had to be someone to protect the trees and answer people's petitions to use their wood. After all, that is how the trolls had breathed life into the changeling hearts made of those same twigs. Without the Elder Mother, the magic would sit dormant inside the trees, unable to be used or given to the trolls with a Blessing-like permission.

One day, I wandered into Time's cavern to see if I could figure out a solution, when I came across the orbs of water that held the vision of how Poppy became Fortune, and The Numina returned. It was the moment I had felt the world shift beneath me, how the feeling of rightness clicked into place. I found that exact moment when it happened in the glade. Sparrow and all her changeling children's chests glowed gold in their sleep on the Eve of Christmastide night. The light shined so bright you could see the shape of their hearts and every twig that constructed them through their skin.

It was an awakening.

The awakening of the same magic Hazel had carried inside her. And the same gift the earth gave to the extinct northern clan her mother hailed from, bestowing her people with extraordinary abilities. Like Hazel's Blessing, the magic inside all the changelings was asleep until the moment that balance was fixed.

Grim and I went to Hazel first, telling her what I saw and what we needed to do to tie up loose ends before she relinquished the position and power of the Elder Mother. That day she willed the majority of her trees to dig up their roots and use them like legs. The whole army of elder trees paraded away from the ring around Hazel's cottage, over the salt-infused path, and into the glade. The trees replanted themselves, burrowing their legs back into the dirt to create a border while the glade's occupants watched in awe.

All six of us Numina were there when the sight of the trees stoked the ember inside the changelings. The hearts sitting in their chests radiated magic that spilled into their veins. Like a crown, Hazel then passed on her title of the Elder Mother to Sparrow. The changeling, in her wheelchair like an enchanted throne, became the keeper of the trees. However, Sparrow would age normally as this magic was her birthright. She'll raise her children to find their gifts and foster their abilities while the trolls create the next body for the baby's heart that Aspen named. Elderflowers rained on the glade at Sparrow's command that day, covering the new year's snow with the creamy blooms. I chased my nieces and nephews through the frosty flowers. Hazel happily threw snowballs at Time's face, laughing as he tackled her into the snow with his wings wrapped around her.

The pieces fell together after that, all of us finding our new roles in life together.

Rush and Sparrow will be expecting another changeling baby any day now, and the kids are as giddy as can be to have another sibling. A couple of their gifts are even beginning to show. Kestrel's hearing is sharpening to the point he can hear every tiny critter rustling about the bushes outside from in the house. I'm tempted to get him a bow and arrow to see how his aim is, but I have a feeling Rush would kill me for giving his child a weapon.

Starling has always been a copycat and a bit of a bully, but his impersonations of certain birdcalls are becoming almost pitch perfect. I've even noticed how some of the winged critters appear in the trees when he whistles. Lark has been singing her little nursery rhymes like always. However, the mood in the room shifts when she does it, brightening or mellowing, depending on her song. Swan and Robin haven't shown any signs of growing their gift yet. But knowing those little trouble-makers, I wouldn't be surprised if one could make bad luck befall someone at her whim, especially when she doesn't get a biscuit before bed. I'd bet the other would become nocturnal, keeping her parents up all night just to play.

And speaking of changes, Poppy makes a wonderful Fortune, creating possible paths to love and ambition. I saw a few flower shops she's planted as an option for some faerie folk and a human or two. Not to mention, she's started searching for her prince in all these opportunities. She still wants the same love Hazel and Time have. Posy, on the other hand, has reignited the crumbled and crisp fate of the Great Library she told me about. It'll be rebuilt in five years. She's also begun dissecting the words on her skin after discovering that they're prophecies. Posy is now assuring the growth of knowledge from many great people being born in the future. My sister is making sure the things they have to offer this new world come to fruition for its betterment.

Being Death has been a work in progress and will be for a while. My past doesn't plague me like it did when I was an ordinary goblin, but I don't think I will ever like blueberries or things made of iron, and I'll always hate cerulean blue. Despite that, now that I have a divine duty with everyone I love at my side, I am free of my confining trauma and fear.

My job until the world is ready for The Numina again is to find the rest of the Pooka. They're all out there, wandering this earth since being freed from Nemain's shackles. Their shadows are kin to my power as Death. I can hear them whispering. When I locate and catch them, they'll stand trial. I am their judge, jury, and executioner. If the past criminals can be reformed like Grim, I will set them free. But if they're still murderers, arsonists, and abusers at heart, then I will dispatch them straight to Purgatory. Grim and I have begun the hunt, but it could take months, years, centuries, or an eternity to find them all. I suppose it's good thing I have all the time in the world.

ACKNOWLEDGMENTS

I'd like to start this section of my book not with acknowledgments but with three long fun facts.

1. There was never meant to be a second Numina Parable book. Heck, there wasn't even supposed to be the Numina Parables. When Whimsical picked up A Daughter of the Trolls, it was a short and sweet standalone story. I'd only sought to write a book featuring disability and mental health representation with a little old European folklore flare. Sparrow and Rush's story was meant to be wrapped up with a perfect 'Happily Ever After' bow, and the curtain was meant to be closed on the glade. Yet here we are. (You'll have to thank Micheline for nudging me to create a continuing trilogy.) Though, because I never intended to write a trilogy and I wanted Sparrow, Rush, and Hazel's tales to stay as they were intended, I needed to expand the meaning behind the Numina Parables. Which is why A Goblin of the Glade takes place ten years later, and the book is narrated by Rose. Just as book three will also take place ten years later from another character's perspective. Yes, this means you will see Sparrow, Rush, and their children again, although a decade older. The triplets will be well into acting as one-half of the Numina. Icarus and Hazel will be happily together, with the latter working as a Healer once more. However, the world will be much different than the one you were thrust into when you opened A Daughter of the Trolls. And I am so excited about that

adventure and the topics it will cover. (Hint: depression and more medical representation!)

2. A Goblin of the Glade was a much-needed therapy for me. ADOTT helped me write about being in a wheelchair and my life with anxiety, while this book tapped into my panic disorder and childhood PTSD. My traumas did not come from being the kidnapped victim of a witch but rather from witnessing one of my older sisters battle cancer and its effects on our family. It was around that time my panic attacks started. I'm sure undiagnosed autism had a large hand in how I processed this time in my life, but I will admit my medical trauma followed me into my adulthood to haunt me when my illness and disability came about. My PTSD is why I found writing about the horrors the triplets faced so cathartic. Sparrow only saw their capture from the outside, but Primrose and her sisters knew what being prisoners inside their own bodies felt like. And I hope that reading about the girls continuing to live with their fears from their childhood, while knowing they can be bigger than their trauma, is as helpful to you as it was to me.

3. My choice of how I portrayed Rose and Grim's relationship is a kind of representation super important to me because I never saw couples like this growing up. I never found it in the people around me, not in movies or tv shows, and definitely not in YA books. Had I known that feeling the way Rose and Grim do about romantic affection is perfectly okay, it would've saved me years of thinking something in me was broken. Sometimes it's not a phase, and this feeling might not change when you find the right person. And. That. Is. OKAY! I've heard people call this preference asexuality, I've heard people call it a trauma response, and I've certainly heard that it's just a part of being autistic. Maybe all of that is true for me, and maybe it's not, but I want to show *you* a new kind of love story that's not told often

enough. I hope some of you found it either comforting, enlightening, or refreshing!

Now to wrap up, let me swing back to the whole point of having acknowledgments and say my thank you's:

Thank you, Whimsical Publishing, for continuing to believe in me and my stories. I'm looking at you, Micheline! Your patience and magic editing abilities never cease to amaze me.

Thank you, Mom and Dad, for forever being my biggest supporters...and for listening to me rant about my plot points for hours on end because I haven't left my house to lay eyes on another person or felt sunlight on my face in weeks.

Thank you, Grimm, for doing your service duties and keeping me company. My numb feet thank you for warming them during the endless hours of staring at my computer screen.

Thank you to my local grocery store for fueling my work hours with endless diet sodas. You don't know how you've contributed to my delicious bubbly addiction, but you deserve thanks anyways.

Thank you to my couch crevice for caressing my old writing gremlin bones and perpetuating my horrible slumping posture.

And, of course, thank you, dear reader, for taking a chance on yet another one of my books. I can't wait for you to read the next one.

About the Author

McKenzie is an award-winning, wheelchair-bound, autistic, published YA fantasy author of the "Numina Parable" series and co-author of "A Traveler's Guide to The Lucky Gryphon: Recipes & Regalings".

She's been an Arizona resident for more than two decades and lives with her doggy soulmate and service beast, Grimm.

McKenzie is also a full-time creative makeup artist and alternative model fighting against disability stigmas one creation at a time. When she's not spending her anxious days writing novels or taking photos in her studio, you can find her over on Instagram sharing her art: @mckenziecatron.

www.ingramcontent.com/pod-product-compliance
Lightning Source LLC
Chambersburg PA
CBHW051956240626
47153CB00005B/1776